BY MARKO KLOOS

Frontlines

Terms of Enlistment

Lines of Departure

Angles of Attack

Measures of Absolution (A Frontlines Kindle novella)

"Lucky Thirteen" (A Frontlines Kindle short story)

To Doug and Helen —

best wishes,

MARKO KLOOS

[signature: Marko Kloos]

Published by 47North, Seattle

www.apub.com

Amazon, the Amazon logo, and 47North are trademarks of Amazon.com, Inc., or its affiliates.

ISBN-13: 9781503950320
ISBN-10: 1503950328

Cover design by Megan Haggerty

Illustrated by Maciej Rebisz

Printed in the United States of America

For Robin: What lucky bastards we are.

PROLOGUE

We now call it the Exodus.

One year ago, a Lanky seed ship appeared in Earth's orbit, humanity's worst nightmare manifesting in the night sky above the North American continent: immovable object and irresistible force all rolled into a glistening black torpedo shape three kilometers long.

The world's fleets were down to the dregs then. We lost half the NAC Fleet in the unsuccessful defense of Mars, which the Lankies took a few months before they showed up at Earth for the first time. Most of the rest is still scattered across the settled galaxy, unable to return home because of the Lanky blockade of our Alcubierre nodes. We had very little left on the board, but we stopped the Lanky seed ship and blew it out of space, only the second time in our half-decade war with them we ever managed to kill one of their ships.

But our victory came with a huge bill.

The last-ditch multinational screening force above Earth lost four ships in the battle. Twelve hundred soldiers and sailors, gone in a few moments of furious and mostly one-sided combat. Five of those sailors were on the NACS *Indianapolis*, which won us the battle by ramming the Lanky at fractional c velocity and damaging the seed ship enough for us to take it apart with nukes. The Lanky ship lived long enough to spew out its seedpods all over North America—each with a dozen settler-scouts in it, twenty-five meters tall and as hard to kill as a building. We followed them down to Earth, and we killed the ones that survived their descent, and we lost even more people. Hundreds of soldiers and thousands of civilians died in one night of heavy, desperate fighting, and we reduced entire city blocks to smoking rubble.

But we beat them, and we survived. Earth won a reprieve.

And now we had something new: Lanky bodies, hundreds of them, and dozens of crashed seedpods. Lots of stuff for our scientists to study and dissect. To figure out how they work, how they can be killed. How their ships can be broken.

Just before the Lankies came to Earth last year, the government of the North American Commonwealth evacuated the Solar System in secret. They took with them a dozen first-rate warships, almost twenty bulk freighters, and the Commonwealth's political and social elite and their families. Nobody knows yet where they went. Fleet rumors say that the Exodus fleet had a secret Alcubierre node to a refuge system prepared long in advance, in anticipation of Earth falling to the Lankies sooner or later. We have electronic intelligence from a cluster of recon buoys Colonel Campbell and *Indianapolis* left when we discovered the secret Exodus staging area just before their hasty departure a year ago. I suppose we need to thank the Lankies for rushing their departure ahead of plan, because they had to leave behind two unfinished warships that are unlike anything any fleet has ever put into space: two heavy battleships, purpose-built for only one job—to close with Lanky seed ships and destroy them.

We spent the last year finishing those battleships and pressing them into service with the hull paint still wet. The Sino-Russians, pragmatic sons of bitches, came up with their own Lanky hammer—orbitally launched antiship missiles, monstrous things with ten-thousand-ton warheads made from a mixture of ice and wood pulp, driven to fractional c velocities in mere minutes via nuclear pulse propulsion. After making new friends on the other side of the fence last year, I am deeply convinced that it must have been a Russian who cooked up the idea of making a pointy block of ice the weight of a heavy cruiser, and then using nukes to propel the thing. It's crude, dirty, and ugly, but, by God, it works. Two more Lanky ships showed up in the Earth-Luna space in one-month intervals a few months after the Battle of Earth, and the Russians blew both of them out of space with their new Orion missiles without any human losses. The Lankies stopped scouting out Earth then.

Of course, using nuke-propulsion kinetic weaponry capable of wiping out half a continent from Earth orbit was a massive Svalbard Treaty violation, but that sort of thing was really low on everyone's priority lists when the Lankies showed up again.

The Orion missiles, as effective as they are, have one major operational drawback. They're too big and heavy to be launched from a starship, so we can't take them through an Alcubierre node. They share that drawback with the new battleships, which don't have Alcubierre drives installed yet. So we finally have viable antiship weapons to use against Lanky seed ships, but they're good only for orbital defense. Mars is still in Lanky hands, and our colonies are still cut off by the Lanky blockade. But we are working around the clock to find a way to take the fight to them for a change. To get revenge for our dead, to reclaim what's ours, and to kick them out of the Solar System for good. And if we can chase them to whatever system they call home and wipe them out altogether, I wouldn't lose any sleep at night.

Humanity's survival is still on the edge of a knife. But we are finally starting to pull on the same end of the rope together, and we are finally killing Lankies in numbers. There's much work left to do, and I know we will lose more people and ships before it's all over, but there is finally a glimmer of hope that the world isn't going to go to shit after all.

Well, at least not any further.

CHAPTER 1

BOOT

I'm not the kind of soldier who has an office. I'm a combat grunt by occupational specialty, a combat controller, a podhead. Among the first molecules on the very tip of the spear. But for the last six months, I have also been a platoon sergeant for a basic training platoon at North American Commonwealth Recruit Depot Orem, and platoon sergeants get offices, so I have an office. It has a desk in it, and it's about twice as big as the biggest berth I've ever occupied on a warship. The first few weeks after I moved in, I felt like a complete fraud every time I walked in to see my name on the door: PLATOON SGT: SFC GRAYSON.

Platoon sergeants are experienced noncoms. Older men and women. But then I remind myself that I am twenty-seven, with almost seven years of service—over five of them as a noncommissioned officer. In the new NAC Armed Forces, made up of what's left after the Mars defeat, the Exodus, and the Battle of Earth, that makes me one of the old and experienced NCOs, and that's a scary fucking thought.

There's a benefit to the office, though. When I can't sleep, which is most nights, I have a place to go and keep myself busy without having to stay in my quarters and have my brain dredge up unwanted memories from godforsaken places a few thousand kilometers or a few dozen light-years away. Not even the good pharmaceuticals can eradicate that particular program in my head.

———————

I look up from my network terminal's holoscreen when I hear footsteps in the hallway outside. The clock on the wall shows 04:14. It's over forty-five minutes to reveille, and too early for someone else to be awake in this place and walking around in the building with boots on their feet.

A few moments later, Sergeant Simer pokes his head through the open doorway.

"Morning, Sergeant Grayson."

"Good morning," I reply. Sergeant Simer is the CQ for the night, the Charge of Quarters NCO manning the little office at the company building's entrance. It's a mostly superfluous tradition in the days of neural networks and computerized access, but it's tradition, and the military has lots of those.

"Real shit sandwich this morning," Simer says.

"Oh yeah?"

I wave him in, and he steps across the threshold and over to my desk.

"Got a call from the base MP just now."

"Uh-oh," I say. "Weekend leave trouble?"

"Bunch of the recruits took the bus into town and hopped a train to Salt Lake on Saturday. They got drunk or baked, one or the other. Chip-jacked a cab, disabled the safety governor, and went for a joyride."

"Oh, no."

"Yeah." Simer makes a pained little grimace before continuing. "Left their travel lane and creamed a hydrobus. Offset crash, one dead, three injured."

"Shit," I say. "Any of ours?"

"Two. One from First Squad and one from Fourth. Privates Barden and Perret. Barden's dead."

I close my eyes briefly and let out a sigh.

"Dumbshit kids. A week and a half before graduation."

I recall Private BARDEN, J. from the personnel roster and the sixty or so times the basic training platoon has stood lined up in front of the building for morning orders every weekday since the beginning of boot camp. He wasn't a PRC kid like most of the recruit pool. I recall that he's a middle-class 'burber from somewhere in the Pacific Northwest. Portland or SeaTac, maybe? I know I'll have to learn everything about Private BARDEN, J. in the next day or two because the platoon leader will have to attend his funeral, and I'll need to brief him for that.

"Thank you," I tell Sergeant Simer. "Kick the boots out of bed early today. Reveille at 0445. Might as well give them a hint something's up. I'll be down at Orders."

The platoon is lined up outside in a laser-straight line, sorted by height. Their uniforms are standard NAC battle camo, boots polished to a spit-shine, haircuts short and neat. My three squad leaders, the drill instructors, are standing in front of the assembled platoon at parade rest. When I step out of the building and start walking toward the line, my senior DI snaps to attention.

"Platoon, ten-hut!"

Thirty-four pairs of boot heels pop together, and the recruit platoon snaps to attention as one. I acknowledge the senior DI's salute and step in front of the assembled platoon.

"At ease."

There's a brief shuffling as the recruits assume a slightly more relaxed posture. I look at them without saying anything for a few seconds, to make sure I have everyone's undivided attention.

"On Friday afternoon, I had thirty-six recruits standing in front of me. Today, I only have thirty-four. I also have one recruit in the intensive care ward at Salt Lake, and one on a slab in the morgue. Recruit Barden was killed over the weekend in an accident. He got zoned and overestimated his driving skills with a jacked vehicle."

There's no noise in the ranks—after eleven weeks of Basic, they know not to make a sound at Orders unless told to sound off—but some of the recruits are trading looks, and most of them seem appropriately shocked by the news.

I pause briefly again to let the news sink in properly.

"This is the new Basic training," I continue. "When I stood where you all are standing right now, the whole platoon slept in a big room. Thirty-six beds and lockers, two rows of eighteen. Six and a half days of training every week, and half a day of downtime. No leaves until graduation. You all know the horror stories from the old-timers."

Some of the recruits smile or grin at this, but they quickly drop back to a neutral expression when they see that I wasn't setting up a joke.

"Now we train you in squads and fire teams. You get to share a berth with your team, two berths per squad. Four recruits per room. We train you that way because that's how you get to live and work in the Fleet or the Spaceborne Infantry, and we have no time to waste in getting you prepared for duty. You even get weekend leave. And most of you know not to abuse that privilege. Most of you."

I fold my hands behind my back and start walking down the line of recruits slowly. They look so young to me, even though most are in their late teens and early twenties and only half a decade younger than I am. But the half decade between us seems like an eternity from where I am standing right now.

"I'm not pissed off because privates Barden and Perret wanted to let off some steam and have fun in town. I'm pissed off because they chose to be stupid about it. I'm pissed off because Private Barden got himself killed a week and a half before he had a chance to pay back the Commonwealth for the time and resources we spent on his training.

I'm pissed off because now we will be two heads short next week when we send you all off to the Fleet or the SI, and four slots that desperately needed to be filled will now go unfilled."

I'm talking in my drill instructor voice and cadence, which I didn't know I possessed until I started my platoon leader rotation at NACRD Orem six months ago. I find that whenever I need that particular voice, all I have to do is channel Sergeant Burke, my own senior drill instructor, whose clipped drawl is still as fresh in my memory as if I had left boot camp last week.

"I know what most of you are thinking," I continue. "You've been around the block in the PRCs, and you think you can handle your shit in the big bad world out there. You think you're smart and tough. You think that dying is for other people. But I'm here to tell you that there are a lot of ways to die out there past those gates. And if you have to kick the bucket, I'd much rather see you go out holding a gun and manning a line against a Lanky advance than braining yourself on a hydrobus bumper while zoned. There are good ways to go and bad ways, and a dumbshit traffic accident just before graduating boot camp is a very fucking bad way."

They all look at me, those young and earnest faces. Quite a few still have that welfare-rat attitude in their expressions, that cocky little streak of defiance that was a survival skill for them in the warrens of the inner cities. But whatever else they are, and whatever thoughts swirl around in those heads right now, they volunteered to be here, to join the thin green line that stands between us and extermination.

"Here's the deal," I say. "Leave is restricted from now until graduation day. You can stay on base or go into town, but you are barred from leaving Orem. And we're having a mandatory chem scan this morning. Anyone with illegal jack in their systems is going to get a bad-conduct discharge and a maglev ride home. Are we clear, platoon?"

"Sir, yes sir!" the thirty-odd members of Basic Training Platoon 1526 bellow in unison. If nothing else, they've learned to stand straight and sound off at top volume.

"I can't hear you," I shout back, even though their combined volume rattled the polyplast windowpane five meters behind me, because that's the sort of thing we do. Establish rituals, hammer them home, drill them to be executed until they become second nature.

"Sir, yes sir!"

"Better," I say. Then I check the chrono on my left wrist.

"It's field day," I announce. "The buses will be in front of the block at 0800 sharp. You will all be geared up precisely according to the checklist. This is the last one of these you'll get to do before graduation. If you graduate. The next time they call you out in combat gear, it may well be for real combat, so keep that in mind. The crucible is a bitch, but it's nothing compared to what you'll see out on a real battlefield, believe me."

I turn to the drill instructors, who are at parade rest to my right and slightly behind me.

"Drill sergeants, take charge of your squads. Chow, then armor up. Weapons issue at 0700. Be ready for dustoff at 0750, including gear checks. Execute."

I walk back into the building as my three drill instructors take over their charges. They'll march the squads back up to the platoon quarters and light a fire under their asses, to simulate having to get ready for combat quickly and under stress. The platoon will spend the last week before the final graduation exercise out on the huge exercise area in the desert surrounding NACRD Orem, simulating an extended engagement against a Lanky landing. Much of our training has been focused on killing Lankies instead of other humans, and I can't say that I dislike this shift in priorities.

I go back to the office and sit down at my desk. Then I pull up the personnel file of recruit BARDEN, J. and look at his picture. He was a cocky kid. Thought he was smarter than everyone else by half, and had a knack for tiptoeing the line with the drill sergeants. In the old NAC boot camp, he would have been sent packing after week two at the latest. But as I told the recruits just now—this is the new Basic training. We can't afford to be ruthlessly selective anymore, at least not in the capricious manner of the old boot camp, where the drill instructors could wash you out for any trivial reason, or no reason at all. But I look at the holoshot of Private BARDEN, J. and find myself thinking that he would still be alive if we still ran Basic like we used to.

Outside of my window, the platoon marches off to breakfast, in a tight and precise formation, with Sergeant Lear calling cadence from the front of the group. Two out of my three drill instructors have no combat experience. Sergeant Lear is a female trooper from the Fleet's military police, and Sergeant Dietrich is from Supply & Logistics. Only Sergeant Fisher, my senior drill instructor, has been in battle. He is a Spaceborne Infantry heavy weapons specialist, an autocannon gunner, and the only member of my drill instructor crew whose service experience is even remotely like my own. Strangely enough, I don't get along with him as much as I do with Lear and Dietrich. He's sullen, clearly suffering from grunt fatigue, and resistant to advice. Lear and Dietrich are motivated, personable, and eager to learn on the job.

There's a protocol in place for everything in the military, of course—including the death of a recruit. This is the first time I've had to follow that protocol, and I hope it's the last. It's shitty enough to lose people on some godforsaken icy rock on the ass end of the universe. It's several orders of magnitude shittier when they're fresh recruits still in training.

I get out my PDP and tap in a message to Sergeant Lear to come and see me after morning chow. Then I start reading Private BARDEN, J.'s personnel file, to come up with eulogy material for the lieutenant when he goes to the funeral later this week.

———————————

Sergeant Lear knocks on my open door twenty minutes later.

"Good God, Lear, did you inhale your breakfast on the run back? I said after chow, not during."

"I eat fast, Sergeant Grayson," she says. "No inconvenience."

"Come in." I make a sweeping gesture and point at the chair in front of my desk. Sergeant Lear walks into the room and sits down, squared away as ever. She's fit and lean, and wears her long hair in a ponytail that reminds me of my old squad mate from the Territorial Army, Private Hansen.

"You are going to head out into the field for the graduation exercise with a short squad," I say.

"Yeah," she replies. "Barden was the leader of my second fire team. Now they're three in that squad."

"Won't be the last time they'll have to patch holes in the squad. I can't get you a replacement. We don't have anyone to slipstream in from the Medical Recovery company."

"We'll manage," Sergeant Lear says. "I'll bump Matteo to fire team leader. They'll just have to work around it."

"Tell me about Barden. They'll send the lieutenant home with him for the funeral. He needs something to talk about over the casket."

Lear shrugs. "He was a cocky little shit, but he wasn't bad. Picked up fast on new stuff. Hardly ever had to show him anything twice, never three times. Had a bit of an attitude sometimes, but which one of them doesn't from time to time. He would have made a decent SI grunt. Maybe even NCO material."

"Damn shame," I agree. "One more week."

"He was a bit of a clown," Lear says. "Always had to crack stupid jokes. The squad liked him okay, I guess."

"Well, that's something. 'He was good-humored, well liked, and a bright and capable recruit.' That will go on the lieutenant's bullshit card."

"I'm just happy I won't have to go. I hate funerals," Sergeant Lear says.

"Same here," I say. "Been to too fucking many lately."

CHAPTER 2
38, SIMULATED

The platoon is geared up in battle armor and full combat loadout five minutes before the assigned time. When I step out in front of the building again, I am wearing my own armor—not the HEBA bug suit, but the standard Fleet laminate hardshell. The only equipment on my body younger than half a decade and unscratched is my rifle, one of the new M-90s. We took the design of the Russian anti-Lanky rifles and tweaked it a great deal for Western sensibilities. The Russian guns are single-shot weapons, whereas our modified copy is a heavy autoloader with a five-round magazine, more than twice the capacity of the old M-80 double rifles we were using before. This new cross-pollinating of ideas and designs between very recent former enemies has been radical and strange, but you can't argue with results.

"This is your graduation exercise," I say when the squad leaders have everyone at attention. "We will board the 'drop ships'"—I point to the buses lined up on the street beside the company building—"and we will do a simulated landing on the training ground ten klicks from this base. Pretend you are twenty light-years away and on a colony moon, because you might as well be. Whether you live through the exercise or die a glorious death for the Commonwealth out there will not determine if you pass. You will pass if you do everything out there according to your orders and your training. Pretend those are real Lankies, and they came to wipe out your families and steal your home world. And then show them why it's not a smart idea to piss off the hairless primates of Sol Three."

The platoon lets out a short, aggressive holler at this, like they're the varsity team about to kick someone's ass in a championship game. They know they can't die out there for real—that it's a sophisticated simulation, the full sensory experience of a real battle, but without the chance of actual death or dismemberment. I would be much more excited and pumped up about combat drops in the real world if I knew I couldn't die.

I step back and let the drill sergeants take over their squads. We use the buses like we would use drop ships in the field, one to a platoon, so everyone files into the bus assigned to us while the other platoons of our Basic training company board the other three buses. As the platoon sergeant, I board last and take the jump seat behind the pilot station. In a combat situation, the platoon commander, Lieutenant Lewis, would sit up front, but our lieutenant is over at training battalion command this morning, undoubtedly for business related to our two dead recruits. I don't envy him the task.

We roll through the base and the huge security lock at the main gate, and then into the desert beyond. NACRD Orem is as isolated as a military installation can be these days. It sits in the desert just a few dozen miles southwest of the Salt Lake City metroplex, on the site of a former military depot, because there's nothing but sand and shrubs out here, and nobody cares when we play war with our noisy toys. Over six years and what seems like several lifetimes ago, I passed the same security lock in the other direction on the way to become a soldier. I thought I knew what I would be getting into, but I had absolutely no idea.

We have several satellite training facilities scattered out here in the dust and rocks. Away from Salt Lake, the area looks a lot like some of our colony planets, so it's close to perfect for drilling off-world combat scenarios. Our platoon bus takes us to OWC Training Facility 38, a re-creation of a typical colony town, complete with a partial mock-up of a terraforming station. As we pull into the facility, the drill sergeants leave their seats and assume drop positions in the aisle of the bus.

"Platoon up!" they yell. The recruits get out of their jump seats and line up along the aisle, rifles in hands, helmet visors snapping closed.

"Check your gear!"

I watch as they go through the proper motions, checking each other's armor latches and equipment. My drill instructors have been on the ball with these kids. They are quick and thorough, and there's very little fumbling or horsing around.

"Charge your weapons!"

Thirty-three recruits cycle their rifle bolts, chambering simulated fifteen-millimeter explosive gas rounds. The training version is a pretend cartridge, stuffed with a computer module and a heavy charge of carbon dioxide to vent into the stock's gas cylinder and simulate the recoil of the real M-90 rifle. I get out of my seat, do a quick check of my own gear, and chamber a round in my own rifle as well. I carry the M-90 and a sidearm, as I would out on a real combat drop against Lankies, but I'm missing my admin deck, which has been an essential part of my real Fleet job for half a decade, and I feel incomplete without it.

The bus comes to a slow stop in the middle of the mock-up colony town. The tailgate opens—not with the hydraulic whine of an actual drop ship hatch, but with the hissing of pneumatic cylinders—and the platoon charges out into the sunny April day, drill sergeants in the lead. I stay in the open tail hatch for a moment and watch their deployment. They split up into squads and fire teams and take up textbook cover-ing positions. The data display on my visor shows the entire platoon fanning out and covering the area 360 degrees around the "drop ship."

In a real battle deployment, I would be taking charge of First Squad as the senior platoon NCO. On field days, I used to do just that in the beginning, to get a feel of the recruits and my drill instructors. But once I was convinced that the drill sergeants had everything firmly in hand, I backed off and started supervising from a distance because I found that everyone deferred to my judgment too much. I've been in combat against the SRA and the Lankies, and two of my three drill instructors have not, so it's a natural tendency, but both my boots and my sergeants need to be able to swim on their own. So while the platoon deploys around the fake colony town, I trot over to the training facility's ops center, a small bunker right in the middle of the place. The computer recognizes my electronic signature and opens the armored hatch for me, and I step into the building.

The ops center is a small two-room structure, stuffed with holo-screens and computer consoles. There's a short row of mesh-backed chairs designed for personnel in battle armor, and I drop into one and turn on the displays and consoles in front of me. The entire facility is lousy with optical and data sensors, and I can keep tabs on every member of the platoon from pretty much any angle. Their suit computers are tied in to the facility's segregated TacLink network, and not only can I see and hear what they see and hear, but I can give them things to see as well. The installation is a giant simulator stage, and I control what goes on out there. If I want them to fight a quartet of SRA drop ships and a company of Russian marines, I can simulate them, and they will become real on their helmet displays and in their headsets. But this field exercise does not involve our old Sino-Russian enemies. They are geared to fight Lankies, so Lankies are what they'll get today.

I check the tactical screen and open the squad leader channel.

"Squad leaders, prepare perimeter defense. Likely threat vector is one-eight-zero degrees."

The squad sergeants toggle back their acknowledgments. The platoon elects to get up on the roof of the terraforming station, which rises twenty-five meters above the desert floor and offers excellent fields of fire. Against the SRA, elevated positions like that are too exposed to air attack or long-range precision fire, but against Lankies, you want to be able to see and shoot as far out as you can, because there's not much room for error when engaging creatures who can cover a kilometer in less than a minute.

I check the visuals I'm feeding to the platoon—dark, rainy skies, a colony world in the middle of having its atmosphere's CO_2 content flipped with its oxygen content. The boots and their drill sergeants don't know it, but the scenario I am letting them tackle today is a rehash of our First Contact with the Lankies, almost seven years ago on a faraway planet called Willoughby. Overhead, it's a sunny day in the desert, but with their visors down and their armor suits controlling their individual climates, my boot platoon is on Willoughby right now, seeing what I want them to see and hearing what I want them to hear.

They all know it's just a simulation, but I can see all of their heart rates climb considerably when I make the first Lanky step out of the squalls to the west and have it approach the terraformer in slow, thundering steps. Twenty-five meters of rain-slick skin the color of eggshells, spindly limbs that look like the thing shouldn't even be able to propel itself on them, joints that bend all the wrong ways, to our Earth-biology knowledge. Even with the right weapons to fight them, they are intimidating opponents, something out of an old monster movie, and I shudder when I think about how utterly unprepared we were to fight them on that day—no idea of what was coming, and armed with weapons that were never designed to kill something of that size and toughness.

The platoon deploys on the rooftop in one long firing line, the new doctrine for fighting Lankies in stand-up battles. The squad leaders shout orders, and the squads take position in a reasonably efficient way for a bunch of kids who were rank civvies just eleven weeks ago. In a regular SI rifle platoon, Third Squad would be the heavy weapons squad, and they'd be setting up a pair of canister-fed autocannons on the flanks of the platoon, but our boot platoon doesn't have training on that gear yet. Everyone has an M-90 semiautomatic anti-LHO rifle. LHO stands for "large hostile organism," and it's the new tactical short-hand for Lankies. As the simulated Lanky lumbers toward the mock-up terraforming station, thirty-three targeting lasers paint the incoming creature with a swarm of green dots visible only to helmet visor displays.

"All squads, on my mark," Sergeant Fisher shouts. "Center mass shots. Don't waste ammo. Three, two, one, fire!"

The platoon's rifles all bark more or less as one, a stuttering drum-roll of thundering reports. The new M-90s are shorter, lighter, fire faster, and are more effective than the old M-80 double rifles. They're also much, much louder. At the last fraction of a second before the sergeant gives the fire command, I cheat a little and make the Lanky lower its head and cover most of its upper body with the large, bony, shield-like protuberance on its head. Thirty-three simulated explosive gas rounds fly out from the rooftop. Most of them shatter and ricochet off the Lanky's cranial shield like pebbles thrown against a concrete wall. The Lanky bellows a wail, shakes its head, and keeps coming, undeterred. They have monstrously long strides when they're in a hurry, easily ten meters to a step, and the three hundred meters between the terraforming building and the Lanky turn into two hundred before the platoon fires the next salvo.

This time, I let the Lanky walk into the defensive fire. At two hundred meters, the rifles' ballistic computers can put the rounds into a sheet of paper that's been folded over twice. The better part of three dozen rounds pepper the center of the Lanky's mass, and the creature's chest heaves out and explodes with a wet and muffled thump. The Lanky's stride falters, and the thing collapses midstep, its body crashing to the ground in an ungraceful tangle of limbs. The platoon's troopers send up a satisfied cheer.

The new rifles have new ammunition, developed by the R&D section at Aberdeen Proving Grounds. With dozens of Lanky bodies at our disposal after the Battle of Earth last year, R&D has had no shortage of ballistic testing material. Lanky skins are thick and almost impossibly tough—even the old armor-piercing shells from our auto-cannons bounced off half the time—but they're not impenetrable. It turns out that shooting grenades or fléchettes at a Lanky is mostly pointless. The new ammo is truly evil stuff, saboted subcaliber pen-etrators that work like hypodermic needles. They hit the Lanky, pierce the skin, release a hundred centiliters of explosive gas, and then ignite the mess. The Lanky on the field in front of the terraformer rolls to one side and lies still, its chest blown out from the inside by a few liters of aerosolized explosive. I've never seen what a round like that would do to a human being, and I really hope I never do, because this ammo can take a hundred-ton Lanky down with just a few well-placed hits.

In theory, I remind myself. We've tested the new rounds on Lanky corpses, but we haven't had a chance to use them in combat yet. It's all conjecture based on dead-meat terminal ballistics, but the gas rounds make an unholy mess out of a dead Lanky, and I have no reason to believe they won't ruin the day of a live one.

The troops on the roof are still in the middle of their self-congratulatory cheer when I send in the next wave. The cheering ebbs when they hear the thundering footsteps in the fog and mist in the distance. Again, I am cheating a little. When I lived through this scenario in real life over six years ago, the second wave was made up of three more Lankies. We had just a squad then, with fléchette rifles, and no hope of stopping three of those things from tearing up the terraformer. Because these troops are a full platoon with much better rifles, I send in not three, but six more Lankies. Let them have a little challenge.

The squad leaders bellow orders again, and the platoon engages the newcomers. I study the camera feeds and the tactical display as they re-form their line and assign fire teams to individual Lankies, just like they should. Two fire teams per squad, three squads per platoon, four rifles per Lanky, five rounds in each rifle between reloads. I'm having the Lankies cross the distance as fast as we know they can move, a kilometer per minute. That doesn't leave much room for errors on the part of the platoon. Alerted and ready for trouble, the Lankies advance with their cranial shields in front of them, and they bob and weave as if they are walking into a hailstorm as the platoon unloads on them. Their head shields are too tough for anything man-portable in our arsenal—even armor-piercing MARS rockets will just chip off bits—and most of the rifle rounds expend themselves harmlessly in small puffs of aerosolizing gas.

"Aim for the joints," Sergeant Fisher yells into his squad channel. The recruits shift their fire, but many of the shots miss the relatively much smaller limb joints of the Lanky bodies.

Not as easy as a static target that doesn't come charging for you, is it? I think and smile to myself. Every last one of these recruits can pot a target the size of a helmet at five hundred meters with those computerized rifles, but it's much harder to aim true when you're scared to death and out of breath.

The Lankies advance into the rifle fire, heads bowed, rounds shattering against their shields, fragments kicking up dust in the dirt beneath their three-toed feet. The closer they get to the terraformer, the more precise the rifle fire from the three squads becomes. At two hundred meters, one of the Lankies falls with a wail and doesn't get back up, its leg joints destroyed by half a dozen exploding gas rounds. At one hundred meters, another goes down, flailing and screaming. A third one falls a mere fifty meters from the terraformer. The other three are at the building a second or two later. Two of them just crash into the wall, sending simulated debris flying everywhere. The third hooks its fingers into the edge of the roof and pulls itself up. The squads retreat away from the Lanky, still firing in good order, but they started their pullback just a second or two too late. Lankies can move much faster than their size and awkward physiology suggests. The Lanky lashes out with a spindly arm and almost casually wipes it across the front occupied by Second Squad. Six of their ten icons on my tactical display are snuffed out as the Lanky strikes a simulated killing blow that takes out over half the squad in a second or two. The Lanky exists only in the computer, of course, so the "dead" troopers didn't get most of their bones broken by a million joules of impact energy. Instead, their suit computers just turn off their optical and audio feeds, lock their visors in the lowered position to render their owners blind and deaf, and freeze the power-assisted joints on their battle armor suits. The six "dead" recruits fall where they died a simulated death, and they'll stay in that spot until I tell the computer to unfreeze them.

The rest of the platoon do a cover-and-retreat drill, rushing back across the expanse of the roof until they reach the single access door to the interior of the terraforming station. At this short range, the rifle fire from the M-90s is a devastating fusillade, and while most of the gas rounds hit the Lanky's impenetrable cranial shield, some make their way past it and blow bits and pieces off the limbs. Three or four rounds hit the upper chest of the Lanky nearly simultaneously and explode, and the Lanky lets out an earsplitting wail and slides off the roof again, mortally wounded. Then the computer decides that the other two Lankies have done enough structural damage to the building to make the front of it collapse. Half the platoon is inside the building, in the hardened staircase, but the other half is still on the roof that suddenly acquires a seventy-degree downward pitch, and a dozen more icons blink out of existence on the tactical display as the computer declares their owners casualties.

The sim is almost perfect. The sensory details are dead-on—the Lanky wails and the thundering sounds of their footsteps, the leaden sky above, the rain squalls and thick mists of a Lanky-occupied world. I have no doubt that the recruits feel as if they really are on a colony world, fighting the good fight for humanity. But it's only almost perfect. I've been in this scenario for real many times, and I know what's missing from the sim. As real as the computer can make it for the recruits, turning the Utah desert into a far-off Lanky world without breaking a computational sweat, deep down they all know they're not in real peril. They don't look up at that ash-gray sky with the knowledge that home is thirty light-years away, and that they are the only humans in the entire star system, the nearest members of their own species a dozen light-years away. They don't have the cold knowledge in the back of their heads that if the battle goes wrong, nobody will ever be around to collect dog tags, or even know about their deaths, for maybe decades, if at all.

The remaining squads do their best to regain control of the situation. First Squad moves down to the shelter of the basement and out to the emergency exit on the east side of the terraformer. Third Squad retreats to the back of the building and calls in for air support from the imaginary carrier in orbit. I decide to complicate things for the platoon.

"Charlie One-Niner, negative on the air support. All assets committed."

Third Squad's sergeant curses into the squad channel and toggles back a reply.

"Copy that, *Enterprise* TacOps. Requesting kinetic strike on marked coordinates, low yield."

I think about the request for a moment and consider denying that one as well, but then I decide that I've thrown this boot squad enough curveballs today. It won't be a complete freebie, however.

"Charlie One-Niner, *Enterprise* sensor array has battle damage. Give me a ten-second marker on the target and upload TRP data, and I'll send two kinetics your way."

"TacOps, copy that. Stand by for TRP data."

I asked for manual target markers, which means that someone has to go out and lay eyes and helmet sensors on the gaggle of Lankies disassembling the station from the outside.

On the tactical display, one fire team from Third Squad leaves the building via the emergency door all the way in the back of the terraforming station, on the opposite end of the part the Lankies are tearing down. I grin when I see that the icons are moving at a much faster speed than a soldier in battle armor can move on foot. The mock-up of the station is built like the real thing, including a pair of all-terrain electric all-wheel crawlers intended for maintenance patrols around the facility. I switch over to the visual feed and see two troopers on each crawler—one in the driver's seat, and one riding shotgun behind him facing to the rear. Only these troops aren't precisely riding shotgun.

The crawlers speed up as they drive up the long side of the building. At about the halfway point, they veer off into the desert, making wide hooks around the far corners to avoid close contact with the Lankies. Then they fire up their helmet-mounted designators and put target markers right into the middle of the group of Lankies dismantling the front of the building.

"TacOps, TRP data uploading."

"Charlie One-Niner, copy good data," I reply. "Stand by for kinetic launch in seven-zero seconds and clear the target area."

The Lankies can sense our vehicles somehow. Anything with an electric motor or fusion plant draws their attention much faster than just a trooper or two in battle armor. Two of the Lankies notice the four-wheeled crawlers and stop what they are doing to pursue the all-terrain vehicles in strides that are slow at first, then longer and faster as the aliens get their enormous mass moving. The drivers of the crawlers goose their electric engine and shoot off into the desert, and even at full throttle, they are barely pulling away from the Lankies. The two rear-facing troops on the passenger seats empty the magazines of their rifles at the pursuers. On a small vehicle going at top speed over rough and bumpy terrain, even the aiming computer isn't a great deal of help. Most of their rounds go wide or kick up dust in front or beside the Lankies. Then two or three rounds hit the lead Lanky, whose lower left limb collapses midstride. The Lanky tumbles to the desert floor in an enormous cloud of dust and gravel.

For a bunch of boots, it's a pretty good plan, and capable execution. It only has one flaw—it makes the Lankies disperse. The two that followed the ATVs are now away from the impact marker for the kinetic strike. When the rail gun projectile from the simulated carrier *Enterprise* hits the dirt right in front of the terraforming station a minute later, the quarter-kiloton impact blows apart the ruined front of the station and the two Lankies that were still working their way through the wreckage. The remaining Lanky, in hot pursuit of the two ATVs, stops and turns around. It's over five hundred meters away from the station now and cleanly avoided the kinetic impact altogether. The two crawlers stop their flight, and the riflemen on the backs of the ATVs reload their weapons. Then First Squad come out of the safety of the basement hallway shelter and takes up firing positions on the east flank of the building. The Lanky acts as if it can't make up its mind where to go next. It's about to find out what it feels like to be stuck between a hammer and an anvil. The ATV teams goose their rides again and swing around wide, and then the remaining Lanky takes rifle fire from three different directions. I watch with satisfaction as their concentrated fire tears into the Lanky, felling it like an enormous alien equivalent of an ancient Earth redwood tree.

When the dust settles, the platoon has lost eighteen out of thirty-three, more than half its number, but it has taken out all six of the attacking Lankies. The terraformer they were supposed to defend is half gone—in the simulation on their helmet visors, of course, not in reality—but I wasn't counting on the building surviving the defense, so I don't subtract any marks for that on the simulation score for the platoon. In the field, for a seasoned platoon of SI, this would have been a near defeat, with half the platoon gone and the facility destroyed. But these are recruits, not even fully trained soldiers yet, and only eleven weeks out of utter civiliandom. All things considered, they did well, but I do have to wonder how many of them I consign to a violent and perfectly unsimulated death on a colony world somewhere by letting this platoon pass their basic training.

The vital signs from the platoon are good, and a lot of them are elated at their victory. No doubt they anticipate this to be the end of their graduation exercise, but it's only the beginning.

"Squad leaders, gather your squads and prepare for egress," I send through the platoon channel. I unfreeze the "dead" soldiers' armor joints. Then I update TacLink with the coordinates for their next waypoint, which isn't the parking spot for the bus that dropped them off. It's the parking lot in front of the platoon building at NACRD Orem, forty kilometers to the northeast.

I smile when I hear the groans and muttered curses over the various squad channels. I've been in their shoes, and I've hated my drill sergeants as much as these recruits hate me right now. But the settled galaxy holds much bigger hardships than a surprise forty-klick hike in battle rattle, and I wouldn't be doing them any favors by going easy on them and making them believe otherwise. They'll be out in the field for the whole week, and they'll hate most of it, but they'll be better soldiers for it. And maybe they'll live long enough to appreciate it one day.

CHAPTER 3

—— GRADUATION DAY ——

On graduation day, the weather is as lousy as our odds against the Lankies. Instead of a big dog-and-pony ceremony out on the central parade ground, we have an abbreviated graduation indoors, in one of the massive vehicle hangars. Every surviving member of the platoon has passed Basic training, which is not like the boot camp I knew. For the ceremony, we actually have visiting families for an audience, which is definitely nothing like the old boot camp. We have a short formation and a long speech from the training battalion commander, and I'm next to the platoon leader in my drill instructor getup, trying to look impressive and soldierly while struggling with the mighty hangover caused by last night's end-of-training instructor party.

"I solemnly swear and affirm to loyally serve the North American Commonwealth, and to bravely defend its laws and the freedom of its citizens."

The recruits repeat the oath of service in loud and clear voices that reverberate through the cavernous hangar. They all look like they mean it. I said the same oath over six years ago, and then again last year for my reenlistment. I suppose I must have meant it, too, back then, because I am still here and wearing the uniform, despite everything that has happened since.

"Welcome to the Armed Forces of the North American Commonwealth," the battalion commander says, and the recruits and their families cheer. My drill instructors, standing at parade rest in front of their squads, stay straight-faced as only drill sergeants can.

"Platoon sergeants, take charge of your platoons and dismiss for liberty."

I step forward, toward the platoon, and my drill sergeants stand at attention.

"Ten-hut!"

The platoon follows suit with practiced precision. They may not be worth anything as infantry yet, but three months of daily formation drills have made them look like soldiers at least.

"Basic Training Platoon 1526—well done," I say in my platoon sergeant voice. "Drinks tonight will be on the house. Enjoy your leave, soldiers. You've earned it. Platoon dis-*missed*."

I watch as the formation dissolves, and the recruits of Platoon 1526—no longer rank civilians, but not yet fully trained and useful troops—rush over to where their families are waiting. About a third of them just mill around in place and talk to each other, recruits whose families couldn't make the trip or didn't want to. The image of the new and reformed post-Exodus military has greatly improved in the year since the Battle of Earth, but there are still plenty of people who think of the armed forces as tools of oppression, jailers and wardens of a vast coast-to-coast prison system. As a former PRC hood rat, and knowing the extent of the old leadership's cowardice and treason, I can't really say I blame the people who still hate the military.

My three drill instructors come over to join me, and we walk toward the gaggle of recruits and civilian families together, to shake hands and answer questions for a while and let the civvies take pictures of their loved ones shaking hands with their drill sergeants.

"Thirty minutes," I tell my sergeants. "Then nudge them toward the buses. Open house at the platoon building for an hour. We'll do unit assignments after midday chow."

"Copy that," Sergeant Lear replies. "And then I'll need a goddamn drink."

I look over the crowd of intermingling recruits and their families and wonder how soon I'll find some of those names on casualty reports through MilNet.

"You and me both," I say.

In the late afternoon, when all the former recruits are off to enjoy their weeklong post-graduation leave, I'm back in my office, closing out records and signing off on branch assignments. As in the past two training cycles, the ratio is 40/40/20 for Fleet, Spaceborne Infantry, and Homeworld Defense. We have lots of warships out of mothballs that need to be crewed, and lots of SI regiments to fill up with warm bodies after the Mars debacle. With the Lazarus Brigades doing most of the heavy lifting keeping order in the PRCs, there's less of a need for HD, so they get just maintenance-level personnel for now.

My finely honed combat vet senses don't even notice Sergeant Lear in the door until she clears her throat. I look up from my screen.

"I thought you were on leave already, Lear. Didn't think anyone was left but me."

"It's a three-shuttle hop to Montana," she says. "If I leave midday, I'll be stuck in some transit quarters shithole for the night. I'll be out with the first bird from Salt Lake in the morning."

"Yeah, transit bunks suck."

I look at her expectantly, but she doesn't walk into the office to sit in the empty chair in front of my desk.

"So what is it?" I say. "Did you come to secure yourself an instructor slot in boot camp flight 1601?"

Sergeant Lear shakes her head with a curt smile.

"Not at all. You, uh, want to maybe get a drink over at the NCO club if you're not too busy? It's past 1700 hours."

"Right," I say. 1700 is the magic hour when they start serving alcohol, or at least what passes for it at a military facility in a cash-strapped country. When I signed up, the food perks were a major incentive to stick it out through boot camp, but now that the military can't be as selective anymore, the culinary standards have dropped a little, to say the least.

I look back at my screen, where half a dozen Basic training personnel assignments still wait for my electronic signature. I can blow them off, but then I'll have to start this boring process again in the morning, possibly with a hangover.

"Why don't you go ahead and grab us a table, Sergeant Lear? I'll need another ten minutes on this admin bullshit. I'll join you when I'm done."

"Copy that," she says. Then she pats the doorframe and walks off. I listen to the sound of her boot soles on the worn but spotless flooring as she makes her way down the hallway.

"Right," I say again, and turn my attention back to the screen with some effort of will.

————————

When I walk up to Sergeant Lear's table in the NCO club a little while later, she already has two bottles of beer waiting. I sit down across the table from her and pop the cap off my bottle. She watches as I take a swig.

"Thanks. I needed that after today."

"Not much for fashion shows, huh?" Lear asks.

"Not much for bullshit," I reply, and she laughs.

"You think it's all bullshit?"

"The training? No. 'Course not. Just sending these green kids out into the force like that. Giving them the idea that they know shit about shit. The time we have, we can barely teach them how not to be a danger to others. Graduating from boot camp with a fucking parade. And families applauding. That shit just makes them feel like they're warriors now."

"They did okay," Sergeant Lear says. "You know what kind of material we get these days from the PRCs. Most of them would have failed boot before the Exodus just for attitude. But there are some tough kids in every batch."

"Tough," I repeat. "For PRC standards, no doubt. One thing to know how to take a punch and jack a hydrocar. It's another level of tough altogether to keep yourself in the fight when you're down to ten percent oxygen and three MARS rockets, and there's half a dozen Lankies coming to stomp you into the fucking dirt."

Sergeant Lear shifts in her seat a little and looks at the label on her beer bottle. Then she clears her throat and looks at me again.

"Sergeant Grayson, I wanted to ask you for a favor. I was wondering if you could give me a recommendation for my transfer request."

"You put in for transfer? What do you have, three tours as drill instructor now?"

"This was number four," she says. "Been at it for a year straight. I'm up for staff sergeant after this flight."

"Senior drill instructor slot," I say. "But that's not what you want."

She shakes her head and takes another sip from her bottle.

"Don't tell me you put in for a transfer to a combat billet, Lear."

I take her shrug as an affirmative response.

"Shit," I say. "Thought you were the smart one. You want to go back into the Fleet right now? Shipboard duty? You're MP, right?"

Sergeant Lear nods. "Master-at-arms."

"Are you out of your mind? You know how many ships we've lost in the last year and a half?"

"Most of the Fleet," she says.

"Most of the Fleet," I repeat. "And that includes almost all the good hardware. They're dragging fifty-year-old frigates out of mothballs and reactivating them with reserve crews and new sailors that have never done an Alcubierre transition. And they need all the atomic warheads for the Orion missiles, so most of the old shit buckets have empty missile tubes right now. You want to trade the fresh air and the weekends off for standing watch in a leaky relic that makes figure eights in orbit just to reassure the civvies on the ground?"

"That's my job," she says. "It's what I trained for. Not this drill instructor stuff. I'm happy standing watch in a leaky relic. I'm a Fleet sailor. I've done my time on the ground in the fresh air. And home's too far for two-day leave anyway, so I just sit here in the NCO club or ride out to Salt Lake on the weekends. I'm bored absolutely shitless."

I chuckle, and she raises an eyebrow.

"Now that last part I believe," I say. "You being bored. Not the soymeal paste about you rather being up there than down here. Nobody in their right mind likes watch rotation on a ship over weekends off and eight hours of uninterrupted sleep every night."

Sergeant Lear shrugs again, but this time with a slight smile.

"You got me there. But don't you feel the same? I mean, don't you itch to get back in the field again sometimes? Knowing that it can all turn to shit in a moment if you don't do your job right?"

I glance at my beer bottle, and my left hand that is idly turning it with just the fingertips. The prosthetics docs at Great Lakes were able to make my hand look like a proper hand again, but the time after our dash back to New Svalbard had been too long, and the damage from the contact salvo too great. The little and ring fingers on my left hand move with the impulses my brain sends over the artificial nerve conduits, and they bend and flex like their biological counterparts, but I have no feeling in them whatsoever other than a coarse sense of temperature and pressure. The replacement is extremely well done, but I can still tell the transition between the real, living part of the hand and the artificial addition. The skin has the same tone and texture, but something about it is just slightly off, and always will be.

"No," I say, and continue to turn the beer bottle. "I don't itch for that. Not anymore."

There's something in Sergeant Lear's expression that almost looks like pity for a moment. Then she lets out a slow breath and leans back in her chair.

"Maybe you're right. Maybe I'm nuts for wanting to go combat again. But I'm tired of this place. Another six months of this, and I'll be a raging alcoholic."

"You can't," I say, and lift the bottle off the table a few centimeters. "Not with this shit. Trust me on that one."

I look at Sergeant Lear, and I'm once again struck by how young she is. Not really in the chronological sense—I only have five years on her at the most—but in appearance. She's had four years of service, but she's in a support specialty, not a frontline combat job. She looks tired, but so do all the other instructors after another twelve-week boot camp training flight of getting up at 0400, going to bed at 2200 or later, and lots of physical and mental stress in between. But she lacks the shopworn look of the grunts. She doesn't have early gray hairs interleaved in that tightly strung ponytail of hers. She doesn't have the wrinkles in the corner of her eyes. And she doesn't have that hallmark of men and women who have seen too much awful stuff, the thousand-yard stare. She doesn't look weary.

I sigh and drain the rest of my beer. Then I put the bottle down and drum a little cadence on the tabletop with my fingertips—three live, two numb. It feels like when your hand has fallen asleep, only without that painful prickle of feeling returning after a few minutes.

"Tell you what, Lear. If you want to put in for a transfer, I'll endorse your request."

"Thank you, Sergeant Grayson," she says, the relief obvious in her face.

"I won't give you the old saw about being careful what you wish for," I say. "But I bet you a bottle of real bourbon that one day you'll look back at this and want to kick your younger self square in the ass."

She laughs brightly. Her teeth are white and even, the telltale sign of a middle-class 'burber upbringing.

"And call me Andrew. Basic flight is done. You're no longer my subordinate. At least not until they shoot your request down, and you get to be senior drill instructor under me for the next batch."

"Okay," she says. "Andrew. Can I buy you another drink? Now it's no longer sucking up to a superior, right?"

I check the battered chrono on my wrist.

"One more can't hurt things, I suppose. We don't have to tuck the little nuggets in tonight, after all."

Someone in the room increases the volume of the large Networks screen mounted on the far wall. I've not paid any attention to the news screen at all since I walked into the NCO club, but now I turn around, because the first words from the speakers are "Mars" and "survivors." Sergeant Lear turns that direction as well.

"Corps Command verified this evening that contact has been established with the largest group of survivors yet located on Mars. The group of holdouts is sheltered in a military bunker underneath Speicher Air/Space Base on the Chryse Planitia plain," the news announcer says. I look around in the room and see that every pair of eyes is fixed to the news screen now.

"Identities of the 1,453 survivors at the shelter have been transmitted and listed on the Corps Command and Department of Colonial Affairs network nodes," the announcer continues. "The survivors include almost five hundred military personnel and their families. The new group of holdouts reports that their supply situation is critical, and that they will require resupply or evacuation within the month, or the shelter's inhabitants will starve to death."

All over the room, people reach for their PDPs to check the mentioned network nodes. Mars is—was—our biggest colony, and almost everyone in the Corps had relatives or friends on Mars or knows someone who does. I do not, and Sergeant Lear doesn't seem to, either, because she continues drinking her beer and leaves her PDP in her pocket.

"Within the month," she says. "No pressure or anything, right?"

I walk into my room a few hours later with considerably more than just one extra beer in me. I close the door behind me and toss the beret onto the bed. Then I sit down at the wall-mounted folding desk next to my bunk, where the screen of my terminal is blinking with an UNREAD MESSAGES notification.

>*Got off duty three hours early. You weren't on the last shuttle. What gives? —H.*

I start typing a response, but decide that my patience level with my prosthetic fingers isn't high enough. I open the drawer of my desk and pull out two small pill containers. One holds the pain meds they've started prescribing after the hand surgery, when I started having aches in the intact part of the damaged hand. The other pills are heavy-duty sleep aids, to make sure I can go through at least half the night without horrendous dreams. I take a pill out of each container, walk over to the sink, and wash both down with a swig of water. Then I return to the terminal and tap on the comms link that will connect me to Halley via vid chat. The screen says BANDWIDTH ALLOCATION REQUESTED for about ten seconds before changing to ALLOCATION GRANTED—CONNECTING.

"You look like crap," Halley says when she sees my face.

"Love you too, dear," I say. "Come and teach the nuggets down here which end of the gun is dangerous, and let's see how you look after three months."

"Like I don't have any experience in that field," she says. "I thought you'd be on the last bird up. Don't tell me they've postponed graduation."

"No, the nuggets are all on their way home," I reply. "I just had a few drinks with one of my drill sergeants. She wanted me to sign off on a transfer order. Wants to go back to regular Fleet duty, if you can believe that. When I got to Flight Ops, they had cancelled the 1900 run to Luna because they have three shuttles down right now."

Halley rolls her eyes slightly and shakes her head. She has the same short, helmet-friendly haircut she's worn since she got into Combat Flight School over half a decade ago, and I have a hard time imagining her with any other cut now.

"Send her up, and I can change her mind in about thirty seconds. So when are you coming up? And what are you going to do to make up for the fact that I'm going to be sleeping by myself in our first night off together in four stinking weeks?"

"Sorry about that," I say. "I'll bring some Scotch. Real, not the synthetic shit."

Halley purses her lips as if in thought and then nods after a moment.

"That would be acceptable restitution. You better make that first shuttle up to Luna in the morning. Remember, we have that thing at noon before we can go down to Vermont."

"Right," I say. "Almost forgot. Where are they holding it?"

"The flight deck on *Regulus*. They're going to park her in geosynchronous orbit over the capital."

"How symbolic. I'll be there, don't worry."

"It'll cost you a lot more than some Scotch if you make me do this alone, Andrew. Fair warning."

"Acknowledged," I reply.

"I'll see you in the morning," Halley says. "I'll go to sleep now. Alone. Most boring."

"Sorry again. I'll make it up to you tomorrow. Love you."

"You too," she says. Then she pretends to stick a finger down her throat and makes a little retching sound. "Have a good night, love."

She air-kisses the vid lens before signing off, and I have a sudden and almost overwhelming urge to be up there and run my fingers through her hair. I lied to Sergeant Lear earlier—I am bored shitless with boot camp instructor duty, too, but I love being posted on Earth because it lets me stay close to my wife. I feel a little selfish for being content with this job just because I get to spend leaves and weekends with Halley, but after all that has happened in the last few years, I think we have damn well earned the privilege.

CHAPTER 4
—— ABOVE AND BEYOND ——

"God, I hate this monkey suit."

"Shut up and clasp your collar," Halley says. "You can look soldierly once or twice a year at least."

"It won't lock. Fucking fastener always takes me twenty tries to get together."

Halley steps behind me and moves my hands aside with hers. Then she clasps both halves of my Fleet dress uniform's stand-up collar with a swift and practiced motion.

"There," she says.

"I hardly ever wear this thing," I say, and check myself in the mirror. Gig line straight, belt buckle polished and perfectly centered, medal rack lined up neatly, combat drop badge shiny. I step aside to let Halley use the mirror. She is wearing the same uniform, the Fleet's Class A dress smock that usually collects dust in a combat trooper's locker until there's a wedding or a formal funeral. My medal rack is topped with a combat drop badge, senior level. Halley's medal rack sports combat aviator wings on top. The new Fleet command saw fit to throw a handful of medals at us after the Battle of Earth almost a year ago. We both have a Silver Star, but Halley's collection of tin-on-a-ribbon is noticeably bigger than mine: Silver Star, Distinguished Flying Cross (three awards), Purple Heart, and half a dozen other Fleet awards for bravery and professionalism and not skipping ahead in the chow line. The longer I'm in the military, the less those colorful ribbons mean to me. Considering what I have to trade every time they give me a new one, those ribbons are piss-poor compensation.

Halley tugs on the bottom of her tunic to smooth it out. Then she flicks a bit of lint from the epaulette on her shoulder, where the three stars of her rank gleam in the light from the bathroom LED fixtures.

"Looking sharp, Captain," I say. "Maybe you ought to represent the both of us. You're senior in rank."

"You are not getting out of this one," she says. "You were a lot closer to him than I was."

"You know he wouldn't give a shit about that medal," I say. "And he sure as hell wouldn't care if we showed up for that dog-and-pony show."

"No, he wouldn't. But the Fleet does. His family does. And I am not going to stand at attention in my dress blues by myself. So get your cover and let's go, Sergeant First Class Grayson. The shuttle is waiting."

"Yes, ma'am."

I walk over to the kitchen table, snatch up my scarlet combat controller beret, roll it up, and tuck it underneath my left epaulette. We've been married almost a year, and by now I know better than to argue with my superior.

The shuttle is full to the last seat. The passengers are roughly half uniformed Fleet or SI, half civilian techs. We are running training cycles at double the rate of the pre-Exodus days, and the fleet yards above Luna are as busy as they have ever been. We lost so many trained soldiers and sailors last year that we are just now beginning to make a dent in the rebuilding of the Fleet. We are building and retrofitting ships, retraining troops, and fortifying Earth around the clock, and we still aren't halfway back to the forces we had before the Lankies took out half the Fleet and the old government absconded with most of the rest.

But there are bright spots in our new line of battle.

"Will you look at that huge son of a bitch," Halley says. She leans across my lap to get a better view of the ships cruising slowly in formation a few thousand meters off the shuttle's starboard side. Her hair smells like the slightly antiseptic three-in-one military shampoo.

"That's a lot of tonnage," I concur.

Off our starboard, the Fleet's latest commissioned warship is escorted by two frigates, which look like divers swimming alongside a whale shark. The NACS *Agincourt* is just slightly under a thousand meters long, half again the length and tonnage of a supercarrier. I don't know much about warship design, but I know people who do, and they told me that the *Agincourt* is basically a really big particle cannon strapped to a bunch of fusion reactors and wrapped in the latest armor. One of Earth's two new battleships, built in secrecy by the same government that fled the Solar System with the Fleet's best gear and a few ten thousand of the NAC's elite. She wasn't complete when the Lankies forced our hand a year ago, so the Exodus fleet left her and her sister ship behind. In the interest of power balance, we gave the other one to the SRA, where it is about to be commissioned as the *Arkhangelsk*.

"Look," Halley says, and points at the aft hull of the *Agincourt*. "They're still not done. There's no armor plating on the port-side ass end."

"Ran out of alloy, maybe?" I offer. "As long as the guns and propulsion work."

"Tell you what. If we ever built a ship that looks like it may scare a Lanky, this one's it," Halley says. "It looks mean as hell."

I look out of the shuttle's scuffed multilayered polyplast window and find myself nodding in silent agreement. The *Agincourt* doesn't share the roughly cylindrical fat torpedo shape of the other warships in the Fleet. She's squat and blocky, with a massive dorsal ridge of armor plates that runs the length of the ship from bow to stern. If the Lankies look a bit like prehistoric dinosaurs, this ship looks like a gigantic approximation of a snapping turtle, flattened and stretched to a kilometer in length. There are no rail guns or sensor arrays cluttering that uninterrupted ride of armor protection. This ship looks like it was built to get close to dangerous things and blow them to pieces.

"Humanity's last, best hope," I say, with dramatic pathos.

"She may just be," Halley replies. "Oh, by the way—I heard through the Fleet rumor network that our SRA pals are commissioning the other one this month."

"Good. The more guns pointed toward the Mars approach, the better."

"They're already calling ours the '*Aggie*' in the Fleet. The other one is '*Archie*.'"

"*Aggie* and *Archie*," I repeat. "Our ticket back to Mars, or a super-expensive way to turn half a million tons of steel and alloy into scrap."

"Always the optimist, huh?"

"Six years of this shit, I'm biased toward 'cynical realism.'"

"It's them or nothing," Halley says. "There's not much left in the construction queue, and those renegade fuckers took everything else worth a shit to God knows where when they left us behind."

"Hope they run into a whole fleet of Lankies and get blown to shit in cold, dark space, fifty light-years from home."

"Better hope we find them before the Lankies do. We need all those ships back. They can have the people. Saves us the trouble of having to kill them ourselves."

Luna is as busy as I've ever seen it, although you wouldn't be able to tell just by looking at the surface. Because it's close to Earth and has low gravity and no atmosphere, the moon is the ideal off-world training ground for all space combat occupational specialties, and both NAC and SRA have their main military schools here. This is where we train our future drop ship pilots and Spaceborne Infantry, and about two dozen other military jobs. I thought the thrill of seeing Earth from the moon would never get old, but I've spent a lot of time here since the Battle of Earth last year, and I find myself conceding that I may have been wrong. But training duty has meant getting to spend time with Halley, and that won't ever get old. Even the normally boring three-hour shuttle ride from Luna to Earth orbit is a welcome respite with my wife by my side. We have spent more time together in the past eleven months than in the five years we had been together before then, and we aren't sick of each other yet, which I suppose is a good sign.

"There's Gateway," Halley says, and points at the main NAC military space hub as we coast into Earth orbit a while later.

We pass within ten kilometers of the station, close enough to see that almost half the docking berths are occupied by warships. Most of those ships are on the small side—frigates, corvettes, a few destroyers, a light cruiser—but it looks significantly busier than it did a year ago, when both Gateway and Independence stations were all but deserted. Most of the ships anchored over there are recommissioned relics from the mothball fleet, but they are armored hulls with missile tubes and working Alcubierre drives, and we need all of those we can get these days.

"Prepare for arrival," an announcement from the flight deck chimes in. "Docking at *Regulus* in one-zero minutes."

"Party time," Halley says. She looks over the ribbon rack and pilot wings on her dress tunic to make sure she didn't miss a piece of lint or a loose thread.

"Some party," I grumble, but do likewise. I don't want to be here, but I need to be. If anyone deserves the honor, it's the man receiving our highest military award today—posthumously.

The enormous flight deck of the *Regulus* has been neatened up for the ceremony. There's a small podium near the forward hangar bulkhead right underneath the large painted ship's seal. Someone set up flagpoles with the flags of the NAC and the Fleet, and there are about a hundred chairs in front of the podium, most of them occupied by a mix of uniformed Fleet personnel and people in civilian clothing.

"Camera crews." Halley points.

Over by the podium, there's a small forest of camera tripods set up, far more than the typical single Fleet newsie recording motivational footage at the average medal ceremony. This is the big one, the one everyone just calls "the Medal," and the fact that the president of the NAC awards it means a far bigger PR circus than usual. Lots of people like to be close to glory. Maybe they hope the shine will rub off somehow. There are probably twice as many people as chairs in this part of the hangar deck.

"Over there," I say, and nod over to a group of soldiers standing a little away from the main gaggle of chatting civilians. In mixed gatherings, combat grunts tend to cluster together, strength and comfort in numbers, just like on the battlefield.

We cross the space between the shuttle's parking spot and the area by the podium. The group of soldiers I spotted has many familiar faces in it. There's almost the entire former command crew of the *Indianapolis*, and some of the Spaceborne Infantry grunts from her old SI detachment. One of them, a tall and lean SI gunnery sergeant, lifts a hand in greeting as we walk up to the group.

"Grayson," he says. "Good to see you."

"Gunnery Sergeant Philbrick," I say, with emphasis on the first word. "Who the hell promoted you?"

"They put promotions onto the trays at chow these days." He shrugs with a smile. "Lots of billets open all over the place. You got bumped too, I see."

I glance at my shoulder boards, which have the rank insignia of a sergeant first class, the Fleet version of the same rank Philbrick is wearing.

"Same deal," I say. "Lots of slots, few bodies to fill 'em."

Philbrick turns to Halley.

"Good morning, Captain."

She waves him off as he raises his hand for a salute.

"At ease. With all the brass on this flight deck, you'll dislocate your arm if you want to be all proper."

"My wife," I say. "Halley, this is Gunny Philbrick. He was on *Indy* with me last year. Everyone else, too." I point to the troopers with Philbrick, who by now have formed a semicircle around us.

"I heard," Halley says. She extends a hand to Gunny Philbrick.

"Thanks for busting this dope out of the brig for me. Would have been a lonely wedding without him there."

"I bet." Philbrick shakes Halley's hand with a grin. "My pleasure, Captain."

"Where's Major Renner?" I ask.

"Lieutenant Colonel Renner," Philbrick corrects me. He nods over to the podium. "First row. She got a ringside seat."

Then-Major Renner was the *Indy*'s executive officer when I spent several weeks aboard last year for our scouting run back to the Solar System. Apparently, when Colonel Campbell gave the order to get into the escape pods, she almost had a physical fight with the skipper in an attempt to stay on board. Almost everyone on *Indy* survived except for five people— Colonel Campbell, the two volunteers who stayed behind with him to man the helm and navigation stations, and two enlisted sailors whose escape pods were never found when the Fleet backtracked on *Indy*'s trajectory and rescued the survivors.

"How's the hand?" Philbrick asks.

I hold up my left hand and wiggle my fingers.

"Looks like a hand again," he says.

"Four days of misery at Great Lakes. Took them three tries to match the skin tone. It's mostly for cosmetics. Waited too long to get the nerve ends fused back together."

"That sucks."

"Yeah," I say. "Could have been worse, though." I look over to the podium, where someone has set up a large printout of Colonel Campbell's personnel file picture. There's a black ribbon tied across one corner.

"Could have been," Philbrick agrees.

There's a minor commotion near the forward hangar bulkhead. We turn to see a group of people entering the hangar through the main access hatch. One of them is a short, slender, white-haired woman in her sixties. I recognize her from the footage of her inauguration ceremony a few months ago.

"That's the president," I say to Halley, who just nods.

"No shit," she says. "She looks shorter in person, doesn't she?"

"Word has it she was a Shrike jock," Philbrick says. "Retired commander."

I've seen the old president—the bastard who left Earth a year back with most of his cabinet and all the good combat hardware left in the Fleet—in Network news broadcasts plenty of times. He always had a phalanx of bodyguards around him whenever he showed up in public. This new president has two guys in civvie suits by her side, but they're too soft-looking for bodyguards. There are also a few uniformed Fleet officers with her, but they're all in dress blues, not combat gear, and clearly just guides. It seems that the new commander-in-chief has no anxieties about mingling with common troops without armed protection. Come to think of it, there are no security checkpoints in sight anywhere on the flight deck. I see lots of holstered sidearms, and the Fleet MPs by the forward bulkhead have their usual PDWs slung across their chests, but the president and her entourage don't seem to care. Most of the new government is made up of veterans, and there's definitely a new wind blowing in NAC state/citizen relations.

"Ten-hut!" one of the general officers near the podium bellows into the audio pickup, and we all snap to attention wherever we're standing.

We watch the president walk up to the podium. The handful of generals by the podium salute her, and she replies with a practiced salute of her own. The president looks a bit tired, but her voice is steady and clear when she addresses the assembly on the hangar deck.

"At ease," the president says. We all relax out of our ramrod-straight attention postures.

"I'm still not used to this," she says. "Flag officers saluting me, I mean. When I was in the service, seeing this many general officers looking at me expectantly usually meant I was in some deep shit."

There's chuckling and some outright laughter in the ranks, and the president smiles curtly. Then her face turns serious again.

"I'd love to tell you that this is my favorite part of the new job, but it isn't. Not by a long shot."

She looks over at the picture of Colonel Campbell, regarding the crowd with that same wryly amused, slightly detached expression I knew well.

"More than half the time, this medal is awarded posthumously," she continues. "As it is today. That means that every other of these awards ceremonies, we have lost someone we could not afford to lose. And there's no doubt that we are all diminished for not having Colonel Campbell among our ranks anymore."

She looks at the data pad on the podium in front of her. Then she picks it up and holds it for everyone to see.

"This is Colonel Campbell's official Medal of Honor citation. I could read it to you word for word, all seven paragraphs of it, but you all know what he did. When we stood with our backs against the wall, when the Lanky seed ship was bearing down to destroy what was left of our Fleet in orbit, he sacrificed himself and his ship to buy us time. We are all still here, putting the pieces back together, because he decided that his life and his ship were a fair trade for the lives of everyone else. That is a debt that we cannot even begin to repay, certainly not with a piece of lacquered gold on a ribbon. But it's a start."

She puts the data pad down again and pauses for a moment.

"Colonel Campbell was supposed to scout out the secret renegade anchorage and retrieve his recon buoys. When he got word that there was a Lanky seed ship headed for Earth and less than three hours away, he made a different call. He set *Indianapolis* on a parabolic back to Earth, and then he burned all his reactor fuel to drive his ship as fast as he could. He had the crew take to the escape pods, and then he flew his ship into the approaching Lanky at close to one-thirtieth of light speed."

Every time I play out the scenario in my head, I wonder what those last few moments in *Indy*'s CIC must have been like. What was going through the colonel's head, knowing he'd blink out of existence in just a few seconds, never knowing whether his actions had made a difference in the end? I'm sure the colonel and the two others in CIC died in a microsecond when *Indy* disintegrated against the Lanky's hull, and that's not a horrible way to go, but the knowledge of their imminent deaths must have been dreadful.

"Colonel Campbell wasn't the only one to die that day," the president continues. "Not by a long shot. We lost so many in that battle last year. Too many. But he did what he did to give us a fighting chance. All of us, here on this planet, whatever nationality or alliance. And for that, a bucket of these medals wouldn't be adequate recognition. But like I said—it's a start."

The rest of the ceremony is mercifully brief. The president does read out the citation for Colonel Campbell's Medal of Honor, because that's what you do at events like this. Then a Fleet major steps up next to her with the medal in a shadow box made of black lacquered wood. To a living recipient, she would present the award by hanging it around his or her neck, but the posthumous awards are given to the closest relative, mounted in a box because only the recipient gets to wear it.

I don't know the woman accepting the award from the president, but I'm guessing it's Colonel Campbell's wife. She's tall, with steel-gray hair that sits in tight curls on her head, and her expression is one of stone-faced detachment. I realize that I know next to nothing about Colonel Campbell's private life. He was the executive officer on *Versailles* for the brief time I was a member of her crew, and then I didn't see him again until our mission to New Svalbard last year, just before the Alcubierre network was deactivated and everything went to shit. I spent a few weeks on *Indianapolis* with him, but I never had the opportunity to talk to him outside of the CIC and our official duties, and now I never will.

When it's all over, they play a slow and somber version of the Commonwealth national anthem over the PA system, the president mingles for a little while to talk to Colonel Campbell's relatives a little more, and the crowd slowly starts to disperse.

"Well, that was uplifting," Halley says. "Let's get back to our quarters and do something fun. We have a day and a half off."

"Hang on for a second," I say. There are more familiar faces in the crowd over by the podium, and one of them looks over to me and waves in recognition.

"I need to introduce you to someone," I say, and pull Halley with me.

"Andrew," Dmitry says in his broad Russian accent when we meet up in the middle of the hangar deck. He grins and holds out a hand, and I shake it firmly. Dmitry's grip is much stronger than his short stature would suggest. I know that he can punch much harder than a guy his size ought to be able to hit.

"Dmitry," I say. "You're about the last person I expected to see here today."

"Here to award battle honors to commander of fine little imperialist spy ship," he replies.

"You're giving an Alliance award to a Commonwealth officer?"

"Alliance general staff gives award," Dmitry says. "I just deliver medal."

I turn toward Halley and nod at Dmitry.

"This is Senior Sergeant Dmitry Chistyakov, Alliance Marines. Dmitry, this is my wife, Captain Halley."

Dmitry doesn't salute Halley, and she makes no motion to extend any military courtesies herself. Instead, they just sort of size each other up for a moment, and then Dmitry extends his hand again.

"I remember picture. You are pilot."

"I am a pilot," Halley confirms. She takes the offered hand and shakes it curtly. "Pleasure to meet you, Senior Sergeant. I hear you had some misadventures with this knuckle-dragger here last year."

"Misadventures," Dmitry repeats with a slight smile. "Yes, we have many misadventures."

Dmitry is wearing the SRA Marines' dress uniform, which looks completely out of place in a hangar full of military personnel in dark blue Fleet and black-and-blue SI dress uniforms. It's a gold-trimmed white tunic paired with black trousers, and black boots that are polished to a mirror shine. Underneath the tunic, Dmitry is wearing a collarless shirt that's horizontally striped in alternating colors of white and blue.

"You came here just for the medal ceremony?" I ask.

"Was here already. On moon, on big Commonwealth training facility." He pronounces the last word very deliberately, as if he has just learned it ten minutes ago. "For observing training of your space infantry. Give advice, take advice, that sort of thing."

I've known for a while that we have started to exchange personnel and training notes with the Alliance—Halley's Combat Flight School is hosting two SRA pilots as observers—but I wasn't aware that Dmitry was one of them.

"You are in an NAC facility, and you didn't send me a message?"

"Has been only three weeks," Dmitry says. "Busy three weeks. Not much time for personal things."

"The world is changing," Halley says with a wry smile. "It'll never go back to the way it was. Not now."

"Not to old ways," Dmitry agrees. "But give time. We find new ways to be *duraky*." He winks at me and pats my shoulder once.

"You come see me at imperialist school of infantry, yes? We drink together, maybe see if you are better now at punching. You look like you need exercise. You get squishy around middle." The word *squishy* comes out exactly like *facility* earlier—as if he had just picked it up not too long ago.

Dmitry winks at Halley and walks back to his own group, a handful of SRA and NAC officers standing in a small gaggle by the podium.

"That little bastard," I say.

"I kind of like him," Halley says, and pats the front of my tunic.

CHAPTER 5

FAMILY MATTERS

Liberty Falls is only fifteen minutes away from the Homeworld Defense Air Station at Burlington, but getting off the maglev train always feels a bit like stepping into an alternate time and reality. I've always felt a bit like a foreign body here, a PRC rat among the upper-middle-class 'burbers, and the feeling is only intensified when Halley and I step out of the maglev terminal in fatigues, with sidearms holstered and our bulky alert bags over our shoulders. The new rules require that we are in uniform and armed while on leave, with a light battle kit in a bag within reach at all times in case there's a Lanky incursion again while we are away from our duty stations. The alert bags hold lightweight armor sets, helmets, comms kit, and DNA-locked personal defense weapons with a thousand rounds of caseless ammunition apiece. If the call comes, we can be minimally battle ready and tied in to TacLink within a minute or two.

"All the gear makes us look like we're planning to annex the business district or something," Halley says when we see the third civvie in as many minutes glancing at us with suppressed discomfort. The armed forces have always been popular in the 'burbs, but even a year after the Lankies visited Earth without invitation, they're still not used to troops in combat gear openly carrying weapons down here.

"You've seen the cops around here," I reply. "They don't even wear hardshell. Two good fire teams could take over Main Street and hold out for three days."

Every time I come here, the place looks unreal to me, like a live museum exhibit or a science diorama blown up to life-size scale. Liberty Falls is a neat and clean little town, old-style brick buildings from two hundred years ago mixed in with new architecture, everything painstakingly designed to harmonize and blend the disparate building styles. The trees and bushes everywhere are real, and they must spend a small fortune every year planting actual grass in the little parks scattered all over town. This is an enclave for the well-to-do and the upper middle class, people who can afford living out among real trees where there are still pastures and empty stretches of wilderness. It's only a hundred kilometers from the Boston-Providence metroplex, but this town might as well be on a colony moon somewhere for all the resemblance it fails to bear to the place where I grew up.

We walk across the small park in front of the maglev station in the center of town. It's fringed by real maple trees—raised in a lab, no doubt, but actual living plants. Halley stops in the middle of the park and kneels on the pathway beside the neatly trimmed lawn. Then she runs her hands across the tops of the grass stalks.

"I know they have that at your parents' place down in Austin," I say.

"Yeah, but we haven't been down there in six months. I always pet the grass when I pass some. Our line of work, you never know when you get another chance."

I watch her with amusement. Then I drop my pack and kneel next to her to do likewise. The grass is soft and pliable, the earth underneath firm and cool. It occurs to me just then that none of the colony moons I've been to in the last few years have had any grass on them. When every gram of interstellar cargo is worth its weight in platinum, you don't waste hold space hauling seeds for decorative plants. You bring seeds that can be turned into food or fuel.

Halley gets up and brushes her hand on the pant leg of her fatigues. "Earth," she says. "It has its nice little corners, doesn't it?"

"Some," I agree. "Give it time. We'll find 'em and burn them to the ground."

Our destination is on Liberty Falls' Main Street, just past the old-fashioned redbrick library and the town offices. It's a small restaurant in a building that looks like it was built before there was a North American Commonwealth. I know that the place, like half the shops on Main Street, is thoroughly modern inside and just looks like it's two hundred years old. There's a blackboard easel outside by the curb that has the specials of the day written on it in colored chalk. Out here, you can still get food that isn't made with soy and shit, and the people who live here can afford meals that would cost a PRC resident a month's worth of black market goods and a commissary chit besides. Even with the fate of the planet teetering on the edge of a sharp blade, there are still those who eat real beef in places where the cops aren't even armored, and those who eat reconstituted crap in neighborhoods where the cops carry more gear than your average Spaceborne Infantry grunt.

"Ready for another dose of family?" I say. Halley pretends to check her nonexistent makeup in an imaginary mirror, then gives me a curt and pilot-like thumbs-up.

"Going in hot," she says.

The inside of the restaurant has a vaguely last-century Mediterranean flair to it: stucco walls, cozy little nooks for the tables, and rustic-looking tables that would be worth tens of thousands if they were made of real worm-eaten antique wood and not its synthetic imitation.

Inside, there are no guests yet. A tall, slender man with a graying regulation-length buzz cut is wiping down tables with a rag. He's wearing a server's apron, and the sleeves of his shirt are rolled up neatly, revealing tattoos on his lower arms. He looks over to the door when we walk in and smiles.

"Well, look what the cat dragged in."

"You don't have one, Chief Kopka," I reply.

"Health and sanitation regulations," he says. Then he shakes out the rag he's holding and drapes it over a shoulder. He wipes his hands on the apron and comes over to us.

"Good to see you, Master Chief," Halley says, and gives him a curt hug.

"And you, Captain," he says. "Still not used to Fleet sailors walking around with ground pounder ranks. You should be called a lieutenant. And wear bars instead of stars."

"Pay grade's the same," Halley says. "That's all that matters."

"I thought you weren't going to be in until tonight?" Chief Kopka asks.

"We got two seats on an earlier shuttle down to Burlington," I reply. "Easier getting spots going down to Earth than coming back up."

"Place is empty," Halley observes. "Did you run out of food?"

Chief Kopka makes a pained little grimace.

"Sort of. We don't open for breakfast anymore, just lunch and dinner. I haven't been getting enough eggs and dairy in. The local stuff is getting stretched pretty thin."

"I need to figure out how to say 'Stretched Pretty Thin' in Latin," I say. "That's pretty much our new motto now."

"Sit down, you two," the chief says. He gestures to one of the empty booths. "Can I get you some coffee, make you an early lunch? Kitchen's warmed up."

"We had food out at Burlington before we hopped on the maglev," Halley says. "But I wouldn't turn down a cup of real coffee."

"How about you, Andrew?"

"I'll take a cup," I say. "And some cream if you have any."

"Not a problem." Chief Kopka walks over to the kitchen door. Before he reaches it, someone else comes out of the kitchen with quick steps.

"You're here," my mother says. "Why didn't you tell me you were coming early? I would have picked you up from the station."

"That's precisely why I didn't tell you we were coming early, Mom," I say. "It's called OpSec. Operational security."

"What, I'm going to pass your location on to the Lankies or something? Give me a break."

Mom comes over to where we are standing and hugs first Halley, then me. She looks relaxed and content. I asked Chief Kopka to get her out of Boston just before things went all upside down last year with Lankies raining down on North America in their pods ejected from a dying seed ship breaking up in Earth orbit. The chief not only got her out of the metroplex in time, he gave her a job at his restaurant and a place to stay. She now lives in an apartment that's smaller than the welfare unit she had in the PRC, but she can breathe fresh air and touch real trees as often as she wants. Her clothing isn't extravagant, but it's clean and tidy and even fashionable, a far cry from the stuff she used to wear out of necessity.

"Sit down, the lot of you," Chief Kopka says. "I'll be right back with some coffee."

We sit as ordered. Mom eyes our sidearms that clank against the backs of the chairs.

"You can take those off and put them in the office in the back if they're in the way," she says. "The chief has a safe back there."

"No can do," I reply. "Gotta have those on our person at all times."

"Even out here?"

"Even out here," Halley confirms. "Last year, those pods went all over the place. Most ended up in PRCs, but a bunch landed in middle-class 'burber towns. Cops with stun sticks fighting Lankies. You can imagine how that turned out."

"We saw some of that on the Networks," Chief Kopka says as he returns to the table with a steel carafe and a fistful of mugs, which he is holding bunched together by the handles. He puts the mugs down and starts pouring coffee. "At that point, I was wishing I had something with a little more pep than that stun gun back in the office. That thing's good for nothing." He slides into the booth next to Mom and pours himself a cup as well.

"A pistol isn't much better than nothing," Halley says.

"Against a Lanky, maybe. But I'm not too worried about those tearing down Liberty Falls. We get PRC riots again, next time they may spill farther north than Concord."

The coffee is as good as I remembered it. There's a world of a difference and a twenty-fold price increase between the soy brew they serve in the military and the stuff here in the chief's little restaurant that is brewed from actual ground beans. Of all the decadences this upper-middle-class eatery has to offer, the coffee is among the cheapest, but my favorite by far. It tastes like liquid civilization.

"How long will you stay?" Mom asks. "Is your training job over?"

"Just a short leave," I say. "We get two and a half days for Earth leave. Then I have to report back to the Depot to prepare for the next batch of recruits and meet my new drill instructors."

"That's not a lot of time," Mom says with a slightly dejected expression. "They are working you to death. After all you have done." She glances at my left hand, resting on the table next to my coffee mug, and averts her gaze again.

"Someone's gotta train the new people, Mom. And there aren't all that many left who can."

We talk and drink coffee without having to watch the clock for once. The chief excuses himself to get back to the kitchen once we've briefed him on the big picture and the little bits and pieces of news that make him feel like he's tied in to the rumor network sufficiently. Mom uses her privileged Network access for military dependents to forward messages to the chief's old shipmates, and we fill in the gaps whenever we're down on Earth for leave. Everyone is starved for information down here. They all want reassurance they won't die tomorrow or next week.

We're on our third or fourth cups when Chief Kopka's place starts filling up with the first lunch customers of the day.

"I have to go back to work for a bit," Mom says. "I've been spending too much time chatting as it is."

"The chief is fine with that," I say.

"Yes, but I'm not. I have to feel like I'm actually worth the room and board, Andrew. Do you two want some more coffee? Something to eat, maybe?"

"I'm good," Halley says. "If I have any more, I'll start humming like a rail gun."

"I've had my fill for now," I agree. "Let's give these folks their table back and go get some fresh air."

"Copy that," Halley says and gets out of the booth.

"Don't worry about lunch," I say to Mom, who collects our coffee mugs and wipes down the table. I feel vaguely guilty for having my mother clean up after me like I'm living at home in the PRC with her again, but she waves me off when I try to take the mugs from her.

"Go for a stroll with your wife and let me do my job, Andrew."

"All right, Mom. See you in a little while."

We walk out of the restaurant, Halley in the lead as usual. When I reach the door, I look back to see my mother watching us from the doorway of the kitchen, a little smile on her face. She turns around when our eyes meet, but I can see that the smile doesn't leave her face as she walks into the kitchen.

"Look at them going about their day," Halley says.

We're walking down Main Street, our romantic little stroll slightly encumbered by the alert bags slung over our shoulders. It's a cool and sunny day, and the clean, cold air is biting my lungs just a little. Halley pats me lightly on the back when I cough.

"Catch something from the boots at Orem?" she asks.

"Nope. It's the air," I say. "Too cold and clean."

"Ah." She chuckles softly. "I can't decide whether that's funny or sad."

"What, me coughing?"

"No, your system so used to breathing shit. Think about it. Most of your life, you've been sucking down either dirty PRC air or the filtered and recycled air on spaceships. Your lungs can't handle the clean stuff anymore."

"You should go to New Svalbard sometime," I say. "If it's still there after all of this. Cleanest goddamn air in the universe. The place is so cold that it never thaws, not even in their summers. It smells like absolutely nothing."

Halley smoothly maneuvers around a civvie family with two kids who are standing on the sidewalk in front of one of the shops. One of the children looks at her, mouth agape. Halley winks at the little boy and cocks an imaginary pistol with her hand. The boy's eyes wander from her face down to the holstered pistol on her hip.

"Don't see that around here too much, do you, kid?" she murmurs when we are well past the family.

"They don't need 'em," I say. "Hundred klicks from the nearest shithole, one way in and out, and lots of cops to guard their 'burbs."

"We might as well be on a Lanky planet," Halley says. "We're total strangers here."

"At least they like having us around now."

"'Course they do." Halley grins without humor. "When your trash is full, you're damn glad to see the garbage crew. Doesn't mean you're going to invite them to your dinner party."

I look back at the family walking down the street, away from us, on the way to some shopping or leisure, maybe a stop at Chief Kopka's restaurant for a long lunch. Even their moderate middle-class wealth is an unobtainable level of luxury for a PRC rat. When I was younger, I would have been resentful to the point of hatred. Now I understand that they are no more responsible for their station in life than I was for mine when I was eighteen and living on two thousand calories of soy and recycled shit every day. Our old grievances are tiny and pointless with the Lankies at the gates.

"We chose to be the garbage crew," I say. "If you signed up to get dinner party invites from the civvies, you picked the wrong career."

"Don't I know it." She hooks her arm into the crook of mine and pulls me closer to her. "My husband, the levelheaded idealist. I like it when you get all principled."

"I don't have those. Well, except for maybe one. Don't let dumb-ass junior officers get you killed in the field."

Halley lets go of my arm and taps the rank insignia on my shoulder with her finger.

"Mark my words, Sergeant Chip-on-My-Shoulder. One of these days, you'll be wearing officer stars, too. And then you'll get to roll your eyes at know-it-all NCOs."

I bark a laugh.

"The day I accept an officer commission is the day you'll see a parade of Lankies tap-dancing down Broadway."

We walk up and down the length of Main Street with our gear bags and our out-of-place attire. It's April, and the day is cool and pleasant, a light breeze from the west carrying the nothing-scent of clean air and melting snow from the Green Mountains. It's not quite as unspoiled as New Svalbard, but it's the closest thing to it on this continent. No wonder the middle-class people are so protective of their little suburban enclaves, unsullied by the uncouth, unwashed masses from the PRCs.

But the people that live here aren't the elite. If they were, they'd have left with the Exodus fleet last year.

When we get back to Chief Kopka's restaurant, it's well past lunch, but the place is still busy. Mom is busing tables, and the chief is in the kitchen, preparing plates and filling orders. He has two waiters who are ferrying meals from the kitchen to the dining room.

"I have the guest room ready for you if you want to lay your heads a bit," the chief says when we walk into the kitchen.

"Thanks, Chief," I say. "We won't take it up longer than we have to. Going back up to Luna in the morning."

"That soon? Getting bored of fresh air and good coffee already?"

"Not now, not ever," Halley says. "No, they're firing the big gun on *Agincourt* at the test range tomorrow, and we have an invite for ringside seats."

"Very nice," the chief says, a bit of envy in his voice.

"You got a second?" I ask the chief, and nod toward his office in the back of the kitchen area. "Got something to give you."

"Sure." Chief Kopka puts down his bread knife and wipes his hands on a towel hanging from the handle of the heating unit in front of him.

We walk over to the chief's office, a tiny space just big enough for a chair, a desk with a network terminal, and a few high-mounted shelves with stacks of analog printouts on them. There's a big security locker underneath the desk, the "armed" light on the biometric lock blinking an unfriendly red.

"Hope you're not going to try to pay me," the chief says. He sits down in his chair.

"I'm not paying you." I close the door behind me and kneel to open the lock on my alarm bag. "I got you a little souvenir from the Fleet."

"Oh?" He watches as I open my alarm bag and take out a small box. It's laminate, tough enough to survive a building falling on top of it, and fitted with a separate DNA lock. It's a portable version of the security locker under the chief's desk. He raises an eyebrow as I put the box on the desk in front of him.

"Go ahead and open it," I say. "Lock's coded to your DNA."

He puts his thumb into the recess for the DNA reader, and the lock of the box snaps open with a click. The chief opens the lid and takes a look at the contents, and his eyes widen in unconcealed surprise.

"I thought those were all under lock and key," he says.

"We issue those like new socks now," I reply. "Everyone's armed all the time when they leave base. New rule since last year."

He reaches into the box and pulls out a standard-issue M109 pistol. With practiced hands, he releases the disposable magazine block and checks the chamber of the weapon to verify that it's not loaded. Then he aims it at the floor of the office, away from me, and pulls the trigger to check for function. The electronic firing module emits a sharp click that would have been a loud bang if there had been a round in the chamber.

"It's coded to you. Well, to me as well because I signed it out. Technically, I am just staging it here for emergencies. Plus seven full magazines."

"How the hell did you get my DNA profile for the lock?" the chief asks.

"I know a guy in Neural who was in tech school with me," I say. "He got your profile from your old Navy personnel file and copied it to the lock when I signed out the gun."

"Pretty sure that's very much against the regulations," the chief says.

"Pretty sure I very much don't give a shit," I reply, and he flashes a grin without taking his eyes off the weapon.

"Keep that in your security locker," I say. "Don't get it out unless there's a major emergency. But if you do get it out, you make those shots count. Protect yourself. And your family. And my mom. You keep them safe. Whatever it takes."

Chief Kopka nods solemnly.

"It's not a fléchette rifle or a rocket launcher," I say. "It won't do much good against a Lanky or someone wearing hardshell battle armor."

"It'll work a lot better than the dumb little stun gun I have in that desk drawer," he says. "And it ain't the Lankies I'm worried about."

———————————

Halley and I spend the afternoon in Chief Kopka's guest room above the restaurant. We hear the din of conversations and clattering silverware from below on occasion as we make ourselves comfortable on the not-quite-big-enough bed in the room and watch Network shows with half an eye as we talk. Sometime around dinner, there's a knock on the door, and the chief brings in two plates with bread and cheese and an almost-full bottle of wine, along with two glasses.

I love spending time with my wife, sharing food with her and making her laugh. I love our unhurried lovemaking, enjoying the act without having to worry about unwelcome visitors knocking on the hatch or overhead announcements in the hallway outside interrupting us. I love the sense that we are home for each other—that it's not a fixed place on Earth or anyplace else you can find on a map, but where we both happen to be together.

But right now, most of all I love knowing that she'll be next to me when I fall asleep, and she'll be there still when I wake up in the morning. It means that I can go to sleep without dreading the shitty dreams that usually come in the middle of the night when I am alone.

CHAPTER 6

RANGE IS HOT

I haven't been on a Treaty-class frigate in at least half a decade. When Halley and I step out of the drop ship and onto the scuffed and worn flight deck of NACS *Berlin*, it feels like I just went back in time. *Berlin* is one of the sister ships of my first Navy assignment, NACS *Versailles*, which went down over the far-off colony of Willoughby seven years ago, the first ship lost to the Lankies.

"Blast from the past," Halley says as we get our bearings and look around. The drop ship we just arrived in is the only bird on the deck. "I didn't think there were any Treaty figs left."

"They must have put a few in mothballs," I say. "I know *Hidalgo* ate it over Mars. I saw her beacon on the tac screen when we passed."

We salute the colors on the aft bulkhead of the deck, a faded painting of the NAC flag above an equally faded ship's seal. NACS BERLIN FF-480: FREEDOM'S DEFENSE. Then Halley, as the ranking visitor, asks the OOD for permission to come aboard.

"The skipper said to send you up to CIC," the officer of the deck says when we have completed the traditional formalities. "Starboard gangway, to the main intersection."

"Central elevator to Charlie Deck," Halley says. "Thank you, Sergeant."

"This takes me back," I say out in the gangway. "Not sure it's in a good way."

"Yeah, last time we were on a Treaty class, things ended up with a lot of running and shouting."

"And near-death experiences."

"I liked *Versailles*," she says. "And not just because that was the only command we ever got to serve on together."

"You liked that relic?"

"Yeah, I did. It was my first ship assignment after Combat Flight School. And the flight ops were tiny. One drop ship and a spare. Three pilots on the whole ship. I was a big fish in a small tank."

"And *Versailles* had a great XO," I say.

"The best," Halley confirms.

We walk up the central elevator and take it up to Charlie Deck, the central command deck on Treaty-class frigates. It houses the heavily armored combat information center right in the middle of the ship, where it's most protected against battle damage. Seven years ago, I reported to her sister ship for my first assignment after tech school and promptly got an ass-chewing from then-Commander Campbell, who was the ship's executive officer at the time. I smile at the memory as we step out of the elevator and onto Charlie Deck. He was wrong, and he apologized immediately when he realized his mistake, and that told me all I needed to know about my new XO.

Berlin looks tired and worn-out. The Treaty figs were in service for fifty years before they started decommissioning them, and this ship looks like it has been ridden hard for most of those five decades. The armored vestibule housing the CIC is painted the regulation Fleet gray, but the paint is scuffed and cracked in many places, and the polyplast of the CIC windows is a bit milky from all the surface wear over the years. We walk up to the SI trooper guarding the hatch and report in. He checks with CIC via an ancient hardwired comms handset, then opens the armored hatch for us and steps aside to let us enter.

Lieutenant Colonel Renner, the ship's commanding officer, stands at the holotable in the pit that makes up the center of the CIC. She looks up when we enter, and I see the tiniest of smiles in the corners of her mouth. She's almost a head shorter than Halley, with sand-colored hair she wears in a much closer crop than she used to have when I knew her on *Indy*. There are more obvious gray hairs in between the sandy ones now, and her face has more lines than it did a year ago.

"Captain Halley and Sergeant First Class Grayson reporting, ma'am," Halley says, and we both give a proper salute. Despite the weary air about her, Lieutenant Colonel Renner returns it with precision.

"Good to see you, Sergeant Grayson. You too, Captain. Sorry we didn't get a chance to talk at the ceremony day before yesterday."

"It wasn't really a social occasion, ma'am," I say.

"No, it wasn't." She looks past us, toward the armored CIC hatch, as if she's expecting someone else. Then she shakes her head lightly.

"Are you ready to go watch some fireworks?" she asks.

"Yes, ma'am. Provided that beast actually works as designed."

"No shit." Lieutenant Colonel Renner smiles wryly. "From what I hear, it took the engineering division three months just to figure out what all the switches did. Let's hope we didn't just piss all that manpower into the wind. Coulda used all those yard apes to get a dozen more cans from the mothball fleet into action."

"Thank you for the invitation, ma'am. It's nice to be able to get back up into space again," I say.

"You're welcome," Lieutenant Colonel Renner says. "We have the space, and by God, you've earned an occasional VIP pass after last year." Her expression clouds over briefly.

"Astrogation, plot a course to Perry Spaceborne Warfare Training Range. Let's get underway so we don't miss the party. It's not like we get to see planet-killing weaponry in live fire every day."

Perry, the Fleet's main live-fire range, is a few hours from Earth orbit, laid out in space in a direction that points away from all intersystem shipping lanes, settlements, and Alcubierre nodes. Some of the stuff the Fleet slings from capital ship launchers can obliterate a deep-space transport or wipe out a settlement if it hits the wrong point in space.

Berlin burns her engines at military power for two hours, then flips for the turnaround burn in the opposite direction. There are several ships in the transit lane in front and behind us, all following the same precise routine. Space travel is nothing like the stuff I watched as a kid on the Networks—ships accelerating and braking on the spot in zero gravity, space fighters banking like airplanes. In reality, it's a lot like trying to stop on a ten-centimeter bull's-eye on a frozen lake precisely from half a kilometer away while on ice skates.

Lieutenant Colonel Renner makes some small talk with us in the CIC as *Berlin*'s icon moves along her computed plot trajectory on the holotable, but she's not quite the same person I remember from my weeks on *Indianapolis* last year. She has never been chatty, but now she's subdued, as if there's a permanent storm cloud living behind those brown eyes now. The CO is perfectly courteous to us, but she keeps the chatter to the barest minimum, and she doesn't bring up the events of last year again after her brief comment to me when we entered the CIC.

"Entering staging point," the helmsman announces when *Berlin* has reached the last tenth of the trajectory line on the holotable's display. "Deceleration complete. Coasting at ten meters per second."

"Contact Perry Control and have them slot us into our gallery spot," Lieutenant Colonel Renner orders.

"Aye, ma'am."

I've never had the opportunity to watch a live-firing exercise out here. With the distances involved in space warfare, there wouldn't be much to see without *Berlin*'s optical gear feeding high-magnification imagery to the holotable in the CIC. We move up to the section of space designated as the observation gallery, where half a dozen other ships are already lined up in ten-thousand-meter intervals, a silent audience of fleet-gray hulls, position lights blinking out of sync.

The star of this particular show is out on the range fifty thousand kilometers away. The massive bulk of NACS *Agincourt* is holding position out in the black, her bow pointed away from us, the lights on her hull flashing a steady rhythm. Further into space, at the far end of the three-dimensional wedge of space designated as live-fire zone, there are targets for *Agincourt*'s main gun, a small and forlorn-looking group of old ship hulls. The biggest in the center of the cluster is an old, heavy cruiser, a sizable ship at probably twenty thousand tons. The other ships are smaller—a frigate and a destroyer, and a civilian unit that looks like an ore hauler from the auxiliary fleet.

"Seems a waste to blow up those hulls when we have so few to go around," I say.

"Those are from the breaker queue," Lieutenant Colonel Renner says. "They were all a few weeks away from the scrapyard. They already stripped out everything worth reusing. We couldn't recommission those if we wanted to."

"Look," Halley says and points to one of the icons on the holographic display. "That's an SRA can."

The icon she points out has the marker SRAS HANOI next to it. The color of the ship icon isn't the customary red we used for SRA contacts until very recently, but the pale blue of a foreign but allied friendly unit.

"One happy human family," Lieutenant Colonel Renner remarks, the irony in her voice more than a little thick.

"Something like that," I say.

"The Russians are mostly all right. The Chinese are hard to figure out. They never give you a direct answer to anything, not even when you just ask them for directions to the head." Colonel Renner shrugs. "Doesn't matter much, as long as they help us kill Lankies."

The line of ships on the holotable orb grows steadily longer over the next ninety minutes as more ships arrive in the gallery section of the firing range and take their holding pattern slots to get a good view of the action. Under normal circumstances, a live-fire weapon test would be an unremarkable routine event, but the stuff that usually goes downrange at Perry consists of light rail gun projectiles or ship-to-ship missiles with half-ton warheads, not plasma bursts moving at near light-speed velocity. The main dorsal cannon on *Agincourt* is by far the most powerful armament ever put on a warship, and the assembled crowd of observers is hoping for some spectacular footage for their data storage modules.

"Red flag, red flag. Range is hot. I repeat, range is hot," Perry Control announces over the general comms channel. "All ships, hold positions as assigned. Live-fire test commencing in t-minus ten minutes. Level Two radiation protocol is in effect."

"Here we go," Halley says. "This thing better be the freaking Hammer of Thor."

"I concur," Lieutenant Colonel Renner says. "'Cause if it isn't, we've wasted a whole lot of scarce resources on a light show."

For something as theoretically exciting as the first test of a city-killer weapon, watching the huge battleship getting ready for the shot is about as exciting as watching paint dry. The *Agincourt* and Perry Control are in a constant chatter involving directional instructions, reactor output levels, and arming procedures. Then the engineering crew members on *Agincourt* are satisfied that all the lights and gauges on the dash look right, and a simulated range horn blast comes over the general comms channel.

"Tracking target, range 125,000 kilometers," the weapons officer on *Agincourt* transmits. "Target locked at point five meters per second, good lock."

"Reactor to pulse afterburner."

"Reactor is at pulse afterburner, output steady."

"Weapons free. Alpha mount, ten-shot burst, fire for effect."

"Firing Alpha in three, two, one. Fire."

We are watching the optical feed trained on the *Agincourt* in high resolution. When the main gun of the battleship fires, nothing spectacular happens. There's no muzzle blast dissipating into space, no launch trail, no fireworks at all from the sending end. For one brief moment, it looks like the space in front of the cannon mount on the ship's centerline distends a little, like a heat shimmer on concrete on a hot day.

A millisecond later, a small, new sun blots out the optical feed momentarily.

The filters of the optical sensors kick in to protect the electronics from the searing intensity of an explosion fireball out in space over a hundred kilometers in front of *Agincourt*. In *Berlin*'s CIC, everyone present utters some declaration of surprise or amazement.

"Direct hit on target," Perry Control sends after a few seconds, quite unnecessarily.

"Holy shit, that thing is gone," Halley says next to me.

"Ten- to fifteen-kiloton range," the tactical officer of *Berlin* says from behind his console. "Target One is stardust. X-ray readings are off the charts."

Where a few seconds ago the sensor feed showed an old thirty-thousand-ton hull floating in space a hundred-odd kilometers away, there's only an expanding cloud of superfine debris and the plasma glow of a high-energy release. There's nothing recognizable left in the part of space where the target hulks used to be. The main gun on *Agincourt* just did to an entire group of target vessels in a millisecond what even a Hammerhead cruiser would need five minutes of concentrated salvo fire and her entire ammunition load to do.

"That, ladies and gentlemen, is what we call a game changer," Lieutenant Colonel Renner says with a satisfied-looking smirk. "Ten times the energy release of an Orion missile, and seconds between shots instead of hours."

"Perry Control, *Agincourt*. We just lost main reactor power."

We all look at the section of the screen showing the massive battleship. Most of the illumination on her hull has gone out, and the fusion engine on her stern is no longer glowing with an exhaust plume. She's slowly drifting backward at maybe ten meters per second, with only her positional lights blinking slowly.

"Uh-oh," Halley says.

A flurry of hectic messages between Perry Control and *Agincourt* follows. *Agincourt* has lost all reactor power and is coasting on emergency auxiliary juice, a bad status for a warship. Without her weapons, sensors, or main propulsion, she would be dead meat in actual combat, regardless of how much power her main armament packs in theory.

"Guess they have some bugs to work out," Lieutenant Colonel Renner says wryly. "Hope they included tow hooks for the tugs."

The end of the live-fire exercise is entirely anticlimactic. Several deep-space tugs and maintenance ships coast out to the helpless *Agincourt* to render assistance. Thirty minutes after the firing of the main gun, the battleship is still under emergency battery power, unable to arrest her slight backward drift.

"Show's over, I guess," Lieutenant Colonel Renner declares. "Helm, get in touch with Perry Control and request departure pattern instructions."

"Aye, ma'am."

On the comms station, a discreet alarm chirps. The comms officer on duty looks at his display and frowns.

"Priority One flash traffic on the emergency channel, skipper."

Lieutenant Colonel Renner frowns.

"Out here? Put it on speaker."

"Aye, ma'am."

The overhead speakers pop to life with a terse and harried-sounding voice.

"All Fleet units, all Fleet units. This is AEGIS."

Halley and I trade glances. AEGIS is the new umbrella acronym for the international planetary defense network. They would only send emergency flash traffic for one specific emergency. The air in the CIC feels like it instantly dropped five degrees in temperature.

"We have a picket breach from the Mars approach. One confirmed bogey coming in at high speed. Time to Orion engagement range is t-minus two hundred minutes. All available units, make emergency speed to Fleet Assembly Point Golf and contact Antarctica Approach for defensive formation assignment. I repeat, we have a picket breach . . ."

Lieutenant Colonel Renner does not wait for the full repeat of the message.

"Plot me a course to AP Golf for a maximum-burn least-time trajectory. Comms, announce our departure to Perry Control. Bring her about and get the reactor up to max. I want every last watt out of that plant."

The CIC crew springs into action, every person in the room attending their duty stations with a sudden urgency. Halley and I look at each other, and I know she is feeling just as anxious and useless in this spot right now as I do.

"Ma'am, I request permission to go down to flight ops and make myself useful," Halley says to Lieutenant Colonel Renner.

"Go ahead, Captain," Lieutenant Colonel Renner says. "See if they can warm up the spare bird for you just in case." Then she looks at me.

"If this blows up and the Lankies make footfall on Earth again, we will need all boots on the ground. Why don't you report to grunt country and see if you can scrounge some armor and a rifle."

"Yes, ma'am," I reply. "Who's in charge down there?"

"We only have a short squad on board. Sergeant Quinones is the senior NCO."

"Understood."

Halley and I leave the CIC and head to the main elevator at a brisk pace. I eye the hatches for the CIC escape pods on the wall of the passageway.

"You don't think she's going to follow Colonel Campbell's lead, do you?" Halley asks when she sees what I'm looking at.

"I don't know. Let's just say I'm glad we'll be in suits and with a drop ship nearby if the Orions miss."

Before we get off the elevator on the flight deck level, Halley pulls me close and kisses me briefly, but with intensity.

"Watch your six. All goes to shit, I'll get us off this thing."

"Let's hope it doesn't come to that."

"Let's," she agrees.

———————————

The SI ready room has a disconcertingly small group of troopers in it, all suiting up in battle gear and cross-checking equipment. I count six troopers, one and a half regular fire teams, not even half the normal SI detachment on a frigate. They all turn and look at me when I step through the hatch.

"You Quinones?" I address the trooper wearing sergeant-rank insignia on the chest plate of his battle armor.

"Affirmative," he says. "What can I do for you, Sergeant?"

"I'm drop-qualified," I say. "Combat controller. Shit goes down and you need to drop, I want to tag along. Got any spare armor I can borrow?"

Sergeant Quinones shrugs. "We got nothing but spare gear these days." He points at one of his troopers. "Corporal Channing," he says. "Go help the sergeant first class here with his gear when you're all latched up."

The SI loaner armor isn't fitted to me, so it's too snug in some places and too loose in others, but latching the hardshell sealed over my battle dress fatigues is a comforting routine nonetheless. The corporal helps me get suited up and then double-checks all my latches.

"Good to go, Sergeant," he says. "Can't set you up with an admin deck 'cause we ain't got any."

"It's okay," I say. "We drop, it's Sergeant Quinones's show. I'm just tagging along to bring an extra rifle."

"Copy that," Corporal Channing says.

"You ever done a Lanky drop before?"

The corporal shakes his head. "Just made corporal two months ago. I was in SOI when that shit went down last year."

Shit, I think. School of Infantry is an SI grunt's first assignment after boot camp. If Channing is a corporal already, we are promoting unseasoned troops to junior leadership ranks after less than a year in uniform right now.

"Well, you can't fucking miss the sons of bitches, so there's that, anyway. Just aim for the weak spots and unload until they drop. Nothing to it."

"Right," the corporal says, but his nervous smile tells me he's not buying the notion that there's nothing to dropping a Lanky.

I don't like facing battle without knowing what's happening around me. On a regular drop, I'd be tied in to the tactical network beyond the squad or platoon level, but this isn't my unit, and I'm not wearing my own armor. When Sergeant Quinones's short squad are all geared up and ready for action, we go down to the flight deck and file into the hold of *Berlin*'s Ready Five drop ship. As we tromp up the ramp, ordnance handlers are busy loading the external wing pylon hard points with heavy ordnance. The drop ship is a Wasp, the older and less capable model still in service, and this one looks about as well worn and tired as its host ship.

"Driving the bus." Halley's voice comes over my helmet headset on a direct channel.

"You bump their pilot out of the right seat?" I ask, relieved to hear her voice.

"Didn't have to. He offered. I have seniority. He was one of my students in Combat Flight School just last year."

"If he graduated last year, he's never done a combat drop," I say.

"Nope. And that's why I'm driving the bus."

"Can you give me a data downlink from Tac so I can see what's going on? I hate being just a blind mudleg."

"Only for you," she says.

A few seconds later, there's a new data stream on my helmet display, and I breathe a small sigh of relief. Then I tap into the TacNet feed and bring up the situational display. I'm only an observer and unable to do all the stuff my regular combat controller gear would let me do, but at least I can see what the CIC holotable is displaying. *Berlin* is accelerating toward the turnaround point, shooting back to Earth at full emergency power. Behind us, more ships are in the return chute toward Earth orbit, but Lieutenant Colonel Renner barreled out of the gallery space first and fastest, so there's a lot of empty space between us and the next ship in line.

"Here we go again," Halley says.

It's been a year since my last combat, but the anxiety returns as easily as if it had merely been lurking on standby mode in the dark recesses of my mind. I watch the icon representing *Berlin* shooting along the trajectory to Fleet Assembly Point Golf and find myself wishing just a tiny bit for the structured boredom of my predictable job down at NACRD Orem, where they are finishing the midday chow in the mess hall right now.

———————

Quinones is the only member of his squad with any combat experience. All his squaddies are either fresh out of SOI, or with minimal status and experience in the SI. None of them have seen anything but training and garrison duty, and none except for Quinones have ever even seen a Lanky outside of a battle simulation. I am in the back of the bus—and possibly only two hours from combat—with a short squad of green troops. I relay this knowledge to Halley in the cockpit, who just lets out an exasperated little huff.

"Do what you can with what you have," she says.

"Best I can hope for is that their squad leader steps aside and lets me take charge, and I can keep these kids alive," I reply. "Half a squad, and they're all fucking boot nuggets."

"It is what it is," Halley replies. "Could be worse. We could have died on Mars last year, or above Earth. So quit your bitching."

"Can't do much else right now," I send back, and she just sighs.

———————

I am tracking *Berlin*'s progress on the plot through Halley's courtesy data link, so there is no need for her to tell me when we get close to the turnaround point, but she does it anyway.

"Will she or won't she?" Halley says when *Berlin*'s icon creeps up on the center point of the trajectory. I know what she means, of course. If Lieutenant Colonel Renner decided to stick it to the incoming Lanky by turning her frigate into a kinetic missile just like Colonel Campbell did last year, she'll drive at maximum acceleration clear past the turnaround point and all the way back to Earth. But right on schedule, the 1MC speaker crackles, and the XO's voice sounds overhead in the hangar bay.

"All hands, prepare for turnaround burn. All hands, prepare for turnaround in t-minus five."

I let out a breath I didn't know I had been holding.

"I guess this is not the day," Halley says from the cockpit.

"It ain't over yet," I reply.

CHAPTER 7

INCURSION

Fleet Assembly Point Golf is lousy with warships when we finally coast into it two hours later. Most of them are smaller warships, but there's a fair number of destroyers, cruisers, and even carriers. It's a much more credible-looking defense force than the motley collection of small orbital combatants that assembled in Earth orbit a year ago to fight off the Lanky seed ship that rained seedpods all over North America.

As *Berlin* slots herself into the defensive formation, I look at the ship names and nationalities of the other units in the vicinity. There's a squadron of European Union corvettes led by one of their frigates, the EUS *Brandenburg*. I know that the Icelandic Coast Guard cutter *Odinn* was damaged in last year's fracas, but she's in formation with two Norwegian fast-attack ships nearby, so they must have hammered the dents out of the hull. There are ships from the Union of South American Nations and the African Commonwealth, even from the Oceanians. I see a Japanese assault carrier, escorted by a cruiser that looks every bit as capable as the NAC's new Hammerheads. The bulk of the defensive wall, however, consists of NAC and SRA ships, dozens of hulls with names like *Ottawa, Minsk, Salt Lake City, Tianchang, Veracruz*.

"Bogey is inbound from the Mars approach, bearing positive zero-one-five by one-seven- five, CBDR. All units, link fire control for barrage fire and stand by. Orion batteries engaging in t-minus forty-five."

The plot in *Berlin*'s CIC shows us in a cluster of blue icons in the middle of the plot, with the combined task force between Earth and the approaching Lanky. When the orange icon for the incoming seed ship pops up on the plot, it doesn't look quite right, and it takes me a second or two to process the information.

"He's coming in fast," I send to Halley. The anxiety that has squeezed the center of my stomach for two hours intensifies. This is not what the Lankies usually do, and every time they do something new and unexpected, we usually end up getting bloody noses.

"Bogey is coming in hot," AEGIS sends. "Closing velocity is ten thousand meters per second, still CBDR."

"Not putting on the brakes, is he?" Halley asks. "The fuck is he doing coming in that fast? He can't eject pods at hypervelocity, can he?"

"Who the fuck knows," I say. "But if the Orions miss, we are in deep shit." At ten kilometers per second, it will take the Lanky less than ten seconds to cross the engagement range of our rail gun and missile fire and plow right through us on the way to Earth.

"They won't miss," Halley says.

They best not, I think. The dreadful possibility has occurred to me that the Lankies have started taking pages out of our playbook. Ten thousand meters per second isn't nearly as fast as the Orions, which accelerate to fractional light speed within thirty minutes, but the Lanky has exponentially more mass than the ten-thousand-ton pykrete warhead on an Orion, or even a water-filled freighter hull.

The warships at the Fleet Assembly Point enter into a slow and cumbersome sort of defensive formation ballet as groups split and re-form according to their AEGIS assignments. The space control units with the heavy ordnance form a firing line to bring all weapons to bear along the likely trajectory of the incoming Lanky. The units without long-range ship-to-ship missiles fall back and form a mobile reserve to engage the seedpods and follow them down to Earth if we need to fight it out in the weeds again.

Berlin is in the group that doesn't have anything in the missile tubes right now, so we join the Earth formation with the carriers while the heavy combatants take up the linebacker position. A little bit of my anxiety falls away as I watch our ship's icon move back toward Earth and out of the way of the Lanky. If there are going to be ship-to-ship exchanges, at least *Berlin* won't be in the thick of it.

"Orion batteries, stand by. Launch in t-minus eight."

The Orion batteries are positioned in high orbit. There are only a handful of them, Earth's only effective defense against the Lankies. Each is a one-time-use item armed with two of the Russian-designed Orion missiles. The missiles themselves are big, ugly things, with dirty gray pykrete warheads in front and bulging bomb magazines around their midsections. They are nuclear pulse propulsion missiles, which means they squirt out nuclear charges and then detonate them to drive the missile forward. One charge per second, ten kilotons each, one-hundred-g sustained acceleration that would turn a crew into fine puree even with artificial gravity systems. They are dangerous and dirty and incredibly brutal, sheer mass driven by atomic explosions to planetoid-shattering speeds in minutes, and they leave a lot of radiation behind, but they are the only thing we have other than the not-yet-ready battleships.

"All units, keep clear of the engagement cone. Level Three radiation protocol is in effect. Bogey still closing at 10k meters per second, bearing unchanged."

"That ship isn't going to slow down to let off passengers," I say.

"Nope," Halley confirms. "He's going for broke."

"To do what?"

"He's either going to hammer down through our picket to check out what's where, or he's aimed right at the planet. Millions of tons at Mach 30, and adios, muchachos."

Out in the black, the warheads of half a dozen Orion batteries train themselves onto an intercept trajectory with the uninvited guest, guided by the best ballistics computers humanity has designed. We only had a few months to cobble the system together, and it's in a constant state of improvement, but the damn things have accounted for two seed ships already, both blown to vapor long before they could get close enough to Earth to do anything dangerous.

Someone in *Berlin's* CIC brings up the optical feed trained on the approaching bogey. Lanky seed ships are very hard to spot even with excellent optical gear unless you know exactly where to look. Since last year, the world's remaining fleets have seeded the Mars approach with enough recon satellites to track anything bigger than a mess hall tray from the outer picket line one quarter of the way to Mars all the way back to Earth. The Lanky seed ship is hauling ass downrange, a matte-black oblong cigar shape three kilometers long and millions of tons in weight. They recovered huge chunks of the Lanky hull that broke up in Earth's atmosphere last year, and they found out that the reason for the ineffectiveness of our weaponry is that the hull of a Lanky ship is twenty meters thick, and made of some material that makes our own laminate armor look like partially frozen whipped cream.

"Orion launch window in t-minus five. All units, prepare for barrage fire. Pursuit units, ready for launch and stand by."

"That's us," Halley says. "*Berlin* TacOps, Bravo One-Two. I am initiating prelaunch."

"Bravo One-Two, TacOps. Copy prelaunch. Godspeed."

A few moments later, the Wasp shudders slightly as the automated docking clamp attaches to the top of the ship. Then the launch system lifts the drop ship off the deck and slowly moves it over to the drop hatch, which is only a very short way from the parking spot on the deck. There's another series of familiar small jolts, the docking clamp stopping the ship over the hatch, then lowering it through the open doors into the launch recess at the bottom of the hull. The upper hatch closes around the clamp to seal off the hangar bay again, and then the outer door opens, leaving nothing but inky black space beneath the hull of the Wasp.

I look around in the cargo hold, where our little three-quarter squad fills pitifully few seats, and most of the green privates are looking like they'd rather be anywhere else right now. One of them is fidgeting, touching the rifle in its holding bracket next to his seat, and looking over to his sergeant nervously. He sees me noticing and gives me a fleeting, embarrassed little grin.

"Not going to tell you it's just like a training drop," I say. "It sure as shit ain't. But this waiting part is the worst. It ain't so bad once you're on the ground and running. Too much to do to think about it."

"Yes, Sarge," he says.

With all the pieces in place on our three-dimensional chessboard, all that's left is the wait. At least I have the privilege of information, tapping into the data link that Halley provided, even if I can't do anything to move those chess pieces around. But there's a different quality now to the pre-battle dread I feel. Before, seeing a Lanky seed ship on the plot meant almost certain death. But we have beaten them now a few times, destroyed four seed ships in the span of a few months. It's still a lopsided battle, but at least now it's not an automatic death sentence. The Lankies are no longer invincible in everyone's heads, and that's making all the difference.

"Orion launch window in ninety seconds."

On the plot, the Lanky is barreling down the trajectory to Earth, course unchanged, still racing along much faster than I've ever seen a seed ship move, ten kilometers per second. Our heavy combatants are lined up like a welcoming committee, obliquely along the projected path of the Lanky, weapons trained on the approach like a gang of robbers ambushing a traveler on a highway. We are more prepared than we were just a year ago, but my mouth is still a little dry as I follow the progress of the blaze-orange icon on the plot, hurtling toward my home planet at hypervelocity.

"Orion batteries, weapons free. Switching to autonomous control."

The seed ship is coming in at ten kilometers per second, but the aspect is directly head-on, a down-the-throat shot that's almost trivial for a computer to calculate. Still, the Orions are made of steel and alloy, and they are propelled by atomic charges, so there's plenty to go wrong even if the computer pulls off perfect aim.

On the optical feed in the CIC, one of the Orion batteries releases its missile from the mount soundlessly. It drifts away laterally, and I can see tiny booster rockets firing on the missile's body. When the missile is a few kilometers away from the mount, the main propulsion system ignites.

"Orion 34, firing."

In space, atomic explosions look nothing like they do on Earth. Without an atmosphere to transmit a shock wave or heat, most of the detonation is radiation energy. On optical, it doesn't look like much, just an iridescent sphere expanding outward from the ignition point. The radiation scanner, however, comes alive with a brightly colored gamma burst that looks like a reverse-polarity shot of the sun. The Orion missile instantly leaps out of the frame, accelerated by the shaped nuclear charge aimed at the pusher plate on its tail end, pulling fifty times the acceleration a human could endure. More gamma spheres appear on the radiation scanner, stringing themselves onto the inter- cept trajectory for the Lanky seed ship like miniature suns. The Orion pumps out one nuke per second, and every time one goes off, the mis- sile leaps forward at a rate no chemically or fusion-propelled object in our arsenal can hope to match.

"Orion 42, firing."

Another Orion mount launches its payload from a different vec- tor, from somewhere over the southern hemisphere. Another missile races toward the incoming Lanky at unbelievable acceleration. These are crude weapons, assembled in space and launched from orbit to save the Earth's atmosphere the fallout from the hundred or so nuclear charges it would take to get an Orion up to escape velocity and out of the planet's atmosphere. They are too large to be mounted on ships and too dangerous for a launching vehicle besides, so we can't use them for anything other than local defense of Earth at the moment, but by God, we finally have a hammer that will crack a seed ship and make it scatter its guts, and I want to cheer every time I see an Orion launch.

"Time to intercept is t-minus twenty. Orion 48 and 71 standing by for second-tier intercept."

Space warfare is a high-stress combination of endless waiting and sudden, overwhelming bursts of extreme force and violence. For the next twenty minutes, all I can do is to watch icons move on a plot while our drop ship hangs in its clamp with nothing but space below. The Orions rush out to meet their target, picking up speed with every second and every nuclear detonation slamming billions of joules into their pusher plates.

"Orion 34 intercept in ten seconds," AEGIS announces when the small, blue, v-shaped icon on the plot has almost reached the much bigger orange lozenge representing the Lanky ship. I hold my breath in anticipation, and the dread I feel at the prospect of a miss squeezes my stomach like a vise. I imagine that everyone else who's tied in to the big picture is feeling the same way.

"Five. Four. Three. Two. One. Impact."

The front of the approaching seed ship disappears in an intensely bright flash of light as ten thousand tons of ice and sawdust smash into the Lanky's bow at over a thousand kilometers per second. The bloom of the impact washes out all the sensor feeds for a few moments. When the noise clears, the Lanky hull—what's left of it—bulls its way through the expanding sphere of superheated matter, but even at this range, it's clear that what's left of the seed ship isn't a functional cohesive unit anymore.

"Target. Direct hit. Orion 34 intercept at 1733 Zulu. Orion 42 intercept in fifteen seconds."

The broken seed ship starts tumbling on its trajectory. Huge chunks of it are still peeling off and adding to a debris tail that extends behind the ship for dozens of kilometers, then hundreds. The ship is broken, but the uncaring laws of physics keep what's left of the Lanky along its original trajectory toward Earth.

"Orion 42 intercept in five . . . four . . . three . . . two . . . one. Miss."

The angry firefly that is the kinetic nuclear pulse propulsion missile Orion 42 just barely misses what's left of the Lanky seed ship and hurtles off into the space beyond at a thousand kilometers per second.

"Fuck," Halley says over our private channel.

"It's all right," I reply. "He's shot to hell already."

"Still got a million tons of mass coming our way."

"Initiate self-destruct on Orion 42. Three. Two. One. Execute."

Out in the blackness of space beyond the incoming Lanky, Orion 42 and its payload disappear in another bright little pinprick of light as the AEGIS launch control crew blows up the missile. It's a dreadful waste of scarce resources, hundreds of nuclear charges that take a lot of time and money to manufacture, but there's no way to retrieve the missile, and it would forever be a hazard to anything it runs into out there, ten thousand tons forever coasting at a few percent of light speed.

"We have hull breach on the bogey," AEGIS announces. "Orion 48 and 71, hold fire."

"Hull breach, no shit," Halley comments in private.

"All units, prepare for intercept barrage. Thirteen minutes to engagement range. Unmask all batteries and switch fire control to automatic."

The seed ship is clearly out of control, and half its original mass is gone, but it's still a chunk of matter at least a kilometer long, and Lanky physiques are so tough that I wouldn't want to bet money on every last Lanky on that wreckage being dead. But with the tough outer hull cracked by sheer brute force, our rail guns and nuclear-tipped ship-to-ship ordnance can reach the softer interior of the seed ship and blow the rest of the ship apart from the inside without having to waste another Orion. The number of intercept-ready Orions is always pitifully low, and if we run out of missiles before the Lankies run out of ships, we'll be back to throwing rocks at mountains.

The broken seed ship enters the engagement range of our fleet's shipboard weapons a little more than ten minutes later. *Berlin* is in the second line of defense, so she doesn't get to contribute her rail gun fire to the fireworks display about to happen, but with so many gun batteries turned on the Lanky, it hardly matters.

"Target in range," AEGIS control sends. "Weapons free, weapons free. All units, commence barrage fire."

The ships closest to the incoming Lanky open fire first, their rail guns pumping out a shot every three seconds in automatic mode. The ships at the front of the firing line are cruisers and destroyers with at least two rail gun batteries each. There are dozens of ships out there, and the gunfire swells to cataclysmic proportions as the Lanky gets into direct-fire range of more and more units. Dozens, then hundreds of kinetic shells streak through the space between the battle group and the Lanky hull. Many glance off the undamaged part of the hull, but plenty find their way through the gaping hole that is the front of the seed ship, bleeding their impact energies into the now-unprotected interior of the Lanky. It still tumbles end over end, bereft of any semblance of control, hurtling toward Earth on a purely ballistic trajectory.

"Cease fire on rail guns. Atomic firing mission commencing. All ships, commence nuclear fire mission."

The ships with atomic ship-to-ship missiles in their tubes launch their ordnance. On the plot, at least a dozen v-shaped blue missile icons pop up in front of the battle group and streak toward the incoming Lanky, slower than rail gun projectiles but much faster than any Fleet unit can hope to accelerate. The launching ships timed their fire to meet the Lanky's destroyed front instead of the still-impenetrable stern section during its out-of-control rotation. The heavy ship-to-ship missiles tear into the shattered hull of the seed ship. A moment later, the entire remaining seed ship comes apart soundlessly and almost in slow motion.

"And farewell, motherfucker," Halley narrates from the flight deck.

"All units, watch out for incoming wreckage," AEGIS warns. "Multiple inbound trajectories."

The Lanky is broken up into countless pieces, but the sheer size of the seed ship means that many of the wreckage chunks still hurtling toward us at several kilometers per second outweigh most of the ships forming the defensive shield. The formation degenerates into barely controlled chaos as each ship tries to get clear of the incoming rain of debris. *Berlin*'s artificial gravity keeps us from feeling the acceleration the way we would in Earth's atmosphere and gravity, but I can see from the optical feed that the frigate is executing a sharp starboard-and-downward turn to get clear. Below us, the familiar dirty-gray-and-blue sphere of our home world swings back into view.

"We get nailed by a chunk of seed ship . . ." I send to Halley.

"Oh, have no fear. I have my thumb on the release button for this boat," she says.

It's nearly pointless to try sorting out the mess on the plot as dozens of ships perform evasive maneuvers. Lanky hull pieces don't show up on radar, but the holographic display in the CIC shows all the bits and pieces that are being tracked by optical gear, and there are too many of them to count.

"Stern section passing through grid Bravo One-Three by Foxtrot Two-Five. *Bersagliere*, expedite evasive, you're right in the trajectory. Expedite, expedite."

The urgent message from AEGIS comes too late, and the remaining piece of stern section, still much bigger than a supercarrier, hurtles toward the icon labeled FF-639 BERSAGLIERE. The hapless EU frigate is turning away from the incoming object at maximum burn, but the Lanky wreck is moving too fast and displaces too much space. I let out a silent curse as the icon for the EU frigate disappears from the plot. The optical feed shows the frigate, position lights blinking and the glow from her engines illuminating the rear of her hull, disappear in the blink of an eye in a cloud of fine debris, five thousand tons of warship splattered against a quarter-million-ton piece of seed ship hull like a bug against the windshield of a fast-moving hydrobus.

"Motherfucker," I say. Halley groans a nonverbal assent. Another two hundred lives gone, faster than you can blink an eye.

"We're going to have a whole bunch of wreckage in atmo very shortly," Halley says. As if prompted, AEGIS chimes in on the local defense channel again.

"Bogey tail section is on trajectory for Earth impact. All pursuit units, commence drops and prosecute."

"Bravo One-Two, TacOps. You are cleared for drop. Repeat, green light for drop. Good hunting."

"Here we go," Halley says. "Hang on back there. *Berlin* TacOps, I am commencing pursuit. Dropping in five. Four. Three. Two. One. Drop."

I don't see her thumbing the button for the clamp release, but I can feel the drop ship falling the last few meters out of the hull and leaving the arti-grav field of the *Berlin*. Halley swings the ship around until the nose is pointed at Earth. Then we are racing back toward our home world at full throttle.

The camera feed shows a spectacular light show, thousands of debris pieces entering the atmosphere and flaring long trails of superheated plasma. The largest piece of the wreckage, the tail section of the seed ship, is spinning slowly as it descends through the top layers of the atmosphere, a chunk of alien matter the size of a city block. Halley is gunning the drop ship at maximum throttle, but the wreckage has a huge speed advantage, and we are merely trying not to fall too far behind as we pursue.

"Trajectory has it coming down somewhere over Greenland," Halley says. "Fucker's going to make a splash when he hits."

"Better Greenland than a PRC somewhere," I reply.

"Tell your mudlegs twenty-three minutes until showtime. We're taking the express elevator down."

"Got it," I say. Then I relay the information to the rest of the squad. The private next to me starts fidgeting with his weapon again, and this time he doesn't even bother with an apologetic shrug when he sees that I've noticed.

"That ship is shot to hell," I say. "Nothing left but Lanky corpses in there. And they're about to hit the dirt at five k per second and make a bitch of a crater. Nothing left alive to fight, I guarantee you."

The private smiles weakly and nods, but I can tell from his expression that he isn't convinced. I can't really blame him because I'm not, either.

CHAPTER 8

GREENLAND

The high-speed descent into the atmosphere is bone-jarring as always. Halley is flogging the drop ship through the atmosphere at the absolute maximum edge of safe speed, and it's not a comfortable ride. There are no windows in the cargo bay, so the green troops with me can't see outside, which is a blessing right now because the superheated plasma streaming by from the direction of the heat-shielded underbelly makes it look like the ship is very much on fire.

The seed ship—what little remains of it—falls through the atmosphere in an entirely nonaerodynamic fashion, tumbling end over end and trailing a stream of fire. Smaller pieces tear off the Lanky hull and are whipped away in the slipstream, and Halley has to keep a close eye on the debris trail behind the seed ship's stern section as she pursues the falling wreckage through the layers of Earth's atmosphere.

On the plot, we are among the vanguard of a large gaggle of craft following the Lanky in. Most of them are drop ships, two dozen at least, but there are a few Shrikes and other attack birds in attendance. If any of the Lankies on that wreckage survive the impact, they'll have a few companies of troops with strike spacecraft in support coming down on their heads instantly. Last year, they managed to land their seedpods in many populated areas, and it took a long night of hard fighting to pry them all off the planet. This time they won't have the luxury of a delayed response.

Below us, the cloud cover above the northern hemisphere obscures the end point of the Lanky's trajectory, but the data feed from the cockpit shows that Halley's assessment was right on the money. The wreck is falling toward the expanse of Greenland in the North Atlantic, mercifully missing the Eastern Seaboard and its massive clusters of population centers by a thousand miles.

"Bogey's still doing six klicks a second," Halley says. "Time to impact, twenty seconds. All pursuit units, back off and stay clear of the target zone. He's going to make the biggest impact plume you've ever seen."

We're still inbound at fifty thousand feet when the Lanky wreck screams down to the surface and smashes into Greenland's interior under a steel-gray sky, and I'm thankful to be so far away. The impact looks like a megaton warhead went off on the surface. I see a rapidly expanding sphere of ice and dust, and then the biggest mushroom cloud I've ever seen rises into the sky. Half a minute later, the sound from the impact reaches the drop ship, a bone-jarring low concussion followed by dull, ominous thunder, a low-frequency rumbling that sounds almost malevolent to my ears.

"Impact. Lanky incursion at 70.446, −42.613, 0420 Zulu," Halley sends over the local defense channel. "Heading down to the deck to check for live targets."

The impact plume looks like something out of an apocalyptic network show. I've seen lots of kinetic impacts and more than a few atomic detonations, and this one is making them all look like wet firecrackers. Halley puts our ship into a wide turn to port as she approaches the impact area, to keep the ship out of the forbidding-looking cloud of debris billowing up at our starboard side. Even though it's only early afternoon, the sky has darkened. Cascades of debris are raining down all over the impact zone. Finally, after ten minutes of gradually skirting the outside of the mess, Halley points the drop ship toward the epicenter.

"Going in," she says. "All pursuit units in the area, follow me. Go optical and scan for movement. You find any, you shoot it until it doesn't move anymore."

As we cross the impact zone, it becomes increasingly clear with every kilometer that nothing is likely to be walking away from this uncontrolled crash. The tail end of the seed ship smashed into the massive glacier that covers most of Greenland at a speed that's unsurvivable for any organism beholden to the laws of physics. Still, we can't take any chances, so we crisscross the map grid for another twenty minutes until Halley is satisfied that nothing is going to pop out of the smoking half-kilometer crater left behind in the ice on impact.

"Ranging gear says the hole down there is two hundred meters deep," Halley says to me.

"I'd call in the locals and have them nuke that crater," I reply. "Just to be on the safe side."

"Already called it in," Halley says. "This is Euro territory. The Danes are going to have their patrol units out here before you know it."

"Going RTB now?"

"Let me do another loop," she replies. "We can't afford to miss even one of those things."

We leave the giant smoking impact crater behind and ascend through the slowly dispersing cloud of ice and dust. Halley scans the area carefully with the sensors on the nose of the drop ship. Out here, Greenland is just a sheet of ice, and any life-forms should be instantly obvious, but Lankies don't show up on radar, and even their thermal profile is far smaller than their size would suggest.

"There's a residual heat signature thirty kilometers to the west," Halley announces. "Could be another piece of wreckage. I'm going to go check it out."

"Uh-oh," she says a few minutes later as we descend onto the spot where a low-level thermal bloom is evident on the sensors. Down on the ice, a Lanky seedpod is half buried in a large crevice, smoke and vapor still rising from the unburied end.

"They managed to eject one," I say.

"If they got one out, there may be more," Halley replies. She switches to the local defense channel.

"All nearby units, this is Bravo Seven-Niner off NACS *Berlin*. We have a Lanky seedpod on the ground at seventy-six degrees, fifty-nine minutes, fifty-three seconds north and negative sixty degrees, forty-seven minutes, twenty-one seconds west. Be aware there may be more seedpods in the vicinity."

She puts the drop ship into a left-hand turn and circles the crash area. The seedpod is an alien edifice that looks out of place on the smooth blue-and-white ice. It's almost as large as a Fleet frigate, with a tapered end and a black, glossy hull. The impact doesn't seem to have damaged the pod much, or if it did, the damage is on the buried end of the pod. The hull piece we saw earlier slammed into the ground at unchecked velocity, but the seedpods have retardation chutes of a kind, and if there are any Lankies in that thing, they most likely survived the impact.

Halley arms the guns on the drop ship and comes to a hover a few hundred meters away and five hundred feet above the seedpod. Then she fires a burst of autocannon grenades at the hull. The heavy armor-piercing rounds would go completely through an armored Mule at this range, but the Lanky seedpod shrugs them off as if they're a handful of thrown pebbles. Tracers glance off the hull and deflect in showers of sparks. When Halley takes her finger off the trigger again, the seedpod's hull is flecked with the starburst patterns of impact marks, but none of the rounds have managed to penetrate the pod.

Halley circles the pod again at low level. The crack in the ice where it became firmly lodged is hundreds of meters long, and so deep that the high-powered searchlights on the nose of the drop ship can't pierce the darkness all the way to the bottom.

"Can't see shit," she says. "No visuals, nothing on thermal or IR. And I can't fit the bird into that crevice."

"Put us down a few hundred meters to the south," I say. "I'll take the squad out and get a closer look. You cover us from above."

"All right. But be careful. If that seedpod starts puking out Lankies, you don't want to be between them and my cannons."

———————

The ramp of the drop ship lowers onto a forbidding and austere landscape. Greenland is one of the few places left on Earth where human settlements are sparse because the climate doesn't support life. It's cold and windy out here, and we all lower our face shields the moment we walk off the ship. We form a perimeter outside, and Halley raises the ramp and takes off again in a swirl of windblown ice and snow.

"Hook around to the right," I tell Sergeant Quinones. "Don't get too close to the seedpod. We don't want to get into the line of fire. Advance to the crevice by fire teams."

"Copy that," Sergeant Quinones replies. He marks the approach on his TacLink display for the squad, and we split into two groups.

The rifle in my hands, optimized for use against Lankies as it is, seems like an insignificant and ludicrously small toy when I look at the bulk of the Lanky seedpod a few hundred meters away, sticking out of the crevice in the ice sheet at a forty-degree angle. The weight of the pod makes the ice underneath creak and groan.

"Keep a real close eye on that thing," I send to Halley. "You know how fast those fuckers can move."

"Don't you worry," she replies.

The crevice in the ice is dozens of meters wide, and the Lanky pod is wedged into it at an angle that looks a bit precarious. The nose of the pod is buried in the ice wall on the far side. I step as close to the edge of the crevice as I dare, and shine my helmet light down into it. The ice walls go from white to a cold blue and then to black at the furthest extent of my light's reach, but I can't see the bottom of the crevice, not even with magnification.

"That's a deep hole," I say. Quinones voices his agreement.

"The Scandis are on the way," Halley sends. "I have the Sirius Patrol on the local defense channel. ETA fifteen minutes."

"The locals will take over in a few," I tell Quinones and the rest of the squad. "Let's take some footage from the other side before they get here and take over."

We start to circle around the tail end of the seedpod, and I'm glad to be moving away from the fissure, which is deep and ominous. It's a polar spring night, and even though it's midnight here on Greenland, the sky overhead is the color of molten lead.

There's another crack and then a loud groan, and the Lanky seedpod's tail end shifts upward a few degrees, then slides into the crevice another five or ten meters with a low grinding sound.

"It's gonna fall in," one of the troopers says.

In front of us, on the flank of the seedpod, thirty meters of hull suddenly disappear. The opening in the seedpod doesn't come with a bang and a piece of hull dramatically blowing off like on the crashed seedpod last year in Detroit. Instead, the hull just silently and quickly folds outward, like footage of a flower opening played in fast-forward. For a moment, we all freeze, and the beams from half a dozen helmet lights dance across the sudden opening in the hull. Then there's smooth and purposeful movement, and a few seconds later, a Lanky unfolds itself out of the opening and steps out onto the ice in a movement that seems deliberate and almost cautious.

"Contact front," I shout into the helmet mike. "Halley, we have interlopers. Coming out of the starboard side."

"I see it," Halley replies tersely.

I don't have to tell the squad to fall back. When a hostile, twenty-meter creature appears in front of you only a hundred meters away, the urge comes automatically. We retreat from the Lanky as we bring our weapons to bear. The Lanky stretches its impossibly long and spindly limbs and unfolds itself to its full height. Huge three-toed feet dig into the ice with steps that sound like huge bass drum rolls. I feel the concussions from the Lanky's steps on the surface through the soles of my own boots.

"Weapons free," Sergeant Quinones shouts.

Six rifles bark out their thundering reports. I aim at the Lanky's midsection and pull the trigger of my own weapon. The anti-Lanky round flies true and hits the creature square in the chest, and the huge head whips around in my direction. Lankies have no eyes, only long and pointed skulls with enormous cranial shields, but I could swear that the thing is looking right at me. It bellows out a wail that overloads my audio feed and makes my computer shut off the suit microphones. More impacts pepper its chest and lower body, and the creature stumbles. Then Halley opens up with her drop ship's cannons, and the Lanky all but disappears in a shower of little explosions. It wails again and stumbles sideways. Then it crashes to the ground in a cloud of snow and ice. Halley follows it with the tracers from her guns without mercy. We add our rifle fire to the barrage, as insignificant as it feels next to Halley's armor-piercing cannon rounds.

There's a sharp crack, so loud that it cuts through the battle din like a knife. Between us and the Lanky, a new fissure appears in the ice. This one is less than a meter wide, but the sudden instability of the ground underneath my feet causes me to shout in alarm.

"Get back," Halley yells into the comms. "Get out of there right now."

We don't need the exhortation. We all turn around and run the other way. I look over my shoulder and see another fissure open up in the ice, this one parallel to the first. There's a rumbling in the air that sounds like a whole mountain is falling down. This time, I can feel the ground start to slant under my feet, and I redouble my efforts to do the fastest hundred-meter sprint anyone's ever done in battle armor.

Behind us, my helmet's rear camera shows the Lanky ship pitching upward thirty, forty, fifty degrees. Then it starts sliding into the large fissure, along with maybe half an acre of Greenland's ice sheet, loosened by the impact or Halley's cannon fire or maybe both. The seedpod and the chunk of ice it has been sitting on since it crashed drop out of sight and into the abyss with a rumble that feels like an earthquake. For just one heart-stopping moment, I think I see some movement in the darkness of the opening in the side of the seedpod. Then everything is gone—ice sheet, Lanky pod, and dead Lanky. The fissure in the ice is now twice as wide as it used to be in this spot. The Lanky pod falls into the darkness with a horrible grinding, thundering staccato that gradually decreases in volume from unbearable to merely painful.

When we are all far enough away from the fissure to feel that the ground won't give out underneath us, we stop and turn around to look at the scene. Halley is hovering above the fissure and sending streaks of cannon fire into the darkness after the tumbling seedpod. There's a huge cloud of ice and snow particles hanging over the crevice, and the searchlights from the drop ship barely cut through it.

"Son of a bitch," Sergeant Quinones pants.

"Yeah," I agree. "That almost went right down the shitter, didn't it?"

"That crack must be half a kilometer deep," Halley sends. "Maybe more."

"I'd tell the Scandis to put a nuke down the hole after that pod," I say.

"You think they can survive a drop like that?"

"You know how tough those things are. Not that they can do much down there in the ice."

"Shit," Halley says. "I've seen plenty of horror films on the Networks. I know exactly how this sort of thing ends."

"The Scandis will deal with it," I reply. "It's their turf anyhow."

"I'm putting down over there on the plateau for pickup," Halley says, and marks the pickup zone on my TacLink display, five hundred meters away. "Sorry for the walk, but I'd rather not put down sixty tons of ship in your vicinity right now, or we'll join that seedpod at the bottom of that fissure."

"No, I'm totally fine with walking," I reply.

The squad and I move over to the designated pickup zone and board the waiting drop ship, glad to have solid steel under our boots again. We strap into our jump seats, and I do an automatic head count as the tail ramp closes. The junior enlisted troops look scared, excited, and relieved all at the same time.

"Heading back up to *Berlin*?" I ask Halley.

"We've been loitering a little too long. I don't have enough juice left to make it back to *Berlin*. I'm heading for the HD base at Thule. Tell your guys fifteen minutes until hot showers and chow."

I relay the news to the squad as we lift off and soar into the bright polar night sky. Then I sit back in my jump seat and wait for the adrenaline in my system to start dissipating. The privates across the aisle from me start chatting in low but excited voices. They've had their first taste of combat, and they came out of it in one piece, which makes them more fortunate than they know. From the way they're talking, I know that this drop will be the topic of many retellings over chow in the next few weeks.

Enjoy it, I think. *Pretty soon you'll get to the point where you'll go out of your way not to have to talk about your drop.*

CHAPTER 9

——— THE FEW THAT REMAIN ———

Two weeks after the Lanky incursion, the talking heads on the Networks still don't talk about much else.

There are Network screens in the rec room—the boots have recreational facilities for after-hours and weekend use now—and there are more in the NCO club and the chow hall, so I get a steady trickle of news updates from the civil world every time I go for a meal or a bottle of crummy soy brew. The zone in Greenland where the Lanky wreckage landed is now a military security zone, and specialists from all the world's big and small alliances are sifting through the remains, hoping for more clues about our enemy.

The civilian Network people are as clueless as ever, but there's a noticeable change in atmosphere on the newscasts these days. People talk about events and military strategies openly and in an unstifled manner. I never realized just how carefully curated the news used to be in the days before the Exodus. Our climate of public discourse seems to have changed. But the civvies still don't understand military subjects very well, and there are only so many well-intentioned but totally misinformed news segments I can take in a week, so I usually get my food to go and eat in the quiet and screen-free privacy of my platoon sergeant office.

I'm halfway through my sandwich when there's a curt knock on the doorframe. I look up and see an officer in CDU fatigues standing in the door. I drop my sandwich and get out of my chair.

"As you were, Sergeant," the officer says. "May I come in?"

"By all means, sir." I sit back down.

The man who walks into my office is someone I've seen before a few times. The podhead community is very small, and some of its members are firm parts of special operations lore. My visitor is one of our branch's celebrities, if the military can be said to have those. His name is Major Khaled Masoud, and he's as much of a legend among Fleet special forces as Sergeant Fallon was among the old Territorial Army. There are fewer than ten living Medal of Honor recipients on active duty across all the branches of the military, and the man standing in my office is one of them.

"Major Masoud, sir," I say. "No offense, but you are just about the last person I expected to see coming through that door tonight."

The major smiles curtly. He is a short guy, about Dmitry's height and therefore half a head shorter than I am. He's probably in his midforties, but the lines on his weathered face and his mostly gray regulation buzz cut make him look a good ten years older. All the lifers in our high-stress, high-exertion field of work have much more physical wear on them than the career soldiers of other branches. The combined physical and mental stresses in the special operations business wear out even the fittest troops prematurely.

"Sergeant First Class Grayson," Major Masoud says. His gaze flicks from the name sign on my desk to the area above the left breast pocket of my CDU tunic, where I'm wearing a combat drop badge in gold. Major Masoud's tunic sports the same badge, but there's another one right above it, superseding it in the hierarchy of awards and badges. It's the highly coveted trident-clutching eagle, the Space Special Warfare badge, by far the hardest of all the specialty badges to earn. There are never more than a few hundred people in the Fleet who wear that badge on their tunics, the Space-Air-Land teams—the first molecules on the very tip of the sharp special ops spear.

"You've never done a drop under me, have you?"

"No, sir," I say. "Not that I can remember. But I've dropped with a lot of your SEALs over the years."

"I have no doubt. You've gotten around a bit since you decided to ditch the consoles and earn that scarlet beret."

"May I ask what brings you here today, sir?"

Major Masoud nods at the empty chair in front of my desk.

"Mind if I sit down?"

"Of course not, sir. Have a seat."

He pulls the chair away from the desk and then sits down, all with a precise economy of movement that would be worthy of a parade formation drill. Major Masoud is not overly muscular, but the arms sticking out of his sharply folded CDU sleeves look like taut steel cables. His uniform's camo pattern is soft and faded—"salty" is what we call a well-worn-in set of fatigues—but the folds are neat and precise, and there's not a loose thread anywhere. I'm suddenly keenly aware of the extra five or six kilos I've put on since I took this training supervision slot. I put the rest of my sandwich back into its wrapper and stow it in my desk drawer.

Major Masoud looks around my office. There isn't anything personal on the walls, just rows of shelves holding hard-copy printouts of training manuals and other deadweight.

"Basic training," he says in a neutral voice. "Do you like what you're doing right now?"

"No, sir, I do not," I reply. "It's boring and repetitive. And I haven't fired any live rounds in months. Getting fat on garrison chow."

He smiles at that—curtly, just the merest hint of an upward tick of the corner of his mouth.

"But it has to be done," I say. "Someone's gotta do it. We need these new boots in the Fleet and in the SI. It's important."

"Yes, it's important," Major Masoud agrees. "Very. But having people with an MOS like yours do it is a terrible waste."

He pulls a folded sheet of paper from the chest pocket of his CDU blouse and unfolds it.

"I went through the personnel database at Coronado last month and compiled this. It's a list of every pod-qualified officer and senior NCO left in the Fleet."

Major Masoud flips the list around in his hand so I can see the print side. It's just a standard-size printout, and the print isn't particularly large or widely spaced, but the two columns of names on the page don't even fill two-thirds of the sheet.

"That's all?" I ask.

"That is all," Major Masoud confirms. "Three-quarters of our qualified special operations personnel were deployed when the Lankies blockaded the nodes and attacked Mars. Forward-deployed on colonies, assigned to carrier strike groups, playing security detachments for high-value extrasolar bases . . . you know the drill."

He puts the sheet of paper away again and carefully closes the pocket on his tunic.

"We lost half our active SEALs and SI recon teams when they threw everything at Mars to stop the Lankies. Most of the rest are cut off from the Solar System, if they're still alive. We may be short on recruits right now, but we are looking at bare cupboards in the podhead section of the pantry. Training basic SI riflemen and -women takes six months. You know how long it takes to train a special ops MOS."

"Yes, sir, I do," I reply. When I switched to the combat controller MOS—the nutcase track, as Halley calls it—I spent the next year in various specialist schools, even though I was already a fully trained and qualified Territorial Army rifleman. And some podhead jobs—SEALs and Spaceborne Rescuemen among them—take almost twice as long to train.

"Some corners can't be cut," I add. Major Masoud rewards this statement with another tiny smile.

"That is a fact," he says. Then he sighs and folds his arms across his chest.

"We are going back to Mars," he says. "The decision has been made. The counteroffensive starts in ninety-eight days, right after this training cycle. One more batch of warm bodies to fill the seats in the drop ships."

The news isn't unexpected, but I still feel a great deal of anxiety welling up inside me at the finality in the major's tone of voice.

"When was this decided, sir? I didn't hear anything about it. Not even rumors."

"Last week. Just days after that Lanky blew through the picket and smacked into Greenland. The new SecDef and the joint chiefs. And everyone in the Corps with gold on their shoulder boards. I snuck in with the SOCOM commander as part of the SEAL delegation."

I'm not nearly high enough in rank or function to be part of joint-chiefs-level strategy meetings, but I'm a little angry at this revelation anyway. With an all-new cabinet loaded with veterans, a combat vet for a president, and a leadership structure that has been completely redone out of necessity, I had hoped that we were beyond having a bunch of old guys decide everyone's fate in secret meetings. But I guess the military still works the way it used to, and that some conventions can't just change in a month or a year.

"With all due respect, sir—I'm not sure we're ready for that," I say.

"No, we are not," Major Masoud says. "Not enough troops, not enough warships. For damn sure not enough of those new missiles. Three months from now is not enough time."

"So we're going to run our heads against the wall again? After what happened last year?"

"Oh, there was debate," he says. "Lively debate. It basically came down to two options. Assault Mars with what we have, as soon as we can, and scrape the Lankies off the planet before they can settle in any further. Use the Orions to shoot down the seed ships and then slug it out on the ground. Hope that we can take them toe to toe once their air and space superiority is gone. After your little adventure in Fomalhaut last year, a lot of people started to see that as a realistic option."

"They are easier to kill with Shrikes and drop ships overhead for close air support. But 'easier' isn't 'easy.' And there are thousands of them on Mars by now."

"There are still human holdouts there," the major says. "If we get back there and kick the Lankies off successfully, we'll not only get the planet back; we may also rescue a few thousand personnel. Maybe a few ten thousand. It's a high-risk op, but I can't blame the people who say that we can't not go."

"I concur, sir," I say, but I'm not sure I even want to know what the major has to say next.

"We know where the Exodus fleet went," Major Masoud says. "They analyzed the comms and data traffic the drones from *Indianapolis* captured while they were on station. We have everything. Coordinates, access codes, ship lists. They finished the decryption last month, right before the Lanky incursion."

"No shit. I thought Fleet encryption was unbreakable."

The major allows himself another tiny smile.

"They beat their heads against the wall with it for six months. Rumor has it they finally asked for help from our new allies in the SRA, and the Chinese crypto division had it cracked in two weeks."

I laugh out loud.

"They didn't just take all the best of the Fleet gear," Major Masoud continues. "They have stuff that never even made it into the Corps. They had their own R&D department. Most of their gear is made to fight Lankies. Those battleships we found unfinished were just part of it."

"Anti-Lanky gear," I repeat. "A whole task force full of it. Would come in handy for the Mars counterstrike."

"Very," Major Masoud says. "I see you are thinking like most of the SOCOM guys at that meeting."

"So why aren't we doing that? Go after the Exodus fleet, reclaim the gear, then use all that to take back Mars?"

"Time," he says. "That op would take time and possibly cost us a large pile of casualties that we can ill afford at the moment. Those traitors took a lot of combat power with them. A dozen warships, all top of the line. And God knows what they stashed in their hideout system before the Lankies forced their early departure. For all we know, they have half a dozen of those new battleships waiting on the other side of the chute when we go after them in force."

"Well, we won't know for sure until we go have a look."

The major gets out of his chair and walks over to the door. Then he pokes his head out into the hallway as if he wants to make sure nobody is eavesdropping out there. Satisfied, he walks over to my documentation shelf and studies the terribly uninteresting spines of the training manuals.

"Like I said—there were two camps of opinion at the joint chiefs meeting. One group favored the 'Mars First' approach. The other group voted to go after the Exodus traitors first and then use the reclaimed assets and personnel to increase the success chance of the Mars assault. We will only get one shot at retaking Mars. Once we are committed, all the chips will be in play. Do or die. Most of SOCOM are in the second camp, but we were outvoted, so Mars First it is."

"However," I say.

Major Masoud flashes a grin that is entirely devoid of humor or good cheer. I know he wouldn't be here if that was all there was to the joint chiefs meeting.

"However," he repeats. "SOCOM got concessions. I am putting together a special operations mission to scout the Exodus system and assess enemy disposition prior to the Mars assault. And I want you on board with us."

It takes me a few moments to process this information. I know I'm a fairly competent specialist in my field, but I also know that I'm nowhere near the top of the field in the podhead community, whether by ability or rank. I'm certainly not high enough in the hierarchy to have a senior SEAL and Medal of Honor recipient personally request my membership on a mission.

"Sir, why would you need a combat controller on a deep-space recon mission?" I ask.

"I don't need you in your primary MOS," Major Masoud says. "I am taking a company of podheads along, and I want you to lead one of the platoons."

I make a mental note to myself to check the sandwich I just ate for contamination. Right now, nothing other than foodborne illness would explain the slide into surreal territory the day has taken since I started eating my lunch.

"Sir, I'm just an E-7, and just barely one at that. I don't have the rank or the skills to lead a scout platoon."

"You are among the most experienced people left on that list." He taps the breast pocket of his tunic. "I went through your mission stats, and you've done 212 combat drops since you graduated from combat controller school, almost half of them pod drops. I need people who have experience doing recon patrols with small teams, and that's pretty much all you've done for the last four years. And you did well at Fomalhaut. I know about New Svalbard and the rescue mission on the SRA moon. Trust me, Sergeant, you have the skills and the attitude I want."

"Sergeants first class are platoon sergeants at best, not platoon leaders, sir. That's an officer slot. Especially in SOCOM."

Major Masoud makes a dismissive gesture with his hand.

"We are short on officers. Hell, we are short on everything. They're putting freshly minted second lieutenants in charge of SI platoons right out of OCS without blinking. Making an experienced NCO a limited duty officer is not a problem right now. I can have you on the priority roster for a promotion to second lieutenant on Monday. One week of LDO Academy over at Newport, and you're done."

I sit, stunned by the broadside I just received, and find myself wanting to check my chrono to see how close I am to being able to get a drink over at the NCO club.

"No offense, sir," I say. "But I've never thought of myself as officer material."

Major Masoud smiles curtly and checks the chrono on his wrist. Then he pulls out the camouflage beret he's wearing tucked under his left shoulder board and slaps it against his thigh to unroll it.

"I have a few more personal calls to make today, Sergeant. And I'm not ordering you, I'm asking. But think on it quickly, because I have a mission to put together and slots to fill. Here's my direct node."

He pulls a clear plastic card out of his pocket and puts it onto the desk in front of me.

"The offer is good for forty-eight hours, Sergeant Grayson. Think it over, discuss it with your wife, but give me an up-or-down vote within two days."

I stand up as Major Masoud turns toward the door. When he is in the doorframe, he turns around and looks back at me, standing in my office, with the overflowing shelves of reference manuals all around me.

"You can choose to stay here and babysit some half-green drill sergeants for another boot camp cycle. And then you'll find yourself in a drop ship in a little over three months, with a platoon of these kids in the bus with you. Dropping onto Mars. Taking on thousands of Lankies and hoping that we have enough Orions in orbit and rifles on the ground."

He puts the beret on his head and tugs it into place over his right eyebrow with a sharp and precise movement.

"Or you can be on the tip of the spear again. Pulling off the hairiest recon mission you've ever done, alongside the best podheads left in the Fleet. Going after those traitor sacks of shit and laying the groundwork for the ass-kicking that's coming their way. You can help us tip the scales in a major way, Sergeant. Make a damn difference."

He nods at the plastic network ID card on the desk in front of me. "Forty-eight hours."

I don't bother with a salute. Instead, I nod, and Major Masoud returns the nod with a stern face. Then he walks off and leaves me standing behind my desk, with the regs manuals piled up on the shelves beside me and the garrison flab I've acquired straining the front of my tunic a little. I listen to the sound of the major's boots as he walks down the hallway toward the CQ office and the building entrance.

Tip of the spear again, I repeat to myself. Only this time that spear is getting poked down a dark bear den, and the bear inside is the size of a horse.

I pick up the network ID card the major left behind and aim for the trash basket next to my desk. Then I pause and think for a few moments. I sigh and stick the card into the side pocket of my CDU trousers with a muttered curse.

CHAPTER 10

— CONCESSIONS —

"No fucking way," Halley says when I break the news to her. She tosses her fork onto the table, picks up the napkin on her lap, and wipes her mouth carefully. Then she laughs out loud.

"Quick, turn on the Network news," she says. "I want to see those Lankies."

"Which Lankies?" I ask. We are in the little kitchen of our joint quarters on Luna, and there's a plate of bring-back chow-hall food in front of me that I haven't touched yet.

"The Lankies you said were going to tap-dance down Broadway before you accept an officer commission."

"I haven't said yes yet," I protest. "I wanted to talk to you about it first."

Halley looks at me and shakes her head, the way you do at an unreasonable child.

"Andrew, I know you too well. We've been together long enough. If you're telling me about it, you've pretty much made up your mind already. If you weren't interested at all, you would have told him so right then and there, and you'd mention it as a footnote maybe over drinks at the RecFac."

I pick up my fork and start poking around on my plate without much enthusiasm. The quality of the once-vaunted military chow has declined over the last year to where PRC rations used to be. The *current* PRC food rations are just a half step above inedible. The people in the PRCs have always supplemented their protein intake with what we used to call "dadot" meat—"don't-ask-don't-tell"—but now I hear they're at a point where sewer rat kabobs are fetching substantial black-market premiums over the shit the ration factories crank out. Too many mouths to feed, not enough left to feed them all properly. Sometimes I still think we kept the Lankies from doing us a giant favor.

"Three months until the offensive, huh?" Halley asks. "How solid do you think that number is?"

"Well, he sat in with the joint chiefs when they nailed it down. I'd say it doesn't get any more solid than that."

"Fuck." Halley picks up her fork again and starts oscillating it between index and middle finger. "That's too damn soon. We have maybe half the pilots we need, and that's with shortening the training as much as possible."

"What do you think of the strategy?" I ask.

"Taking Mars first? Yeah, I really think we have no other choice. Not if there are still people holding out underground. And God only knows what those ugly motherfuckers are going to throw at us once they are settled in all the way. That incursion two weeks ago still gives me the willies."

"Why? They didn't get through. Fleet blew 'em to shit."

"The change in tactics," Halley says. "They came in way faster than usual. Few kilometers more per second, they could have sailed right through our defensive screen. All it takes is one Orion miss, and we have that mess like last year again, only a hundred times worse. We would never get a lid on a thousand Lankies right in the middle of a metroplex. Not without nuking our own cities."

"And then what's left to save," I say.

"We can't let them keep a staging base in our Solar System," Halley says. "We kick them off Mars, or we are done within a year or two. I just wish we had a lot more time to prepare. Much as I don't want to be stuck at Drop Ship U for another twelve or twenty-four months."

In our living room nook, there's a large screen on the wall that's supposed to make up for the lack of windows and viewports on the lunar base. It shows the feed from the nearest environmental camera on top of this building's dome. Right now, the blue-and-gray orb of our home world is rising above the low mountains on the lunar horizon. So many nicer, bigger, cleaner planets in the galaxy, I think. Why can't they just leave us this one? It's not much of a prize as it is, anyway. But maybe it's not really about colonization to them. Maybe they just want to see us gone from the universe as much as we want to be rid of them.

"You must have made a name for yourself among the podheads," Halley says. "One of the top-dog SEALs coming and asking you personally."

"I don't think it's that," I reply. "I think they're at the point where they can't be picky. He said as much."

"So you're going to accept?"

She studies me with an expression that I know to be carefully calibrated to neutral.

"You'd rather I didn't."

"Of course I'd rather you didn't," she says. "I'd rather have you here with me for a while longer, even if we only see each other on the weekends. That's much more than most military couples get."

"But you aren't telling me I can't go. You're not going to resent it if I accept the promotion and go off on that mission."

"I'll have plenty of resentment, Andrew. But you know what it is I'll resent? The fact that you'll get to do frontline stuff again while I'm stuck in the instructor grind for God knows how much longer. I am tired of teaching and grading and standing in front of a holoscreen with a goddamn wand while others do the jobs they were trained to do. The jobs they're best at."

She sighs and pushes her plate away. "But no, I can't tell you not to go."

"Sure you can. You're my wife."

"And we both chose to wear the uniform," Halley says. "We chose to keep wearing it when we had the choice. On that rooftop, a year ago, when we had the chance to disappear and join the Lazarus Brigade."

"We thought about it for days," I say.

"We really didn't. I think we both had made up our minds already when we were still up on that roof. We both kept those uniforms on. That means we both agreed to keep dancing to this tune. And we go where they need us, when they need us to."

"It's not even a fighting mission," I say. "It's a recon run. Against people, not Lankies. And not even against SRA troops. Worst-case scenario, they bag us and take us as POWs."

Halley gives me that indulging look again.

"Worst-case scenario, they wipe out your recon team. Or they bag you and then decide to line you up against a wall. These people aren't our own anymore, Andrew. They deserted Earth. All of us, civvies and the Corps. Left us all to deal with the Lankies by ourselves. They catch you on their new home, wherever that is, they're just as likely to flush you out of an airlock than to waste food and a cell on you. They don't play by our rules anymore."

"They're still people," I say. "I'll take my chances with those over Lankies any day. Nobody's ever been taken prisoner by a Lanky."

"It's a combat mission, Andrew." Halley gets up and carries her plate over to the kitchen nook. She scrapes the little bit of food left on the plate into the protein recycler and puts the plate into the sonic cleaning unit.

"They're all combat missions," she continues. "You know that as well as I do. But you want to go. You love that the SEALs are asking you to come along. You want to prove to yourself that you still have what it takes to play around with the tough kids. I understand that. I really do."

"You would do the same," I say.

"Damn fucking straight I would," she replies, without a moment of hesitation.

She walks over to the door of the bedroom and stretches with a yawn.

"I'm turning in early," she says.

"I thought we'd go over to the RecFac and grab a beer or two before bedtime."

"You go ahead. I am wiped out. Been doing simulator training all week. Sitting in a chair and looking at screens all day."

"You sure?"

"Yeah," Halley says. "Just keep it down to a dull roar when you get back in."

I know she's upset, but I also know she's not upset at me directly, and that I can't do anything right now except to give her a bit of elbow room and stew a bit on her own. Still, I feel a sense of guilt as I watch her kick off her boots and slide the bedroom door shut behind her.

———————

Halley's Combat Flight School is just one of the tech schools here on the lunar base, which is as big as any Corps base down on Earth's surface. The main difference is that there's no outdoor space, so moving around here feels a lot like moving between a bunch of moored and interconnected starships. I go over to the nearest service hub, which has a chow hall and several recreational facilities. The closest NCO club is almost, but not quite, packed to the last seat, so I take two bottles of soy beer to go—the maximum allowance per head and evening—and drink the first while I'm standing at the bar and looking around.

Most of the personnel in the NCO club are Fleet sailors or SI troops in tech school. All of them are young and green, mostly corporals and three-stripe sergeants, kids that have been in the military for maybe a year or two at the most. They're here to learn how to fly a drop ship or lead an infantry squad in zero-g EVA combat, or perform any of the thousand other specialties in a modern, spacefaring military. I spot the occasional small cluster of senior NCOs at some tables—staff sergeants, sergeants first class, a master sergeant or two—but overall, the room is full of troops with brand-new stitching on their rank stripes. These are the most seasoned of the emergency replacements they started to funnel into the Corps right after Mars and the Exodus last year. These kids will be the backbone of the counteroffensive, leading privates and PFCs even younger and greener than they are into battle. And with the planned Mars assault, we are once again willing to risk so many lives on a single roll of the dice.

"Excuse me, Sergeant."

Behind me, a female corporal walks up to the bar, and I step aside a little to make space. She holds her dog tags out for the bartender to scan. He swipes his handheld scanner over the tags and nods.

"One," she says. He passes her a bottle of soy beer, and she puts it to her lips and swigs about half the bottle on the spot.

"Been looking forward to that all day," she says. I turn around to look at her. She's wearing a Fleet flight suit with corporal-rank insignia, two slanted stripes on each shoulder board.

"Rough day at tech school?" I ask, and she lets out a little snort.

"Rough month," she says.

"What are you flying?"

"What am I learning to fly, you mean. Retraining for spaceflight on the Wasp. I used to drive a Hornet for HD."

"And they moved you to the Fleet?"

She nods.

"Interservice transfer. Guess we need more Wasp pilots than Hornet jocks right now."

"I was an interservice transfer too, once," I say. "Same direction. Came from HD when it was still called Territorial Army."

"Wow. That was a while ago. Long before I joined."

"Not that long," I protest. "Just a little over five years ago."

"I was still in middle school five years ago," she says. "It was a while ago."

"God," I say. "Thanks for making me feel like a fucking relic, Corporal."

"You don't look that old," she says.

But you look too fucking young, I almost, but not quite, say out loud. Instead, I just take another swig from my bottle. Then I notice a tattoo on the corporal's wrist. It's clearly hood rat ink, the sort you can get in the alley shops down in the PRC warrens for three thousand calories and half a dozen rimfire cartridges. She's wearing a red number superimposed over a scanner pattern on the inside of her wrist. I know the red number signifies the network node ID of the part of the PRC where she lived. It's a gang badge. When I was a hood rat, I had many opportunities to pick up a similar decoration and often only barely managed to avoid it.

I nod at the tattoo.

"Where are you from, Corporal?"

She glances at the tattoo and shakes the sleeve of her CDU fatigue jacket over it to cover it up.

"Pittsburgh. 23-East." She looks at my wrist, which is free of skin art. "You?"

"Boston. 7-North. Never ran the alleys, though."

"It's harsh," she says. "But you know how it goes in the Clusters. This is much better. Real food. My own cot. And I don't have to worry about someone round the corner ready to jack me for my two-k cals."

I do know what life is like in the Clusters, and I know the kind of shit the girls in the gangs have to deal with every day. I know that getting jacked for her ration wasn't the worst thing she had to worry about back home, not by a long shot. But I also know that she doesn't really know just what she traded in exchange for this temporary status of relative safety. Or maybe she does, and made the trade gladly. A lot of these new recruits from the worst PRCs are far tougher than I ever was.

"Well, good luck, Corporal," I say and put my empty bottle onto the bar. "Maybe I'll see you in the Fleet in a few months when you drive my bus for a drop."

"Can I ask you a question, Sergeant?" she asks as I turn to leave.

"Go ahead," I say.

For a moment, she drops the tough-kid swagger and the unconcerned expression, and I can get a glimpse of the tense girl underneath. She hesitates for a moment or two before continuing in a slightly lower voice, even though the T-pop music in the place is almost drop-ship-engine loud, and nobody around us pays even the slightest bit of attention to our conversation.

"We heard rumors about a big op coming up."

"Soon," I tell her. "Right after this training cycle."

"Shit." She looks a little relieved and deflated at the same time. "Is it Mars?"

I shrug in reply.

"It's Mars," she says. "Fuck."

"Pay attention at Combat Flight School," I say. "First assault wave, they'll send everything that can ferry troops down to the surface. You'll have forty mudlegs in the back who rely on you to get them down in one piece so they can fight those bastards. And then you and your gunner will be the main support for your platoon. Just like your old job in HD, only with bigger targets."

"Nothing to it," she says and lets out a shaky little laugh.

"Plenty to it," I say. "But you'll get it done. And you'll enjoy blowing those spindly motherfuckers apart. And if it turns out to be that day, you make sure you don't have a single round left in your bird before you go in. Because fuck 'em, that's why."

She nods solemnly.

"Because fuck 'em," she repeats. "Damn straight."

"You'll be all right," I say. "Just get your grunts on the ground."

"Yes, Sergeant. Thanks for the intel."

"Don't spread it around," I say, even though I know that she'll start doing just that before I've even made it out of the NCO club.

The female corporal from the Pittsburgh PRCs walks off with her bottle of crummy soy beer, and I watch her make her way through the crowd.

Twelve weeks, I think.

Where do I want to find myself in twelve weeks? In the back of a drop ship descending into the Mars atmosphere, with that young corporal or someone just like her in the pilot seat, and more of these green kids in charge of my platoon's squads and fire teams? Or do I try to help shuffle the odds for the assault in our favor, even just a little bit, by joining the recon team?

And if I decide to go with the recon mission, how much of my motivation is the desire to just be somewhere else when we start stuffing the meat grinder with all these new troops?

Or you could be at the tip of the spear again, I hear Major Masoud's voice in my head.

As I look over the crowd, all these young and newly minted corporals and sergeants, I concede to myself that despite all the bitching over the years, I took the nutcase track because deep down inside, I like it out there on the tip of the spear. I feel more alive on a hostile world in battle armor hundreds of kilometers from the nearest support ship, and billions of kilometers from the rest of humanity, than I do anywhere else. And I've never once had a shitty dream while I was deployed.

Back in the quarters I share with Halley, I check on my wife, who is fast asleep in the bedroom, or at least pretending to be. I slide the door to the bedroom shut again and sit down at the network terminal between the kitchen nook and the living room. Then I pull Major Masoud's network access code card out of my pocket and let the terminal scan it.

BANDWIDTH ALLOCATION REQUESTED flashes on the screen for about a second and a half before the line changes to PRIORITY ALLOCATION GRANTED—CONNECTING.

It's 2100 hours already, and I expect to be connected to a static image of the recipient asking me to leave a video message, but when the screen changes to a video feed, it's the live Major Masoud, in his worn but pressed CDU fatigues, sitting at a desk in what looks like a staff office.

"Sergeant Grayson," he says when he sees my video feed. "You've considered my offer."

"I have, sir," I say.

"And what is it going to be?"

I take a breath and let it out slowly before I continue.

"I'll accept the assignment. Under one condition."

Major Masoud raises an eyebrow almost imperceptibly.

"Condition," he says. "Well, what's your condition." He doesn't inflect the word like a question.

"I want to recruit my own command staff. Platoon sergeant, squad leaders, platoon guide. You can pick the rest, but let me choose my own senior NCOs."

He looks at me with an unreadable expression for a long moment.

"You have specific people in mind?"

"I do," I say. "Proven personnel."

"I have a hard time scraping together a full NCO complement as it is. You can pick your own sergeants, unless I've already slotted them in somewhere else in the company."

"That's unlikely, sir. Thank you."

"And they have to be fully drop-qualified and in a suitable MOS, of course."

"The ones I have in mind wear gold drop badges, sir."

"Then talk to them and get me their names and personnel numbers if they accept. No later than Monday morning, Sergeant, or I'll fill the slots otherwise."

"How soon will I have to report to LDO Academy?"

Major Masoud checks something on his screen.

"Monday morning," he says. "I am putting you in a priority slot. You'll get orders for Newport first thing in the morning. And your fast-track commission is going into effect by Friday so you can meet the prereqs."

"That's fast," I say.

"We have no time to waste," Major Masoud replies. "It's amazing how quickly you can cut through paperwork bullshit when the wolf is at the door, Sergeant."

He checks his chrono.

"Have those names and numbers to me by Monday," he says. "Earlier, if possible. And pack your gear for Newport. You'll be wearing stars before the weekend."

"Yes, sir. You'll have the roster by Monday."

Major Masoud nods and terminates the connection without ceremony.

I didn't hear the sliding door opening behind me, but I sense Halley's presence in the doorway of the bedroom. I turn around in my chair to see her looking at me with a mocking little smile, arms crossed in front of her chest.

"Lankies on parade," she says.

"Right down fucking Broadway," I agree.

"Well." She leans against the doorframe and tips her head toward the darkened bedroom behind her. "Why don't you wash up and come to bed with me, Lieutenant. Looks like I won't be seeing you again for a while after this weekend. Might as well make the best of short time."

I think about a snarky reply, but then decide against it. I know Halley is still pissed off, but I'm glad she's not pissed at me, or at least not too much.

"Yes, ma'am," I reply and get out of my chair, leaving the second, unopened bottle of soy beer on the little terminal desk. Sometimes, the smartest possible thing to do is to shut up and do as you're told.

CHAPTER 11

———— RANK BEGINNINGS ————

Lieutenant Colonel Laroux unfastens my epaulette loops and pulls the rank sleeves off them. He hands them to the master sergeant standing slightly behind him and takes a new set out of his pocket. The new rank sleeves each bear a four-pointed star standing on a point, the post-reform unified rank symbol of a second lieutenant. He sticks the new sleeves onto my epaulettes, fastens them again, and then pounds his hand down on each rank sleeve firmly and ceremonially. Then he holds out his hand.

"Congratulations, Lieutenant Grayson. Welcome to the NAC officer corps."

I shake his hand, careful to calibrate the force of the grip to match his own.

"Thank you, sir."

We are in his office, back at the Depot's headquarters building. My berth in the platoon building is cleared out, and my gear is waiting for transport to the airfield, where someone is going to toss it onto a shuttle bound for the East Coast. With some luck, my gear bag may even arrive at the LDO Academy in Newport before I get there on Monday.

Lieutenant Colonel Laroux takes a folder from the master sergeant and opens it.

"Your commissioning certificate," he says. "I wish you good luck in this new chapter in your career."

He closes the folder and hands it to me.

"Thank you, sir."

"You did good work here at the Depot," the lieutenant colonel says. "Three tours as a platoon sergeant. Your personnel sheet has nothing but good marks. I hate to lose you to the Fleet again."

"Yes, sir. I apologize for making you find a new platoon sergeant for 1552 two weeks in."

"Orders are orders . . . Lieutenant." I can tell from the tiny pause before the *Lieutenant* that he meant to say *Sergeant*. I suspect it will take me a good while longer than that to think of myself as an officer.

"A priority assignment means that you have more important things to do for the Corps. And you sure as hell put in your time down here this year. Bet you are glad to be going into the black again."

You have no idea, I think.

I tuck the folder under my arm, stand at attention, and salute the commanding officer of what is now my former training battalion. He returns the salute almost casually.

"Best of luck to you, Lieutenant. Dismissed."

I turn on my heel and leave the CO's office. When I am outside, I breathe a small sigh of relief. Whatever lies ahead, I am officially done with NACRD Orem, and between my boot camp and the year I've spent here training new troops, I've had more than my fill of the place, this dusty and busy patch of military property where I've spent more time than in any single place since I left the PRC what feels like half a lifetime ago.

———————

It's Friday morning, not even two hours past morning chow. Under normal circumstances, I'd rejoice in a longer-than-usual weekend. But

I have to report to the LDO Academy for my officer indoctrination on Monday, so I won't have time to go up to Luna to spend the weekend with my wife. Not if I want to try to recruit my squad leaders in person. I could send them messages via MilNet and backdoor channels, but it's harder to turn someone down in person.

On the way to the shuttle pad, I get out my PDP and scroll through my notes until I reach the short list of candidates for platoon leadership positions I put together after Major Masoud offered me the assignment. I decide to sort them from easiest to hardest to convince, and start with the low-hanging fruit first.

———————————

The shuttle to Lejeune is full to the last seat on a Friday, and I am glad to be on the ground again two hours later, even if the heat out here in coastal North Carolina is much more humid and oppressive than the dry desert air at Orem.

Camp Lejeune has been around for almost two hundred years. It used to be a wet-navy Marine base in the old United States, back before the NAC even existed. In the new Corps, it's the largest Earthside base for the Spaceborne Infantry, the main training facility and home for most of the SI troopers not currently assigned to Fleet ships or colonial bases. I've been here only a few times on exercises, years ago, and the base is so massive in its sprawl that it's all new to me again when I try to find my way around.

I walk into the company building of Alpha Company of the Spaceborne Infantry's 25th Colonial Expeditionary Unit right around chow time. As I step through the double automatic doors at the entrance, two NCOs, a staff sergeant and a corporal, walk out and salute me in passing. It takes me a second to recognize what they're doing even as I reflexively return the salute. I glance at the stars on my epaulette sleeves, which still vaguely make me feel as if I am committing some sort of fraud.

The company office is staffed by a lone corporal at the moment. He's sorting printouts into mail slots when I walk into the room.

"Good morning, sir," he says.

"Good morning," I return. "Lieutenant Grayson, Fleet. I'm looking for one of your NCOs."

"Yes, sir," the corporal says. "Who is it you're looking for?"

"Gunnery Sergeant Philbrick. I was told the company's in garrison this week. Please tell me I won't have to hoof it up into orbit to catch them at SOI or something."

"No, sir." The corporal checks the large personnel status screen on the wall of the company office. "Gunny Philbrick is out at the firing range with First Platoon this morning."

"Great," I say. "How long a walk is that?"

"Range Four is right by the beach. Ten klicks, sir."

"Great," I say again, with a little more emphasis.

"The mess sergeant is going to run out lunch to First Platoon in a few, sir. You can hitch a ride with him if you want."

"Do I ever," I reply.

The firing range is just a few dunes away from the Atlantic Ocean, which I have not seen in years, except from space. The breeze is warm and muggy, and out on the water, I can see cargo vessels in the distance, their solar sails reflecting the diffused sunlight poking through the perpetually overcast sky here by the big eastern metroplexes. There are a few wet-navy warships, too, fast hydrofoil corvettes from the HD's naval arm, making high-speed runs across the waves and dragging rooster tails of water spray.

I can tell from the thundering reports coming from the range lanes that the First Platoon is live-firing their anti-LHO weapons today. I don the ear protection offered to me by the mess driver and walk over to the safety zone of the live-fire range.

Range Four has five large firing lanes, hemmed in by massive earthen berms on three sides. Most of the small-arms training in the Commonwealth Defense Corps is done on computerized ranges with simulated rounds and holographic targets, but simulator ranges are still no full substitute for firing actual live rounds at destructible targets. No matter how good they make the simulations, there's nothing like launching real tungsten and high explosives and feeling your weapon buck with the recoil of a caseless propellant charge.

There's an SI trooper with an M-90 rifle in each of the firing lanes, and short lines of more troopers waiting their turn behind the firing positions. I watch from the edge of the safety zone as the SI troopers fire their rifles at distant polymer targets that are geometric approximations of Lanky shapes. The sand underneath the firing stations bounces with the muzzle blasts from the rifles every time a trooper fires a shot.

Another group of SI troopers are sitting together in the middle of the safety zone, and there are NCOs standing near them and supervising their charges. Gunnery Sergeant Philbrick is standing near the ammo-issue booth by the firing lanes with another sergeant. The sergeant with him sees me stepping up to the safety zone and points me out to Philbrick. He turns around and startles.

"Take over for a minute, Staff Sergeant," he says to the trooper next to him. "You have the deck."

"I have the deck," the staff sergeant confirms. Philbrick trots over to the edge of the safety zone and extends his hand with a grin. Then he sees my rank insignia and smoothly converts the attempted handshake to a salute.

"Lieutenant Grayson," he says. "Good God, they got you, too?"

I return the salute, feeling slightly silly. Up until this morning, we were equals in rank and pay grade.

"It appears that way," I say. "Just wait. Your turn is coming."

"Not in a million years." Philbrick laughs.

"That's what I said, too. My wife is going to make fun of me for months after all my shit talk about officer commissions."

"Field promotion? You an LDO now?"

I nod. "I'm getting a platoon."

"Better you than me," he says. "But at least you're a mustang. NCO experience makes good lieutenants."

"Let's hope."

Behind Philbrick, the troopers on the firing line open up with their anti-Lanky rifles again. The sledgehammer reports bounce off the berms and reverberate back to where we are standing. Without hearing protection, I'd be deaf for days. Philbrick nods to the rear of the range, and we walk away from the safety zone. I lead the way and go over to the nearest sand dunes to get a view of the ocean again.

"Lovely day," I say. "I never get to come out to the water anymore. Not since I enlisted."

"I don't care for it," Philbrick says. "I'm from Vermont. Went to boot camp right there at PI." He nods down the beach to the south, where I know NACRD Parris Island sits on the same coastline, two-hundred-odd kilometers away. The Commonwealth Defense Corps only has four recruit depots—Orem, Parris Island, San Diego, and San Antonio. Like everything else in the military, they have informal rankings stacking them up against each other for desirability. San Diego is considered the best draw of the lot, followed by Orem and San Antonio. Parris Island is the roughest of the four, but the troops who graduate from PI have a defiant sense of pride about having weathered the short end of the stick.

"Fucking swamps and sand fleas," Philbrick says. "We wipe out every species on this planet, those things'll be the last ones standing. Give me the Green Mountains over this any day of the week."

"I like the mountains," I concur. "There's something about the ocean, though."

"What brings you out here? Pretty sure you didn't come all the way to the ass end of Lejeune to talk geography. Not that I mind the diversion today."

"I see they have you hitting the live range."

"Yeah, finally. Got a bunch of new privates who never got to fire live rounds until today. We're conserving resources, see. At least we almost have a full battalion now."

"You know we are heading to Mars soon, right?"

Philbrick folds his arms in front of his chest and looks out over the ocean. Then he turns his head away from me and spits into the sand by his feet.

"I suspected as much. Been drilling mostly LHO tactics for the last few weeks. There's no official word from division yet, but you know how the lance corporal underground works."

"Only thing faster than light speed is the rumor network," I say, and Philbrick grins.

"We're not ready," he says. "We weren't ready a year ago, when we got our asses kicked. We sure as shit aren't ready now."

"But we're going anyway."

Philbrick looks back toward the firing range, where his new privates are hammering apart harmless polymer Lankies with explosive gas rounds.

"Gonna end up collecting a lot of dog tags," he says.

"What if we can keep that number down?"

He looks at me and raises an eyebrow.

"And how do you propose we do that? A new gunnery sergeant and a new second lieutenant? Did they hand you the key card to the strategy room at Defense?"

"There's a mission in the works," I say. "I signed up for it because I think it may tip the scales for Mars."

"Do tell," Philbrick says.

———————

I describe the visit from Major Masoud in as much detail as I can. When I'm done, Philbrick laughs and shakes his head.

"Figures," he says. "Always some podhead shit going down ahead of the main event. One company?"

"It's a scouting run," I say. "We don't need to bring enough to beat them down. Split the platoon by squads and fire teams. Four-man recon teams with heavy weapons for backup. Fast and mobile, in and out."

"Far away from home," Philbrick says. "No supplies except what you bring along. And if you get discovered, you're in a world of shit."

"In other words, just like old times," I say, and he laughs again.

"Maybe for a podhead like you. Ain't going to be a ship in orbit, I'm guessing. This will be a long-range recon thing. And I mean really long range."

"I've done it before," I say. "And when the darts start flying, does it really make a difference if your evac ride is a thousand or a million kilometers away?"

"You know it doesn't. But why are you coming to me with this? You sure as shit don't need advice from an E-7."

"I am putting together my own command team for the platoon. I need squad leaders who know what the fuck they're doing out there. Someone I can trust." I hold up my left hand and wiggle my fingers.

"You want me to be one of your squad leaders?" Philbrick asks.

"Affirmative," I say. "I know you're above rank for the job, but this isn't going to be a cookie-cutter recon platoon. Everyone's going to be senior rank for their slots. Except me, I guess."

"Shit," he says. "I'm assistant platoon sergeant for this outfit now."

"These aren't your troops from *Indy*," I say.

"No, we got broken up and reassigned. I have a few people from the old crew. Humphrey and Nez. The rest are new. I'm locked into that slot right now, though."

"SOCOM has a ton of pull. If I can make the reassignment happen, will you take the slot?"

Philbrick looks over to the live-fire range again and purses his lips.

"I can't leave my guys alone," he says. "Been through too much. The green privates, they're not going to give a shit if the platoon gets a new gunny tomorrow. But I can't just up and leave Nez and Humphrey with them."

"What if I can get them transferred, too?"

Philbrick doesn't answer for a while. At the range, the staccato of heavy-caliber gunfire continues, the echoes rolling across the dunes like thunder in an intensely angry storm.

"Train for another few months, and board the bus for Mars," I say. "Hope it all turns out. Or come with the recon team and play for higher stakes." I feel a little bit like I'm recycling Major Masoud's talking points trying to sell this mission, but I know that Philbrick is as tired of garrison duty as I am, and I know he's as flattered to be asked to join as I was when Major Masoud asked me.

"At least it ain't Lankies," he says. "And there isn't a grunt left in the Corps who would pass up a chance to take it to those chickenshit cowards."

"So you're in?"

He drops his shoulders with a sigh.

"Yeah, I'm in. But only if you get Nez and Humphrey in as well. You get me that, I'll take a squad. Let you boss me around."

"Outstanding," I say, trying not to show my relief.

"You have the other squad leaders squared away already?"

"No, you're the first one," I reply, and he laughs.

"Who else? Anyone I know?"

I tell him the name of my other candidate, and he laughs again, but this time his laugh has a distinctly incredulous note to it.

"You have got to be shitting me."

"Not even slightly. You two are not going, we're not going."

"Holy hell." Gunny Philbrick shakes his head. "There's no way they'll let you do that."

"Watch and see," I tell him. "Watch and see. And pack your gear bag just in case."

CHAPTER 12

———— TOLEDO TERMINUS ————

Last year, right after the PRCs exploded in the wake of the Exodus, the maglev rail system suspended all traffic into or out of the PRCs out of necessity. The Lazarus Brigades asserted control over the Clusters one by one after that, and the new government was more than happy to let them. But it took months for the transportation arteries to go back to some semblance of the pre-Exodus normality, and a lot of them still aren't fully tied back into the network. If you want to make it into Detroit, you'll get as far as Toledo, Ohio, which is as far as the maglev goes now. And the closest Homeworld Defense air station to Toledo is my old duty post of Fort Shughart in Dayton.

———————

I have the strangest déjà vu when I step off the shuttle on the landing pad in Dayton. I was here, seven years ago, gearing up on the drop ship pad just across the taxiway, on a hot and muggy summer night that is still vividly seared into my memory. Our company went out to quell a food riot, and my squad came back with two of us in body bags and most of the rest wounded. I never got to come back here after that night. They ferried me to Great Lakes Medical Center, and I was discharged from what was then the Territorial Army while I was still at the hospital. I went straight from Great Lakes to my new duty station for Navy indoctrination, and never even got to say good-bye to any of my old squad mates.

Shughart is all the same except in one critical aspect now: The 365th Autonomous Infantry Battalion is still here, but Sergeant Fallon told me last year that my old platoon got dissolved and dispersed all over the brigade in the wake of a minor mutiny. The hard cases, like Sergeant Fallon, got shipped off to a penal battalion of sorts, and then into exile to far-off New Svalbard from there. The rest were dispersed and slotted into line companies all over the continent. I don't know where Hansen, Priest, and my other squaddies are right now, or if they're even still alive. I do know that Stratton and Paterson are resting in little stainless steel cremation cylinders, filed in tiny burial plots in the memorial halls of their respective hometowns. The 365th is still here, in the same building, but it's a different unit now, with a new commanding officer and unfamiliar faces in my old platoon. I could stop and visit, but it would be pointless. Some of the old-timer NCOs may still be there and recognize me from my six-month stint with the 365th seven years ago, but the people that would have been glad to see me are no longer here. Seven years ago, we were all together on this airfield, joking around and boarding the drop ship that would take us to disaster, but now they are just ghosts of the past to me, and I to them.

I never left Shughart when I was still stationed here because I never had a reason. There's a tube station right by the main gate that feeds into the Dayton public system. The train cars are old and beat to shit, but they run. I scan my military ID at the ticket computer and drag my alert bag onto the next city-bound train with me.

At the Dayton station, I switch platforms from the military-only level to the public system. Upstairs, where the civvies intermingle with the uniformed HD troops and cops, the station looks like a PRC street market. It's far busier and livelier than the last public transport station I visited, back home in Boston over a year ago. There are still civilian police all over the place, but they wear only light armor, not full riot gear, and the atmosphere isn't as tense and hostile as I remember Boston last year. I check departure tables and go up the stairs to where the fast maglev trains depart. At the top of the stairs, a civilian police officer checks my ticket slip and waves me through.

"You're not going to scan my ID?" I ask. They usually check ID to make sure you're the same person who printed the slip at the ticket computer, to keep military personnel from buying free rides for friends and dependents.

"Scanner's broke," he says. "No worries. Where you're going, nobody in their right mind goes in uniform 'less they are legit."

The maglev ride from Dayton to Toledo only takes half an hour. It's early in the evening, and the summer sun is setting outside. I'm tired and want to use the opportunity for a nap, but the knowledge that I'm getting four kilometers closer to the Detroit metroplex with every passing minute keeps me just anxious enough that sleep won't set in despite my bone-deep fatigue. On the other side of the scuffed and stained polyplast windows of the maglev train car, the streets are still lined with single- and two-story houses, but I know that soon enough, I'll pass that threshold between the old suburbs and the new PRCs, that demarcation line between tenuous order and controlled anarchy, and then the buildings will get progressively taller and filthier. I see my own reflection in the window, and my face looks as tired and shopworn as the faded and fraying cloth covering of my seat.

The train glides into the Toledo station and comes to a slow stop that has an air of finality to it.

"Toledo Terminus," a computer announcement says from the address system in the train car ceiling. "This is the final stop on this line. All passengers are required to disembark. I repeat, all passengers are required to disembark. This is the final stop."

I know that the line used to go all the way into Detroit before the Exodus, but things have changed since then. I gather my alert bag and line up in the aisle with the rest of the remaining passengers who have business in Toledo or beyond. Everyone else in this maglev car is a civilian, and they all look as tired and beaten down as I do. There's something about being this close to a PRC that just saps the cheer and the energy out of most people.

The military and police presence here in the Toledo terminus is heavier than it was in Dayton, and the station doesn't have the same market square atmosphere to it. Instead, the civvies go about their business past small groups of policemen and HD troops, and the ones out here are in heavier gear. Some of them eye me curiously as I make my way through the station with my alert bag on my back, and I do my best to appear unconcerned. This is the atmosphere I'm used to from the pre-Exodus days, distrustful cops on edge safeguarding what remains of orderly state functions here on the edge of official NAC control.

At the exit door to street level, there's a checkpoint set up, half a dozen HD troopers with sidearms and PDWs manning a cordon funnel and checking IDs. I step up to the line of guards and hold out my military ID for them to scan.

The sergeant who scans my ID looks genuinely concerned.

"Sir, are you sure you want to leave the secure area at this hour? It's almost 2100 hours."

"How far does the secure area extend?" I ask.

"Hundred-meter perimeter around the station, right up to the riverfront. Everything on the other side is militia-controlled. You go out that set of doors and across the bridge at the other end of the transit plaza, and there's a militia checkpoint on the other side. They won't let you through armed and in cammies."

"I've got a pickup waiting," I say. "I'll be all right, Sergeant."

The sergeant shrugs and hands my ID card back to me.

"If you're positive, sir. We won't be able to do much if they decide to detain you, though. Their turf over there."

I stick my ID card back into my document pocket and try to look confident.

"Can't wait until the morning, Sarge. Pressing business."

"Must be some top-level shit, sir. Sorry," he adds after a moment.

"It is some top-level shit," I say. "Trust me, I wouldn't go out there by myself if I didn't have to. I'm not a dipshit."

I walk through the cordon funnel and head for the doors. When I reach them, I take a brief look back at the HD troopers manning the checkpoint, and most of them are watching me and talking amongst themselves in low murmurs. The sergeant who checked my ID gives me a nod, but I can tell by his expression that I do in fact qualify as a dipshit in his opinion. I take a deep breath and step through the automatic doors and out into the evening air.

Walking across the bridge into the militia-controlled part of the city is an almost surreal experience. There are forty-story buildings lining the riverbank on both sides, and I hear and see the noisy pulse of a large city all around me, but the bridge itself is dark and quiet. I am the only pedestrian crossing the water right now, and I feel uncomfortably exposed out here in the dark. Above the city, the streetlights are illuminating the cloak of haze that hangs over the city.

On the other side of the bridge, there's another checkpoint. This one is made up of waist-high concrete barriers. There's a squad of militia troops standing guard out here, all in the same olive-drab uniforms adopted by the Lazarus Brigade. They look anachronistic in their fatigues, with the rank insignia of the old pre-NAC United States Army, but their common equipment makes them look a lot more professional than the ragtag band of armed civvies that ambushed my platoon just a few dozen kilometers north of here seven years ago.

As I approach the checkpoint, I make sure I keep my hands away from my sidearm or the alert bag on my back. Whether they are antiques or not, I am greatly outnumbered and unarmored, and if things get sporty with these militia guys, I'll be hugely outgunned. But they all just look at me with mild curiosity, not hostility. Things have changed since last year, it seems.

"Good evening," I say when I am in hailing distance. The squad leader wears the old insignia of a sergeant on the sleeves of his olive-drab fatigue jacket, three chevrons pointing up. To my surprise, he sketches a salute, albeit a perfunctory one.

"Evening," he says. "What brings you to our side of the river, Lieutenant?"

"I hear the food is better," I say, and some of the militia troopers nearby laugh.

"No, it ain't," the sergeant says.

I look at the way he carries his rifle, suspended from a single-point sling and hanging diagonally in front of his body. He has his finger properly indexed alongside the trigger guard.

"You prior NAC service?" I ask.

He nods. "Two years HD."

"I'm here to see someone," I say. "I was told to ask you to contact this network node and tell them that Lieutenant Andrew Grayson is asking for a pickup."

I pull my PDP out of my pocket, unlock it with my fingerprint, and show the screen to the militia sergeant. He looks at the device with mild surprise.

"Deion," he says to one of the other militia troopers. "Get on the link and send a message to node 679-Alpha. Tell them there's a Lieutenant Grayson from Fleet asking for passage."

"Copy that," the trooper says and walks off toward the nearest alley mouth behind the barriers. Maybe a minute later, he returns.

"They're sending a ride for you, Lieutenant. ETA forty-five minutes."

"Any place I can sit while I wait?" I ask.

The sergeant points to the nearby concrete barriers. I sigh and take off my alert bag. Then I walk over to the nearest barrier and sit down in front of it, too tired to care or argue.

———————

A little over an hour later, two noisy military vehicles show up at the end of the street on the militia-controlled side and roll toward the checkpoint. They're ancient, gasoline-burning designs straight out of a military history book, utility all-terrain vehicles of the kind that were once used by the army of the old United States. They're square and flat-bottomed, with large, knobby, honeycomb tires. There's a gunner standing up in the roof hatch of each vehicle, and they are both manning pintle-mounted automatic guns with air-cooled barrels. The small column comes to a halt twenty meters short of the checkpoint, and the headlights from the lead all-terrain illuminate the scene harshly until the driver kills the lights. The doors of the lead vehicle open, and three militia troopers climb out. I recognize the one from the passenger seat right away.

"Major Jackson," I greet the tall, dark-skinned woman wearing gold oak leaves on her collars. I offer a salute, which she returns before holding out her hand to shake mine.

"Good to see you again," she says, and startles a little when she sees my shoulder sleeves. "Lieutenant. Moving up on the ladder."

"Not as high as you, Major."

"And you thought they were going to arrest you last year," she says. "Told you they got bigger fish to fry."

"Precisely why I'm here to talk to the general," I say.

"Well, jump in and take a seat," she says. "Just don't crack any windows on the journey. Some rough neighborhoods on the way, Brigade or not."

"You're going to take my gun bag and dog tags for the ride?"

"No need. We're not hiding out anymore. And you'll need that buzz gun if we take a wrong turn."

———————————

On the ride into Detroit proper, we pass many scars in the rows of houses and tenement high-rises lining the streets. There are half-gone buildings standing next to occupied ones, and ruins that amount to not much more than charred foundations and twisted steel sticking out of concrete rubble piles. I always thought I'd never go back into this city unless ordered at gunpoint, right until last year when Halley dropped her ship and the platoon in its hold right into the middle of the place in pursuit of a Lanky seedpod. I didn't have much time to reflect on my fear a great deal then, but I definitely have unwelcome flashbacks as we roll through the summer night.

"Those guys back at the checkpoint were agreeable," I tell Major Jackson. "Almost courteous."

"Fleet remnants got a lot of credit last year when you showed up and went right after the Lankies," Major Jackson says. "SI, too. Defending the civvies, that went over well. You didn't run like the rest of 'em did." Her expression darkens. "Deserting the planet. Leaving us to clean the mess."

"What about HD?"

"We don't kill each other on sight, if that's what you mean. But no, HD ain't precisely very welcome around here on most days. Didn't hear shit out of Dayton the night the Lankies dropped in. You Fleet and SI people made it all the way from orbit, but they couldn't be assed to come the hundred fifty klicks from Shughart to help out. If Homeworld Defense don't defend the home world, the fuck are they good for?"

An hour into our ride, we are right in the middle of Category 5 PRC country, the latest and greatest residence clusters with high-rise towers that are a hundred floors tall. Without a suit computer, I have lost my bearings, so I have no idea where in Detroit I am, and the Cat 5 blocks all look the same wherever you go. Our battle against the Lankies last year took place in the middle of a few Cat 5 blocks. One drop ship, one platoon of troops, half a dozen Lankies, and tens of thousands of frightened civilians. I wouldn't have bet anything on our survival if someone had told me the odds before the battle, and I'm still amazed that we walked out of there alive. But I take some solace in the fact that throughout our sixty-minute journey, nobody fired a single shot at us as we passed through much of Detroit's outskirts.

Our ride ends at the foot of a residence cluster. The all-terrain cars descend down a concrete ramp that leads below one of the enormous three-hundred-meter towers that make up each corner of a Category 5 PRC cluster. We pass through a set of steel doors and then into a subterranean passageway wide enough for two cars side by side. Then the space opens up, and we come to a halt in a large underground garage. It's well lit, and there are at least a dozen more of the old all-terrain vehicles lined up alongside the walls in individually marked bays. More militia troops in olive-drab fatigues are milling around down here, working on cars or loading gear, and a few of them even spare our little column a second look as our driver kills the engine, and we disembark.

"Safe the guns and stow the ammo," Major Jackson tells her crews. "Come with me, Lieutenant. I'll take you upstairs."

"Aye-aye, ma'am," I reply and follow her dutifully, not keen on drawing attention in this place by stepping a foot away from where I'm expected to be.

"Upstairs" really means upward. We step into an elevator that whisks us to the fiftieth floor of the PRC tower. Then we walk a small gauntlet of checkpoints, all guarded by very fit-looking and heavily armed militia troops that wouldn't look out of place in an SI ready room. I notice that up here, the troops carry more modern weaponry, current-issue PDWs and M-66 fléchette rifles—stuff that will defeat modern battle armor at close range.

We take another elevator that carries us the rest of the way up the tower to the hundredth floor. There's a final checkpoint up here, but the armored militiamen step aside and let us through when they see Major Jackson. Nobody has even asked me to surrender the alert bag on my back or the sidearm on my hip. With all the armed personnel around here, I suspect I'd have a really short life expectancy if I pulled out my weapon and started popping off rounds.

Major Jackson leads me into an empty briefing room. There's a large table with a bunch of mismatched chairs around it, and the major gestures toward it.

"Have a seat, Lieutenant. I'll let the general know you're here. Shouldn't be long."

"Thank you, Major. Good to see you again."

"And you." She exits the room and leaves the door open as she walks out.

The briefing room has tall floor-to-ceiling polyplast windows that look like they're about five centimeters thick. Outside, the sprawl of the PRCs extends as far as I can see, which isn't very far despite my vantage point three hundred meters up. There's a perpetual haze over the large metroplexes that gets illuminated from all the city lights below at night. The incandescent, dirty fog surrounds and envelops the city like an impenetrable dome. From this height, it has a certain beauty to it. I sit down in one of the chairs next to the window, put my alert pack aside, and watch the city outside for a little while. I've been in a PRC many times before, but this is the first time as a soldier where I'm by myself, a hundred kilometers or more away from the nearest brothers and sisters in arms. If there's any trouble tonight, I'll be on my own, with nobody around to help me or even bite the bullet with me. I look up into the sky, but the glowing haze above the city is dense, and I can't see the moon, where Halley is probably sleeping in our quarters right now.

A short time later, General Lazarus walks into the room, a data pad in his hand and a tired look on his face. I get out of my chair, but he waves me off curtly before I can salute.

"As you were, Lieutenant. Sit down."

I do as I am told and put my butt back into the chair. General Lazarus walks over to where I am sitting, pulls out another chair, and sits down in front of me with a small sigh. Then he puts the data pad onto the conference table next to him and stretches his neck.

"Long day," he says. "They all are, lately."

"Yes, sir," I say.

The general looks older than he did last year, more so than the time since our last meeting would justify. His close-cropped hair has quite a bit more gray and silver in it, and there's deep fatigue evident around his eyes. But he's still muscular and taut, and he still radiates competence. I don't know what his name was before he called himself Lazarus, and I never checked the database to ferret out his service record from his Marine days, but I know that his occupational specialty involved breaking people and their stuff. There's an air of quiet danger around him that tells me he wasn't a personnel officer or supply group supervisor when he was still wearing a Marine uniform.

"What brings you here tonight? Have you reconsidered my offer from last year? Ready to get out of the Fleet and make a contribution here on the ground?"

"Sticking with the Fleet for now," I say. "At least until the job is done."

"It's never done," he says. "Even if we get the Lankies out of the Solar System, there'll always be a new furnace to feed new recruits into. Sooner or later we'll kill each other again if we have no Lankies to shoot at anymore."

"How well are you tied in to Corps intel?" I ask. General Lazarus shakes his head slightly and smiles.

"Let's just say 'well enough,' and leave it at that."

"Then you know there's a major operation coming up."

"You don't need to have your finger on the pulse of the Intel division to know that. It's the next logical step. Stop the Lanky incursions, push them back before they figure out to send everything they have at us at once one day. But yes," he continues, "I have heard about the operation."

"Three months," I say. "I just spent two training cycles at Orem to help churn out new bodies for the infantry and the Fleet. I can tell you that we're nowhere near ready for an op of that size."

"It's a gamble," General Lazarus says. "The eternal generals' dilemma. Go too soon, risk failure. Wait too long, risk losing initiative to the enemy. I don't think there has ever been a military campaign planner who was happy with what was on the board when the campaign kicked off."

"There may be a mission in the works. One that could put more stuff on the board before this whole mess begins. Maybe even enough to influence the outcome."

"But you can neither confirm nor deny," General Lazarus says with a tiny smile.

"That's correct," I say with an equally measured smile.

"I'm guessing that's what that new rank is about." He nods at the stars on my shoulder boards.

"I'm trying to staff a platoon," I say. "And I'm here because I want to ask your permission to borrow someone under your command. To serve as my right hand for that mission."

General Lazarus's right eyebrow takes a slight upward angle for a moment.

"And who did you have in mind?" he asks, even though I'm certain that he knows exactly which one of his troopers I intend to recruit.

"Master Sergeant Fallon," I say. "No better infantry platoon NCO in the entire Corps. Or what's left of it."

General Lazarus chuckles. Then he leans forward, rests his elbows on his knees, and steeples his fingers. He studies me for a moment or two while lightly tapping his chin with his fingertips.

"Master Sergeant Fallon," he repeats slowly. "Master Sergeant Fallon is one of my most important assets. She is in charge of the NCO development for the Brigade. She trains all my new sergeants. I consider her indispensable at this point."

"I was hoping I could convince you to let her join me for a few weeks," I say.

He looks at me and folds his arms in front of his chest, a little smile playing in the corners of his mouth as if he's trying to decide whether I am joking, or just incredibly brazen.

"And why would I give up one of my senior noncommissioned officers to go on a Fleet mission? What are you putting on the table for me as an incentive? What do I get out of it?"

"If we're successful, you may never have to worry about fighting Lankies down here again," I say.

"And if you're not, I may lose the primary mentor of my noncom corps." He shakes his head. "I want to see the Lankies gone as much as anyone, but loaning you Master Sergeant Fallon is a lot of certain risk for very uncertain reward. You're going to have to do better than that."

"What is it you want?" I ask. "I don't have any pull with the general staff. I can't get you any new gear."

"We have gear," General Lazarus says. "Lots of it. HD has transferred a lot of the old reserve equipment to us. It's not the most modern, but it's sufficient, and it allows us to standardize. No, you'll have to put something more useful on the table. You know our needs. I discussed them with you last year when I made you the offer to join us."

I know where he's going with this, of course. He has me over a barrel, and I know that he knows it by the tiny smile that never leaves the corners of his mouth even as he pretends to be nonplussed.

I let out a small sigh.

"Fine. Fine. You let me borrow Master Sergeant Fallon for this mission, I will take that training slot you offered me. I'll train your guys for one year, get a program off the ground."

"Two," he says.

"Eighteen months," I say. "A year and a half. And only after we've taken care of the immediate threat. After Mars."

General Lazarus puts the tips of his steepled fingers to his lips again and studies me for a few moments as he ponders my offer.

"Done," he says.

"Thank you, sir," I say, trying not to let my profound relief show in my voice.

"Don't be too thankful just yet," the general says. "That's only half the battle. The other half is going to be convincing Master Sergeant Fallon. I can only give her permission to join you. I can't order her to join you. That sell is all up to you, Lieutenant."

CHAPTER 13

—— BREAD AND CIRCUSES ——

"This is a sad fucking day for the military," Sergeant Fallon says when I step out of the elevator and into the tower atrium. She's waiting in the elevator bank vestibule in immaculate parade rest, hands behind her back, feet spread a shoulder's width apart. Then she steps forward and gives me a rough and quick hug.

"Been a while, Andrew," she says.

"That's a fact," I say.

"I suppose I should have saluted you instead," Sergeant Fallon says. "A fucking lieutenant. Of all the NCOs I've known, I would have put money on you being the last to accept a commission."

"You're exempt," I say. "And not just because of the blue ribbon."

As a Medal of Honor recipient, Sergeant Fallon has the prerogative to receive salutes from anyone regardless of rank difference, so she wouldn't have to salute me anyway. But even without the medal, I would have felt odd about receiving a salute from my old squad leader, a woman who has been in the service since I was in elementary school, and whose combat record makes mine look like I'm a towel-counting supply jockey.

"What are you doing here, Andrew? Thought you had enough of this turf for the rest of your days."

"I came to see you," I say. "Got something to ask you."

"Must be important if you're all the way out here in Shitville. Is your wife with you, too?"

"No, she's up at Luna, still training pilots."

"Well, she did all right last year. Guess they're learning from someone good."

The atrium is an enormous square that makes up most of the ground floor of the residence tower. The buildings have a hollow core, for convection cooling and ventilation, and you can see all the way from the atrium floor to the reinforced concrete roof. Tonight, the halves of the roof are open to let the warm summer air circulate. Out on the atrium, people are milling about alone and in small groups, and nobody is paying any particular attention to us.

"I was about to walk over to the interchange to grab a drink and watch the race. Why don't you come along? We can drink shitty beer and talk a bit."

"Watch the race?" I ask.

"Yeah. Come, and I'll show you. It's what passes for Friday night fun around here now. Beats firefights any night of the week, let me tell you."

We walk out of the residence tower and into the plaza in the center of the block, which is quite a bit livelier than the atrium. It's a warm night, and people are out as they usually are when the weather is good. There are vendor stalls lining the sides of the plaza, and the noise level is raucous but not hostile. It feels a lot like the safer parts of my old PRC back home, where you can spend an evening drinking with your friends without having to worry about ending up in a crossfire between gangs or contraband dealers.

"That took a shitload of work," Sergeant Fallon says when I tell her so. "When we dropped here the night we lost Stratton and Paterson and

MARKO KLOOS

I lost my leg, this place was a free-fire jungle. People killing each other over rations. Food riots. TA raids. This was the worst of the worst."

She points to our right, past the next cluster of residence towers visible beyond the retaining wall of the block we're in.

"That neighborhood is about five klicks that way, by the way. In case you ever want to do some fucked-up sightseeing."

"No, thank you," I reply. I have no interest in seeing the street again where my squad mates died, or the building entrance where we huddled for our last stand and I almost bought the farm after getting shot three times.

"I did, a few months ago," Sergeant Fallon says.

"Why the fuck would you do that?"

"I don't know, really. To understand better? To come to terms with it? Fuck, I have no idea. Maybe I wanted to see if there were still blood-stains on the asphalt where that round blew off half my leg."

"And?"

She shakes her head.

"Nope. Place looks a lot different in daylight. I hardly recognized it. Remember that high-rise you blew up with a thermobaric?"

"Yeah," I say, and the memory triggers a sudden twisting feeling in my gut.

"It's still there. Just a little shorter than before. You took out the top ten floors. They just cleared the rubble and put a new roof on."

"Let's keep that little detail to ourselves," I say. "I don't care to broadcast that around here."

"It was collateral damage," Sergeant Fallon says. "You can't put a gun emplacement on a building and then complain when it gets return fire. None of the Brigade guys would give you shit for what you did. Well, not much."

"So how did they turn this place around like that?" I ask, eager to move on to a different subject.

144

"Brigade took over the policing. Recruited from the neighbor-hoods. Veterans only, at first. Then the locals who weren't complete shitheads. The trainable ones, not the hard cases from the gangs. Treat 'em right, teach 'em how to do their jobs, crack down on the ones who can't handle the power. Street by street. Block by block. Work with the hood rats, not against them."

"Looks like it worked out well."

"Eventually," Sergeant Fallon says. "Took years of blood and sweat. And parts of the city still aren't Brigade-controlled. Probably never will be. Too hard-ass even for the general to crack. Can't police people who don't want to be policed. But here in the quiet part, you can be out past 2200 again without getting stomped into the curb."

"I see you all have matching gear now," I say, and point to the M4 carbine Sergeant Fallon wears slung over her shoulder.

"We have an arrangement with HD now. They gave us all the old United States surplus from the wartime reserve depots. Vehicles, rifles, ammunition. Billions of rounds. It's all ancient as fuck, but it still works. And we can finally standardize our training and issue. Hard to even come up with a weapons training manual if your army uses whatever they can find," she says.

"Mind-blowing," I say. "A few years ago we were shooting at each other. Now HD is providing weapons."

"It's a good trade for them," Sergeant Fallon says. "We keep the peace in the PRCs for them, and all they're out is a few storage depots full of obsolete gear. We still don't have the firepower to match the HD or SI battalions, but it's more than enough to keep a firm hand on the PRCs. I'd call that a win-win situation for the new government."

From beyond the retaining wall on the far side of the plaza, I hear loud engine noises, the raucous, thundering racket of old combustion engines. It echoes and reverberates in the canyons of the streets between the high-rises.

"What the fuck is that?" I ask.

"The race," Sergeant Fallon says. "You'll see."

In the street that separates this residence block from the next, there's a crowd lining the sidewalks, and there are barriers on both ends of the block to close this section of road to traffic. Someone laid out an ellipse shape on the asphalt with orange polyplast fencing, the sort used for temporary traffic control. There are LEDs set up on the retaining walls of the adjoining residence blocks to illuminate the scene beyond what the street lighting can contribute. It's an ad hoc temporary racetrack a hundred meters long and maybe thirty meters wide. On the track, two vehicles are revving their engines next to each other. Both are old Army all-terrains, but these look like they've been stripped of everything that isn't strictly necessary for driving. They're barely more than frames with driver seats and engines.

I shoot Sergeant Fallon an incredulous look.

"We had more vehicles than we needed all of a sudden," she says with a shrug.

"And they use them for racing?"

"*Panem et circenses*," she replies. "Bread and circuses. Nothing wrong with a little fun. Don't tell me they never had stuff like this where you grew up."

The noise from the racetrack and the surrounding crowd is impressive, and we stay a good distance away—close enough to watch the action, far enough away to still be able to have a conversation. On the track, the stripped-down all-terrains send up dark clouds of exhaust fumes as they continue to gun their noisy engines. Then they release their brakes and barrel down the makeshift racetrack, and the crowd cheers.

"People make their own fun, whatever shit they find themselves in," Sergeant Fallon says. "Let them watch these things go fast around a circle. Beats the shit out of watching them shoot each other in the alleys."

Sergeant Fallon walks over to one of the nearby vendor stalls and returns with two bottles that don't bear any labels. She hands one to me and uncaps her own. Then she takes a swig, closes her eyes, and sighs.

"Needed that after today."

"What is this stuff?" I ask, eyeing the bottle suspiciously. The plastic is green and opaque. I pop off the cap and smell the contents. It has a familiar artificial fruit tang to it.

"They call it Bug Juice. The base is fruit juice made from ration packet powder. Then they add a few shots of ethanol. A few liberal shots."

I take a swig, surprised to find that the concoction is actually not awful. It certainly beats the soy beer we can get in the military clubs.

"It's no Shockfrost," I say. "But it's all right."

Sergeant Fallon winces. "Nothing's a Shockfrost 'cept a Shockfrost. You could run a drop ship with that stuff. Best thing about that god-forsaken ball of frozen shit."

She's talking about New Svalbard, of course, where we got stuck for months last year just before the Exodus. Whenever I remember that little ice moon and the rough crowd that settled it, I vacillate between dread and something that feels strangely like homesickness. It's a lonely, harsh, frozen colony, and it's on the ass end of settled space and terribly vulnerable, but there's something clean and pure and simple about it. The more complexities this profession throws at me, the more I find myself thinking that New Svalbard would not be the worst of all choices for a retirement colony. But I keep that opinion to myself, because Sergeant Fallon would have me forcibly committed to the mental ward at Great Lakes if I shared it with her.

"You didn't come here to discuss the relative merits of local booze production," Sergeant Fallon says matter-of-factly. She nods over to some nearby concrete barriers, and we both sit down, a little out of the way of the crowds that have gathered to watch the noisy race.

"There's a special mission in the works," I say. "Deep-space recon."

"Where to?" she asks.

"I have no idea," I say. "Yet. But I can tell you who we're going after."

I make a sweeping gesture with my bottle to encompass the scene around us—the racetrack, the high-rise residence towers, the city as a whole.

"The fuckers who ran away just before the Lankies dropped on our heads. The ones who were supposed to hold the fucking line. The ones who left us to clean up the mess they left behind."

"That a fact." Sergeant Fallon takes another swig from her bottle and grimaces. "We found out where they went, huh?"

"Colonel Campbell's recon drones did. The ones he left on station at that secret anchorage right before we came back to New Svalbard. They recorded all the message and data traffic right up until their whole fleet took off and made Alcubierre."

"Well, I'll be dipped in shit," she says. "Corps intel actually good for something for a change."

"I hear they had some help from the Chinese."

"And you're going to check out their new cozy home."

"That's the idea," I say. "Get eyeballs on the place so we can call in the rest of the Fleet and spoil their little party."

"I would pay good money to be there when they drag the old NAC administration back home by their scruffs. Give 'em a trial, then hang 'em for treason. Or better yet, shoot them over to Mars and let the Lankies settle that account for us."

"You want to be a part of that? Come with me. I need a platoon sergeant I can trust. Someone who knows the job."

Sergeant Fallon barks a laugh.

"You want me to serve under you?"

"You're the best platoon NCO I've ever had. I know it's a lowly job for a master sergeant, but you know it better than anyone else I know."

"Andrew, you can get any number of gunnery sergeants in SI who would jump at that chance. You don't need me to ride herd on a bunch of space apes for you."

"Look," I say, and turn the bottle in my hands slowly. "I'm a fresh second louie. I've never been in charge of anything more than my battle armor and my radio set. I need people with experience 'cause I sure as fuck don't have any. Not when it comes to leading thirty-six troops."

"You've been in the shit for half a decade, Andrew. You're a damn sight more qualified for the job than some boy wonder fresh from Officer U. Don't fucking worry about it too much."

"But I do," I say. "I worry. Because if I find that I'm in over my head, I can't call a time-out and have them fly in another guy to take over. I fuck up, three dozen grunts are going to bite it."

"Your day job involves calling down airstrikes. Giving the cruisers targets to shoot nukes at. I think you can deal with the stress of commanding a grunt platoon."

She puts her bottle to her lips and chugs about half the remaining contents.

"Besides," she continues. "You know how I know you'll be a good officer? Because you do worry. I've never met a second lieutenant fresh out of the academy who didn't think he was God's gift to tactical warfare. You'll be just fine."

"Come with me," I repeat. "It's a two-week mission. Maybe three. Keep the squad leaders on task and watch my back if things start going sideways. Keep me on the straight and narrow if I start going sideways."

She doesn't say anything. Instead, she keeps watching the crowd reacting to the events in the race we can't see from our vantage point.

"They thought they got away clean," I say. "Left us here to die. Never came back to check on the mess they left behind. As far as they know, we're all dead by now, and Earth is Lanky real estate. Think about how much fun it would be to go after them and help fuck up their little paradise."

"How many ships did they take with them?"

I think for a moment.

"A Navigator supercarrier. A cruiser. Three frigates, I think. And a destroyer. Along with a dozen freighters from the auxiliary fleet."

"And that's not counting what they may have squirreled away in their new home system before the Lankies cut their timetable short."

"Correct," I say.

"So we'll be ludicrously outnumbered and outgunned," Sergeant Fallon says.

"Almost certainly."

"Fuck." She grins. Then she looks back over to the crowd watching the race and lets out an exaggerated sigh.

"Two weeks," she says. "Maybe three."

"That's the plan."

"Did you talk to the general about this?"

"I did," I say. "He says it's up to you, but he gave his permission if you decide to come along."

"What did you have to leave on the table for that?" she asks with a smile.

"Told him I'd join the Brigade and do training for a year and a half."

She chuckles and drains the rest of her beverage.

"Man, you must really want to hang your nuts back over the fire."

Sergeant Fallon chucks the empty bottle aside. It clatters to the concrete and bounces off a nearby barrier.

"Ah, what the hell. I've done nothing but whipping these hood rats into shape for the last year. This will be like an adventure vacation for me."

She sighs again. Then she stands up and pats the concrete dust off the set of her fatigues.

"I'll be your platoon sergeant, Andrew. As a personal favor. For what you did on New Svalbard, and everything after."

I suppress the urge to jump up and cheer. Instead, I get to my feet in a dignified manner and merely allow myself a satisfied grin.

"Thank you," I tell Sergeant Fallon. "I didn't have a backup plan in case you turned me down."

"Fuck my soft and squishy heart," she grumbles. "As if I don't have enough of my old squad nuggets ordering me around already."

CHAPTER 14

ON OUR TERMS

The Limited Duty Officer Academy at Fleet Station Newport is one of the most taxing schools I've taken in my time in the service. It's only a week of classroom instruction, and there's almost no physical component involved, but getting lectured on officer uniforms, etiquette, and Fleet history and regulations is hard to endure. I know that while they're teaching me stuff I mostly know already, my new platoon is getting ready for deployment without me. They already cut down the LDO indoctrination to one week instead of two because of our personnel situation, but it's still a week I could be spending getting to know my new troops and training with them instead of looking at a holoscreen while some Fleet desk jockey drones on about tropical and cold-weather uniforms and how to handle your fork at a formal dinner.

Most of the new officers at LDO Academy are shipboard specialists. There are only two infantry grunts in my class, a new SI lieutenant and a Fleet Security officer. Whenever you stick a bunch of troops from all over the service into a class together, the grunts will naturally gravitate toward each other, and we spend our off time swapping battle stories and running together to remain in fighting shape. I've not been back in a classroom setting in years, and it just reinforces to me that humans weren't meant to sit on their asses for eight hours a day, especially not combat soldiers.

On the second day at LDO Academy, I get an incoming message on my PDP at evening chow. I check the screen to see an inbound connection request from Major Masoud at SOCOM. I leave my half-eaten meal behind and step out of the mess hall to respond to the call.

"Your SI sergeant and his two junior NCOs are in," Major Masoud says. "Not a problem. They have the chops for the job."

"They do, sir. What about Sergeant Fallon?"

"It's your choice," Major Masoud says. "And I know Sergeant Fallon's service record, of course. But she's HD and barely space-qualified. You want to take an HD NCO on a mission out of system?"

"There's no better platoon sergeant left in the Corps," I say. "Yes, I want her to come along. We've been in combat together off-world. I assure you that she knows her business. On this planet or any other."

"Oh, I have no doubt," Major Masoud replies. "Your pick. You want to bring her, you get her. But your platoon may not be altogether happy with a platoon sergeant from Homeworld Defense, regardless of her reputation in the Corps."

"I don't need Sergeant Fallon on my team to make the platoon happy," I say. "I need her to keep the platoon alive and on the job."

Major Masoud flashes a curt smile.

"Fine," he says. "She'll be your platoon sergeant. But be very careful, Lieutenant. This is an unorthodox platoon composition, to say the least. It's not a common thing to give your platoon-sergeant slot to an HD NCO with minimal space-warfare training. You may be setting yourself up for circumstances that are beyond your ability to control."

"Yes, sir," I reply. "With all due respect, that has been the case ever since I signed my terms of enlistment."

He looks at me as if he's considering how to reply.

"Your orders are on the way for Gateway on Monday," he says. "We have absolutely no time to waste. Prepare yourself, Lieutenant Grayson. This may be the most important operation you'll ever be a part of."

He disconnects the link, leaving me to look at the momentarily dark screen of my PDP.

"Aren't they all," I say to the battered little device.

My LDO Academy class ends with a fizzle instead of a bang. We're all experienced former NCOs with a low tolerance for dog-and-pony shows, so there's no corny motivational ceremony, no formation in dress uniform under the eyes of the academy commander with guidons flapping in the wind and long-winded speeches about duty and leadership. Instead, we have a quick little step-out-and-shake-hands affair that lasts all of three minutes, as if our instructors are fully aware of the fact that we are itching to get back to work after a week of learning stuff that's of very little importance to the war effort. I say a quick good-bye to my infantry running mates, and we dissolve and head out into the weekend quickly and separately, just the way we arrived. I'm on a shuttle back to Luna not forty minutes after I received my official blessing to go forth and be an officer in the NAC Defense Corps, and I feel that I've mostly wasted a perfectly good week.

The shuttle schedules are once again all fucked to hell, so it's Saturday morning before I get back to Luna and the married quarters I share with my wife.

When I unlock the security pad at the door and walk into the place, Halley is asleep in the bedroom, with the sliding door to the sleeping berth open. I put down my gear quietly and step into the kitchen nook to coax a cup of soy coffee out of the personal brewing unit on the counter, a small, officer-only luxury perk Halley got from the supply group a few months ago. There are only a handful of coffee capsules left in the little drawer underneath the unit. As shitty as the military coffee is, we're running short even on that horrible stuff. Too many mouths to feed, not enough to feed them with.

"You're home," Halley says in a sleepy voice from the bedroom as I sit down at the kitchen table. The table is piled high with stacks of printouts and other instructor paraphernalia, and I shove it aside to carve out a little bit of real estate for my coffee mug and my PDP.

"Good morning," I say. "Coffee?"

"Affirmative," she answers.

I get back up and drop another capsule into the brewing unit. Halley's mug is on the kitchen counter, half full of cold coffee. I dump her mug out into the sink, rinse it, and place it underneath the brewing unit.

"Almost out of coffee," I say.

"No need to try and order more." Halley comes traipsing out of the bedroom, dressed only in her PT shorts and a green flight suit undershirt, her hair tousled and as unruly as her short cut ever gets. She hugs me from behind and kisses me on the back of the neck.

"Look at you," she says. "Second lieutenant. I'm no longer poaching among the NCO corps."

"One week of shake-and-bake school," I reply. "And I think I may have been asleep half the time."

"Well, we gotta celebrate tonight while we can. Maybe I can talk the handsome corporal in the O Club out of a bottle of fizzy stuff. He's been checking me out coming and going for weeks now."

The coffee brewer spits out its finished product into Halley's mug. I take it out of the brewer and hand it to her. She takes the mug with both hands and sits down at the kitchen table. I sit back down in front of my own mug.

"Want to do breakfast?" she asks. "It's 0730 already, but if I get ready quickly, we can catch the tail end of morning chow."

I look at my wife, at the way even the baggy and unflattering military-issue underwear can't completely conceal her shapely form underneath, and find that powdered egg and soy sausage patties are not quite the first thing on my list of desires.

"Or I could get out of these sweaty CDUs, hop into the shower, have my way with you in the cot, and take my chances with lunch later."

Halley looks at me and smiles with her lips on the rim of the coffee mug.

"Plan B it is," she says. "Go rinse off."

A good while later, when we're back in the sleeping nook, with our limbs all tangled up in the sheets and each other, Halley starts humming a tune with her head resting on my shoulder.

"You're in a good mood this morning," I observe. "Something I did?"

"Mmmm-hmmm," she confirms. "That, too. But I got great news yesterday after morning orders."

"And what are those?"

"I'm handing the keys to the shop to someone else for a while on Wednesday. I got orders for a new assignment."

I turn to look at her. "Combat unit?"

"No clue. Orders say to report to the 160th at Campbell on Wednesday morning."

"Down on Earth?"

"Mmm-hmmm," she says again. "Don't know what for, but it's probably to qualify on a new bird, or to do some snake-eater shit for HD. The 160th has all the top-flight hardware. The important thing is that I'll be free. I've been in that instructor slot for too fucking long. Over two years of classes, simulator, flight lessons, classes, simulator, repeat ad nauseam."

"If they have you flying combat drops for HD, things might get a bit hairy," I say, remembering all too well the night in Detroit seven years ago when a shot-down drop ship cost us half a squad of dead or wounded.

"You are going out of system on a recon run against God knows what," Halley says. "Don't talk to me about hairy. I can handle myself, you know."

"Better than anyone else I know," I concede.

We lie in silence for a few moments. Outside in the hallway of the residential pod, an announcement interrupts the quiet hum of the environmental system, inconsequential administrative crap.

"Isn't it fucked up?" Halley chuckles. "We have a year of married residential bliss, getting laid every other weekend and spending more time together than ever before. And we both can't wait to get back into combat. What the fuck is wrong with us?"

"I'm not looking forward to battle," I say.

"Bullshit."

"No, really. I don't. But Mars is going down soon. All hands on deck. All bets on one hand. And I don't want to just sit and wait for that to happen. I don't want to babysit recruits until we all get orders to file into the drop ships and hope the Orions do the job."

"You want to control your fate," Halley says.

I hold up my hand, the left one that was shot to ribbons last year by a security police officer on Independence station. It's impossible to tell by looking at it where the flesh ends and the prosthetics begin, but I can feel the precise fault line between living matter and cosmetic synthetic material without fail.

"This stopped hurting six months ago," I say. "But I'm still taking the pills."

Halley reaches up with her own hand and runs a finger down the center of my palm.

"Why?"

"Feels good. Helps me sleep. Cuts down on the dreams. I take that stuff, I sleep through maybe half the night instead of waking up every other hour."

"You talk to the Fleet shrink any?"

"Sure." I shrug. "Felt like I was wasting her time. The fuck do I have to complain about, really? Made it through Fomalhaut and Earth last year. Get to live on base with my wife. Low-risk training job. Bunch of new ribbons on the smock. So what if I can't sleep through the night anymore? I didn't suffocate on Mars. Or get blown up on Long Beach last year when we all transitioned into the middle of a Lanky battle group."

"You shouldn't feel guilty for making it," Halley says.

"I don't feel guilty for making it," I reply. "But a lot of people died so I could make it back to Earth. Come back to you. Do something worthwhile. I don't want to feel like I'm not holding up my end of the deal."

Halley doesn't reply. Instead, she keeps caressing the soft tissue of my palm with her fingertip. Then she takes my hand into hers and puts it onto my chest.

"So we go do our jobs again," she says after a while. "Our real ones. And if things go to shit, we'll kick ourselves for not joining the Lazarus Brigade last year."

"If Mars fails, there won't be a safe place left anywhere. Least of all in the PRCs. Might as well do this thing on our terms."

Halley rolls over onto her side and props up her head with her arm. I'm expecting one of her usual wry jokes, but her expression isn't humorous at all.

"Whatever happens, Andrew—know that I'm glad for the time we've had. Every minute of it. I'd teach mind-numbing classes for the next fifty years in exchange if I had to."

"Best years of my life," I say. "Despite it all. Don't ever doubt it."

Halley smiles. Then she leans in and kisses me.

When we separate again, she moves in closer and drapes her leg over my body with a contented sigh.

"Well," she says. "You'll go off into the black again on Monday. I go dirtside on Thursday. But until then, let's make the best of the time we have."

"Affirmative," I say, and pull her against me.

CHAPTER 15

——— TAKING COMMAND ———

"Of all the shit I've had to tolerate, this ranks right up there with the worst, Lieutenant."

Master Sergeant Fallon puts a little bit of acid into the last word as she tugs on the bottom of her fatigue tunic to straighten it out.

"I told you there'll be less friction if you wear Fleet CDUs for this run," I say. "Besides, the Fleet camo isn't so bad."

"I don't have a problem with the camo," she grumbles. "I have a problem with the fact that this thing just came from Supply. It still has starch in it. It's like wearing sheets of cardboard."

We are walking on the main passageway along the central spine of Gateway station. Sergeant Fallon is wearing brand-new Fleet-issue CDU fatigues with the rank insignia of a master sergeant. She looks very out of place in the Fleet's digital black-blue-gray pattern instead of HD's distinctive urban camouflage or even the solid olive green of the Lazarus Brigade uniforms. Her smock is almost sterile—there's only a name tape, the rank sleeves, and her gold combat drop badge, but no unit or specialty patches.

"Well, you can't be running around in your Brigade uniform up here," I tell her. "You'll be fine once it wears in."

"By the time this thing gets soft enough to not creak when I fold it, we'll both be twenty-star generals."

Gateway is busy as always, and the concourse is pretty packed with transitioning personnel, but most junior enlisted and NCOs give us a bit of a berth when they see our rank sleeves or the less-than-happy expression on Master Sergeant Fallon's face. We are both dragging our personal kit boxes, which follow us on wheels like obedient puppies.

"What kind of ship is it?" Sergeant Fallon asks.

"Not a clue. All I have on our orders is the docking collar number. Echo Five."

"Echo Five better have something big and comfy docked on the other side."

"Doubtful," I say. Sergeant Fallon hates the idea of space travel, and the ship large enough to qualify as "big and comfy" in her book would have to have the interior volume of a small planet.

Docking collar E5 is in the section of Gateway reserved for capital ships, ten thousand tons or more, which bodes well for the size of our assigned ride.

E5 is guarded by two SI troopers in light armor. They check our credentials carefully. While they decide whether we have any legitimate business on board, I look at the OLED display above the docking collar that usually shows the name and hull number of the ship that's docked on the far side of the collar. This one only reads "CLASSIFIED."

"Strangest name for a ship I've ever heard of," Sergeant Fallon comments dryly. "Welcome aboard the *Classified*. Lead ship of her class. Sister units are the *None of Your Business* and the *Piss Off*."

We walk down the docking collar and onto the ship. The entrance corridor behind the main hatch is wide and spacious. The ship's seal is painted on the bulkhead, and her name and motto are stenciled underneath: NACS PORTSMOUTH AOE-1: BEANS AND BULLETS.

"*Portsmouth*," I say to Sergeant Fallon. "Remember her?"

"All those Fleet cans look alike to me. But I recall the hull number. Been seeing it often enough on the tactical screen down in the ops center in New Svalbard. She was part of the Midway task group."

"The task group's main supply ship."

"We're riding into battle on a fleet oiler?"

"Hey, you wanted room to stretch out," I say.

The Fleet's fast supply ships aren't defenseless, but they're designed to resupply warships, not take their place in the line of battle. I know that *Portsmouth* has self-defense armament, but I also know that she has next to no armor, and that even an old frigate could soundly beat the shit out of her in a one-on-one engagement. The AOEs are also not terribly stealthy, and nowhere near fast enough to outrun a destroyer or a space-control cruiser. As we walk down the corridor to our assigned report point, I find myself hoping that this unit is just a staging point for now instead of an integral part of the mission.

"Lieutenant Grayson," the Fleet sergeant guarding the main passageway intersection says when he checks my orders. "First platoon. Your guys and girls are in Module One. Down the topside spinal, and it's the first hatch on your right."

———————

"It's got room to stretch out, all right," Sergeant Fallon says when we step through the hatch of Module One. The Portsmouth-class supply ships are completely modular, with space for sixteen mission modules that can be swapped out according to the needs of the task force. I've never set foot into a crew quarters module before, and for sheer space, it beats any crew berthing system I've seen.

We step into an entrance area that's easily ten meters square. Beyond, there's a gangway leading further into the quarters module, and hatches for individual berthing spaces on each side of the gangway. Four of the individual berths are separated from the rest and set on the entrance side of the module. Three SI troopers in fatigues are already here, sitting around a low table in a corner of the entrance area. I recognize all three at once.

"Ten-hut!"

Gunnery Sergeant Philbrick gets up from his chair and snaps to attention, and the two troopers with him follow his lead.

"As you were," I say, after my customary half-second delay in which my brain processes that they're standing at attention for me. The three SI troopers relax their postures.

"Gunny Philbrick," I say. "How are the new digs?"

"Palatial," he says. "The AOE containers are all right."

"Gunny Philbrick, Master Sergeant Fallon," I introduce them. "She's your platoon sergeant for this run."

"Yes, sir." He nods at Sergeant Fallon. "Ma'am."

The two troopers with Gunny Philbrick are Humphrey and Nez. Humphrey was a sergeant last year, and now she wears the rank sleeves of a staff sergeant. Nez, now a sergeant, was a corporal when we served together on *Indy*. I introduce everyone to Sergeant Fallon, who is the only newcomer to the group.

"You'll be leading my First Squad," I tell Philbrick. "Normally I'd slot you into platoon sergeant with your new rank, but I need Master Sergeant Fallon in that spot. We'll just have to be a little rank-heavy in the platoon leadership." *Except for me*, I don't add. "I've never been in one of these. Care to give me the tour?" I ask Philbrick.

"Affirmative, sir."

We follow him back to the passageway on the opposite side of the entrance hatch.

"Squad berths," he says, and points to the individual hatches all along the passageway. "One to a fire team, four troopers per berth. Squad leaders get their own. And no hot-bunking."

"Excellent," I say. Hot-bunking—the sharing of one bunk by more than one trooper and sleeping in shifts— is a necessity on smaller ships, but wildly unpopular among the Fleet for obvious reasons.

"Head and shower are in the back. The open area up front is for assembly and downtime. And your berths are on the other side. Away from the riffraff." He smiles.

The four individual berths in the front of the crew quarters module are already labeled on the hatches—by job title, if not by name. One says PLT MEDIC, the one across the passageway from it PLT GUIDE. The two adjacent ones closest to the entrance hatch are marked PLT SGT and PLT CO.

As far as accommodations go, my new berthing space is downright luxurious compared to what I've had on most other ships in the Fleet. The Platoon CO berth is the biggest of the spaces in the crew quarters module. I have a sleeping nook, a private shower and toilet that are little clamshell capsules in the corners of the berth, and a small office space right in front of the entrance hatch. The crew quarters module seems to be brand new. I can't see any wear or dirt anywhere, and the mattress on the cot still has a protective plastic wrap covering it. I open my personal gear container and sort what little stuff I brought along into the personal locker next to the sleeping nook.

The wired comms handset on the wall of the office space lets out a muted buzz. I walk over to it and pick up the receiver.

"Lieutenant Grayson."

"Welcome aboard *Portsmouth*, Lieutenant," Major Masoud's voice comes over the hard wire. "Stow your kit and report to me in *Portsmouth*'s ops center at 0900. Bring your platoon sergeant, too."

"Affirmative, sir."

I check the chrono on my wrist and synchronize it with the one on the bulkhead above the entry hatch, which shows 0757 hours.

On the other side of the hatch, there's a small commotion as more troops arrive in the quarters module. I can hear Gunny Philbrick's voice greeting them. Whatever the composition of the rest of the platoon will turn out to be, I know that Philbrick will be my de facto third in command as the leader of the platoon's First Squad.

I pick up the comms receiver and punch up Sergeant Fallon on the little screen next to the wall mount.

"Fallon," she answers curtly.

"Grayson," I reply. "Gunny Philbrick is herding the new squaddies right now. Keep an eye on things. Have them assemble and come get me when the platoon is accounted for."

"Affirmative," she says. Then she pauses for a moment. "Weird, isn't it? Me reporting to you all of a sudden."

"It is weird," I say. "I'm still worried you'll jump my ship if I fuck up, like I'm your junior squaddie."

"Oh, have no fear, Lieutenant," she says. "That'll definitely still happen if the situation calls for it."

———————

At 0830, there's a knock on my hatch. I open it to see Sergeant Fallon outside in the passageway.

"Platoon assembled and in formation, sir."

"Thank you, Master Sergeant," I reply. Then I check myself in the stainless steel mirror next to the hatch and step out into the passageway with her. Everything about this seems incorrect—the lieutenant's stars on my rank sleeves, my old squad leader calling me "sir" and deferring to me, the sudden weight I feel resting on my shoulders at the thought of being in charge of forty lives. But reality is what it is, so I nod at my friend and platoon sergeant, and walk out into the common area with her.

The platoon is lined up in three rows, with Gunny Philbrick and the other three squad leaders front and center.

"Atten-hut," Gunny Philbrick rasps when Sergeant Fallon and I step into the room, and thirty-odd troopers snap to attention. Gunny Philbrick comes to attention in front of me and salutes.

"I report the platoon ready and in formation, and all personnel present and accounted for," Gunny Philbrick recites.

"Thank you, Gunnery Sergeant." I return the salute, and Gunny Philbrick joins the formation with the rest of the squad leaders.

I step in front of the assembled platoon, and thirty-eight pairs of eyes rest on me.

"Good morning, platoon," I say.

"Good morning, sir," they not-quite-shout back at me.

I look at the faces in front of me. Other than Philbrick, Nez, and Humphrey, I don't know a single one of them. Most look terribly young, privates and PFCs not too long out of SOI.

"I know what you're thinking," I say, and lift one of the lapels of my camouflage smock. "Wrong camo pattern. Holy shit, a Fleet puke."

Some of the junior enlisted in the back of the ranks laugh.

"I'm Second Lieutenant Grayson. And yes, I am Fleet. I am not, however, a console jockey. I'm a combat controller by trade, and I've done over two hundred combat drops. So if you have doubts about your new Fleet lieutenant, rest assured that he knows what he's talking about when it comes to the stuff we're here to do."

I know I'm probably just imagining the barely concealed relief on the faces of the other squad leaders. The speech I'm giving is a little bit chest-thumping, but it's the sort of thing I'd want to know if it were me standing in formation as a junior NCO. Inexperienced officers can get you killed anywhere, but the infantry platoon is an especially unforgiving learning environment.

"I will share the specifics of our mission with you as soon as I have authorization," I continue. "All I can tell you right now is that we are going out of system, and that this is important, with a capital *I*. Until I get to brief you in detail, square your gear away and take care of any business you may have on the network. It may be a good while before you get to catch up on mail again."

Sergeant Fallon is standing behind and to the right of me. She's at perfect parade rest, like a drill instructor at boot camp.

"I will now turn you over to your new platoon sergeant. You have the luck to serve under Master Sergeant Fallon for this mission. And I mean that without irony. Those of you up on your NAC military history may remember the name, and yes—she is *that* Sergeant Fallon. When she tells you to jump, I highly suggest you are in the air before you even ask for an altitude parameter."

I can tell from the faces of the junior personnel that most of the troopers in the formation aren't up on their NAC military history, but I know that some of them have been in the service long enough to know the names of the small handful of living Medal of Honor recipients. In any case, those who don't know her will without a doubt be thoroughly educated by those who do, and some of the half-whispered anecdotes may even have some basis in reality.

"Too much?" I ask in a very low voice when I turn toward her to give her the floor.

"Too much," she replies in the same low voice. "But good enough."

"Good morning, platoon," she addresses the formation.

"Good morning, Master Sergeant!" they shout back.

"The lieutenant is too kind," she continues. "I'm really rather easy to get along with. You won't find me policing the head for soap scum or your uniforms for loose threads. I have a super-low tolerance for pedantic bullshit."

Some of the troops allow themselves a chuckle at this.

"But there are things I won't let slide even a millimeter. Stuff that matters. You will at all times give everything you have to make the mission succeed. You will not shirk your duty or shift the blame for poor performance to someone else. You will not let others pull your weight. You will not leave a comrade behind on the field in training or in battle, whatever the cost. And you absolutely will not doubt that I will kick you out of the nearest airlock personally if you disobey or disrespect your squad leaders, your senior NCOs, or your platoon leader.

"When we are out there, we are all we have. Backup will be too far away to save us if things go to shit. It's just going to be us and whatever we bring to the party. Let's make it so that things don't go to shit. Use your time wisely. Train with your squad mates, get to know them, and run a few miles together if you have downtime instead of sitting on your cots and griping about Fleet chow or that bitch of a master sergeant. We're just one platoon, part of one short company. We can't have anyone slacking off or screwing up. So don't slack off or screw up. Understood?"

"Yes, Master Sergeant," the reply comes from the platoon.

"Squad leaders, take over your squads. Gear and kit check at 1130." Sergeant Fallon nods at the squad leaders standing in front of their charges and steps back to make space for them in the assembly area. The squad leaders step out and take over their respective squads.

"What do you think?" I ask Sergeant Fallon in a low voice.

"Bunch of kids," she says. "Nobody under the rank of corporal older than twenty, and none of the corporals look like they've been in much more than twelve months. I'd feel better with the old crew from Shughart here, I'll tell you that."

"At least we have seasoned NCOs," I say. "Philbrick's been around the block. And he has two good fire team leaders."

"Yeah, they'll do," Sergeant Fallon says. "They'll be scared out of their wits, but they'll get over it. You did, back in the 365th."

"Just did what I had to," I say. "Didn't want to let the rest of the squad down."

"The universal motivator," she says. "That has always been what makes a squad function under fire. Not honor or medals or promotions. As long as they make us pick up rifles and go to war together, it'll always be about the grunt next to you."

I check my chrono.

"Time to go see the boss," I say.

"Ready when you are."

"Gunnery Sergeant Philbrick," I say in a loud voice, and Gunny Philbrick turns toward me.

"Sir."

"You have the deck," I say.

"Aye, sir. I have the deck." He returns his attention to the squad in front of him.

"Let's go see the man," I say to Sergeant Fallon.

Sergeant Fallon and I walk into *Portsmouth*'s ops center at precisely 0859 hours. The ops center is a large room with an impressively big holotable and situational display in the middle. It's not precisely a CIC, as *Portsmouth* isn't a fighting ship, but even a fleet supply unit needs to have situational awareness. Most of the consoles in the room are unmanned right now. Major Masoud is standing by the holotable and flicking through lists and readouts on the holographic screen in front of him. There's a Fleet officer in camouflage standing next to him, and as we get closer to the holotable, I see that he's wearing the rank sleeves of a captain. The gold insignia above his left breast pocket is an eagle clutching a trident in front of a planetary hemisphere. Major Masoud wears the same thing on his smock—the badge of a qualified

Space-Air-Land special warfare operator, the Fleet's very small and highly selective SEAL community.

I salute the major, and he returns the courtesy briskly.

"Lieutenant Grayson reporting as ordered, sir. This is my platoon sergeant, Master Sergeant Fallon."

"Yes," Major Masoud says. "I know about you, of course."

I am briefly curious how this almost unprecedented situation—two Medal of Honor recipients in the same room and command chain—will play out as far as military courtesies are concerned. Technically, neither needs to salute the other regardless of their rank difference, and yet both are obliged to render a salute to a recipient of the NAC's highest award for valor. Major Masoud chops through this particular Gordian knot by extending a hand to Sergeant Fallon.

"Welcome aboard, Master Sergeant. I'm happy to have someone with your reputation on the team."

Sergeant Fallon shakes the major's hand.

"Thank you, sir. Glad to contribute."

The SEAL captain salutes Sergeant Fallon.

"Captain Hart. Pleasure to meet you, Master Sergeant."

"And you, sir," Sergeant Fallon says as she returns the salute.

With so much military acumen in the room, I feel thoroughly superfluous, like I'm a kid pretending to be a soldier surrounded by real soldiers who are indulging my play.

Behind us, more troopers enter the room. They're all in SI camo, two officers and two senior NCOs. They join our little group clustered around the holotable, and the brief but time-consuming ritual of formal greetings and reciting of courtesy formulas begins anew.

We exchange courtesies and size each other up as we do. Every one of the officers and senior NCOs in the company is an experienced and drop-qualified combat soldier. I may be the most junior officer in rank seniority, having worn stars for just a little over a week, but the second lieutenant in charge of Second Platoon looks like I have a few years on him chronologically.

"Now that we're all here, let's get to it," Major Masoud says. "We are on the clock, and time's running short. We clear moorings at 1400 and proceed to the assembly point, where we will meet up with our escort and wait for some assets that are still in transit right now. Then we will proceed to the transition point at maximum burn and make our way to the target system. You won't have much time to get to know each other, I'm afraid."

"Sir—we are going to battle in a supply ship?" I ask.

"That's affirmative," Major Masoud says. "I couldn't get much hardware out of Command for this one, but they did give us *Portsmouth*. We'll also bring along a combat escort."

"If this ends up being a fight, this ship won't last long. Not against what they can put on the board."

Major Masoud smiles at me, and it's the same humorless smile I've seen on his face a few times before.

"She's not a heavy cruiser, but she has a few tricks up her sleeve, Lieutenant Grayson. And where we are going, we'll be happy for all the extra supplies an AOE can haul along."

"And where is that, sir?" Lieutenant Wolfe, Second Platoon's commanding officer, asks.

"Later," Major Masoud answers. "Operational briefing will commence once we are on our way to the transition point. Report readiness to the ops center by 1300 and tell your platoons to take care of any comms business while we're still docked. Once that collar comes loose and we're underway, we are off the network and running under blackout protocol. Any questions?"

"Who's going to ride shotgun?" I ask.

"Operational briefing," Major Masoud says.

"Yes, sir."

"Anything else?" he asks, in a tone that leaves no doubt that he's not terribly interested in answering anything else in detail. When none of us speak up, he nods.

"Readiness report by 1300," he repeats. "Until then, prepare for departure and see to your platoons. Dismissed."

"Major Khaled Masoud," Sergeant Fallon says when we walk back along the topside spinal passageway toward the modular cargo section of the ship.

"You know the man?" I ask.

"Not personally. Not until today, anyway. But I've heard stories."

"He has probably heard stories about you as well."

"Not those kinds of stories." She looks around to check this section of the passageway, which is empty except for us right now.

"How much do you trust your platoon, Andrew?"

"I trust you," I reply. "I don't know the other squad leaders yet, but I know I can count on Philbrick and his two. Why?"

"If shit goes down, keep them close at hand," Sergeant Fallon says. "Because I trust Major Masoud about as far as I can throw a drop ship."

"Why? You don't know the guy. You've been TA and HD all your life. Don't tell me you served with him before."

"No, I haven't," she acknowledges. "But I've heard things."

"You've heard things," I repeat.

"Read up on his Medal of Honor citation if you haven't already. You know those mission reports where things go to shit, and there's only a handful of survivors making it back to the drop ship?"

"Yeah."

"Well," she says. "He seems to be a magnet for those kinds of drops. He gets off on doing suicide runs, I think."

She sighs and scratches the back of her head.

"Well, however this mission goes down, I feel pretty safe predicting that boredom isn't going to be one of our problems," she says. "Shoulda stayed in my safe and cozy welfare city."

CHAPTER 16

—— SPECIAL ASSETS ——

A few hours later, we meet up with our combat escort.

"Now hear this: replenishment personnel, stand by for transfer operations. NACS *Berlin* is now coming alongside to port. I repeat, stand by for transfer operations on port stations."

As platoon leader, I have limited access to the tactical feed from the ops center. When I hear the announcement from the 1MC back in my office, I switch on the display of my terminal and check the situational plot. The center of the display shows a representation of *Portsmouth*. Nearby, in close formation, two ships are taking up position alongside *Portsmouth*: NACS *Berlin* and NACS *Burlington*. I consult the database on *Burlington* and see that she's an older Fleet supply ship. I tap into the audio feed from the ops channel and listen to the strangely soothing comms traffic between *Portsmouth* and *Berlin* as the frigate is taking up position alongside the much larger supply ship.

"*Berlin*, decrease bow angle by one-half degree. Reduce speed by three meters per second."

"*Portsmouth*, copy. Negative one-half on bow thrusters. Reducing speed to fifty meters per. Separation rate negative three meters per."

"Burn lateral for positive three on my mark."

"Burning lateral for positive three, copy."

"Three, two, one, mark."

I watch the slow ballet unfolding, a five-thousand-ton frigate maneuvering itself into parallel formation next to a fifty-thousand-ton supply ship in zero gravity with no external reference points, using only short bursts from the propulsion system's thrusters to get into position. It amazes me every time I get to witness such a feat of engineering and training. We are so incredibly skilled at adapting to even the most hostile of environments, and so often we use those skills to be more efficient at killing each other.

There's a knock on the hatch of my quarters, and I get up and walk over to unlatch it. Outside, Sergeant Fallon is leaning against the frame of the hatch.

"Sent the squaddies off to chow," she says. "I'm going to take the NCOs over to the noncom mess and make sure we're all on the same frequency."

"I'll be right along," I say.

"Uh-uh." She shakes her head with a little smile. "You, sir, are an officer. You get to dine in the officers' mess with the other platoon leaders. Lieutenants have no business in the NCO mess. You know the rules."

I want to protest, but then I close my mouth again. She's right, of course—it's a breach of unwritten protocol and courtesy for an officer to intrude into NCO space like that—but I can't help feeling a little wounded. I've eaten in the NCO mess or at the noncom club for years now because that was my crowd. And now the stars on my rank sleeves lock me out of my usual places of refuge and socialization while on duty.

"You're the boss now," Sergeant Fallon says. "You have to keep your distance. Not just to the privates. To the NCOs as well."

"Is that your advice as my platoon sergeant?"

"As your platoon sergeant and as your friend," she says. "You don't want the junior ranks to get too friendly with you. It'll make your job much harder when you have to send them into harm's way later."

What she says makes perfect sense, but I still feel like I've just been locked out of my old clubhouse. I sigh and nod toward the module's exit hatch.

"Go calibrate the squad leaders, Master Sergeant," I say. "I'll go check out the luxuries in the officers' mess."

The officers' mess is not a bad consolation prize. Because *Portsmouth* is designed to accommodate mission personnel in addition to her regular crew, the mess halls are much bigger than I would have expected even from a ship of her size. And the chow is decent—not the fare we used to eat before everything went to shit last year, but not the almost-welfare food they're doling out in the enlisted mess these days. There's not even a line at the chow counter, so I grab a tray and choose from the small variety available: rice, chicken, and some leafy greens. At least the rank comes with a few perks.

Two of the other platoon leaders from my new company are sitting at a table in a corner of the room. I take my tray and walk over to them.

"Mind if I join you?" I ask.

"Not at all," Lieutenant Wolfe says. "Plenty of space."

"Yeah, this chow hall is something else."

"Where's the other Fleet guy?" Lieutenant Hanscom asks. "He too good to eat with us or something?"

"I have no idea," I reply. "Haven't swapped ten words with him since we came aboard."

"Same here. If he's out of SEAL country, he's trailing the major."

"I wouldn't take it personally. SOCOM folks are a little weird. You think the branches are tribal, you don't know how insular the podheads are."

"You're a podhead," Lieutenant Wolfe points out. She nods at the beret tucked under the rank sleeve on my left shoulder. "And you're slumming here with us."

"Yeah, but I'm a combat controller. Most of my job is running around dirtside with SI teams. Slumming," I add, and she grins.

"Spaceborne Infantry. Fleet SEALs. Combat controllers. And a mixed command crew. This is one strange company they've cobbled together," Lieutenant Hanscom says.

"Here come some more of your Fleet guys," Lieutenant Wolfe says and points over to the entrance hatch. I have my back turned to the hatch, so I have to turn around in my chair to see what she's pointing at. A group of Fleet officers in flight suits are entering the officers' mess. One of them is a woman with short, dark hair and captain's insignia on her rank sleeves. I drop my fork as if someone suddenly electrified it.

"Son of a bitch," I exclaim.

"What is it, Grayson?"

"That's my wife," I say and get out of my chair. Halley looks around the mess hall to get her bearings, and her eyes widen ever so slightly when she spots me. By the time she does, I've already covered most of the distance between us.

"Huh," she says and grins at me.

For a brief moment, three conflicting emotions struggle for dominance in my head: joy at seeing my wife unexpectedly, anxiety at the thought of both of us being on the same dangerous mission, and anger at the fact that she didn't tell me the exact nature of her assignment. Then the joy wins out. But kissing a fellow officer in the middle of the mess wouldn't be appropriate or professional, so I just return her grin and shake my head at her.

"What the fuck," I say. "What are you doing on this ship?"

The pilots who came in with Halley just sort of stream around us like the tide around a rock in the surf, but not without some of them shooting us curious looks.

"Flying a drop ship, silly," she says. "It's what I do, remember?"

"Why didn't you tell me you were assigned to the recon mission?"

"I swear I didn't know, Andrew. I went down to Fort Campbell this morning, and they briefed us and gave us new ships to take into orbit not two hours later."

"Tell me you're just ferrying."

She gives me an incredulous look.

"They don't use experienced senior flight instructors for ferry flights. Any flight cadet with brand-new wings can do that." She smiles. "I'm along for the ride."

"So what did you bring?" I ask. "Wasp-A out of mothballs?"

Her smile morphs into a wicked little lopsided grin.

"Oh, no," she says. "Something with a little more punch than that." She looks over to the rest of her pilot group, now standing in line at the chow counter.

"Want to come and take a look?"

"I'd love to," I say.

———

I get a powerful sense of déjà vu as I walk down the main spinal passageway with Halley. In all our years in the Fleet, we have never actually served on a ship together officially since *Versailles*, seven years and several lifetimes ago.

"Whoever's in charge of this run must have a lot of pull," Halley says to me.

"Major Masoud is in charge of the ground component," I say. "*Berlin* is coming along as our bodyguard. Lieutenant Colonel Renner."

"It's like reunion week," Halley says.

"Oh, you don't know the half of it. Why do you think the major has pull?"

"Because you kids are getting the very best battle taxi in the Fleet. In any fleet."

"Dragonflies?"

"No," she says. "Not Dragonflies."

We walk back into the mission module space of *Portsmouth*. Halley leads me down to the ventral passageway, where I know the SEAL platoon is quartered in a crew module just like the one my own platoon occupies. She checks the status display next to one of the access hatches to verify that the module is pressurized and unlocked. Then she opens the hatch and gestures for me to follow her through.

"Whoa," I say when I step into the module.

The module is mostly open space, a miniature hangar with an automated refueling station and service carts lining the bulkhead. There's a docking clamp mechanism on the ceiling, a smaller version of the ones I've seen in flight decks all over the fleet. Sitting on the deck in the middle of the hangar module, and taking up most of it with its considerable size, is a very large and unfamiliar drop ship. It has some resemblance to a Dragonfly, but it's quite a bit bigger, and it looks about five times as mean, which is no mean feat considering the aggressive looks of the Dragonfly class.

"What in the hell is that?" I say. "I've never seen one of these in seven years in the Fleet."

"That is a Blackfly," Halley says. "Don't bother looking it up on your PDP. They don't exist."

"SOCOM project," I say, and she nods.

"We brought four. That's half the existing inventory. They belong to the Special Operations Aviation Regiment."

There are maintenance personnel working on the bird in front of us. The refueling probe is latched on to the fuel port in the wing root, and I can see the thick umbilical of a service line snaking underneath the ship and terminating in a port hatch on the underbelly. The ship is all black, but it isn't the rough, nonreflective paint they slapped onto *Portsmouth* to make her low-observable. This hull is almost mirror-smooth, and something about the way it reflects the light from the overhead fixtures looks familiar.

"Polychromatic armor plating?" I hazard a guess, and Halley nods.

"Same stuff they use for the HEBA suits. It's made for long-range special operations insertions. Fast, agile, and freaking invisible."

"How long have those things been in the Fleet? I've never even heard rumors about them, and I've done a shitload of drops with SOCOM."

"The 160th used modified Dragonfly birds for their drops until this year. These just came off the assembly line maybe six months ago."

"So they're not battle tested," I say.

"The prototypes have a few combat drops," she replies. "Trust me, they do what they were built to do."

"And how is it that you know about these and I don't?"

"Because I'm one of the pilots who's checked out on that type," she says. "Most of the rest are eating lunch over in the officers' mess right now. We have more of these birds than we have pilots who are cleared to fly them."

The Dragonfly drop ships are aggressively angular and look like they're spoiling for a battle. This Blackfly has a much more streamlined hull, all curves and very few angles, but somehow it looks meaner still. The windows of the cockpit are smaller than on the Dragonfly, their edges are rounded, and the polyplast—if that's what it is—has been coated with an opaque layer that makes it impossible to see into the cockpit itself. On the Blackfly's underside, I see the telltale seams of ordnance bay doors, all faired into the body and fit so tightly that I have to look very carefully to see the general shape of the doors, stretched octagons with rounded corners.

"That's going to make a really small radar target," I say.

"You have no idea," Halley says. "It has the radar cross section of a fucking wedding ring."

"Can't shoot what you can't see."

"Precisely. I'll take a stealth profile over bigger guns any day of the week. Of course, she does have some big guns, too. Retractable chin turret, triple chamber autocannon mounts on each side of the centerline, and internal bays for fireworks."

"And we have only eight of these," I say.

"They each cost about as much as four Dragonflies," Halley says. "And they're so classified, I'll have to kill every surviving member of the platoon once the mission's done."

"Any idea which platoon you're ferrying?"

Halley shakes her head. "We just got here. Got orders to grab chow and stand by, and that's it."

"Well," I say, and look at the lethal lines of the hulking drop ship that takes up most of the aviation module we're standing in. "If this mission fails, it's not going to be for a lack of kick-ass gear."

"Now hear this," the 1MC blares overhead. "Platoon leaders, pilots, and senior NCOs, report to briefing room Delta at 1100 Zulu. I repeat, all platoon leaders, pilots, and senior NCOs, report to briefing room Delta at 1100 Zulu."

I check my chrono, which shows 1014 Zulu.

"Let's get back to the chow hall and grab breakfast," I suggest. "And then we can go and find out where and when we're going to die this time."

———

"Good morning, ladies and gentlemen. Welcome to Operation Paradise Lost."

Major Masoud is standing at the lectern in front of the briefing room, elevated on a little dais. The briefing room is one of the nicer ones I've seen in the Fleet, comfortable reclining chairs set up in a stadium fashion, each row a little higher than the one before it. A huge holoscreen takes up most of the wall behind the major, and he touches a control on his lectern to bring the display to life. It shows the seal of the ship for a few moments until it changes to the SOCOM logo.

"We are a day out of Gateway, and our remaining assets have arrived at the assembly point and are being squared away at present. We had to get out of observation range and to a SOCOM assembly point because the neighborhood doesn't need to know what kind of toys we're putting onto *Portsmouth*."

Sergeant Fallon and I are sitting in a row with the leader of Second Platoon, Lieutenant Wolfe. We've barely had time to get to know each other in the day since we cleared moorings at Gateway, but Lieutenant Wolfe seems all right. The two SI lieutenants commanding Second and Third Platoons have stopped by more than once for a chat or to get advice, and I suspect it's because they're at least somewhat starstruck by Sergeant Fallon, whose Medal of Honor makes her a member of the military's most exclusive and prestigious club. Only Captain Hart, the leader of the SEAL platoon, hasn't been around much since we met in *Portsmouth*'s ops center yesterday. He disappeared to wherever they berthed his SEAL platoon, and I haven't even seen him in the mess at chow time yet.

"Situation. We are about to enter the target system, where a renegade faction of the former NAC government has fled with a substantial percentage of the remaining NAC fleet. We don't know what awaits us on the other side of the transition, but we do know which units are involved in the treason."

He brings up a list of ships on the screen behind him, along with hull numbers and small 3-D models that slowly spin in place.

"They are the destroyer *Michael P. Murphy*, the cruiser *Phalanx*, the frigates *Acheron*, *Lethe*, and *Styx*, and the carrier *Pollux*. They also took along twelve freighters from the auxiliary fleet, transporting unknown cargo—most likely passengers for resettlement. In addition, they have two fast Fleet supply ships, the *Hampton Beach* and the *Manchester*."

One of the officers lets out a low whistle.

"That's an awful lot of tonnage to go up against," I tell Sergeant Fallon in a low voice. With the Corps scraping the bottom of the barrel for ships, we'd be very hard-pressed to match that renegade force in combat power in a head-to-head engagement. We have more ships now, but they're mostly fifty-plus-year-old frigates and cruisers, and a few ancient carriers from the mothball fleet.

"Needless to point out," Major Masoud continues, "we cannot hope to force them into a stand-up fight and represent enough of a threat to make them surrender."

Most of us laugh at this, and Major Masoud smiles. Every time he does, it looks like the gesture is causing him physical discomfort.

"So we are going to do what SOCOM does best. We'll fight dirty. We'll sucker punch and keep hitting below the belt.

"Mission. We will transition to the target system. We will gather intelligence for a future assault by the rest of the Corps, and conduct pre-strike preparations to facilitate future action. And if the situation turns out favorable, we will plan and execute hit-and-run raids on essential military infrastructure."

There are some murmurs of approval in the room. Major Masoud changes the holoscreen over to a much shorter list of ships.

"Assets. The flagship for this mission is NACS *Portsmouth*, an AOE-class fast Fleet supply ship. Our combat escort, NACS *Berlin*, is on the way and will rendezvous with us in three hours."

That's it? I want to voice out loud, but I manage to keep it in my head instead. One of the other officers in the room has no such inhibitions.

"We're taking a forty-year-old frigate as our combat power against a reinforced modern carrier task force, sir?"

"We are," Major Masoud says.

The new round of murmurs in the room sounds considerably less approving than the one before.

"We can't match them for hulls or gun barrels," Major Masoud says. "And even if we could, it would mean a bloody fight and a lot of destroyed ships. So we go in light. The smaller the force, the harder it is to spot. *Berlin* has more than enough firepower to deal with any minefields or picket ships we may stumble across. Any more ships would be a liability, not an asset. Keep that in mind: we are not going up against a modern carrier task force. We're going up against all the stuff they're trying to guard."

He changes the screen again, this time to a schematic of *Portsmouth*.

"And I believe I told Lieutenant Grayson yesterday that this ship has a few tricks up her sleeve. *Portsmouth* spent almost a month in our SOCOM fleet yard before she docked at Gateway. Allow me to point out a few enhancements."

The schematic of *Portsmouth* changes to an outside view of the ship. The hull looks very different from the standard Fleet gray paint scheme. It's a rough, pebbled black that looks like the *Portsmouth* took a dip in a mud puddle before drip-drying.

"Ideally, she would be wearing polychromatic hull plating right now, like the new Orbital Combat Ships," Major Masoud says. I feel a twitch of sorrow at the thought of *Indianapolis* and her skipper.

"But we didn't have the time or resources for that kind of refit. So we did the next best thing. *Portsmouth* is wearing a coat of nonreflective, radar-absorbent paint. You can't hide a ship this size as well as a tiny little OCS or corvette, but you can make her a lot harder to spot."

The image on the screen changes back to a schematic. *Portsmouth* has the same general flattened cigar shape of most other Fleet ships, but three-quarters of her length are dedicated to cargo and supplies.

"As some of you will know, the new AOEs are fully modular. *Portsmouth* has sixteen mission pods." He points them out on the screen.

"Eight each on starboard and portside, four pods in each quadrant of the hull."

The pods on the schematic detach from the rest of the ship and fly outward. Without the pods in their recesses on the hull, *Portsmouth* looks a lot like the skeleton of a fish—big head, but nothing but bones and ribs beyond that until you get to the tail end. Where a fish would have a rear fluke, *Portsmouth* has its engineering module with the fusion rocket propulsion system.

"These modules can be swapped out and configured any way the mission requires. We have about half of them full of supplies—food, water tanks, fuel, and ammunition. Four are configured as crew quarters for your platoons. Four are for our aviation assets. And two are holding special surprises courtesy of SOCOM research."

"What kind of aviation assets, sir?" Lieutenant Wolfe asks.

"One drop ship per platoon," Major Masoud says. "We are bringing along four brand-new Blackfly covert-ops drop ships. You are most likely not familiar with them, but I guarantee you that you will come to love them intensely."

"How are we going to launch four drop ships off an AOE? The hangar deck on this thing is tiny."

"That is correct," Major Masoud says. "*Portsmouth*'s hangar deck doesn't have the space for the drop ships we are taking along."

"So how are we taking them along? Are we strapping them to the hull?"

There's some muted laughter in the room, but Major Masoud doesn't join in.

"We are taking them along in cargo modules," he says. "And when it's time, we can launch all four of them at the same time without the help of *Portsmouth*'s hangar. We are launching them directly out of their modules."

He zooms the display in on one of the cargo modules on the screen and taps a sequence onto the control pad in his hand. The cargo module turns to reveal a sliding hatch in its side. As we watch, the doors retract, and a boom with a drop ship hanging off it extends through the opening in the module. Then the doors close behind the extended boom, and the drop ship detaches and flies away.

"We developed these for special operations," Major Masoud says. "They're standard cargo modules adapted for autonomous flight ops, to give force-projection capabilities to ships that usually don't have any. We can launch drop ships out of these modules, and we can retrieve them. It's nowhere near as fast as launching from a proper flight deck, but it beats the hell out of strapping them to the hull. And we can launch all four ships at once without having to waste time waiting for one hangar clamp to cycle through the launch procedure four times."

"Sneaky," I murmur to Sergeant Fallon. "Son of a bitch turned a fleet oiler into a tiny assault carrier."

There are general sounds of approval coming from the room. I look over at the SEAL captain, who's sitting all the way on the right side of the room, leaning against the wall next to him with arms folded in front of his chest. He doesn't look the least bit excited or surprised. I conclude that none of this is news to him.

"Execution," Major Masoud continues. "As soon as we rendezvous with *Berlin* and the aviation assets are in the barn, we are making best speed to the transition point. We will refuel and make a combat transition under maximal EMCON. Once on the other side, we will assess the tactical situation and begin our scouting run."

"Where exactly is 'the other side,' Major?" I ask. "Or is that classified until after the transition?"

"I was waiting for someone to ask." The major allows himself a thin-lipped smile. "The big secret. The one that took us a year to figure out. Where they went."

He clears the schematics from the display behind him and brings up a new screen, this one a chart of a star system. I've been all over the colony systems for half a decade, but I've never seen this particular system map.

"They went to the Leonidas system."

The room erupts in conversation that's definitely above the common courtesy level for briefings, but Major Masoud just watches the small crowd assembled in the briefing room without comment.

"Sir, Leonidas is an unsettled system," Halley says. "That's a hundred and fifty light-years away. It hasn't even been remote-surveyed yet."

"Correct on one count, Captain," he replies. "It's a little over a hundred and fifty light-years away, yes. But it's not unsettled, and hasn't been for a while now."

As far as I know—as far as everyone knows—the furthest expansion of human colonization before the Lanky invasion was at Tau Cygni B, not quite seventy light-years from Earth. We've never made it any further into space, and that colony fell to the Lankies three years ago, with the loss of three hundred thousand colonists and a reinforced battalion of Spaceborne Infantry. I've never even heard rumors of a colony so far out past the Thirty, more than twice as far as what we've been told was our outer limit.

"That is where they went, without a doubt," Major Masoud continues. "And that is where we will go in eighteen hours if *Berlin* and the second supply ship are on time."

One hundred fifty light-years, I think. In the cosmic scale of things, it doesn't really matter whether we're ten or a hundred light-years from Earth—both are right around the corner and an eternity away, depending on your perspective. But something about that number seems unsettling. When I was in combat controller training, we had to do survival exercises in a deep indoor pool designed for dive training. I've been in pools hundreds of times in my life, but standing on that tower and looking at the water below knowing that the bottom of it was over a hundred meters deep instead of just five or ten made a difference to my primate brain. If our Alcubierre drive fails while we're in system, we'll never make it back home alive, not even going at fractional c while in cryosleep.

"Questions," Major Masoud says.

"Sir," Halley says. "What if we reach the Leonidas system and find it crawling with Lankies?"

"Then we will consider the problem solved and transition out again as fast as we can spool up the Alcubierre drives," Major Masoud replies. "Our job is not to engage Lankies. Our job is to scout and lay the groundwork for reclaiming NAC assets for the Mars offensive. If we show up and the Lankies own the place, we can safely assume there aren't any NAC assets left in that system to reclaim."

"That would utterly break my heart," Sergeant Fallon says in a low voice, and I nod solemnly.

"Can we expect backup if things go to shit, sir?" Lieutenant Wolfe asks.

Major Masoud shakes his head.

"We'll be a long way from anyone else. The transition alone takes over twenty-four hours. I can't imagine a tactical situation where we'd have time to send for help and wait for a task force to make it through. We will be on our own, and we'll only have what we bring along."

"Another day at the office for SOCOM," Captain Hart says. He looks like the briefing details are boring him a little. I'm sure that's an impression he wants to cultivate among us junior ranks from lesser branches.

"Any more questions?" Major Masoud asks.

Some of the other people in the room have a few. I listen and make mental notes as Major Masoud answers inquiries about logistics and rules of engagement. Sergeant Fallon watches me as I make notes on the scuffed screen of my battered little PDP.

"What are your thoughts?" I ask her.

"My thoughts," she repeats and scratches the back of her head. "My thoughts are that I am way out of my element any which way I turn out here. But I will tell you this. I know staff officers, and I know bullshit when it comes out of their mouths."

I look up and make sure Major Masoud didn't overhear this statement, but he's in the middle of answering a question, and the people in the chairs in front of us are having their own low-volume conversation.

"Which part was bullshit?" I ask.

"Can't quite put my finger on it," she says. "But if he has told us half of what's in those holds and what he plans to do with it, I'll eat a drop ship with a big side of noodles."

When the questions from the group cease, Major Masoud wipes the information on the screen behind him and resets the display to the holographic image of the ship's logo.

"This concludes the initial mission briefing. We will have a post-transition briefing once we have assessed the situation in the target system. In the meantime, prepare for combat transition. All personnel will be in battle armor prior to Alcubierre. All unit heads, report readiness to me by 1400. Dismissed."

We get out of our chairs and file out of the briefing room. On the way out, I rejoin Halley, who is at the tail end of her group of drop ship pilots.

"What do you think?" I ask her.

"Deep-space recon with experimental hardware," she says. "Going into a system that's further away from Earth than anywhere we've ever been. No backup, and a ship full of SOCOM toys and SOCOM troops." She drops her voice a little. "Right now I can't decide whether to be scared out of my mind or piss myself with excitement. Probably a little of both."

Behind us, Sergeant Fallon rasps out an amused little cough.

CHAPTER 17
LEONIDAS

"All hands, combat stations. I repeat: all hands, combat stations. Alcubierre transition in t-minus thirty."

After the most tedious Alcubierre trip I've ever had to suffer through, Task Force Rogue transitions into the Leonidas system like a pair of thieves slipping into a dark alleyway. We pop back into normal space at slow speed and under full EMCON. I'm in *Portsmouth*'s ops center, along with Dmitry and most of the other officers except for the pilots, who are strapped into the seats of their respective drop ships and attack boats in the hangar modules.

"Transition complete. Give me a passive sensor sweep," *Portsmouth*'s skipper orders. He's a lieutenant colonel named Boateng, a tall black man with a graying regulation haircut and a close-cropped beard. The holographic display in the middle of the room pops into life silently. The blue lozenge-shaped icon in the dead center is labeled AOE-1 PORTSMOUTH. Right next to it, so close at the current magnification scale that the icons almost seem to be touching, is the blue lozenge representing FFG-480 BERLIN, where Lieutenant Colonel Renner is undoubtedly running her own sensor sweep of the neighborhood.

We wait as the sensor arrays on *Portsmouth* search the area for traces of activity—optical, infrared, gamma radiation, radio waves. With every sensor sweep, I expect a cluster of nearby threats to pop up on the holotable any second—a welcoming committee of advanced frigates, or a space control cruiser, or a nuclear minefield surrounding the Alcubierre transition point. A few minutes later, however, the plot is still blank except for *Portsmouth* and *Berlin*.

"Neighborhood is clear, sir," the tactical officer says. "No activity out to at least ten thousand klicks."

"Keep scanning," Lieutenant Colonel Boateng orders. "Contact *Berlin* on low-power near-field comms and request data link."

"Aye, sir."

A few moments later, the holotable updates and the scan range increases as the data link goes active and *Berlin* adds the feed from her superior sensor suite to the tactical situation display.

"Astrogation, let's have a fix, please."

Five minutes pass, then ten, without anyone springing a trap on us. The holographic orb of the tactical display remains blank except for our own two ships. Finally, *Portsmouth*'s skipper is satisfied that the transition point is safe for now.

"*Berlin* reports fuel reserves at eleven percent, sir. That's with the emergency fuel."

"Let's clear the neighborhood and find a good spot to commence refueling ops," Lieutenant Colonel Boateng says. "Another two hours in Alcubierre, and they would have run dry. I guess we found out how far a frigate can go on full deuterium stores."

"Astrogation fix is in," the astrogation officer says. "We are in the Leonidas system, two hundred million klicks from the parent star and just outside the debris disk."

"1MC line," the skipper orders, and picks up the handset.

"1MC open, sir."

"Attention, all hands," Lieutenant Colonel Boateng announces. "Welcome to the Leonidas system. We are still alive, and will remain so for the immediate future. Helmets off, but keep 'em close. Replenishment personnel, stand by for transfer operations."

Next to the skipper, Major Masoud releases the seals for his own helmet and pulls it off his head, and I do likewise.

"*Berlin* Actual on near-field, sir," the comms officer announces.

"On speaker," the skipper orders.

"Aye, sir. Go ahead."

"Looks like they didn't set a tripwire," Lieutenant Colonel Boateng says.

"As far as we know," Lieutenant Colonel Renner replies. She sounds a little tired. "Let's hope they're not doing any long-range surveillance of the node. I'd hate to see a task force popping up on Tactical in a few hours."

"Or worse, a flight of standoff nukes," *Portsmouth*'s skipper says.

"My tanks are almost dry. I want to come alongside for a refuel ASAP. If we need to clear the neighborhood at high speed, I want to have full stores."

"Affirmative. I propose we find a cozy nook somewhere on this side of the debris disk and give you a refill," Lieutenant Colonel Boateng says.

"In the meantime, I'm launching the recon drones for a full sector scan," Lieutenant Colonel Renner says. "I want to get a good picture of what's out here before we move around too much and run face-first into a battle group."

"Or a Lanky seed ship," Lieutenant Colonel Boateng says, and my stomach does a little somersault at the thought.

Looking around in *Portsmouth*'s ops center, I am keenly aware that we are in hostile space in a ship that isn't really a warship. *Portsmouth* lacks armor and weapons, except for a CIWS system to intercept incoming missiles. The ops center has no weapons officer station, and there are no SI troops guarding the door. *Berlin* is old and tired, but she's a proper combat unit, and all things considered, I find myself wishing they had berthed my platoon on *Berlin* instead. If missiles and rail gun rounds start flying out here, this ship won't be half as survivable as the frigate that's keeping pace with us on our port side, no matter how many state-of-the-art drop ships *Portsmouth* has tucked away in her mission pods.

Three uncomfortable hours later, we are slowly and silently coasting further into the Leonidas system, and *Berlin* is once again docked alongside *Portsmouth* for replenishment. The supply ship *Burlington* topped off the tanks on both *Portsmouth* and *Berlin* right before our transition, to make sure we got into the system with the maximum amount of reactor juice on board, but the twenty-four-hour Alcubierre run has taken its toll on *Berlin*'s fuel reserves. The tactical sphere above the holotable in *Berlin*'s ops center is expanding gradually as the recon drones from *Berlin* move away from our little task group, but so far, all they survey is empty space.

"Stand down from combat stations," Lieutenant Colonel Boateng finally orders. The XO picks up the 1MC handset and makes the general announcement, and I can practically hear the chorus of relieved sighs all over the ship.

"Have your troops get out of armor for now and grab some showers and chow," Major Masoud tells us. "But expect trouble to show up on short notice. This system shouldn't be this quiet."

"What's the word from upstairs?" Sergeant Fallon asks when I walk back into the platoon pod.

"Dressed up for nothing, luckily," I reply. "Everyone in their squad berths?"

"Armored and ready for go-time."

"Let them ditch the hardshell and assemble on the quarterdeck, please."

"Copy that." Sergeant Fallon pops the release latches on her own armor on the way to the back of the pod.

Three minutes later, thirty-nine troopers are lined up in front of me on the quarterdeck and looking at me expectantly. I find that I'm still not used to this kind of attention, but the three tours I spent as a drill instructor supervisor at least gave me a lot of practice in addressing full platoons.

"As you've heard, we're in the Leonidas system," I say. "You are now officially the furthest-deployed Spaceborne Infantry troops in NAC history. Nobody's ever been out this far except for the people we're trying to track down."

There's some muted cheering, but most of the troops look apprehensive instead of excited, which is exactly how I would feel in their spot.

"We are in clear space for now, but that can change in a hurry. The recon drones are probing ahead, and we may have to jump back to alert status in very short order. We'll step down just a little for now. Chow break, one squad at a time. Keep your armor close."

Sergeant Fallon takes over to sort out the chow schedule, and I walk back to my own quarters to get rid of my armor. The battle armor is climate-controlled, but the environmental controls don't kick in until the suit is fully sealed, and we've been riding out combat stations for the last few hours with our visors raised and the suit envos off, to save battery power for emergency use. The hardshell doesn't breathe, and when I unfasten the armor modules and drop them on the floor in front of my bunk, the ballistic liner underneath is moist with sweat on the inside. When I peel it off, I can feel the warm air release that had been trapped between my body and the liner for hours now.

Having a private shower is an almost unimaginable luxury. I've had my own berths before, but never one that included a wet cell, even if it's just a tiny little clamshell capsule. I clean the accumulated sweat from hours of standing around in armor, and conclude that being an officer does have a few decent perks after all.

Thirty minutes later, we are back in the briefing room on *Portsmouth* for the post-transition briefing. Freshly showered, and without the constant dull ache of the Alcubierre field pulling on my bones, I feel much more comfortable.

"They are here," Major Masoud announces. "Wherever they are hiding, they are keeping very tight EMCON, but we know that they have set up refuge in this system."

He brings up a tactical display on the holoscreen behind him. It's a chart of the system, a distant yellow star and five planets in elliptical orbits around it. We are between the third and fourth star of the system, near the large debris disk that bisects the system on the ecliptic plane.

"As you can see, Leonidas has five planets. Only two of them are suitable for habitation, and three are gas planets. But all of the planets in this system have terraformable moons. Leonidas a has three, Leonidas b has two, and Leonidas c has seven. Leonidas d and e have one moon each. That means we have two planets and fourteen moons to scout for human activity, all without being discovered ourselves."

I look over to Halley, who shakes her head slightly. We all know the logistics involved in scouting that many celestial bodies properly, and if we start flipping over rocks on every moon in this system, we'll be busy for months.

"There's no radio traffic out there, at least nothing loud enough to reach us out here. But our recon drones did sniff out something interesting in our neighborhood. A single source of occasional transmissions, right . . . here."

Major Masoud rotates the map and zooms in to a section of it, not too far from where we transitioned into the system.

"There's an asteroid field right here, half a million klicks off our current trajectory. And something in that field sent out a one-second encrypted burst transmission not too long after we arrived."

He marks the location on the holographic map and zooms the map back out so the icons for *Berlin* and *Portsmouth* are back in the scale.

"We redirected two of the drones to make a closer pass. Visuals indicate it's either a relay station or an observation outpost. They're making directional transmissions every time the asteroid they're on makes a full rotation and the station faces toward the interior of the system. It's a low-power tight beam, really hard to pick up, but one of the drones caught it."

Major Masoud opens another display square on the hologram behind him and flicks a grainy video feed onto it. It's a maximum-magnification shot from a recon drone's camera system—the craggy surface of an asteroid, and a clearly man-made structure protruding from it. It's a low-slung cross-shaped structure, a central pod with four spokes projecting from it that connect to smaller pods on the ends of each spoke.

"That," he says, "is where we'll get the intel we need to save us having to comb through the system moon by moon."

"Sir, they'll see us coming and send for help," Lieutenant Dorian interjects. "With all due respect, should we be advertising our presence in the system this early?"

"They'll see *Berlin* coming," Major Masoud replies. "They'll certainly see *Portsmouth* coming, black paint or not." He smiles sharply and nods at the corner of the briefing room where the drop ship pilots are sitting in a row together.

"But they won't see a single Blackfly coming from the dark side of the asteroid they're on."

A general buzz of excitement goes through the briefing room. I look over to the pilots, and Halley and her fellow drop ship jocks are exchanging glances, undoubtedly already trying to figure out how to beat each other to the pilot seat for that particular run.

"Small installation like that, we can secure it with two SEAL teams, maybe three," Captain Hart says. He sounds confident to the point of slight boredom, and I decide on the spot that I'll probably never get around to liking him. But then Major Masoud shakes his head, and I see with some satisfaction that the captain's little smirk disappears from the corners of his mouth.

"It's an unarmed station. It may even be an automated relay. Either way, it's a tiny outpost, and it doesn't support more than a tech or two, if they have it staffed at all. The SI can take this one."

He looks over to me.

"Lieutenant Grayson, I want you to get two squads from your platoon together and report mission readiness by 1730. One squad on the ground, one in reserve in case things go to shit. No point taking the entire platoon. You won't be able to fit them all into that tiny little station anyway. You'll be taking along one of the Fleet Neural Networks people to get the intel off the station once the place is secured."

"Aye, sir," I say, trying to hide my surprise. I would have bet on Major Masoud picking someone from his pet SEAL platoon for a mission like this. The SI are trained for this sort of assault, of course, but this sort of cloak-and-dagger stuff is right in the center of the SEALs' competencies. But I know better than to answer in any other way than the affirmative.

Major Masoud turns his attention to the pilot section.

"I want First Platoon's drop ship warmed up and ready for skids-up at 1800. We are going to nudge *Portsmouth*'s course to match the asteroid's rotation so you can launch and approach from the station's blind spot. *Berlin* will provide overwatch from a distance. Any questions?"

"I'm not sure I'm comfortable with the amount of premission recon," Halley says from the flight section. "Feels like we are rushing in."

"We have to rush in, Captain," Major Masoud replies. "For all we know, that outpost spotted us when we came out of Alcubierre. We need to assume they already know we are here. We need to grab what we need and go."

"Understood," Halley says, but I know her facial expressions, and I can tell she's still not entirely happy with the situation.

"Let's get to it," Major Masoud says. "I want to be gone from this neighborhood before the big kids show up to give us a bloody nose."

"Squad leaders, to me," I call out when I get back to the platoon pod. My NCOs obey and come across the quarterdeck to where I'm standing.

"Gear up two squads," I say, and look at the candidates: Philbrick, Wilsey, and Welch. I make my decision in a heartbeat.

"Gunny, suit up. You're going in. Sergeant Wilsey, your squad will be backup. The rest can stay out of armor and stand by."

Gunny Philbrick and Sergeant Wilsey both nod and walk back to the squad berths, this time with urgency in their steps.

"Am I coming?" Sergeant Fallon asks.

"I'd just as soon have you here and keep Sergeant Welch and Third Squad occupied. Do a CQB drill on the range. Have them go running on the concourse. Get their blood flowing a little."

"Copy that," she replies. Then she shakes her head and grins. "Still not used to you calling the shots and telling me what to do."

"Tell me about it," I say.

CHAPTER 18

— RAID ON THE RELAY STATION —

It feels good to be gearing up for a concrete mission again after days and days of uncertainty and tension. With my battle armor and my weapon, I have a tiny bit of control over my existence again out here in the black. First and Second Squads are ready and waiting in precise lines on both sides of the passageway outside when I leave the platoon pod. *Portsmouth* has very wide passageways because of the freight and supplies that need to be moved from pod to pod in the ship, and even two full infantry squads in combat gear don't clog it up.

"What in the fuck is that?" one of the troopers says in astonishment when we walk into the aviation pod, where the Blackfly drop ship squats on the deck with her engines silent, warning strobe at the rear of the tail boom painting the inside of the pod with bright orange streaks.

"That's the state of the art in battlefield transportation, Giddings," Philbrick answers. "So secret, it doesn't even exist."

"Sure as shit looks real to me," Corporal Giddings says, his eyes firmly glued to the exotic and unfamiliar shape of the Blackfly.

The tail ramp of the Blackfly is much narrower than the ones on the Dragonflies and Wasps, despite the fact that the ship is quite a bit larger than either. As with the ship, there are no straight lines and right angles on the ramp, either. Its edges have a sort of serrated look to them, facets with round corners, and the ramp is slightly narrower at the bottom than it is at the top. It's coated with some absorbent material that muffles our steps as we trudge up the ramp, which feels all wrong. I like the reassuring clatter of boot soles on steel whenever I board a drop ship with a platoon, and its absence is an unwelcome change in pre-battle ritual.

As big as the Blackfly is on the outside, the hold seems smaller than the one on the Dragonfly. Where the other drop ships have two rows of seats on each side with the troopers facing each other across the hold, this ship also has two rows on the centerline of the ship, seats that are arranged back-to-back so the troopers sitting in them face the outside rows.

"First Squad, center left," the crew chief of the drop ship directs. "Second Squad, center right."

The squads file into the unfamiliar ship as instructed, one squad per row. Platoon leaders usually have a seat up near the front bulkhead, and I look for my assigned spot. The crew chief points me toward it.

"Command console," he says. "Data jack is by your right knee when you sit down."

The command console in the Blackfly makes the ones in the older drop ships look like rows of cans on strings. I have no fewer than four large display panels in front of me, with several smaller ones arranged in a row overhead. I can command the whole platoon with the comms suite in my suit, of course, but it's much easier to keep an eye on the big picture when you have hardwired twenty-inch display flats instead of simulated ones projected into your field of vision by your helmet. I strap myself into the seat in front of the console, connect the data umbilical from the console's jack into the receptacle on my armor, and let my tactical computer connect to the ship's much more powerful neural network. I'm facing the port side of the hull, so the rows of squad jump seats are to my left. Behind me, the crew chief sits down at his own control console on the other side of the drop ship's aisle.

"Ramp up," he announces. The Blackfly's tail ramp creeps upward into the closed position with a soft hydraulic hiss and seals itself into place.

"Passengers aboard, verify hard seal on the cargo hold," the crew chief sends to the flight deck. My heart skips a beat as I anticipate the reply from the flight deck, hoping to hear Halley, but the voice that replies is male and unfamiliar.

"Copy hard seal on cargo hold," the pilot sends back. "Stand by for undocking. Turning one and two."

The ship's engines spring to life with a sort of whooshing roar, which is barely a whisper here in the cargo compartment. I can feel the hull vibrating slightly as both of the drop ship's main propulsion units come online.

"Holy shit, this thing is quiet?" I say to the crew chief, who nods with a grin.

"Quieter at full throttle than a Wasp at idle," he says. "She has noise-absorbing mounts on her noise-absorbing mounts."

I return his grin and turn around to check my network link.

"Rogue Ops, Rogue Actual. Comms and data link check."

"Rogue Actual, Rogue Ops. You are five by five on voice and data."

I toggle into my platoon's network and select the squad leader channels.

"Rogue squads, Rogue Actual. Give me a comms and TacLink check," I say.

"Rogue One Actual, check," Gunnery Sergeant Philbrick sends back his verification.

"Rogue Two Actual, check," Sergeant Wilsey replies.

Twenty-six individual trooper names pop up on my display in two rows of blue lettering, two squads with three fire teams of four troopers each, along with both my squad leaders. We're only going in with one of those squads, but it still seems like overkill to send thirteen fully geared SI troopers in to take over one little relay station. On the other hand, things in this line of business have a habit of going to shit on the ground once the mission starts, and there has never been a platoon leader in battle who thought he had way too many troops on hand to deal with a problem.

"Rogue Ops, Rogue Actual. Comms cross-check complete," I send back to ops. "Ready for showtime."

Outside in the aviation pod, I hear the faint blaring of a warning klaxon.

"All personnel, clear the pod for flight ops," the overhead announcement comes. "Depressurizing pod in t-minus thirty. I repeat, all personnel clear the pod for flight ops. Depressurizing in t-minus twenty-six."

The modular flight pod is a big compromise solution. It doesn't have the standard docking clamp arrangement of a proper flight deck, and there's no double airlock to enable a drop ship to launch out of the bottom hull without depressurizing the hangar. Instead, there's a docking clamp overhead that's attached to a rail mounted to the ceiling of the pod. As we wait for the depressurization to start, the clamp extends from the rail and attaches to the receptacles on the top of the hull. Then the clamp pulls the drop ship off the deck a very short distance.

"Depressurization in ten. Nine. Eight. Seven . . ."

The aviation pod doesn't depressurize gently and slowly like an EVA airlock. Instead, orange warning strobes flash, and then the entire outward section of the pod opens out and into space, the outer hull panels unsealing like a huge clamshell. The drop ship rocks slightly in its clamp as all the air in the pod escapes into space at once. The pod doors swing out of the way, and the boom above the drop ship extends into the space beyond. I watch on the camera feed as the boom folds out to twice its original length and then comes to a stop.

"Launch prep complete," the pilot announces. "*Portsmouth* Ops, Blackfly One requesting permission to launch."

"Blackfly One, *Portsmouth* Ops. You are cleared to launch off Starboard Pod One. Initiate launch sequence and maintain heading of relative nine-zero by zero-zero after launch."

"*Portsmouth* Ops, copy initiate launch and assume relative nine-zero by zero-zero. Initiating launch sequence."

The docking clamp puts itself into motion and moves the Blackfly out of the aviation pod and into the open space beyond the clamshell pod doors. The ship takes up most of the space inside the pod, so our ride on the launch rail doesn't take very long. Then we come to a gentle stop at the end of the rail. I check the camera feed and see the hull of *Portsmouth* disconcertingly close to the end of the Blackfly's tail boom.

"Drop in three, two, one. Drop."

I'm used to drop ships falling away from their launching hosts as the launch airlock is normally still inside the artificial gravity field of the bigger ship, but the Blackfly gently releases from the clamp and slowly floats away from *Portsmouth* as the pilot throttles up the engines very slightly. When we are several dozen meters from the launch boom, he increases thrust, and we accelerate away from *Portsmouth*. The ship is astonishingly quiet, as if someone had wrapped the engines in the world's biggest blanket.

"Launch sequence complete," the pilot sends to *Portsmouth*. "We are go for mission profile burn."

"Blackfly One, resume own navigation and enter mission profile trajectory at your discretion," *Portsmouth* Control sends back. "Good luck, and Godspeed."

I look back toward *Portsmouth* on the camera feed, and I realize with some discomfort that I've never left a host ship via drop ship while my wife was still on board. Every time we were on the same Fleet vessel together and left it on a drop ship, she was in the pilot seat of that ship.

On the other side of *Portsmouth*, *Berlin* is keeping station several kilometers away. The pilot puts the Blackfly into a wide turn to port, and we accelerate ahead of *Portsmouth* and then cross in front of her bow. The rough black paint is working well—with all the position lights and hull illumination turned off, she's pretty hard to spot against the backdrop of deep space with the naked eye even from just a kilometer or two away.

"Burning for intercept trajectory," the pilot announces. Then he throttles up all the way, and the drop ship practically leaps away from our two-ship task force. I take another look back when we are several hundred kilometers downrange, and even the big *Portsmouth* with all her size and amenities looks almost insignificantly tiny in the black void behind us.

———————

The transit to the target asteroid takes four hours, which is a long time when you are wearing battle armor and you're strapped into a spartan jump seat that wasn't built for long-term comfort. The pilot seems to know what he's doing—every time the asteroid is at the point of its rotation where the relay station is on the side away from us, he burns the engines to accelerate us or make trajectory corrections, and whenever the station faces us, we are coasting, like a black hole in space. Seeing a ship in polychromatic camouflage from the vantage point of its hull-mounted lenses is the weirdest visual. I can tell roughly where the outlines of the ship are, but the Blackfly itself is undefined and blurry, as if it's partially translucent. I've seen the effect before on a smaller scale, while wearing my bug suit on Lanky-controlled worlds, but to see it on this scale is both amazing and a little disconcerting.

On our approach, I spend my time collating camera visuals from the relay station. Every time the asteroid turns the station toward us and we cut out the propulsion, we are a little bit closer and the camera images get a little bit sharper. I share the images with my two squad leaders, Gunny Philbrick and Staff Sergeant Wilsey, to come up with a plan of attack on the fly.

"Central section looks maybe twenty-five meters across," Philbrick says. "Ain't much of a habitat. If it's manned, they have a half dozen guys there."

"Civil or military, you think?"

"What would you put there?"

"If it's a listening post, military. If it's a comms relay, civvie techs," I say.

"No need to stash a full squad away on that," Philbrick says. "They're not there to fight, just to rotate watch shifts. Four to six, tops. Infrastructure won't support more."

"Worst-case scenario, we have a reinforced fire team in there. Plus side, they don't know we're coming. We coast up and do a stealthy insert, we catch half of them asleep or on the shitter."

"Even if not, we'll be ready for trouble and they won't be," Philbrick says. "Whatever they're watching for, it ain't gonna be us."

I look over the pictures of the relay station again and mark the visible airlocks for my squad leaders.

"That hatch right there on the main would be ideal," I say. "Gets us in right next to the reactor, and I bet their command consoles are right near there."

"Yeah, but it'd be a bitch to coast this thing in next to the hub," Wilsey says. "There's not a ton of clearance between the spokes right in that spot."

"Then we go in on that end over there," Philbrick suggests, and marks a secondary hatch on one of the outer pods at the end of a station spoke. "Jack the hatch or blow it open. That looks like a fifty-meter dash to the central module once we have the airlock open."

"I wish we could send Second Squad around to pop into the hatch on the other side at the same time, but we only have one bird and one docking collar." I circle the hatch Philbrick suggested. "That'll have to be the one. Get First Squad briefed and ready to be on the bounce."

"Copy that, LT," he replies, and it takes me half a second to process that he means me.

———

The target asteroid is large, maybe a kilometer from one end of its vaguely football-shaped bulk to the other. Our drop ship pilot matches course and rotation with the asteroid as we approach, still on the far side from the relay station, and begins his approach to the target.

"At the apex of the next rotation, we're moving in right above the deck," the pilot says to me over our local tactical channel. "That gives you nineteen minutes before the station rotates back toward the system interior and they start sending again."

"Copy that," I reply before relaying the information to my squad leaders. With the ship under full EMCON, we are on our own right now, and I have to make all the tactical decisions without being able to consult with Major Masoud or anyone else in our task force, which is standing by four hours away.

"Station over the apex in thirty seconds. ETA two minutes."

"First Squad, lock and load," I order. "Form up for entry in the EVA lock."

Gunny Philbrick and his squad unbuckle and get out of their seats to move up past me and into the EVA lock that's between the bulkhead to my right and the cockpit section. Like the Dragonfly class, the Blackfly has a separate airlock system for its two exterior access hatches in the flanks of the ship, to enable personnel launch or retrieval in zero-atmosphere environments without having to open the tail ramp and decompress the entire cargo hold.

I swivel around in my chair and check the squad as they file by. Sergeant Humphrey gives me a jaunty little thumbs-up. Gunny Philbrick brings up the rear, and we exchange nods.

"Careful out there, Gunny," I say as he walks by.

"Always," he replies, and pats the hard plastic of his M-66 carbine.

We approach the station right above the deck, so low that I can make out the texture of the asteroid's surface in sharp detail on the camera feed. The pilot weaves the Blackfly through the little crags and nooks formed by the asteroid's irregular surface, and his deft hand on the stick reminds me of Halley's flying skills.

"Two hundred fifty meters," he sends. "Eighteen minutes until the next rotation apex. Two hundred meters. One hundred fifty meters."

We coast into position next to one of the station's outlying pods. The station itself is a modular construction, pods and access tubes anchored to the asteroid's rock surface with heavy bolts. Our pilot expertly slows down the drop ship and then brings us exactly parallel to the target pod's external airlock hatch. I don't know how fast this asteroid is moving through space or at what rate it is spinning around its own axis, but the pilot of our ship has matched the velocity and rotation rate perfectly with a seventy-ton drop ship on the first try.

"Extending docking collar."

With the drop ship's starboard hatch right next to the airlock of the station, the pilot extends the flexible docking collar from the hull of the Blackfly to the exterior wall of the station pod. There are many ways for SI troopers to enter an enemy space installation, and this one is the fastest and most preferred way—making a hard link between the assault ship and the target to be boarded, and then just cutting open the hatch or hacking it open electronically.

The collar attaches itself to the hull around the airlock soundlessly.

"Collar extended and latched on," the pilot sends. "Stand by for pressurization."

There's now a flexible black umbilical connecting the drop ship's starboard hatch to the airlock of the station pod, just big enough for a squad to rush through in single file. I know that Philbrick and his squad will still have their helmet visors down and their suits' oxygen supply switched on, because any incoming fire or emergency maneuvering will tear the docking collar from the hull or depressurize it.

"Pressurization complete. You are 'go' for main hatch release and EVA."

"Copy clear for hatch release and EVA," Gunny Philbrick replies.

As First Squad gathers behind their leader and prepares to exit the ship and assault the station, I bring up all their visual feeds on my command console, then arrange the feed windows to make a row slightly above my field of vision. With the command feed, I can see what the squad sees and monitor everything from my jump seat without even turning my head, and I can selectively talk to the squad as a whole, the fire team leaders, or each individual trooper. It's a lot like my regular job as a combat controller, only now I'm directing people with rifles rather than air assets or artillery batteries.

"Pressurization confirmed. Opening main hatch." Sergeant Humphrey wrestles the lever for the hatch control downward, and the hatch moves out and away with a soft hiss.

The squad moves out in single file, Sergeant Humphrey in the lead. There's air in the docking collar, but no gravity, so they all use the hand- and footholds set into the side of the collar at regular intervals to move with practiced swiftness through the zero-gravity tunnel formed by the collar. While she's using her left hand to grab the assist loops and pull herself forward, Sergeant Humphrey's right hand holds her fléchette carbine, and the green dot from her targeting laser never wanders off the outer airlock door of the station.

"Hack it," Gunny Philbrick tells her. "Thirty seconds. Then we'll go in the hard way."

"Copy." Sergeant Humphrey pulls herself up to the outer hull of the station and opens the external protective cover of the airlock control panel. Then she gets her PDP out of the pocket on her armor and attaches it to the data jack.

"As soon as that lock cycles, they'll know they have visitors," Gunny Philbrick says to the squad. "Through the outer lock, open the inner lock, and then into the pod by pairs. Humphrey's team, left side. Nez, right side. Giddings, you have the tail end. And if you have to shoot in there, watch your fucking fire. Not a lot of space for stray rounds."

"Head for the main control cluster," I add. "Should be in the central pod. Secure any personnel and make sure nobody flips any switches."

"Copy that," Philbrick replies. "Ten seconds, Humphrey."

"Stand by a sec. And . . . got it."

Humphrey drops her PDP and lets it dangle by its data cord. The outer airlock door moves inward with a resonating thump. Then the door halves slide back into their wall recesses. Inside, the lights of the station's airlock come on with a flicker. At least half a dozen green targeting lasers appear on the inner airlock door as Philbrick's troopers bring their rifles to bear.

"Up and at 'em," Humphrey says. She pushes off the wall, grabs the edge of the airlock hatch opening with one hand, and slingshots herself into the space beyond, aiming her rifle with her free hand. Behind her, the rest of the squad follows.

The feed from the squad's individual helmet cameras turns into a collage of disjointed, rapid movements as the squad fans out into the station pod. The interior of the station is lit by overhead light strips, and the SI troopers have powerful helmet-mounted illuminators that add their lumens to the enclosed space, making shadows dance and washing out one another's camera feeds intermittently.

"Pod is clear. Cover the tube."

I hear the hard breathing from Philbrick's squad as they clear the pod and then advance into the connecting tube that links this pod to the main section of the station. I see equipment racks, control panels, a desk with a coffee mug and a switched-off data pad on it, the trimmings of a boring garrison post on the ass end of nowhere.

I look at Humphrey's feed because she is the trooper in the lead. She moves down the access tube methodically, shining her weapon light into every nook and cranny. Then I see movement in her field of vision—a human silhouette, right at the hatch to the main section of the station.

"NAC Defense Corps," Humphrey shouts. "Freeze and show me your hands!"

She barely finishes the command before I see muzzle flashes at the end of the corridor, and the report from an automatic weapon reaches my ears twice—once from Humphrey's audio feed, and then again muffled a fraction of a second later as the sound travels through the docking collar and the EVA lock of the Blackfly.

Several more rifles cut loose in the narrow passage. Their rapid reports make my audio feed go cataclysmic, and the computer dials down the volume automatically to preserve my hearing.

"Contact front!"

"Motherfucker!"

"Watch your fire, watch your fire!"

"I'm hit," someone else adds to the chatter. I check the voice tag to see that it's Sergeant Nez, in the middle of the group and on the right side of the wall. Two of his squad mates move up and over to him. There are too many troopers in too narrow a space, easy targets for someone at the other end to just hose down with automatic fire, but the SI troopers under my command know ambush drills and give back about five times as much as they're receiving.

"First Squad, advance," I shout into the comms. "Second Squad, cover Sergeant Nez and support."

"On it," Sergeant Humphrey shouts back.

First Squad rushes forward, charging out of the killing zone, text-book response to an ambush. The gunfire ahead of them ceases, and the hatch to the main part of the station closes just as Sergeant Humphrey reaches it and throws her weight against it. The hatch pops open again, but only a few centimeters. I see shadows moving in the space beyond. Someone on the other side curses, and the hatch slams shut again, propelling Sergeant Humphrey back into the connector. She shouts a curse back at the hatch.

"Blow the hatch," Philbrick orders. "Right now."

Two of First Squad's troopers swiftly retrieve plastic explosive charges from their leg pouches and slap them against the hatch hinges. Then they prime them with remote detonators.

"Back," Sergeant Humphrey orders. "Fire in the hole."

The charges explode with a muffled bang and blow the door inward, where it lands on the deck of the main station pod, trailing wisps of smoke. The troopers from First Squad take no chances. As soon as the hatch hits the floor on the other side, Humphrey follows it up with a contact flash-bang grenade. It explodes in the main pod with a crack that's loud enough to make my helmet's built-in audio cut out momentarily. First Squad follows the flash-bang into the room not half a second after it explodes.

"Clear left!"

"Clear right!"

The main section of the station is empty except for scattered equipment and a body near the hatch First Squad just opened violently. It's a male trooper in SI armor, wearing the rank insignia of a corporal. The dead trooper wasn't wearing a helmet when the shooting started, and it looks like several fléchettes from First Squad caught him in the neck and head during the brief but violent firefight. His weapon lies nearby, a standard M-66 carbine just like my own SI troopers are carrying. Sergeant Humphrey picks it up, ejects the magazine block, and works the bolt to clear the firing chamber of the weapon.

"The fuck did they go?"

"Clear every corner of this place," Philbrick orders. "Second Squad, move up. We have one enemy KIA, but there's at least two more of theirs running around in here."

"Three, I think," Humphrey says.

"Suit controls say pressure's dropping," I warn. "You have air escaping somewhere. Someone must have shot through the station hull."

Humphrey and two of her troopers check one of the nearby hatches leading to the next pod's connecting tube. As she puts her hand on the release handle, there's the unmistakable sound of explosive decompression on the other side, and the status light on the hatch panel jumps from green to red.

"Got a lot of air escaping nearby," the drop ship pilot sends. "One of the other satellite pods, on the other end of the station from me."

A new noise fills the station. It's the ascending whine of a dual-mode engine going from cold start to operating pressure. The hull of the station shakes a little as the vibrations from whatever the engine is attached to transmit through the steel and alloy. On a table near Gunny Philbrick, a coffee mug starts dancing near the edge of the desk. It falls and bounces on the rubberized floor plates, splashing coffee against Philbrick's leg armor.

"Blow that hatch open," Philbrick orders.

"We'll decompress the rest of the station," Corporal Giddings says. "Nez has a busted face shield. He can't seal his armor."

"Second Squad, get him back to the ship," I order. "Blackfly One, do you have a visual?"

"Negative. Angle's all wrong. But someone opened a big hatch over there."

"Second Squad, get Nez back to the ship now," I send.

Something akin to an earthquake goes through the framework of the station. The floor shakes so hard that some of the troopers lose their footing and crash against walls or shelves inside the main module. The engines of the drop ship increase their pitch as the pilot tries to keep the Blackfly in formation with the airlock, which makes an unexpected leap sideways and upward with the rest of the station.

"We have a launch," the pilot says matter-of-factly. "A shuttle just launched from the far pod. Small craft, looks like a Fleet mail bird."

"Fuck," I say to myself, loudly.

"He gets past the dark side of this rock, he can transmit our location."

"I know," I reply. "Goddammit. Do you have a bead on him?"

"Negative. I'm tied to the airlock and he's moving away at a ninety-degree angle on my three o'clock. I only have guns."

"Rogue Actual, Rogue One-Niner," Corporal Giddings sends over the squad channel. "We're in the EVA lock with Nez."

"Lock the hatch," I order. "Third Squad, secure that airlock now. Blackfly One, tell them to cut thrust immediately and keep radio silence."

"Attention, renegade Fleet shuttle. Turn off your propulsion and keep your comms cold, or we will shoot you down," the pilot sends out.

I check the video feed from our starboard hull. The firefly glow of the shuttle's engine is already a few hundred meters away from the station. Right now, the bulk of the asteroid is preventing him from sending a signal out to whoever's listening in the inner system, but as soon as he gets clear, he can scream for help as loud as he wants, and there won't be anything we can do about it at that point.

"Don't shoot," the reply comes. "We are unarmed."

"I don't give a shit," the Blackfly's pilot sends back. "Cut your engine right the hell now."

"Don't shoot. We are unarmed."

"He's playing for time," the pilot says to me. "Thirty seconds, and he'll be in the clear."

"Third Squad, status," I shout into the platoon channel.

"Securing airlock. Ten seconds."

"Hurry the fuck up. Blackfly One, cut yourself loose from the airlock and bring your weapons to bear."

"I'll tear the collar off," he says.

"We'll do an EVA recovery when the dust settles," I reply. "Fucking do it."

"Copy."

"Airlock secure," Third Squad sends, and I let out the breath I've been holding for the last twenty seconds or so.

"Blackfly One, go."

The pilot increases thrust and pitches sharply away from the station. On the external video feed, I can see the soft gray tunnel between our own hatch and the station's airlock stretch, then rip away from the hull around the airlock. The pilot cuts the collar loose from our ship, and it drifts away slowly as the drop ship picks up speed and moves away from the station.

"Twenty seconds until he's clear. Coming around," the pilot says.

I toggle comms to the Fleet emergency channel the pilot just used for his own transmission, and address the fleeing shuttle directly.

"Renegade Fleet unit, this is your last warning. Cut propulsion and come about, or we will destroy your ship."

"Don't shoot at us, goddammit," the shuttle's pilot replies, and now there's more than a little panic in his voice. "We are unarmed."

"Speed and direction unchanged," our pilot says. "Fifteen seconds."

"Goddammit," I shout. On the optical feed, I see the shuttle rushing away from us, eager to reach the edge of the signal-blocking rock we are currently circling.

"Call it, Lieutenant," the pilot says.

If I order him to fire, he'll wipe out a ship that can't fight back, and kill several people who aren't shooting at me or mine right now. If I don't give the order, they'll scream down the house and alert the neighborhood, and a whole task force will come looking for us. They may come looking anyway, or they may not even hear the transmission. Too many mays and ifs for life-and-death decisions. And there's no time to consult with *Portsmouth* or Major Masoud, who wouldn't reply anyway because the task force is running under radio silence to avoid giving itself away. I have to make that call, and I have to make it right now.

I close my eyes.

"Weapons free," I say. "Shoot him down."

"Copy," the pilot says, with what sounds like genuine regret in his voice. "Engaging."

"For the love of God, don't shoot! We are unarm—"

The Blackfly's forward turret raps out half-second bursts of armor-piercing grenades. They're meant for ground support use, not space combat, but a shuttle isn't a tough nut to crack. The burst chews into the tail end of the shuttle and extinguishes the firefly glow of its engine. The plea from the shuttle crew turns into brief, disjointed screams before the transmission ends abruptly when the fuel tank or the engine or maybe both decide to let go. Almost a kilometer away, the shuttle disintegrates soundlessly. The pieces of the wreckage continue on their trajectory, driven by inertia, and quickly disperse in a wide cone of debris and frozen air. I don't look too closely at the results of my order. I don't want to see the bodies of the people we just killed, NAC troopers just like us, maybe people I've trained and dropped into combat within the last few years.

"Target," the pilot says. "Splash one. Fucking idiots."

I want to shoot back an angry retort, but part of me agrees, so I bite my tongue and hold fire.

"Gunny, frisk the place and secure the intel. We're going to have to do an EVA transfer from the airlock once you're done. Docking collar's ripped to shit."

"Understood," comes Philbrick's reply. "Give the Networks guy about thirty to do his thing."

"Tell him to expedite," I say. "Just in case someone noticed all the commotion. I want to be gone before we get bounced by some frigate coming to investigate."

"Copy that. I'll keep you updated."

———

It takes the Networks guy twenty-one minutes to get all the data off the Neural Networks console in the station's control center. By then, we are in the middle of an unfavorable rotation, where the station is pointed into the system interior and ready to send whatever updates they were burst-broadcasting every hour. This time, the transmitter stays quiet. We wait out the rotation until we are beyond the apex, and the station is once again hidden by the bulk of the asteroid that plays host to it.

Back in the cargo hold, the platoon medic is patching up Sergeant Nez, who took a fléchette through his face shield that shattered his cheekbone and sliced him open from the side of his nose to his earlobe. Despite the mess that is the left side of his face, he takes the treatment sitting down while joking around with the medic, even though I know from experience that this sort of injury hurts like hell. Four inches to the left and up, and Nez would be in a body bag right now, and yet he's joking around as if the medic is merely patching up a paper cut. But I know why he's doing it—I've been in the same place, and blowing it off with jokes is much better for your mental health than admitting to yourself how close you just came to getting your dog tags folded.

We retrieve the SI squads one by one by catching them with the open EVA lock of the drop ship, a retrieval method that takes much skill on the part of the pilot and a lot of courage and trust on the part of the troopers who have to push themselves out of the airlock of the station and into open space. But the pilot knows his job, and so do Philbrick's three fire teams. Just before the next rotation apex, we have the whole squad back on the Blackfly, along with the data we came to take.

The trip back to the task force takes three and a half hours, lots of time for me to review the mission in silence and reflect on the choices I made. We don't know how many died on the ship we shot down—more than two, and five at the most, which is as many as that type of shuttle can hold. Three to five KIA among the renegade forces—I still have a hard time designating them as "enemy"—and one wounded among our own ranks. We accomplished the mission with minimal casualties on our side, but somehow it doesn't feel like a success to me. In fact, when we dock with our aviation pod in *Portsmouth's* flank again, I feel like I've fucked up on a grand scale.

CHAPTER 19

— ROLLING WITH THE PUNCHES —

"You had to make a tough call, Lieutenant," Major Masoud says. "But it was the right call."

"Yes, sir," I say, even though I am not nearly as convinced as my company commander. I am standing across the holotable from him, and he is sifting through the mission data the drop ship computer uploaded to *Portsmouth*'s tactical network a little while ago.

"You kept EMCON and had your platoon execute a successful assault on an enemy installation. You retrieved the mission objective and eliminated a potential threat to the task force before it could become a problem. And you had no casualties of your own."

"One wounded," I object. "Sergeant Nez took a round through his face shield that broke some facial bone."

"How's the sergeant doing?"

"He's in Medical right now, but the corpsman had stitched him together all right on the trip back already. He'll have a nice scar to show off."

"Good." Major Masoud turns his attention back to the data stream in front of him. "You did flawless work on your first platoon leader mission, Lieutenant. For what it's worth, your performance validates my choice to bring you on board. I don't think the SEAL platoon could have pulled this off any better. Go square yourself away and take care of your troops. Dismissed."

I salute the major and turn around to walk out of the ops center, strangely offended by my company commander's praise.

———————

Back in the platoon bay, Sergeant Fallon and Gunny Philbrick are supervising the post-mission gear maintenance. The quarterdeck—which is what we've come to call the open space between enlisted berths and the quarters for the platoon leadership—is full of troopers cleaning weapons and running diagnostics on their gear. The room is abuzz with the usual post-mission chatter. I look over the room for a moment, see that my sergeants have the place well in hand, and go back to my berth, where I close the hatch behind me and strip down for a long shower at maximum water temperature.

The hot water makes me feel marginally better. I'm in the middle of getting dressed in clean CDUs when there's a knock on the hatch.

"Stand by for ten," I shout, and finish buttoning up my CDU blouse. Then I walk over to the hatch and open it. Outside, Sergeant Fallon stands in the passageway, arms folded across her chest.

"How did it go?"

"We got it done," I say. "One WIA, Sergeant Nez."

"How many of theirs?"

"Three at least. Wasn't pretty."

"It never is." She looks at me with a slightly quizzical expression. "You okay?"

I could invite her into my office and talk about what happened, but I suddenly feel that Sergeant Fallon isn't the right person to unload my concerns onto. So I just shrug and nod.

"I'm fine," I say. "Just tired. First mission where I got to do nothing but fly a chair with my ass, and I'm worn out more than if I had cleared the damn station by myself."

"I hear you. I got to babysit the rest of the platoon and take Third Squad for some cardio while you guys went off to kick in doors and shoot people. But I guess my days of leading assaults are coming to an end. Too many damn rank stripes."

"I'm pretty sure you'll get your chance on this run sooner or later," I say.

"Out here, I'm okay with babysitting," she says. "I know my limitations."

She pauses and looks at me as if she wants to say something else. Then she glances over to the quarterdeck and nods.

"They're not a bad bunch. I may have to revise my opinion of the SI as a bunch of overconfident space monkeys."

"When they're done cleaning and stashing their shit, have them grab chow and enforce some rack time for First and Second Squads."

"Copy that," she says. "You should do the same. Grab chow and head for your rack."

"That's all that's on my mind right now," I lie.

Sergeant Fallon walks back to the quarterdeck, and I close the hatch and get my PDP out of my pocket. Then I send Halley a message.

>*Are you free for chow right now? Need to talk.*

Her reply comes back maybe twenty seconds later.

>*Be topside in 10.*

It's strange, but for once I don't want or need my former squad leader's counsel, even though she has been the closest thing to a mentor I've had in my military career. Instead, I just want to talk events over with my wife instead, even though she is not an infantry trooper—or maybe partly because she isn't one.

Halley and I meet up in the officers' mess ten minutes later. I grab a meal tray and a drink while she finds us a table, and then I give her the rundown of the mission in between bites while she listens and silently eats her own meal.

"Second Lieutenant Dorian," she says when I am finished. "That's your drop ship pilot."

"He's good," I say. "He really knows how to handle his bird. And he didn't hesitate when I told him to shoot that shuttle down."

"You were the mission commander," Halley says. "Had you told me to, I would have done the same thing in his stead."

"Without flinching?"

Halley stabs her food absentmindedly without taking her eyes off me.

"Is this bugging you? Like Detroit did?"

I consider her question for a moment.

"A little," I say. "I mean, it's not like Detroit. Not really. That was a military target. And they had their warning. Several warnings."

"But."

"But," I repeat. "I just feel like I've stepped over a line somehow. These are our own guys. And we drew first blood. I did. Not directly, but I ordered my guys to, and they listened."

"Of course they did. You're the officer in charge. But you didn't draw first blood, Andrew. They did. You said they fired first. Injured one of your NCOs."

"Yeah, they fired first," I say. "Humphrey told them to freeze. They opened up. And then we did. But that ship? They were unarmed and running away. And I told Lieutenant Dorian to shoot them in the back."

"They fired on your guys before they boarded their alert bird. And they would have given you away the second they cleared that rock and had line of sight to wherever their home base is. Count on it. I would have," she adds, and pokes her soy patty again for emphasis.

"I know," I say. "I know all of that. That's why I told Dorian to fire." I shrug. "Still doesn't mean I'll ever feel great about it."

Halley looks at me and shakes her head with a smile.

"See, Andrew, this is one of the reasons why I married you. You don't just follow orders. You don't pull that trigger lightly. But you do make the call when you have to. And then you agonize over whether you've made the right call."

"Self-doubt." I smile. "Not very officer-like, is it?"

"That's how I know you're a good person. You doubt yourself. But it's a good thing when you're in the killing business. Only a sociopath is always and absolutely sure he'll always make the right call."

"Thank you," I say.

"Don't mention it," she replies. Then she puts her fork down, reaches across the table, and puts her hand on mine.

"But remember that they chose this. That crew chose to disregard your warning and keep going. Everyone you'll come across in this system, they made the choice to blow up our comms relays and steal a trillion dollars' worth of gear. They made the choice to take their own and then leave us all to die. They had their choice, and they chose to fuck the rest of us. Keep that in mind when you go up against them. Because I sure as hell will. And don't you lose a single night of sleep over that shuttle."

At that moment, I feel a profound swell of gratefulness that Halley managed to get herself assigned to this mission, and that I can sit here with her, over this crummy Fleet lunch, and have her give me reassurance. I knew the things she's telling me all along, of course, but it's liberating to hear them from my wife, who knows me better than anyone else in the world. We can't share a berth on this ship, so I won't be able to fall asleep next to her, but she's here with me, a hundred and fifty light-years away from Earth, and whatever is going to happen while we're out here is going to happen to both of us.

"You look like you've been awake for a week, Andrew. Finish your damn food and hit the rack while you can, will you?" Halley says in a gently chiding tone.

I am tired—more so than I usually feel after a mission, even though I didn't do very much, physically speaking. In fact, hitting the rack has a lot more appeal to me right now than finishing the other half of the cheese-and-bologna sandwich and the dollop of fortified vegetable blend next to it. I push my tray across the table toward Halley, who is almost finished with her own food.

"You want this?"

She looks at the remaining half of my sandwich and sticks out her tongue a little.

"I'm good," she says. "Had enough of the Classic Number One Lunch Combo at Drop Ship U to last me until retirement."

"Fine." I pick up the tray again and look for the dish drop. Halley looks up at me with an amused expression and shakes her head slightly.

"Leave it on the table, Lieutenant. The orderly will clean it up. Rank perk, remember?"

"I've been an NCO for too long," I reply, and put the tray down again. "I'm not sure I'll ever get used to this officer thing."

"Sleep," she repeats and nods toward the exit hatch. "You need to be rested next time the balloon goes up."

———————

Mercifully, the balloon does not go up while I am in my bunk and in a deep, dreamless sleep. Sergeant Fallon either doesn't need me for platoon business for a watch cycle and a half, or she noticed how much in need of sleep I seemed. When I wake up, it's not because some ship alert or overhead announcement wakes me, but because my body decides that I am rested enough.

I check the chrono and find that I've been out for over eight hours straight, an almost indecent luxury for someone on a warship in the middle of a hot zone. I get up from the bunk, which I never turned down before falling asleep, straighten out the cover blanket, and change into a fresh set of fatigues. Then I check the terminal on my desk for messages and alerts. There are about fifty or so, but none of them are urgent or require immediate replies.

On the other side of the hatch, I hear muffled cheers and the sounds of physical activity out on the quarterdeck. I unlock the hatch and step over the threshold to see what's going on.

The platoon has converted the quarterdeck into a fighting ring. In the absence of a proper ring with ropes and posts, they have rigged a virtual one with tape markers and about two dozen individual thermal foam pads from their personal gear, magnetically connected to make a square the rough size of a SIMAP ring. The Spaceborne Infantry Martial Arts Program is the close-combat system they teach the SI and Fleet grunts as soon as they get out of Basic, and it's wildly popular as a communal exercise and intra-unit competition sport among the troops. On a warship, you don't usually have the space to be able to run a few kilometers every day, but there's always a five-meter-square patch of deck free somewhere to set up a SIMAP ring. In this particular makeshift ring, Corporal Giddings is currently fighting one of the privates from Second Squad. They are locked in an embrace in the center of the ring, trying to keep each other's arms down while attempting to push the other off balance. Giddings has the better technique, but the private from Second Squad—Minie?—has probably thirty pounds on the corporal, and wins the pushing contest by sheer physics. Giddings loses his balance and stumbles backward, then falls into the crowd lining the edge of the ring. The watching troops cheer.

Sergeant Fallon is watching the scene from the edge of the little passageway between the staff berths and the quarterdeck. She's leaning against the bulkhead, arms crossed in front of her chest, and she looks mildly amused. I walk up next to her, and she nods at me.

"Up from the dead, I see."

"You should have roused me earlier. I look like a sloth."

"No need to get you up," she replies. "The NCOs had everything well in hand. Be glad you got to tune out for a good stretch."

"You must be bored to tears. Babysitting junior NCOs, and you can't even take a break to go see the evening race."

"It's a change of scenery," she says. "And I don't mind this. Beats getting shot at."

The next pair on the mat are Sergeant Humphrey and Private Rogers, which seems like an unfair matchup from the start. I've served with Humphrey before—she was part of the SI detachment on *Indianapolis* last year, and I've been in the ring with her myself a few times during our long transit back to Earth. Humphrey is much stronger than she looks and rock hard when it comes to taking punches. She's not in my weight class, but I remember how she almost cleaned my clock twice in the ring last year. Her opponent, Private Rogers, is a female SI trooper about Humphrey's height, but without her athletic build. Rogers has blond hair she keeps in a tightly tied ponytail, a hairstyle that isn't quite against SI regulations, but that involves considerably more maintenance hassle than the standard "helmet-short" style that Humphrey is sporting.

It seems that this particular fight would last the ten seconds it ought to take for Humphrey to make contact and punch her lighter, less muscular opponent out of the ring, but Rogers is holding her own. She's faster and has a little bit more reach than Humphrey, and she has learned to put those advantages to use. They circle each other, and when Humphrey bulls in to flatten Rogers with a combination, her opponent moves out of the line of attack and counters with her own combination that catches Humphrey off-center. They don't give each other much leeway, but I can tell that Humphrey is holding back just a little, turning the bout into a training opportunity for the younger private.

Sergeant Fallon and I watch as the seemingly uneven fight develops into a fluid, dynamic engagement that is fun to watch. Rogers knows that Humphrey can clean her clock at any point if she leaves herself open or slacks off, and she puts all her heart into the fight. The troopers around the ring cheer when Humphrey drops her guard just a bit near the end of the round because her arms are tired, and Rogers exploits the momentary weakness by moving in and firing off a fast left-left-right combo. The straight right makes it through Humphrey's guard and smacks her in the mouth. The reply comes swiftly and forcefully, Humphrey returning the favor with a left jab and a powerful right cross that plows into Rogers's gloves and makes her hit herself in the nose with her own padded fist. Then the buzzer sounds, and both fighters break off the engagement and bend over with their hands on their knees, panting and gasping for air. Humphrey is bleeding from the lip, Rogers from the nose, but both are grinning as they tap each other's gloves.

"Not bad," Sergeant Fallon concedes. "My little hood rats would wipe the floor with 'em, though. They don't do rings. Or rules."

"Why punch someone when you can shank them," I say.

"Precisely."

"Hey, Lieutenant," Gunny Philbrick calls out from the other side of the quarterdeck. I look over and see that he's putting on a pair of gel gloves. "Want to go a round?"

"Mind your rank," Sergeant Fallon says. "You don't mix it up with the enlisted."

"This is SIMAP," I reply. "There's no rank in the ring. It's a tradition."

"There's always rank," she cautions. "Especially when there are bloody noses involved."

Most of the troopers turn their heads to see how their platoon leader is going to respond to the challenge. If I accept, I may get my chops busted by my own platoon sergeant. If I refuse, I look like I'm chickening out. I don't know most of the junior enlisted, but I know Philbrick, and I suspect he's offering me a chance to show my PFCs and corporals that their leader isn't some soft Fleet console jockey.

"Toss me some gloves," I shout back, and some of the enlisted holler their approval. Someone else chucks a set of gel gloves in my direction, and I catch them and take off my CDU blouse.

"Can't pass up a dick-measuring challenge, can you?" Sergeant Fallon says in a low voice and shakes her head, but she smiles dryly as she does it.

"Ain't about that, Sarge," I reply, and fasten the integrated wrist wraps of the gel gloves.

"Sure it ain't."

Wearing just the thermal undershirt on my upper body, I am keenly aware of the extra ten or fifteen pounds of garrison flab I've put on since I started the basic-training supervisor job last year, but the gloves still feel good on my hands. Stepping onto the mat is like walking back into a favorite rough-but-friendly watering hole. Something in my brain just switches gears whenever I feel the gel cushions over my knuckles and the tight wrap of the stabilizer around my wrist. I was never a fan of physical violence back home when I was still a PRC hood rat, but I've come to love the SIMAP sessions with the SI guys on deployments. It's a simple, primal contest of skills and physical ability, and it engages your body and brain completely, with no room for mental baggage or bullshit.

"You sure you want to get punched in the face by an officer?" I ask Philbrick when we meet in the middle of the mat to touch gloves.

"Can't find anyone else to fight," he says. "Nez is out. And all these wimps are too chicken to punch the gunny."

I've seen Philbrick fight many times in the SI rec room on *Indy*. I fought him myself at least a half dozen times, back when we both had the same rank. He's slightly taller than I am, has more reach than I do, and he's surprisingly nimble for a tall guy. We tap gloves and take up fighting stances, and then the fight is on.

I haven't been in the ring for over a year, and I can feel it. Just twenty or thirty seconds of trading punches with Philbrick and I'm panting for air. He has long legs with plenty of reach, and he likes to use them in the ring. A snap-kick connects with my upper thigh and makes me grunt with the pain of the impact. I reply with a sideways kick that makes him dodge backward, but that throws him off balance a bit, and I step in and follow it up with a left-right combination that rattles his cage. Then we are close enough to each other to trade body shots for a few seconds. I dole out two and collect as many before we push apart again. On the periphery of the makeshift ring, the troopers are cheering us on, but I'm barely aware of them, tunnel vision in full effect.

In the ring, two minutes are practically an eternity. By the time the signal sounds, I'm sweaty and as worn-out as if I had run a few miles in full battle armor, and my thigh and jaw hurt from where I collected some solid, painful hits from Philbrick. But I know I got him back in roughly equal measure, and I'm glad that I was in good enough shape—or he was cautious enough—that none of us humiliated the other in front of all the junior ranks. We tap gloves again, a little worse for the wear than at the beginning of the round, and the enlisted troopers all around us voice their approval again.

"You've gotten slower," Philbrick says, panting.

"And you've gotten uglier," I pant back.

Overhead, the ascending two-tone trill of a 1MC announcement sounds, and the room goes quiet instantly.

"Now hear this. Platoon leaders, pilots, and senior NCOs, report to briefing room Delta at 1730 Zulu. I repeat, all platoon leaders, pilots, and senior NCOs, report to briefing room Delta at 1730 Zulu."

I trade looks with Sergeant Fallon, who checks her chrono and makes the hand signal for "double-time."

"Looks like fun's over for me," I say to Gunnery Sergeant Philbrick. "Gunny, you have the deck."

"I have the deck," Philbrick confirms. Then he raises his voice to address the rest of the platoon.

"On your feet and get the gear stowed, people. Let's get ready for infantry business again."

CHAPTER 20

THE WEIGHT THAT TIPS ── THE SCALE

There's a familiar face in the briefing room this time, and seeing Lieutenant Colonel Renner sitting in the front row with her senior personnel is evidence that this briefing is going to kick off something big. I take a seat next to Sergeant Fallon again, and when Halley walks in with her fellow pilots, she picks the row right in front of mine. We exchange glances as she sits down, and she gives me a brief smile and a furtive thumbs-up.

Major Masoud is already at the front of the room in his worn but immaculate fatigues, the sleeves sharply folded without a single crease or wave, his camouflage beret tucked underneath the rank sleeve on the left shoulder with the beret badge precisely facing up and out. The golden thread of the drop badge sewn above the left breast pocket is so worn and faded that it looks like silver, but as far as I can see, not a single thread on his tunic is out of order.

When the entire leadership echelon of the company is in the briefing room, Major Masoud turns on the holoscreen behind him, which pops into life showing *Portsmouth*'s logo again.

"Dim lights," he says, and the environmental AI obeys and turns the overhead lighting down. The low conversations in the room come to a halt.

"Ladies and gentlemen, we have them by the balls," he says.

Some of the present officers and senior NCOs let out muffled laughs or chuckles, but Major Masoud's face does not let on that he was joking in any way.

"You think I am being facetious," he says. "Rest assured that I do not have any interest in humor at present."

He taps the screen of his remote control, and the ship's seal disappears from the holoscreen. In its stead, there's now a three-dimensional situational display, with the parent star of the Leonidas system in its center and the closest three planets in elliptical orbits around the star. There's an asteroid belt just past the orbit of the third planet, and a small pair of blue icons shaped like lozenges standing on point are on the outer edge of it.

"Task Force Rogue," he says, and circles the ship icons on the screen. Then he zooms part of the display in on the task force ships to show their labels: BERLIN and PORTSMOUTH.

"We are just outside the substantial asteroid belt that is orbiting Leonidas between the orbits of the third and fourth planet. The station we raided yesterday was an observation post and communications relay on one of those asteroids. Lieutenant Grayson's SI team made successful entry and obtained the intelligence off the station's data nodes with no casualties on our side." He nods at me, and heads turn in my direction, which makes me feel more than a little uncomfortable.

"We have the coordinate data from their antenna array, so we know which way the antennas were pointed whenever they made a transmission. We also have all their message traffic. The traitor settlement is here, on the third moon of the third planet, Leonidas c."

The Major zooms the map out again and pans over to where the holographic representation of Leonidas c is wobbling along on its elliptical orbit. If the hologram is an accurate depiction of reality, Leonidas c is a bright blue gaseous planet.

"The moon in question is a little over half the size of Earth. The renegade sons of bitches call it Arcadia."

The conversations in the briefing room start again at low volume. Major Masoud observes the room while he zooms the display in on the hologram depicting the third moon of Leonidas c.

"We don't have detailed maps of the place—yet. But the stuff we got off the data nodes in that relay station is good enough to plan a full recon drop. And while I wish we had more time to send out drones and prepare the field before we go in, we don't have any time to spare."

He increases the display scale until the star map is showing a large enough slice to show our task force at the edge of the asteroid field on one side and Leonidas c in its orbit on the other side. There's a lot of empty space in between, but I can see that the asteroid field orbits along the same sort of long ellipse as Leonidas c, only with a few million kilometers of space in between them.

"We know what they have in this system, but we don't know where they're keeping it. Lieutenant Colonel Renner?"

The skipper of *Berlin* gets up from her first-row chair and joins Major Masoud at the front of the room.

"Our best guess is that they are keeping the defensive force concentrated near their home base," she says. "They don't have the number of ships needed to have an effective patrol pattern in a system of this size, and their force composition practically requires them to operate in task groups. But whatever's out there, it's running silent like we are. We haven't picked up any radar or active radiation source in this system except for the burst traffic the drone caught when we discovered the relay station. Not that I'm complaining, mind." Lieutenant Colonel Renner allows herself a small smile.

"And this is where we have the advantage right now," Major Masoud adds. "We know exactly where they are, and what they have in-system. They don't know where we are. If they even know we are here."

"Figure they'll come checking when they notice their relay has gone off the air, sir," Halley says, and several heads nod in agreement.

"Of course they'll come check. We already have the drones looking along the likely line of approach," Lieutenant Colonel Renner replies. "We're kind of hoping they'll check soon, because then we can verify without a doubt where they've staged their little fleet."

"But we have to proceed with the battle plan either way, because we don't have the time to sit and wait. Not when our fuel and food stores get depleted more every day while we are a hundred and fifty light-years from our supply lines." Major Masoud takes over the holographic map again and zooms in on the third moon of Leonidas c.

"We know where they are," he repeats, and stabs the hologram with his index finger. "Leonidas cs3. Arcadia." He pronounces the name the renegade settlers gave their new home with a sarcastic little bite in his voice. "Whatever we call it, it's their little clubhouse. And Rogue Company is going to sneak in and spoil the party."

———————————

The briefing is long, but far from boring. In fact, in all my years doing rash and daring podhead missions in the Fleet, I've never seen someone put together such a breathtakingly bold and cocky mission plan. But not everyone seems convinced that the major still has all his marbles.

"You are going to send the drop ship wing on a three-million-kilometer insert?" Halley says in an incredulous voice when the major diagrams the insertion plan for the company—all four drop ships, launched from *Portsmouth* while she's making an elliptical orbit just out of the predicted optical detection range of the known units in the renegade fleet.

"The alternative is to get this ship closer to the target moon and risk detection and destruction," Lieutenant Colonel Renner replies for the major. "The Blackflies can make that run, and they are a hundred times stealthier."

"That's way out of range even for a minimum acceleration burn, and that would take us weeks," Halley objects. "Unless we load the external hard points up with fuel tanks and take absolutely no external ordnance along. And then we can't do fire support once we're dirtside."

"You'll carry all the fuel you can cram into the externals," Major Masoud says. "If you need to do fire support on the ground, you'll be limited to cannons and wingtip containers. And *Berlin*'s two Wasps will fly along with buddy tanks in the hold and refuel your flight about halfway to the target."

Halley ponders the major's statement while her fellow pilots talk to each other again in low, excited voices.

"I've never made an insert from that far out. Not even close."

"Nobody has, Captain. You'll be setting a new Fleet record."

"If we make it back," the pilot sitting next to Halley says to her in a low voice, and she rewards the comment with a smirk.

"Look, you know your hardware better than I do," Major Masoud continues. "The Blackflies are the stealthiest small units in the entire Fleet. Whatever they have in orbit, I am certain you are going to be able to sneak past it and deliver the grunts dirtside."

"Oh, I'm not worried about being seen," Halley replies. "I know that I can coast right past a cruiser and take samples of the hull paint without being seen. It's the 'getting back' part that worries me. Even if the Wasps top us off on the way in. Atmospheric flight burns a lot of fuel."

Major Masoud nods at Lieutenant Colonel Renner, who steps up to the display.

"Optimal launch point for low-energy trajectory to Arcadia is here"—she marks the point on the task force's orbit—"and pickup point is going to be here." She marks another point on the other side of the orbital ellipse. "That's nine days later. *Berlin* and *Portsmouth* will remain on the far side of the asteroid field and keep using it as cover against optical detection. Subtracting transit time, that will give you seven days to accomplish your mission on the ground. You are to keep enough emergency fuel to make orbit and set yourself on a low-energy trajectory to the rendezvous point, and we will send the Wasps back out to meet you and refill your tanks."

Halley and the pilot next to her exchange looks again. From Halley's carefully neutral expression, I can't really tell what she thinks of that plan, but she doesn't object outright, which I know she'd do if she found the idea idiotic, no matter what the rank of the officer who proposed it.

"One company, four drop ships, one week in enemy territory," Sergeant Fallon says next to me. "Bringing only what fits into the ships. No backup. And if things go to shit, no friends overhead."

"In other words, business as usual," I reply.

Of course, Sergeant Fallon and I know from personal experience that when things really go to shit for the squad on the ground, it doesn't matter much whether the support ship is thirty minutes or thirty light-years away. Still, as I study the plot on the holoscreen, I can't help but notice just how big this system is, and just how isolated and far from home we're really going to be.

We spend the next hour or so in the briefing room going through the details of the mission with the whole command team, Fleet and SI alike. It's a bold mission, but other than the extreme range of the drop ship insertion—which according to Halley is three times longer than any infiltration run she has ever done—it's a fairly standard long-range reconnaissance run in company strength, the kind that is pretty much the bread and butter of the podheads. And knowing that we are going up against other humans—and fellow North Americans at that—makes the whole thing feel a little less perilous. But when I say this out loud to Sergeant Fallon, she laughs and looks at me as if I just told her a dumb joke.

"You of all people should know better," she says. "Like your own people can't shoot you up just as well as the SRA."

"Point taken," I concede, and touch the spot on my side where I have scars from fléchettes fired by an NAC Defense Corps rifle, with a hand that has two prosthetic fingers that replaced the ones shot off by an NAC security officer last year.

Major Masoud concludes the briefing by clearing the holoscreen of all ancillary windows and projections until only the system map remains. He zooms out the scale until it includes the target moon— Arcadia—and our orbital trajectory. The lonely little blue icons labeled BERLIN and PORTSMOUTH are inching along on the dotted ellipse that marks our course.

"Jump-off is in thirty-nine hours," he announces. "The company will be ready to embark at t-minus thirty-six hours. Double- and triple-check your kit. If it isn't on the drop ships when we push off, it might as well be on the other side of the Alcubierre node. Pilots will cross-check and synchronize their navigational data with *Portsmouth* Ops."

He looks at the assembled officers and senior NCOs in the room with a stern face.

"Make no mistake, ladies and gentlemen. I know this is going to sound like most motivational prejump pep talks you've heard, but this is probably the single most important mission you'll ever be a part of. This isn't about taking some dusty piece of shit moon away from the SRA, or scraping some Lanky town off the face of a colony planet. Our success or failure may decide the outcome of the greatest battle in the history of humanity. Our hundred and fifty troopers can be the weight that makes the scale tip one way or the other."

He smiles grimly.

"And if we can serve these traitorous, thieving sacks of shit the bill they deserve for leaving the rest of us at the mercy of the Lankies, then I'm going to count that as a perk. Dismissed," he shouts into the chorus of cheers that follows his declaration.

Next to me, Sergeant Fallon does not cheer. Instead, she looks at me and smiles her sardonic little lopsided smile.

"Ooh-fucking-rah," she says mockingly.

CHAPTER 21
—— INTO THE BLACK ——

Thirty-nine hours—it's amazing how they can simultaneously feel like an eternity and no time at all.

As an enlisted podhead, you mostly only have to worry about yourself and your own gear prior to a drop. I am not used to having to worry about forty troopers and their gear, but Sergeant Fallon is, and she gently waves me off after I check on the platoon for the tenth time in as many hours.

"Leave the nuts-and-bolts shit to your NCOs," she says. "You need to learn the magic word. Delegate."

"Delegate," I say.

"That's right. Now get the fuck off my quarterdeck, sir. The junior enlisted get jumpy when the lieutenant looks over their shoulders too much."

"Carry on then, Sergeant," I say. "See? Delegating."

She makes a sweeping-away motion with her fingers, and I resist the urge to make a one-fingered motion in return, just in case some of the privates are looking our way.

The module section of the ship is abuzz with prelaunch activity. The platoons are checking their gear and putting on battle armor, and the drop ship crews are loading their birds and checking systems. Halley is the pilot of Second Platoon's drop ship, and I meander over into their section of the ship, astern from ours. I find my wife in the aviation module, where she is checking the gear her platoon has tied down in the cargo hold of her Blackfly.

"Shouldn't you be checking on your platoon?" she says when she spots me by the hatch. She gives one of the tie-down straps on the pallet next to her an experimental tug and then walks down the tail ramp and over to where I am standing.

"Sergeant Fallon kicked me out because I was doing too much of that."

Halley is dressed in her combat flight suit, which is a one-piece jumpsuit with about a million external pockets. Over the suit, she's wearing a light armor vest. Her sidearm is strapped to her thigh, and she's as dressed and ready for battle as drop ship pilots get, minus her helmet. For my taste, that armor vest doesn't cover nearly enough essential parts of her anatomy.

"That's a lot of fuel," I say and nod at the enormous external fuel tanks hanging from the wings of the Blackfly. Like everything else on the drop ship, they don't have straight lines or right angles anywhere.

"I've never taken along four drop packs," she says. "That thing is going to handle like a wallowing swine when we hit atmosphere."

"I wish you were in the driver's seat of my bus."

"I don't," she replies. "Too much pressure. You have Lieutenant Dorian. He knows his shit. He'll get your mudlegs down into the dirt in one piece."

"He can handle that ship," I concede. "But I like having you close."

"I'll be close, Andrew. We're going in ten-minute intervals. I'll be right behind you." She looks around the hangar pod and flexes her hands. "God, it's been a while. First combat drop since Earth last year."

"Good times," I say, and she laughs and shakes her head.

"God help me, but I do love it. All of it."

"You aren't right in the head," I say.

"You love it, too," Halley says. "And don't pretend that you don't. You wouldn't have taken that mission otherwise. You love it just as much as I do. Getting ready for a fight, being scared shitless, all your nerves on edge. But you feel more alive than ever."

"I guess we're both nuts," I say.

Halley looks around the hangar pod again. There are techs near the front of the drop ship, unhooking hoses and data umbilicals, but nobody is paying any attention to us this very moment. Then she pulls me close and kisses me.

"I am so glad for all of this. You, me, us being here, everything that happened to us since Basic. I wouldn't trade it for the world, Lankies and all. If we end up a frozen cloud of stardust today, I know that I've fucking lived." She lets go of my tunic and straightens out the fabric gently with her hand. "And we'll be together out here until the universe collapses. Beats the shit out of having your ashes packed into a stainless steel capsule and shoved into a hole in the wall."

"Now, see," I say, "and you thought you had absolutely no romantic bones in your body."

"Go and gear up," she says. "I'll see you out in the black. I'm right behind you. Wherever it is we're headed."

Standing there in the hangar pod with my wife, her excitement and her confidence, surrounded by all this gear and about to drop into combat and mortal danger again, I suddenly feel a brief and powerful gladness as well. Halley is right, of course. We may die today, or we may live to be a hundred and fifty, but we will have directed our own course a little, and that's much more than most people get these days.

"Now hear this: t-minus fifteen to launch. All mission personnel, board your ships. I repeat: all mission personnel, board your ships."

The platoon has been ready and assembled on the quarterdeck for a while, double-checking each other's armor latches and equipment while engaging in the traditional predrop joshing and trash-talking. Now the mood turns businesslike and serious as the squad leaders line up their charges to get ready for the short walk over to the flight module.

"All right, people. It's showtime. Time to do something for the exorbitant salaries they pay us," Sergeant Fallon declares.

We file out of the platoon bay by squads and cross the passageway outside to enter the flight module, where our drop ship is waiting with its tail ramp open. Because the flight module is so small, they can't fire up the engines while there are still personnel in the pod, so the boarding process is eerily quiet aside from the chatter of the infantry grunts as they trudge up the ramp and take their seats in the hold.

"Remember the good old days back at Shughart?" Sergeant Fallon says as we watch the loading process from the back of the module.

"We had that huge airfield," I reply. "And they used to play motivational music while we boarded."

"Those were the days," she replies, with a slight tinge of nostalgia in her voice. "Back when we only had to worry about hood rats with guns, not this deep-space alien invasion shit."

"Back in the old Corps, things sure were different," I say in a creaky, old-guy voice, and she laughs.

When all the troopers are in their jump seats inside the cargo hold, we follow up the ramp. We pass through the rows of battle-ready troopers to the front of the hold, where Sergeant Fallon takes a free seat at the top of First Platoon's row, across from Gunny Philbrick. I take the command chair in front of the bulkhead and plug myself into the console with the data umbilical. The screens turn on and immediately start feeding me status reports.

"All aboard," the crew chief says. He pushes the control for the tail ramp, which closes quietly. For some reason, this time it makes me think of a lid closing on a coffin.

"Passengers aboard. Verify hard seal on the cargo hold," the crew chief sends to the flight deck.

"I show hard seal on the hold," the pilot replies.

The now-familiar muted whine of the Blackfly's engines starts up outside. The inside of the hold is far more crowded than during the raid on the relay station a few days ago. We have a full platoon on board, and all the jump seats in the hold are taken. In addition, half the empty space between the seat rows and the forward bulkhead is taken up by supply pallets that are strapped to the floor of the cargo hold. I have a pallet parked right behind the command chair, blocking my view of the crew chief, who is manning his own console on the starboard side of the ship.

"Comms and data check, people," I send to my squad leaders and platoon sergeant. "Let's make sure the wireless stuff works before we have to go EMCON."

My squad leaders send back their acknowledgments. Sergeant Fallon adds her own virtual thumbs-up, and I check the data stream from thirty-nine armor computers. Everything is working the way it should, and everyone is in the link, connected to me via low-power wireless data streams.

"Rogue Ops, this is Rogue One Actual. Comms cross-check complete. First Platoon is ready for showtime."

"Rogue One Actual, Rogue Actual," Major Masoud sends back from the cargo hold of his own ride. "Copy that. You are five by five on comms and data."

The company command section is riding with the SEALs in Blackfly Four, which doesn't come as a big surprise to me. The major and his SEALs have been segregating themselves from the SI platoons all along, and it's no shock that they're not going to start mingling with us right at go-time.

Outside in the flight module, klaxons start blaring again, followed by an overhead announcement.

"All personnel, clear the pod for flight ops. Depressurizing pod in t-minus nine. I repeat, all personnel clear the pod for flight ops. Depressurizing in t-minus nine."

"Anyone need to hit the head before we launch best hurry up," Sergeant Fallon says to the platoon, and there's laughter.

At launch time, the flight module goes through the same cycle as before. The air in the module is vented into space all at once when the clamshell doors of the pod open. Then the launch boom extends, and the Blackfly trundles outward on it, carried by the docking clamp overhead. We reach the end of the boom and come to a stop with a slight shudder of the hull.

"*Portsmouth* Ops, Blackfly One is locked in and ready for launch sequence," the pilot sends to our host ship.

"Blackfly One, copy. Stand by for remote launch initiation. In ten . . . nine . . . eight . . ."

I think of Halley, who is in the pilot seat of Blackfly Two, on the other side of *Portsmouth*'s hull and slightly astern from us. She'll be directly behind us on our trajectory, ten minutes apart. On a normal drop, she'd be well in visual range, and I could probably see her cockpit with enough magnification from the stern camera array, but these are Blackflies, and their polychromatic armor plating will make them practically disappear. Still, I know she's going to be out there with me.

". . . three, two, one. Launch."

We drop free and float away from the hull of *Portsmouth*. Our pilot increases thrust on the engines and clears the ship by a few hundred meters before he turns the nose around. We pass underneath *Portsmouth*, and I watch the supply ship continue on its course with the drop ship's dorsal camera array until she's just a small black dot, emitting a faint glow from the shielded engine nozzles in her stern.

"Burning for intercept trajectory in three . . . two . . . one. Burn."

Our pilot fires up the engines for acceleration burn. Once again I am amazed at the low noise level inside the cargo hold. The Blackfly really is quieter at full throttle than all the other drop ships are at idle. Combined with her polychromatic armor, she's the perfect tool for high-risk commando stuff. I've been a podhead for years, and the fact that I've never even heard of this new class of drop ship makes me a little anxious. If they could keep these drop ships secret even from the rest of the podhead community, what else is floating around out there with the renegade fleet that we've never encountered?

"We're on the way," I send to Sergeant Fallon. "Just like old times, huh?"

"Not really," she replies. "I'm used to breathable air on the outside of the hull."

———

The transit to the vicinity of Leonidas c is one of the most taxing experiences I've had in my time in the service. No drop ship is designed to make an insertion from that far out, and I've never spent this much uninterrupted time in a cargo hold. The troops spend their time talking on private channels or playing the limited variety of diversionary games loaded on their PDPs. At the midpoint of our transit, twelve hours into the flight, we take on fuel from the Wasps to top off our tanks, and the squads take turns unstrapping from their jump seats and stretching their limbs. The Blackfly has a tiny galley and a toilet right next to it, but we are under combat stations and therefore in armor, and nobody is willing to risk a quick death in the event of a hull breach just for the convenience of using a proper toilet instead of the armor's built-in waste elimination system. Long missions in armor forcing you to take a piss into your armor's auto-cleaning underlayer aren't something they mention in the recruiting office or in the war flicks on the Networks.

Leonidas c is an ever-growing presence off our port bow. It's a big blue gas planet, quite beautiful to look at. The atmospheric swirls and patterns on the planet surface are mesmerizing at high magnification, and I'm glad for something other than inky black space to look at. On the tactical display, the other three drop ships are lined up behind us on our intercept trajectory, roughly ten minutes apart. If something happens to Blackfly One on the ingress, the rest of the platoon will have plenty of warning to avoid the same fate. Without radar and under full EMCON, we are limited to the optical gear, and we don't pick up anything else in the system at all until the stretched ellipse of our intercept course brings us around Leonidas c a bit.

"There she is," our pilot sends. "Port bow, three hundred by negative twenty-five. Popping up just over the planetary horizon by the equator."

I check the optical feed and zoom in on the section of space Lieutenant Dorian pointed out. Leonidas cs3—Arcadia—is just barely visible as it peeks around its much bigger planet.

"Huh," I say. "It looks like—Earth."

"It does, doesn't it?"

Arcadia is a little green-and-blue orb that looks nothing like most other colony moons I've seen. It very clearly has an atmosphere—even from tens of thousands of kilometers away, I can see the white patches of sporadic cloud cover.

"Anything on the radar detector?" I ask, even though I have access to that information through my data link.

"Not a thing," Lieutenant Dorian replies. "I hope we have the right neighborhood. Be a bitch to have come all this way for nothing."

A warship or military base can be seen—or more accurately, heard—long before you cross into the range where it can detect you in return. That's because radar and radio emissions can be picked up from very far away with passive threat detectors. But we've been through a good part of the Leonidas system without picking up so much as a whiff of active radiation. Unless the renegade faction has discovered a revolutionary new way to discover far-off threats, they seem to willingly accept blindness in exchange for near-invisibility.

"This is the place," I say. "Unless they had that relay station set up with the wrong data on purpose. Throw off anyone coming after them."

"I don't think that's likely," Lieutenant Dorian says. "They're not keeping quiet 'cause they're worried about people finding them."

Ten minutes later, our pilot lets out a satisfied little shout.

"Contact," he says. "Visual contact, three thirty by negative five. Three . . . five . . . six ships."

"Battle group?" I ask.

"Big one's a carrier. Navigator class. Too big to be anything else. Can't make out the smaller ones yet. And there's a structure."

I check the optical feed and pan over the area at maximum magnification. There, in the orbit of that little blue-and-green moon, I can make out a familiar shape. I've seen it before, last year, when *Indianapolis* followed the damaged destroyer *Michael P. Murphy* on its run from Gateway Station.

"It's an anchorage," I say. "Same as the one they left behind in the Solar System. Where we found those battleships."

The structure looks like two giant letters E joined at the spines, a central axis with six tines jutting outward. All those outriggers have ships docked at their ends, and smaller ships take up the spaces between the outriggers. One of them is definitely a Navigator, the Fleet's premier supercarrier, which would make that ship NACS *Pollux*. The other ships are too far away and still too small in the optical feed to positively identify them without doing an electronic IFF interrogation or lighting them up with active radar, which wouldn't be a wise course of action right now.

"Looks like we found the task force."

"Most of it," I concur, glad that we didn't make a twenty-three-hour trip in a cramped drop ship for nothing.

"Look at them all tied down in anchorage. They're not expecting trouble."

"That's only six. We still have four unaccounted for, plus all the auxiliary fleet freighters they took."

"Oh, I think we'll see them around sooner or later," Lieutenant Dorian says.

As we coast closer to Arcadia, the image of the anchorage becomes clearer with every minute. I let the computer cross-check the visuals of the anchored ships with the list of Fleet units known to have gone with the renegade fleet a year ago. The cruiser-size hull has to be the only cruiser they took along, NACS *Phalanx*. There's a frigate that looks small enough to be a Treaty-class ship, which would make her NACS *Lausanne*, sister unit to our *Berlin*. The task force has way more combat power in this system than we do, but I'm happy to see that most of it is tied up at the anchorage and inert at the moment.

"That would be a juicy nuke target right there. Six for the price of one," Lieutenant Dorian says.

"Yeah," I agree. "If we didn't need all those ships for Mars."

"Shame," he says, with what sounds like sincere regret. "We could— hang on. Contact. New contact on optical, bearing zero-zero-five by positive zero-five-two. Distance one hundred thousand and change."

A new icon pops up on the tactical display in the cockpit, marking a spotted ship in high orbit above the northern hemisphere of Arcadia. Even with the lenses at maximum zoom, I can't make out the type or class, just a Fleet-gray hull with position lights blinking.

"Is he flashing station lights?" I ask.

"Yep," Lieutenant Dorian replies. "Full Christmas tree. Not getting any active radiation from him, either. He doesn't want to be heard, but he sure doesn't give a fuck about being seen."

I look at the trajectory projection for the newcomer to see if he's on an intercept course. He's not headed our way, but he's not aiming for the anchorage, either. With every passing minute, we get closer to Arcadia and our orbital insertion. I know that Lieutenant Dorian does not want to risk a corrective burn and give us away on infrared or whatever else the renegades have aimed at the approaches to Arcadia, but we also don't want to get too close to a patrolling unit, polychromatic armor or not.

"It's one of those new frigates," he says after a few minutes. "Those Greek underworld ones."

"You sure?" I consult the optical feed again to look at the hull of the patrolling ship, now a few ten thousand kilometers closer.

"It's the right size. And the shape looks off for a Treaty."

When the renegade fleet made their escape, they left behind the two unfinished battleships that are now *Agincourt* and *Arkhangelsk*, but they also had a trio of frigates nobody had ever seen or heard about before—*Styx*, *Acheron*, and *Lethe*, identified through their IFF transponders by the *Indianapolis* when we discovered the renegade anchorage. We know very little about these frigates and their capabilities, but if they were meant to be escorts for those battleships, they're built to go up against Lankies. As I look at the far-off maybe-frigate on the optical feed, silently coasting along in front of the blue-and-green backdrop of Arcadia, I wonder just what kind of new surprises they kept secret over the years.

"Orbit insertion in forty-six minutes," Lieutenant Dorian says. "Going to aerobrake and see if we can set up orbit on the other side of the moon from that station. I don't want to have to use the burners to slow us down."

The drop ship needs to slow down for a stable low orbit, and since we can't fire the engines to counterburn on the way in, the only other option is aerobraking, using the friction from atmospheric entry to slow us down gradually. As stealthy as the Blackfly is, we can't hide the superheated plasma that surrounds and flares behind us like a fiery rooster tail as we start skipping through the first dense layers of Arcadia's atmosphere. Anyone looking our way with enough magnification will see the light show, and the ships following us in ten-minute intervals will light up the sky again in the same obvious fashion.

"Hitting atmo," I inform the platoon, quite unnecessarily. The drop ship is buffeting and bouncing roughly as we descend at the fastest safe rate, bleeding speed and kinetic energy. Pod landings are rougher still, but in a pod, you can't get bounced against anything, so it seems less jarring. By far the most shoot-downs and accidents occur in this phase of an orbital insert, when the ship is on a fixed trajectory and very visible. I scan the threat sensors obsessively, even though they're almost useless while the drop ship is ensconced in superheated plasma. Finally, after what seems like an eternity but took less than thirty minutes according to my suit's chrono, most of the buffeting stops, and we are soaring through a deep-blue sky, with the stars above us and the blue-green surface of Arcadia below. The horizon in the distance has a pronounced curve to it at our altitude, and there's an iridescent light blue band of atmosphere shining on the far-off boundary between moon and space.

"We'll be below the line of sight horizon to the anchorage in seven minutes," Lieutenant Dorian says. "We should be able to get the rest of the flight on near-field comms."

"Copy that," I say. "Just give the word when we're in the clear."

A hundred thousand feet below us, the colony moon spreads out like a surreal tapestry. It looks like one of those environmental holograms they project onto the walls in the RecFacs or medical facilities to relax people and let them pretend there's an unspoiled world beyond. Arcadia isn't a frozen ball of ice and rock like New Svalbard, or a craggy, brown-and-red desert like Fomalhaut's SRA-owned moon or precolonization Mars. There's blue water and green land, mountains and rivers, the sun glistening off hundreds—thousands—of bodies of water, lakes and streams and seas. And there isn't a single trace of human activity anywhere—no contrails crisscrossing the skies, no lights or exhaust plumes, and no permanent smog haze over most of the land below. Instead, we are cruising above a broken cover of white clouds. I share the video feed with the platoon just so they can see what they're about to drop into. Imaginations can run a little wild when you're descending into hostile territory in a windowless cargo hold.

"Look at that," Sergeant Fallon says. "It's friggin' paradise. Never seen anything like it. No wonder most of the welfare rats want to win the colony lottery."

"Most of 'em don't look like that," I say. "None of them do, actually. None that I've ever set foot on, anyway."

The other three drop ships enter the moon's atmosphere in five-minute intervals behind us, each trailing bright and obvious tails of fire on their way down. On the way into low orbit, our flight was neatly lined up, but aerobraking in the upper layers of the atmosphere isn't a precise way to slow down. By the time Blackfly Four has made the transition into atmo, our flight is dispersed in a rough diamond formation, with more than a hundred kilometers between us.

"Threat detectors still showing zip," Lieutenant Dorian says. "No active radar, no radio traffic, no nothing."

"Maybe they all dropped dead, and we can just waltz in and call the Fleet for a pickup," I offer.

"Wouldn't hurt my feelings any."

A few minutes later, Lieutenant Dorian chimes in over the shipboard intercom channel again.

"We're in the radio shadow of the anchorage, and there's nothing on the scope. I'd say we're safe for low-power tight beam comms."

I send a coded message to the rest of the flight, a two-digit number that takes a millisecond to transmit. A few seconds later, we get three separate transmissions back.

"Rogue Actual, this is Rogue One Actual. The threat board is green. Transmitting tactical now."

Our ship is in the lead, so our optical sensors can see a good hundred kilometers further into the distance than those of the following ships. Our Blackfly's computer sends its sensor information to the three other ships in a millisecond burst.

"Rogue One Actual, Rogue Actual," Major Masoud replies. "Confirming data link. Proceed to your deployment point and commence mission."

I send my acknowledgment back and slowly let out a long breath. The riskiest part of the ingress is over, but we are still way behind enemy lines, and a very long way from any backup.

"Let's head to Deployment Point Alpha," I tell Lieutenant Dorian. "So far, so good."

"I'll reserve judgment until we have our skids on the ground," he replies, in a very Halley-like burst of realistic pessimism.

Deployment Point Alpha is in a river valley between two low mountain chains. The mountains in this place are wild and craggy, bare of vegetation or snow. They remind me of the landscape I've seen while flying over Iceland on Earth.

"Holy shit," Lieutenant Dorian says when we crest the ridge and drop into the valley beyond. "Look at the goddamn greenery outside."

The valley in front of us has a stream running right through the middle of it, and both sides of the riverbed are lined with trees, many square kilometers of them. The sight is so surreal that it makes me feel like I've come down with a sudden flash fever. None of the colonies we've settled have had vegetation on them that wasn't raised in a hydroponic greenhouse and used for food purposes, but the trees whose tops we are skimming over at only a few dozen feet altitude are most definitely not food. They look like fir trees, Earth firs, something I've never seen away from our home planet.

"What the fuck," I say.

"That's thousands of trees," Lieutenant Dorian says. "How the hell did they get all those out here?"

"Beats me," I reply. "I don't suppose there's a chance they're native flora?"

We put down the ship in a clearing in the middle of this surreal forest. Lieutenant Dorian uses the retractable wheels on the Blackfly's landing skids to roll the ship underneath the tree canopy to camouflage it from above, and I give the platoon the signal to get ready for disembarking.

"Get them out and set up perimeter security," I tell Sergeant Fallon.

"On your feet, and let's get out of this fucking thing," Sergeant Fallon says to the troops. "Charge your weapons and stand ready to deploy by squads."

Thirty-eight troopers get out of their jump seats and cycle the actions on their carbines. The light above the tail ramp jumps from red to green, and the crew chief punches the controls to open the ramp. It lowers itself with that soft hydraulic hiss particular to the Blackfly, and First and Second Squads are on the trot before the bottom of the ramp even hits the dirt.

It's almost comical to watch the SI troopers rush out of the cargo hold and down the ramp, only to slow down perceptibly once they have their boots in the dirt and their eyes on the environment outside.

"Stop the sightseeing," Philbrick shouts from the rear of First Squad. "Perimeter, eight to twelve o'clock, numbskulls."

First Squad swarms out on the port side of the drop ship, and Third Squad deploys to the starboard side. Second Squad takes the tail end, and within twenty seconds of the first set of SI boots on the ground, the troopers have established a 360-degree security perimeter around the drop ship, fifty meters away, weapons pointed in all directions.

I charge my own weapon and follow Sergeant Fallon out of the hold and into daylight. As I step off the ramp, my boots land on a soft cushion of soil and discarded pine needles. Sergeant Fallon raises her visor and looks up at the crowns of the trees.

"Pop your face shield," she tells me.

I raise the shield on my helmet. The air smells like pine resin—the real thing, not the artificial scent from chemical dispensers. The only thing that's missing to make the scene completely surreal is the chirping of birds, but there are no sounds other than the wind rustling the trees and the engines of the drop ship behind us whispering in idle mode, ready for a hasty departure if it turns out to be needed.

I walk over to the nearest tree, let my rifle hang from its sling, and touch the bark. It feels rough under the gloves of my armor. If it didn't take a minute or two to unseal the armor, I'd take the gloves off to check the feel with my bare skin, but they look and smell and feel real enough. These are Earth trees, without a doubt. Whether they were transplanted here or grown in this spot, their seeds came from our home planet, a hundred and fifty light-years away.

"What the fuck," I say again.

Sergeant Fallon walks up next to me and touches the trunk of the tree as well. She runs her hands up and down the bark almost lovingly. Then she looks up at the crown of the fir and squints.

"How tall do you reckon this thing is? Eighteen, twenty meters?"

"More like twenty-five," I reply, using the known scale of a Lanky as a guide.

"Twenty-five-meter trees," she says, and pats the trunk. "I know you kids don't know shit about trees these days. But even if that's a fast-growing variety, that tree is twenty years old."

"You mean to suggest they planted these things two decades ago? That this place has been colonized for at least twenty years, and they've managed to keep it a secret from the rest of us?"

"Well, the trees are here, without a doubt," she says. "Which means they planted them here, or took saplings or older trees from Earth. You really think they had the space to ship thousands of fir trees a hundred and fifty light-years?"

"No, I don't," I say. Transporting cargo over interstellar distances is insanely expensive—by far the most costly aspect of colonization is hauling the five thousand tons of material for each ready-to-build atmospheric terraforming unit. Cargo weight is so controlled that SI and Fleet personnel have a fixed and very low weight limit for personal possessions. Nobody would try to haul a million tons of trees when they can take along the seeds for a tiny fraction of the weight.

I look around, at the hundreds of trees in view. With the nearby mountain ridge in the background and the fluffy white clouds in the clean blue sky, it looks beautiful, pastoral, prettier than anything I've ever seen on Earth. From the air, it looked like the valley is full of these trees, thousands and thousands of Earth plants that have no practical purpose beyond just being here.

Beyond making the place look like Earth, I think.

"How long have they been fixing this moon up?" I wonder out loud.

Sergeant Fallon picks up her rifle from where she had propped it against the trunk of the nearby tree, and checks the loading status again out of habit.

"Apparently, since just after you were born," she says. "And nobody knew a goddamn thing about this place until now. Makes you wonder what the hell else they've kept for themselves all these years, don't it?"

CHAPTER 22
VISUAL CONTACT

"What in the high holy hell are those?" Sergeant Fallon asks when Gunny Philbrick and his squad open one of the modular equipment cases they carried out of the Blackfly's armory.

The case contains three dozen tiny, spindle-shaped devices that look like toy versions of Fleet warships. They're set into protective foam and neatly lined up in three rows of twelve. Gunny Philbrick takes one out of the case and rests it on his palm. It's barely longer than his hand and half as wide.

"That's our little eye in the sky," he says. "RQ-900 micro-drone." He turns it in his hand and holds it out to Sergeant Fallon, who looks at it with interest. "Surely you had something like that on hand in the Territorial Army."

"Something like that," she says. "But they weren't that small. That thing is tiny."

"Bigger on the inside." Philbrick grins. "Full passive sensor package. High-res camera array with thousand-millimeter lenses. TacLink integration. Whatever these things see, we'll see a few seconds later."

"Neat," Sergeant Fallon says. "What's the range?"

"A hundred kilometers' mission radius, give or take a dozen depending on altitude. But you can cover a lot of ground with those cameras from fifteen thousand feet up. Saves us a lot of legwork."

Philbrick and his squad set up the thirty-six recon drones with a speed and efficiency that comes from practice. We'd get more coverage from a recon run with the drop ship, but it's much larger and more obvious, and it would burn too much of the fuel we may need for close air support later. The drones are designed to do the same job but far stealthier, and their built-in battery-driven electric motors cost us almost nothing to run. After only ten minutes of assembly-line work, all three dozen drones are lined up on the tail ramp of the Blackfly. Their propulsion package is a little dual-rotor assembly that is as silent as hummingbird wings.

"Units one through thirty-six, function check complete," Private Rogers announces. "All systems are 'go' for launch."

"Here's the pattern," Philbrick says, and brings up the topographical map of the area. Every drone has a hundred-kilometer patrol route mapped out for it that takes the terrain into account. "Figure a hundred minutes for both legs. You want them to go live link or storage mode only?"

In live-link mode, the drones will broadcast their recon data in real time using a low-power encrypted data link. In storage mode, they'll save the recon data to their internal memory modules and download them to our local TacLink setup when they've returned from their flight. Live link gets us earlier warning of threats because it's immediate, but it does involve transmissions that can potentially give us away. Storage mode means we get the information with a hundred-minute delay, and if a drone goes down, we'll have a blind spot in our recon coverage.

"Go live link," I say. "Didn't spot anything on the threat board on the way in. I don't think we have to worry about the comms from the drones right now, and I want to know ASAP if something is coming our way."

"Copy that, sir," Philbrick replies.

The drones take off one by one, in three-second intervals, whirring off into the clear blue sky like inoffensive little bugs. They don't have polychromatic plating, but they're so small that their little gray-and-blue bodies are just about invisible when they're only barely above the treetops. Not even the hearing augmentation in my helmet is picking up the soft buzz from the tiny double rotors.

"Birds away. Live link up," Gunny Philbrick says. "Good data on all thirty-six."

Almost instantly, the TacLink display on my map updates as the drone cameras push out our awareness bubble a few meters per second. Then the drones accelerate to patrol speed, and the bubble grows more quickly, filling blind spots on the tactical map and drawing the surrounding area in high resolution.

"Now I just have to resist the temptation to lie down in this soft grass and take a long nap," Sergeant Fallon says to me.

———————

The recon drones take almost an hour to reach the maximum range of their patrol patterns. Thirty-six drones mean that each is covering a ten-degree wedge, but that wedge grows wider the further the drones are away from our landing site. I'd have an easier time monitoring the feed from the big screens of the command console inside the drop ship, but I don't want to go back into the cargo hold where I just spent twenty-four uncomfortable hours. Instead, I walk around outside in the sunshine and keep the tactical display up on my visor overlay. All around me, the SI troopers are still arranged in a circle to cover the drop ship, but with no immediate threat detected by the drones, some have taken the opportunity to take off their helmets and chew on some ration bars.

From twenty-five thousand feet up, the drones can see for hundreds of kilometers with their cameras and passive sensors. The computer does the work of filtering the information and presenting it to me for review every time one of the drones picks up something worth looking at. The first obviously man-made structure pops up on my display from drone 11, which is humming along in its high-altitude patrol loop to our east-southeast. I check the location marked by the computer and immediately rush over to the drop ship to get in front of a bigger display. Sergeant Fallon notices my hurried gait and follows me into the ship.

"Problem?"

"Not yet," I reply and plug my armor back into the console. "One of the drones spotted something. Hang on."

I bring the imagery up on the bigger command console screens and zoom in. Even with its 1,000mm lens, the target looks small from five kilometers up, but it's very clearly a human-built structure, a nearly square concrete building with rounded corners.

"The fuck is that?" Sergeant Fallon says. "Looks like a bunker."

"Gunny, check the feed from unit 11," I send to Philbrick. "Get that drone down closer, but keep an eye on the threat display. Anything goes active down there, you go the other way."

"Copy that," Philbrick replies. "Stand by. Rogers, over here and fly me that drone for a minute. Bearing one hundred, get her down to five thousand, nice and easy."

We watch the feed as the drone swings its nose a little further to the north and descends toward the unidentified installation. I can make out more and more detail with every minute, but I still don't know what I'm looking at, and Sergeant Fallon doesn't have any idea, either.

"Computer says it's fifty meters square and ten meters tall," Philbrick says. "Nothing on infrared or UV."

"Looks abandoned," Sergeant Fallon says. "The sides have green spots on them. Like there's vegetation growing around it."

"Why would you use that much concrete for a building at the ass end of space and then abandon it? That makes no sense." I have to think of Lieutenant Dorian's suggestion that maybe everyone on this colony dropped dead somehow. They couldn't have gotten a Lanky visit, because then the whole place would be crawling with the bastards, and the atmosphere would be much heavier on the carbon dioxide. If some calamity befell this secret colony, the Lankies had nothing to do with it.

"Holy shit, it's a terraformer," Private Rogers says. "Sorry, sir," she immediately adds.

"What makes you say that, Private?" I ask.

"Look right there." She uses her light pen to mark the display in front of her and then sends the annotated image through TacLink. "There are exhaust vents. Four on each side. You just can't see them all that well because they covered the openings up. But you can see where the vent louvers are." She points to the features she described.

"I can't really make that shit out," Sergeant Fallon says.

"Me neither," I concede. "Private, drop her another thousand feet and do a slow loop around the place."

"Yes, sir." The drone's video feed shakes a little as the drone reorients itself, but the targeting crosshair of the camera array stays dead center on the roof of the unidentified installation.

"I think she's right," Philbrick says after a little while. "Those are exhaust vents. Way too big for environmental stuff. And there used to be a power conduit running right here. They took it down, but you can still see the service road. It's a terraforming unit with a feed link for the fusion plant."

"It's tiny," I say. "I've never seen a terraformer that small. The Class III units are the smallest I know, and that down there is half the size of those."

But as the drone drops into an even lower orbit around the facility, I can see that Private Rogers must be correct. The building is clearly a fusion reactor with atmospheric terraforming vents. It has all the components of a terraformer, only at reduced size.

"Why'd they switch it off?" I wonder.

"What do you do with those when you're done terraforming?" Sergeant Fallon asks.

"You turn the unit to maintenance mode and keep it around as a fusion reactor for nearby settlements," Gunny Philbrick says.

"And if you don't need the fusion power?"

"You mothball it so you don't have to staff it."

Sergeant Fallon looks at me and shrugs with a smirk.

"Okay, fine. It's a terraformer," I concede. "And it's deactivated. Mystery solved."

There's a red blip on the tactical display, and I turn my attention back to the screen.

"We have something else," Private Rogers announces. "Drone 34 has some big-time infrared source up ahead."

I change the screen to the sensor feed from drone 34, which is tooling along at fifteen thousand feet to our northwest. There's cloud cover between the drone's cameras and whatever it has spotted, but the infrared sensors in the nose show big, regular patches of thermal energy on the ground, eighty or ninety kilometers ahead of the drone.

"Now that doesn't look abandoned," Gunny Philbrick says.

"Get unit 34 below the cloud ceiling so we can get visual," I say. "And see if we can get a little closer."

"We let the leash out too far, we may lose the unit on the way back."

"Do it, Gunny. We can spare a drone. But I want to get eyes on that."

"Copy that. Get her in closer, Rogers. Just until you're through the clouds."

It's a foregone conclusion that the drone has found a settlement or other big installation on the moon. The infrared emissions aren't scattered and blotchy, but large and regular, big buildings powered by a lot of energy. But without getting eyes on target, we can't guess what we have out there just by infrared emissions alone. Thankfully, it doesn't take the drone very long to descend ten thousand feet and break through the cloud cover.

"Visual contact from unit 34," Private Rogers says, a little bit of excitement creeping into her voice. "Multiple buildings. Dozens."

"We have found us a settlement," Gunny Philbrick says.

———

The settlement is a lot more obvious than the lone, deactivated terraformer the other drone spotted. We see a tight cluster of colonial architecture, a little town of one-level structures with a few taller buildings here and there. At the edge of the settlement, maybe half a kilometer away from the main cluster, a terraforming unit similar to the one we discovered stands on a little hilltop, and much of the infrared radiation the drone detected is coming from the fusion plant part of the terraformer and the atmospheric vents lining the sides of the unit.

"Drop her another two thousand and make a little loop to starboard," Philbrick instructs Private Rogers. "Let's get some beauty shots from all angles."

The tactical computer diligently updates the map with the information fed to us by little drone 34, turning a racetrack pattern in the sky over a hundred kilometers to our west. The settlement is two hundred and fifty kilometers away, in a wide plain with rolling hills. There's a river just a few hundred meters outside the settlement, making a loop around it and forming sort of a natural moat on three sides. On the other side of the river and opposite from the hill with the terraformer, there's a separate cluster of large buildings, and a long runway that stretches out behind them.

"O-hooo," Philbrick croons when the drone's camera pans over the area around the runway. "Look at that. Hangars. And Shrikes parked in front of them."

An icy trickle runs down my spine when I see the unmistakable shapes of the NAC's lethal ground-attack craft lined up on the tarmac between runway and what I'm guessing to be a pair of hangars. We have one drop ship and a platoon of troops, and one single Shrike could turn us all into finely shredded hamburger if we found ourselves on the receiving end of its weapons. And there are four of them sitting on the tarmac, with God knows how many more stashed away in the hangars behind them.

"They must have offloaded the attack birds from the carrier for ground use when they got here," I say. "That's bad fucking news."

"Only if they get wind of us," Gunny Philbrick replies. "So let's keep a low profile."

Next to me, Sergeant Fallon chuckles.

"I don't think we're here to keep a low profile, Gunny."

The drones return to Deployment Point Alpha an hour later, whirring back into the clearing and setting down on the grass one by one with computerized precision. The last one to return is drone 34, which puts down with Private Rogers's display showing two percent of power left in its battery pack. Philbrick's squad collects the miniature aerial flotilla, dismounts the propulsion units, and plugs the drones back into their case for recharging and automatic servicing.

"Those just saved us a week of foot patrols," Sergeant Fallon remarks. "Handy little things."

"Yeah, we use 'em on Lanky worlds where we can't get regular aerial recon," Philbrick says.

With the drones back in the barn, we have a full tactical picture of the situation on the ground in a three-hundred-kilometer circle around Deployment Point Alpha. With the other three platoons at their own deployment points sending out their own drones, our little recon company will have scouted several thousand square kilometers of ground in just a few hours, without any of our squads ever moving more than a few hundred meters from the drop ships. If we stay out of sight of those Shrikes and don't draw any undue attention in this place, we will have mapped the entire moon in detail within a week. I send the data from our TacLink out to the other platoons via data link, which takes less bandwidth and transmitting power than voice comms.

>*ENEMY INSTALLATION LOCATED AT PLANETARY GRID DELTA-28. SETTLEMENT, EIGHTY-PLUS BLDGS, AIRFIELD, FOUR PLUS GROUND ATTACK CRAFT-TYPE SHRIKE. RECON DATA FOLLOWS. REQUEST INSTRUCTIONS FOR NEXT DEPLOYMENT POINT. ROGUE ONE MSG ENDS.*

The reply from Major Masoud comes not even fifteen minutes later. I bring the message window up to read the content, and immediately sit up straight in my jump seat, jolted wide awake.

>*ACK RCPT OF RECON DATA 5/5. ROGUE ONE PLT IS ORDERED TO PROCEED TO PLANETARY GRID DELTA-28. PLAN AND EXECUTE ASSAULT ON ENEMY AIRFIELD. IMPERATIVE RPT IMPERATIVE PLT DESTROY OR DISABLE ANY GROUND ATTACK CRAFT. ACK RCPT OF ORDER AND PROCEED NO LATER THAN 2200Z. ROGUE CMDR MSG ENDS.*

"Gunny!" I shout. "Sergeant Fallon. To me, double-time."

Both my senior sergeants rush up the ramp and over to where I am staring at the display, reading the message from our company commander a few more times to make sure I didn't misunderstand it.

"What gives?" Gunny Philbrick asks. "Incoming visitors?"

I rotate the display so Philbrick and Sergeant Fallon can see the text on the screen. Philbrick does a little double take. Sergeant Fallon just folds her arms across her chest and smiles the tiniest bit.

"Well," Philbrick says. "I guess this isn't strictly a recon mission anymore, is it?"

He turns to Sergeant Fallon and shakes his head.

"Are you some sort of damn psychic, Master Sergeant?"

"Negative," she says. "I just have a really good bullshit radar."

CHAPTER 23

—— SUCKER PUNCH ——

Ten minutes to target.

I don't know how Sergeant Fallon can stand in the cargo hold while we are doing a nap-of-the-earth run over rolling hill terrain at full throttle, but it seems to be a particularly developed skill of hers. She's hanging on by a single hand strap, swaying along with the jolts and bounces of the Blackfly, and drilling the platoon on the details of our speedily concocted battle plan for the second time while I can barely manage to keep my lunch in the command console jump seat.

"First Squad—ingress on foot along the riverbed from Drop Zone One. You are setting up a blocking position by the bridge and greasing anyone and anything that tries to make it across to reinforce the airfield. If needed, you will play backup to Second Squad. Second Squad—you are with me. We are going in from Drop Zone Two along the unfinished fence perimeter and past the refuelers. Once we are in, we set demolition charges on anything in there with wings on it. Egress via the slope on the south side of the field and to the bridge, where we meet up with First Squad. Third Squad—you are moving west half a klick from Drop Zone Three and providing long-range fire support from the hill overlooking the runway and east end of the apron. Anything tries to take off, you shoot it down."

I check the video feed from the Blackfly's nose array and immediately wish I hadn't. We are barreling across Arcadia's landscape in the darkness that descended on this hemisphere an hour ago, and we're so close to the ground that I swear I can count individual blades of grass. The pilot is flying the bird with the terrain-following radar disabled because we don't want to give our approach away with emissions, so he's flying the seventy-ton ship by hand, just using night vision and raw skill on the stick. I used to think Halley was by far the best drop ship jock in the Fleet, but it turns out I just didn't have enough exposure to her SOCOM colleagues yet, because this kid is just about as good as she is.

"The drop ship will circle around and stand by in case things go to shit. We don't want to burn the fuel or use the ammo unless we absolutely have to, and we don't want to risk having to walk all the way home."

Some of the troops laugh nervously. The junior enlisted look particularly anxious—I know that the senior NCOs are just as tense, but they've learned to mask their fear. I don't sense any fear on Sergeant Fallon, masked or otherwise, and I don't think I ever have, not even when we were hobbling down the street together in Detroit almost eight years ago, gunfire coming in from all directions.

"Loadouts," Sergeant Fallon continues the litany. "First Squad—rifles and MARS rockets. Two launchers per fire team and at least four rockets each. Rifle grenades, as many as you can carry. Don't start bitching about the weight—you'll be happy for it if they start rolling armor. Second Squad—rifles and demo packs. Two packs per head. We want to be able to blow up everything essential twice. Third Squad—two AMRs and two MARS launchers per fire team. If one of you sons of bitches gets killed for lack of shooting back because you ran out of ammo, I will personally violate your carcass. Understood?"

"Yes, Master Sergeant," the enlisted grunts shout back. I grin behind the shield of my visor. Nobody does motivational premission pep talks better than Sergeant Fallon. I have come to believe that everyone alive has one talent, something they were born to do, and which they can do better than most other people. For Halley, it's flying a drop ship. For Sergeant Fallon, it's leading small groups of young men and women into the teeth of the dragon.

"This will be a sucker punch," she continues. "They have no idea we are coming. They're loafing around, watching some canned network shit, stuffing their faces at chow, or jerking off in the head. They have no idea about the world of shit that is going to rain down on them. They are garrison troops. They were not picked for this job because they're good at what they do. They were picked because they can follow orders and keep their mouths shut. We are not garrison troops. We are in the business of killing people and breaking their shit. So let's get ready for business."

We got the attack order only three hours ago, so we didn't have much time to come up with a battle plan for the assault, but improvisation is the name of the game for SI most of the time, so the platoon rolled with the punches. I don't know what caused the major to shift the focus of our mission from recon to commando raid, but I know that he wouldn't have shared his motivation even if I had asked. I can only trust that the other platoons are involved with something that requires the neutralization of that air power, even if it means blowing up Shrikes that would have been assets in the upcoming Mars battle.

"Three minutes to Drop Zone One," Lieutenant Dorian says from the flight deck. He sounds tense and focused. I check the tactical display again and watch as the little arrowhead icon representing Blackfly One creeps across the topographic map inexorably toward the red rectangle in map grid D28.

"First Squad, get ready," Gunny Philbrick shouts. "Tail ramp goes down, you grab your gear and hustle. I don't want to see those skids on the ground for longer than a second."

I've not been in real battle for over a year. The raid on the relay station was a brief battle for one of my squads, but I sat it out in this jump seat in front of a console while my troops did the fighting. This time, I'll be out there with them, holding a rifle and sticking my head into the line of fire again. It's the scariest thing in the world, but Halley was right—it's also the most exhilarating, and I did miss the intensity of it all, that sustained push of adrenaline that makes you feel vividly and intensely alive.

The pilot pulls up the nose sharply, banks to starboard, and almost reverses course for a few seconds before swinging the ship back to its original heading. The tail ramp starts coming down before we are at zero airspeed, and by the time we are hovering a meter or two above the ground, the ramp locks in the horizontal position.

"First Squad, move, move, move!"

The troopers of First Squad file out of the ship at a fast shuffle, every trooper carrying personal gear and probably fifty pounds in extra weaponry or ammo. They leap off the edge of the tail ramp one by one and disappear in the darkness beyond.

"Kick some ass," I send Philbrick over private comms. The tall gunnery sergeant gives me a thumbs-up without turning around or taking his hand off his gun. Then he's gone, out in the darkness with his troops.

"First Squad delivered," the crew chief sends to the flight deck. The Blackfly launches itself upward and forward again.

"Second Squad, get ready," Sergeant Fallon calls out. She checks the loading status of her rifle and the locking hood on her sidearm's holster. Then she looks over to where I am sitting, and we exchange a glance. For just a moment, I have a powerful premonition of my old squad leader dead on a rubble-strewn tarmac, fléchette holes in her battle armor, dark blood pooling underneath her. I look back at my console and shake my head to clear the entirely unwelcome vision. I shouldn't be here, sitting in this chair, pulling the strings that may lead her—and everyone else—to that fate. But I am, because somebody has to, and they follow me willingly, because I asked them to.

The drop ship changes directions as it follows the river that snakes past the settlement—right, left, then right again. Then we are over Drop Zone Two, coming to a hover once more.

"Second Squad, go," Sergeant Fallon orders. They file out of the ship and off the edge of the ramp. Six seconds later, the second row of seats in the Blackfly's cargo hold is empty as well. Sergeant Fallon follows her troops out into the night, and she doesn't look back or give a thumbs-up.

"Second Squad delivered," the crew chief calls out. The Blackfly roars upward and pitches forward to pick up speed again.

"One minute to Drop Zone Three," Lieutenant Dorian sends.

"Third Squad, get ready." Sergeant Welch gets out of his seat and grabs one of the overhead handholds. The troopers of Third Squad check their weapons one last time, even though I know their loading status has been checked several times already since we left the deployment point almost an hour ago.

The Blackfly descends again and touches down on the ground almost gingerly. I hit the quick-release button on my seat's harness, grab my rifle from its storage bracket next to the seat, and stand up to join Sergeant Welch and his troopers.

"Good luck," the crew chief says behind me. I give him a thumbs-up. In front of me, Third Squad is rushing down the ramp, with Sergeant Welch bringing up the rear. I take a quick look around the hold, nod at the crew chief, and run down the ramp to join the rest of my platoon.

The night outside isn't as pitch-dark as it had looked from inside the cargo hold. The moon's parent planet, Leonidas c, is coming up on the eastern horizon. Just the top of the planetary orb is peeking over the far-off mountain ridges, and the planet's iridescent blue glow gives the nighttime landscape on this moon an eerie, otherworldly quality.

Drop Zone Three is a depression behind a low hill that sits three hundred meters from the river that passes by the colony settlement, and close to five hundred meters from the runway of the airfield. Third Squad scales the hill and splits up into fire teams, four and four. Two troopers in each team have MARS launchers in addition to their regular rifles, which they lay out on the ground next to them, along with the rocket cartridges they brought for the launchers. The other two in each team have AMRs, which are large precision rifles for long-range fire support.

I crawl up to the crest of the little hill and switch my helmet optics to night vision and maximum magnification. The settlement is a typical colony town, prefabricated buildings lined up in a regular pattern along two main roads that meet in the middle of the town. The installation next to the town is very clearly a military airfield. There's a three-thousand-foot runway, two hangar buildings with large sliding doors, and a main building with a small control tower at the top. Parked on the apron outside the hangars are the four Shrikes we saw on the drone footage. They don't have ordnance on their pylons, and their engines and gun muzzles are capped with red maintenance covers. I check the range from the hilltop to the nearest Shrike with my rangefinder: 477m.

"Look at that fence they're putting up," Sergeant Welch says. He points out the unfinished fence line we spotted with the recon drone. There's a partial fence structure running in front of the airfield's cluster of buildings, support posts that are thirty meters tall.

Some supports have heavy-duty steel mesh fencing strung between them, but most don't, and we can see construction supplies stacked up nearby.

"What are they looking to keep out with that?" one of the troopers asks, and Sergeant Welch snorts.

"Let's think about this for a second, Benavides. What's about that tall and likes to wreck colony towns?"

"Benavides's mom," someone else contributes in a low voice, and there's muffled laughter on the squad channel.

"Cut the chitchat," Sergeant Welch says. "Check your fields of fire and dial in that main building over there. Benavides, park yourself fifteen meters further left so you can get better dope on First Squad once they set up shop by the bridge. And nobody touches a trigger until I say so."

"Copy that, Sarge." Benavides grabs his gear and sets up in the spot indicated by his squad leader.

"I can't believe what sort of shit security they're running down there," Sergeant Welch says. "Bunch of mess cooks with butter knives could walk in there and fuck shit up."

"I don't think they're expecting people," I say.

Below us, the two other squads are moving into position. First Squad is making its way along the river and up the incline toward the spot where the flat steel bridge connects the settlement promontory with the military airfield. Second Squad and Sergeant Fallon are almost at the unfinished fence line that borders the airfield perimeter.

"Watch for perimeter surveillance," I warn the squad leaders and Sergeant Fallon. They send back their acknowledgments silently.

Philbrick's First Squad reach their position first. They cross the bridge swiftly and quietly, then take up covering positions on the far end, facing both town and airfield with their two fire teams. Two of Philbrick's troopers return to the bridge a few minutes later and rig something up in the center of the steel structure. I check their video feeds to see that they're preparing demolition charges, flattening out two strips of plastic explosives and weaving them through the weight-saving holes in the steel of the bridge surface. When the charges are prepped, the two troopers rush back to their fighting positions, a hundred meters away.

"Vehicle patrol coming in from the west," one of the Third Squad troopers warns. Instantly, a red icon pops up on our TacNet screens, a fast-moving lozenge shape coming down the airfield on the runway side. I look over in that direction and see the familiar shape of an MAV, a multipurpose assault vehicle. It's an electric all-terrain runner that seats four troops, with big knobby tires designed for unpaved ground, and a remote-controlled autocannon mounted in a modular weapon station on the roof. They have their headlights turned off, which means they're using their night-vision gear to find their way around.

"Bogey is running augmented," I caution. "Everyone keep your head down."

My long-range riflemen are tracking the MAV with their guns as it comes down the airfield next to the runway and then turns toward the town, where First Squad have set up their blocking position near the bridge. If he crosses over, he may notice the demolition charges if he's very alert or we are very unlucky. Sergeant Fallon and Second Squad take cover among the stacked-up construction gear by the fence site. My heart is pounding as the MAV turns toward them and cuts across the apron between runway and hangars, pausing briefly at the spot where the Shrikes are parked. Then it starts rolling again, and the driver makes a left and passes to the right of the main building, which puts the bulk of the structure between him and Second Squad. The MAV rolls across the unfinished fence line and down the hill toward the river, seemingly in no particular hurry or alarm.

"Let him pass. They're just out for a nighttime cruise," I say.

"Copy that," Philbrick answers. "Holding fire."

Between our three squads, we are tracking the MAV with enough firepower to reduce it to shrapnel in just a few seconds, but that would alert the entire installation and scuttle our plan. On the other hand, the autocannon on that MAV can chew up a squad just as quickly if we are spotted, so I am tracking the MAV's progress and the direction of its roof-mounted gun very carefully. The MAV rolls down the slope toward the river, then makes a left turn and accelerates along the bank of the slow-moving stream. Then they're around the bend of the hill and moving off toward the back of the airfield again, and I let out a long breath.

"First and Second Squads, proceed," I send. "Bogey is moving off to the west again and has lost line of sight."

Second Squad emerges from the cover of the construction stacks and moves around the corner of the nearby main building. I zoom in on the control tower, which has large, tinted polyplast windows.

"AMR gunners, check the tower for me," I say. "Go infrared."

"It's clear," one of them replies. "Nobody in there."

"We're in," Sergeant Fallon sends. "Starting to deliver the goodies. Cover our asses for about five."

"Copy that."

The troopers of Second Squad set up a small overwatch perimeter in whatever cover they have available on the airfield apron. Then some of them move in and start setting charges on the parked Shrikes. Each of those costs tens of millions of dollars, and I wince inwardly at the thought of how many mouths we could have fed back home in the PRCs with the money for the war machines we're about to blow sky-high.

"Got a minor problem," Sergeant Fallon says to me.

"What is it?"

Instead of replying, she sends me the feed from her helmet camera. She's at the door to one of the hangars, which is opened maybe two meters wide. The hangar isn't lit inside, so the image from her camera has the emerald tint of low-light magnification. Parked in the hangar are more Shrikes, standing wingtip to wingtip in two rows that face each other.

"Eight more. If the other hangar has as many, we didn't bring enough boom."

I think for a moment, adding up in my head the explosives they took along.

"Blow up the outside ones with full charges. Split the charges for the rest and go for mission kills. Landing gears, engine intakes, weapons mounts. See how many spare parts they brought for those birds."

"Copy that," she replies.

The squad spends the next few minutes sticking remote-detonated explosive charges to the Shrikes in the hangars. No lights come on in the tower upstairs. We hear noises coming from the settlement a quarter kilometer away, the regular nighttime sounds of an active town, but the base itself is quiet as a tomb, which is fine in my book. For just a few minutes, I find myself embracing the possibility that we may actually pull this off without any bloodshed tonight. Once the birds are spiked, Second Squad will withdraw and join up with First Squad, and then we will blow the charges and egress to the pickup point.

On the edge of my zoomed-in tactical map of the airfield, a little red caret comes rushing down the side of the map again, and I mutter a curse.

"MAV's coming back," someone from Third Squad cautions. "He's hauling ass right down the center of the runway."

I train my optics onto the runway. The MAV is barreling down its length at top speed, still without headlights. The cannon on the vehicle is still in its travel position on the centerline, as far as I can tell.

"The fuck are they doing?" Sergeant Welch says.

"Incoming from the runway," I warn Second Squad, even though they undoubtedly already see the information on their TacLink screens.

The MAV shoots all the way to the end of the runway, then whips around in a tight turn, rear wheels squelching, and comes to a stop. Then the headlights of the vehicle come on, and the MAV starts rolling again at a more sedate speed.

"They're fucking joyriding," Sergeant Welch says. "Doing donuts on the runway."

The breath of relief that escapes my mouth isn't halfway out when the nose of the MAV swings toward the hangars, and the vehicle slowly rolls toward where Sergeant Fallon and Second Squad are hunkered down.

"First Squad, things are about to go rodeo," I send to Gunny Philbrick.

The MAV stops in the middle of the airfield apron, fifty meters from the hangar doors. All around me, the troopers of Third Squad are drawing a bead on the stationary vehicle almost five hundred meters away.

"He comes any closer or turns that gun, we're lighting him up," Sergeant Fallon warns in a low voice.

The MAV starts rolling forward, then stops again abruptly. A searchlight pierces the darkness and stabs into the space between the hangar doors. Then the MAV starts backing up, the electric drive whining with a high-pitched sound. The gun turret on the roof of the MAV releases the autocannon from its travel lock, and it swivels left, then right.

"Shit," Sergeant Welch mutters.

My hope of remaining undetected evaporates in the muzzle flashes of half a dozen rifles from Second Squad as they open fire at close range. The lightly armored windshield of the MAV is peppered with hundreds of fléchettes. The MAV backs away from the incoming fire at top speed now. The cannon on its roof raps out a five-round burst, the reports from the heavy gun reverberating across the airfield and bouncing back and forth between the buildings until it sounds like a platoon of vehicles just opened fire. Some of the grenades go wide and strike the front of the hangar roof in bright little explosions. Two more go through the open door of the hangar and explode inside. A second or two later, the base's alarm klaxon starts blaring, the harsh sound carrying cleanly all the way to the hill where I am observing with Third Squad.

"Third Squad, weapons free," I bellow.

Four AMR rifles fire almost simultaneously, sending laser-guided, armor-piercing rounds into the side of the MAV, which comes to a shuddering halt just as it reaches the runway again. Then it lurches forward. The cannon mount hammers out another salvo, which tears into a corner of the main building and sends concrete shards flying in big clouds of dust.

To my right, I hear the distinctive pop-whoosh of a MARS launcher. I look over just in time to see the rocket streak downrange. It covers the almost five hundred meters to its target in a little less than two seconds. The MAV disintegrates in a huge fireball, spewing fragments everywhere. The gun mount tears loose from the exploding vehicle and tumbles through the air, the long barrel flipping end over end. It clatters onto the airfield apron in front of the Shrikes.

"Second Squad, clear out and blow those charges," I shout into my helmet mike. "Fall back to First Squad's position."

There's a new swell of rifle fire, but it doesn't seem to come from the guns of Second Squad. On the tactical display, I see red icons designating enemy personnel popping up near the main building, on the side we can't observe from our hilltop.

"Taking fire from the building," Sergeant Fallon says. "Boy, we stirred the shit now."

For the next few minutes, all I can do is track the progress of the firefight on my TacLink screen because most of it is taking place in the line-of-sight shadow of the base's main control building. Both sides are using the same weaponry, so I can't even tell by the report who is firing at whom. Then there's movement on top of the control building as a hatch opens, and armed troopers spill out and onto the flat surface of the roof.

"They're trying to get at you from above," I warn. "Four, five, six on the roof, heading your way."

"Well, get 'em off of there," Sergeant Fallon replies with a distinctly annoyed timbre.

"AMRs, pick them off," I order.

The four precision rifles boom again, one after the other, and every time one of them barks its sharp and authoritative report, a trooper on the rooftop falls. After the second of their number is down, the rest of them notice they're under fire from behind and go prone to try to spot us for return fire. The AMR riflemen don't need more than a few seconds to draw a bead on the stationary targets, and then there's no movement anymore on the rooftop. We have gone from a quiet egress to appalling bloodshed in just three or four minutes, and the casualty count keeps increasing.

"We have incoming from the town," Gunny Philbrick warns. "Armored vehicles, look like Mules. They are rolling toward the bridge."

"Don't let them cross and get Second Squad in the ass," I say.

Mules are bad news for an infantry squad. They carry their own squads, but they also have reactive armor and sophisticated fire control systems for their autocannons, and they are on the whole much harder to kill than a soft-skinned MAV. Under normal circumstances, I'd call in close air support to eliminate the risk to Philbrick's squad, but these aren't normal circumstances, and I don't want to commit our one ace in the hole unless I absolutely have to.

The Mules are coming down through the main settlement and out onto the perimeter road that circles the town. They're wedge-shaped, brutal-looking things, with six wheels and a remote weapon station on top that's bigger than the one on the MAV. Only these weapon stations aren't configured with the usual all-purpose long-barreled 35mm autocannon. They are fitted with box launchers for heavy antiarmor missiles—a lot of destructive power, but not particularly useful against entrenched infantry.

"Hold your fire until they are on the bridge," Gunny Philbrick cautions.

The Mule pilots are picking speed over caution. They roll down the road at a good clip, their big knobby tires spitting gravel and dirt. There's just a little more than three vehicle lengths between the two Mules when the first one reaches the bridge and rolls onto it without slowing down. The second Mule stops at the far end to let the lead vehicle cross first.

"Blow it," Gunny Philbrick shouts.

There's a dull, ugly crack coming from the bridge. The structure collapses without much flash or drama. It merely folds in half when the first Mule is almost all the way across, and the armored vehicle tilts backward with the collapsing bridge. It slides down the steep bank rapidly and splashes into the river ass end first. Then it flops over backward and disappears underwater. The wheels slip below the surface of the river, leaving foamy swirls behind. The driver of the second Mule throws it into reverse and backs away from the destroyed bridge. Up at First Squad's position, I hear the muffled reports from two more MARS launchers, and two rockets scream out from their launch tubes and smash into the front and side of the Mule. The exploding warheads savagely rock the vehicle. It keeps reversing, two of its wheels on the right side blown out and on fire, smoke billowing from the underside of the Mule. The weapons mount swivels as the gunner is looking for a target, but there's nothing for him to shoot at with heavy AT rockets.

The Mule makes it a hundred meters in reverse before Philbrick's MARS gunners have reloaded their launchers. Two more missiles fly out to meet the smoking Mule. One goes wide and shoots out into the darkness. The other hits the tiny armored windshield dead center with a bright flash, and the Mule rolls to a slow stop. Black smoke starts pouring out of the destroyed windshield. There's movement on the back of the Mule, as if someone is trying to lower the troop hatch, but the movement ceases when two loud, sharp, bright jets of flame shoot out of the windshield and tail hatch at the same time, like a gigantic blowtorch.

"Kill," Philbrick says. "Two down."

It takes me a few seconds to be able to tear my eyes away from the ghastly spectacle. The Mule's fuel or ammo or both are burning up in the vehicle and adding copious amounts of fuel to the fire started by the MARS's dual-purpose antiarmor warhead. At a minimum, we just killed a three-man crew. If the troop hold was full, fifteen troopers are now burning up inside the destroyed Mule. Traitors or not, that's a shitty way to go, and I have no desire to check on the contents of that troop compartment.

The firefight around the main base building and the runway apron is still in full swing. Fléchette rifles are rattling in rapid-burst fire, punctuated by the dull crack of exploding rifle grenades or tungsten shotshells. I can read the flow of the fight from the picture painted by the TacLink screen—Second Squad in a defensive position at the corner of the hangar building, shooting around corners and through the open hangar door.

"Clear out of there and blow the charges," I tell Sergeant Fallon. "Then link up with First Squad at the bridge."

Sergeant Fallon clicks her acknowledgment without bothering to use voice comms. Twenty seconds later, a drumroll of explosions drowns out the rifle fire, which slacks off instantly. The four Shrikes on the apron disappear in clouds of dust and fragments. When the dust clears, all four are on the ground, undercarriages blown away, smoke pouring from the engine air intakes, service covers blown off and scattered on the ground. Shrikes are heavily armored and extremely resilient, and even a well-placed charge won't destroy one outright, but these birds will need factory rebuilds before they can take to the skies again. Inside the hangar, a fire alarm bell is playing its harsh one-note alarm, and a mix of smoke and fire-retardant vapor is coming out of the crack between the open double doors.

"Blackfly One, prepare to dust off and head for the pickup point," I send to Lieutenant Dorian.

"Give the word, and I'll be there in two mikes," our drop ship pilot replies.

From the far end of the runway, I hear the ominous sound of powerful dual-purpose aviation engines. I zoom in on the area on maximum magnification, but the source of the noise is partially obscured by the bulk of the second hangar and the refueling station in the foreground.

"Someone get me eyeballs on the west end of the runway," I say.

"I hear it, too," Sergeant Fallon says. "Wilsey, take Ponton and Gilroy and double-time to the corner. Give me a visual."

She marks the corner in question on the TacLink map unambiguously, and Sergeant Wilsey and his two troopers dash over to it to get a clear line of sight to the end of the runway. As soon as they reach it, I toggle to the feed from their helmet cameras. There's a pair of low bunkers at the far end of the runway, connected by two short taxiways, and a Shrike is rolling out of one of those bunkers and across the taxiway at a good clip. Even from a thousand meters away, I can see that this Shrike has its hard points loaded with air-to-ground ordnance.

"Shit. They have a Ready Five bird."

"Don't let the motherfucker take off," Philbrick sends. "He'll waste us from above in about three minutes flat."

I've been on the receiving end of Shrike attack runs, and I know Philbrick is overestimating our chances. Even with the thermal camouflage afforded by our armor, the Shrike will spot us and engage, because that's what they're designed to do, and there's nothing we brought with us that will touch a Shrike once it's in the air. There's only one way to keep this from turning into disaster, and that's to keep the attack bird from taking off. But time is running out—the pilot knows his base is under fire, and he is wasting no time rolling his ship onto the runway and swinging the nose around for a takeoff run.

"MARS rockets," I bellow at Third Squad. "Whatever you have in the tubes. Right the fuck now. Blackfly One, we need an intercept now."

The MARS gunners bring their launchers to bear, but I don't have to consult the map to see that it's a very long shot to the end of the runway, which is almost two thousand meters away from our little hilltop. The MARS rockets have a maximum range of just a little over half that, and because they are unguided, the hit probability falls drastically past five hundred meters or so.

"Don't have the range," Corporal Kennedy says. "I'll waste the shot if I try."

"Lead him, and fire when he's halfway down the runway on the takeoff run," Sergeant Welch replies. "And stand by on that reload. You miss, I'll have you scrubbing the shitter with a toothbrush for a week."

Sergeant Welch and I both know that the reload won't come fast enough if the first salvo doesn't do the job, and that nobody in Third Squad will be scrubbing anything ever again if that Shrike gets into the air.

At the end of the runway, the Shrike jock has lined up the nose of his ship with the centerline of the runway. He doesn't stop for a preflight or to get his bearings. He just throttles up, and the Shrike leaps forward and begins picking up speed. The distant whine of the engines turns from a low whine to a shrill howl.

When the Shrike is a third of the distance to the end of the runway, the first of the MARS gunners touches off his rocket. It shoots out of the launcher and across the thousand-plus meters between us and the rapidly accelerating Shrike. The MARS slams into the concrete of the runway a little in front and to the left of the Shrike, which continues its takeoff run undeterred. Next to me, the AMR gunners start shooting as well, emptying the magazines of their rifles in a rapid shot-per-second cadence. The other three launchers open fire simultaneously. One goes above the Shrike and soars off toward the Ready Five bunker at the other end of the runway. Another hits the concrete just in front of the Shrike's nose gear, and the ship lurches and swings to the side, but the pilot steps into his rudder and corrects the way of the nose before the Shrike can run off the asphalt and flip over. The fourth MARS rocket strikes the armored fuselage right between the cockpit and the engines, but the angle of the impact is too steep, and the warhead glances off in a shower of hot fragments.

"Motherfucker," Sergeant Welch shouts. Next to me, the MARS gunners frantically reload their launchers, but I know they'll never get them reloaded fast enough before the Shrike is off the ground. The AMR gunners are still shooting their rifles at the ship, hoping for a lucky hit. I aim at the Shrike with my rifle and add my fléchette fire to the barrage because it's all I can do, even though the ship is at the outer range of my rifle's effective range and armored like a Mule besides. On the runway, the nose of the Shrike lifts off the ground as the pilot starts his takeoff rotation.

Above and behind us, I hear the unmistakable deep, rolling thunder of large-caliber automatic cannons. I don't even hear the Blackfly until the drop ship is almost overhead, its engines barely above a whispering rumble even at full throttle. A stream of tracers races out like laser beams from the old space war shows on the Networks. It peppers the Shrike's fuselage and churns up concrete dust on the runway surface below. The attack ship lifts off the ground a few meters, now at two hundred knots or more, and yaws to the right. One cannon shell clips off half a meter of wingtip on the Shrike's port wing. Two or three strike the nose and the cockpit area. Another blows off the front landing gear, which disintegrates and spews its parts wildly all over the runway below. The Blackfly pulls out of the attack run with a graceful turn to the right, away from the Shrike. The polychromatic armor reflects the night sky behind and above the ship, and it disappears into the darkness again like a ghost, its engines all but inaudible from a kilometer away.

The Shrike pilot makes a valiant effort to save his ship, but he's too low and too fast to straighten out the Shrike's lopsided attitude. The right wingtip strikes the ground and throws up a puff of dirt and gravel. Then the attack ship careens tail over nose and cartwheels along the right side of the runway, engines still screaming at full throttle. I wait for an ejection capsule to arc into the sky and deploy a triple-canopy chute, but none appears. Then something on the Shrike explodes and triggers a chain reaction—fuel, ammo, probably both—and the whole thing blows up in a giant, cataclysmic orange fireball. The thunderous explosion is so loud that it drowns out every other sound on the battlefield. It rolls over the hillside and across the town like the throat-clearing of a pissed-off god. A few seconds later, I can feel the heat from the fireball on the exposed skin of my face even from almost a kilometer away.

"Splash one," Lieutenant Dorian sends, matter-of-factly. There's no triumph in his voice.

An eerie silence settles over the battlefield when the echoes of the explosion have died down. We still hear the commotion from the settlement, but the rifle fire has ceased. The Shrike is a burning wreck in a fiery patch of ground a good fifty meters across, bright orange flames and billowing black smoke. Somewhere in that small inferno, a pilot is being reduced to ashes and charred bones.

"Second Squad, regroup and join up with First. Exfil to the pickup point. Let's get out of this place before they send in reinforcements." *If they have any*, I think. We just crippled a wing of Shrikes and killed the better part of a garrison platoon.

"Second Squad has casualties," Sergeant Fallon sends back. "We'll be a little slower on the exfil."

I check the platoon biometrics with dread. One of the troopers has weak vital signs, Private Best. Another trooper has no vital signs at all.

"Private Gilroy is KIA," Sergeant Fallon reports. "Took a cannon round to the armor from that fucking MAV."

"Copy that," I say. "Leave his kit and haul him out."

Sergeant Fallon clicks back her acknowledgment.

"Time to leave, people. Blackfly One, expedite to pickup zone."

"On the way," Lieutenant Dorian replies. "ETA three minutes."

I've been around death many times in the military. I've lost people close to me, and came close to my own violent demise more than once. But I've never had a KIA in my unit who died doing what I ordered him to do. I know that I didn't kill him personally because I didn't pull the trigger on the gun that ended his life, but that knowledge doesn't let me feel a great deal of absolution. I told him to be in that spot with the rest of the squad, and now he's dead.

We watch over First and Second Squads as they join up and make their way down the steep riverbanks to reach the exile point where the drop ship will land in a few minutes. By all standards, we have dealt the local garrison a major ass-kicking. They lost at least two dozen troops and three armored vehicles. We disabled or destroyed all their offensive airpower because we caught them mostly unprepared, and we were ruthless about inflicting damage. It was a sucker punch, just as Sergeant Fallon predicted. But as I look over the carnage we are leaving behind as my two squads retreat from the airfield, I can't shake the feeling that we are the bad guys for a change.

CHAPTER 24

KICKING OVER THE HORNET'S NEST

Arcadia is easily the most beautiful of all the colony moons and planets I've seen in my entire career. It has an abundance of fresh water, rivers and streams and about a thousand lakes. Two mountain ranges crisscross the only continent on the moon, which takes up maybe a third of the planetary surface. The rest is ocean, dotted with many large and small islands. It's a pretty big place, but you can see a lot of it when you are on the run and trying to hide from aerial patrols.

"Bogey at eleven o'clock high," Lieutenant Dorian sends. It's his fourth contact report in two hours, and I no longer feel crippling dread when he calls out a Shrike in our aerial neighborhood. "Fifty klicks out, reciprocal heading. I'm going to drop down another five hundred and hide us in the ground clutter."

I check the outside view, which doesn't look like we have another five hundred feet to drop. The Blackfly is flying up a narrow valley in one of Arcadia's main mountain ridges. They're not the Himalayas, but the peaks of these mountains are three thousand feet above sea level, and right now I have to look up to see those peaks. Since our raid on the airfield two days ago, we've had to relocate the drop ship four times already to avoid direct overflights by Shrikes. They don't have active radar running, but Lieutenant Dorian is familiar with their passive surveillance gear, and he isn't keen on the idea of letting one closer than ten kilometers, polychromatic armor or not.

"I'm going to go out on a limb here and say they know we are around now," Sergeant Fallon says dryly from her jump seat to my left.

"Now, see, that's pure speculation," Gunny Philbrick replies. "Those explosions could have been equipment malfunctions."

With the carnage of that raid two days behind us, the collective shell shock most of us suffered is slowly wearing off. For a bunch of garrison troops caught unprepared, the renegade troops we faced managed to get into action fast and cause us some hurt in exchange for the sound beating they received. There's a sealed green body bag tied to the deck of the drop ship's cargo hold between me and the crew chief. Judging by what I saw of his body when Second Squad brought him back from the airfield, Private Gilroy must have been dead before he hit the ground.

The MAV's remote autocannon was only the light 25mm module, not the beastly 35mm they put onto the armored Mules, but that 25mm is the same gun we use at squad level for heavy fire support, and individual armor is no match for it. Gilroy took a single shell to his chest armor, slightly below and to the left of his sternum, and turned everything from his collarbone to his waistline into bloody mush. It was most likely a lucky hit—or supremely unlucky, from Gilroy's perspective—but he's just as dead as if it had been a deliberately aimed shot by a skilled gunner instead of a spray-fired round triggered by a panicking garrison trooper under fire.

"We need a data link to Company," I tell our pilot. "Let's pick the next place somewhere up high."

"Copy that," Lieutenant Dorian says. "We'll see them coming from further away."

"What's the status on the go juice?"

"Not horrible. Yet. Aux tanks one and four are almost dry. Then we'll be down to aux two and three, and the internal. But trucking around in the weeds burns it up fast."

If we don't keep moving, we greatly increase the chance of a Shrike patrol finding us on the ground. But moving burns up fuel we will miss later when we have to return to *Portsmouth*. I like the safety afforded by mobility under stealth—the polychromatic armor doesn't work when the engines are off and not generating power—but we can't stay on the run and relocate twice a day forever before we run the bird dry and become sitting ducks. At least the ship is lighter than it was when we entered the atmosphere. Not only did we burn through half of the external fuel tanks we brought, but we also used up a fair bit of ammunition and food. The pallet in the hold behind me has fifty boxes of field ration packs on it, a dozen meals per box, and it's already almost halfway gone.

"What about the little plateau near the top of that ridge?" I ask, and mark the area in question on the TacLink map for Lieutenant Dorian.

"Let me check it on optical once I'm through this valley," he replies.

A few minutes later, he sends me his own marked-up shot of the map via TacLink.

"Looks good. Just enough space to land the bird, and we're shielded by that ridge. We can set up OPs on that crest. Anything comes, we should be able to see it from a long way out."

"Let's do it, then."

"Copy that. ETA four minutes," Lieutenant Dorian says.

I relay the news to the platoon, who make relieved noises. The drop ship's mobility and armor means safety, but bumping around at low level in a crowded hold is tiring and unpleasant, and when you are merely a passenger, you have no control over your own fate at all.

We set down on a small, rocky plateau high up near a craggy ridge that runs roughly southwest to northeast. The soil up here is ochre-colored, and so fine that it clings to our boots as we file out of the drop ship's hold and onto the surface. We are sheltered by the nearby ridgeline, which is between us and the location of the airfield we raided. Anyone looking to spot us would have to fly directly overhead or come up the valley behind us.

Outside, the sun is shining. The Leonidas system star looks a lot like our own sun from Earth does. The only thing that makes it very obvious that we aren't on Earth is the large, iridescent blue planet that takes up a quarter of the sky on the opposite horizon. When we are rotated toward it, Leonidas c is visible day and night because it is so close and bright.

The plateau where we landed is roughly two hundred meters long and a hundred wide, and Lieutenant Dorian rolled his Blackfly to the very northern edge, where the ridgelines meet at a sharp point that forms a narrow, craggy canyon that shelters and conceals most of the drop ship's bulk. The platoon sets up the usual perimeter security while I discuss deployment locations with Sergeant Fallon and my squad leaders.

"Gunny, get First Squad up on that ridge and set up an OP," I say to Philbrick and mark the map on TacLink for everyone to see. "Five hundred meters, out there, between that big peak and the little one. Looks like there's a good flat spot up there."

"Be a bit of a climb," Philbrick says and eyes the steep walls of the ridge.

"We need to get a data link to Company, so take the big comms kit and relay back to the ship."

"Copy that. Want to launch the drones from up there, too?"

"No, we'll do that from here. No point having your guys drag up the extra weight. That's a thirty-second flight for the drones."

"Fine by me," Philbrick replies.

"I suggest you send along a few MANPADS," Sergeant Fallon says to me. "If we get bounced by a low-flying bogey, that might buy us the time to get our own bird back in the air."

"Good idea. Gunny, add a pair of Tridents to the list. However many you think you can haul up there."

"Half a dozen if I don't take any MARS tubes. I don't think we have to worry about pursuing armor too much in this landscape." He nods over to the rocky ravine beyond our plateau, which drops forty degrees or more and would be utterly impassable for a Mule or even a lightweight MAV.

"Do it," I say, and he nods.

"Sergeant Wilsey, you take Second Squad down the ravine and over to the other side of it. Go down a klick, see if you can find a good spot right about here." I mark the location on the map for him. "That way you can see anyone who tries to make it up the valley toward us, and spot any aerial traffic to the south. Sergeant Welch, take Third Squad and climb that ridge to the east. Take at least a pair of Tridents. I want you to set up shop on the far side and to the north of our position so you can cover Second Squad's blind spot in that direction. Any comments or questions, let's hear them."

The squad leaders have neither. I dismiss them, and they walk off to gather their fire teams and move out. Sergeant Fallon nods her approval.

"That's as close to all-around coverage you're going to get with three squads. I would have put them into the exact same spots."

"I've been looking at TacLink screens for years now," I reply. "Air defense coverage angles, defensive fire sectors, all that stuff. My brain just sort of does it on autopilot now."

"A second lieutenant with a clue. Never thought I'd live to see the day."

"It's a brave new fucking world," I say, and she grins.

While the three squads are climbing the ridges on either side of our hiding spot with hundreds of pounds of weapons and equipment between them, the crew chief and I set up the recon drones for deployment. When they are all out of their case and have their propulsion packages installed, I check their function over TacLink and program their little onboard computer brains with preset patrol patterns. Then I activate them, and, one by one, they buzz off into the cool mountain air and accelerate away to start their patrols. Almost immediately, the uplinks are feeding me data. I tap into the visual feed of drone 22, which is climbing the ridge right above where Philbrick and First Squad are struggling up the steep incline. They are loaded down with comms gear and several Trident air-defense missile launchers. Then the drone is past the squad and over the nearby ridge, gaining dozens of feet in altitude every second. I drop the window for the visual feed and go back to the TacLink map, where my sensor awareness bubble slowly expands again as the drones are zooming outward and away from the plateau and the drop ship.

Sergeant Fallon comes trotting down the drop ship's ramp with a ration bag in her hand. She walks over to where I am standing, closes the lid of the service case for the drones, and sits down on it. Then she pulls open the ration pack and rifles through the contents.

"Ha. Beef and noodles."

She pulls the main meal pouch out of the bag and pops the little capsule at the corner of the bag that heats up the contents chemically.

"Those boys bitch about the rations, but compared to the shit we have to dole out in the Clusters, this is manna from heaven. Kids these days don't know what real shit food is."

The pouch changes color to indicate that the heating process is finished. Sergeant Fallon pulls the opening tab and takes a plastic spork out of the ration bag. Then she begins shoveling the contents into her mouth.

"Remember the stuff we used to get?" I ask. "Back before the Lankies, when they still fed us all the good chow?"

"Do I ever," she says with a full mouth. "I haven't had a fresh cut of real beef in almost two years. Not even the vat-grown stuff."

"I remember my first meal at Basic. We ate until it started coming out of our ears, and then we ate some more. And then the DIs made us run two miles, and everyone puked."

She chuckles around her mouthful of imitation beef and noodles.

"Those were the good times. I think those are gone forever."

"I'm not sure they were the good times," I say. "Food was better. No Lankies to worry about. But look at the shit they had us do for that good chow."

Sergeant Fallon shrugs and pokes around in the meal bag with her spork.

"I guess you are right. I'm eating the same crap as everyone else in the Clusters, but I sleep better at night."

I walk over to the drop ship and step into the cargo hold to get myself some food as well. One of the boxes on top of our dwindling stack of rations is open, and I rifle through it to check the variety. I pick the least objectionable one—chili with beans—and then go forward through the drop ship's central passage to the cockpit to check on our pilot. The armored cockpit hatch is open, and Lieutenant Dorian is snoring in his pilot seat, helmet on the empty copilot seat next to him. I decide not to bother him and walk back to the cargo hold. To get past the half-finished pallet of rations, I have to step over the sealed green body bag we tied to the floor to prevent it from sliding all over the place. The plastic bag in my hand is the same olive-green shade as the body bag, which makes the meal look disturbingly like a miniature version. I never noticed the similarity until just now.

––––––––––––

"OP Alpha is up and running," Gunny Philbrick reports an hour later. "The relay is live. Tridents are in standby mode."

"Copy that," I send back. OP Alpha is set up on the ridge half a kilometer to our west, two fire teams spaced a hundred meters apart.

Their TacLink updates don't tell me anything the drones didn't already see, but even with autonomous recon drones and all the other whiz-bang technology at our disposal, there's still nothing that can fully substitute for ten sets of trained eyeballs and the experience of a few seasoned NCOs. And each of those fire teams has a Trident antiair missile launcher and two reloads. If a Shrike discovers our hiding spot and makes an attack run, we have a credible defense in place. Trident missiles have a warhead that deploys three laser-guided explosive tungsten darts. The little missiles leave the launcher tube and kick it up to Mach 10, and they have a ten-kilometer range, enough to intercept a Shrike and damage or destroy it before it gets into cannon range.

The drones have reached the outer limit of their patrol range and are on the way back to us. We are seven hundred kilometers to the northeast of the airfield we raided two days ago. The cameras on the drones have spotted two of the strange, small-scale terraforming units to our west and north. One is inactive, but the other one is putting out heat, which means it's in use and generating power. There's no settlement nearby to receive the electricity from the station's fusion plant, but the imagery from the drone cameras shows a cleared site that is under construction, maybe in preparation for putting up another town. Arcadia isn't very large, but it's very empty, like most colonies its size. Fifty or a hundred thousand people don't even begin to fill up a place half the size of Earth.

With the comms relay up on the ridge, I use the drop ship's systems to send out a low-power communications burst in the general direction of the other platoons. We don't have any units in orbit, so we have to rely on whatever comms gear we brought, and all of it has limited range without an orbital relay to distribute the signal.

The first reply comes from Third Platoon, two hours later. It's the first thing I've heard on the Company-level channel since we landed on Arcadia.

"Rogue One, this is Rogue Three Actual, do you copy, over?"

"Rogue Three Actual, this is Rogue One Actual. I hear you three by five. What's your status, over?"

"One Actual, we are on the move. The place just got lousy with Shrike patrols about thirty-six hours ago. We did our initial recon run and are heading to an alternate deployment point."

"Three Actual, send me a TacLink upload so we can see what you're seeing. We may have had something to do with those Shrikes swarming all over the place."

"We figured as much. Stand by for TacLink upload. Let's evaluate and pick up comms again in five."

"Copy that, Three Actual. One Actual out."

The computer updates the TacLink map with the data from the uplink a few moments later. Just like that, our window on this world grows two-thirds in size as the data collected by Third Platoon is added to our own. In a regular combat drop, when the platoons are within a few miles of each other at the most, the TacLink sharing is instant, but this recon mission is anything but regular.

The "known world" recon data on my TacLink map forms a crescent that's several hundred kilometers wide and almost a thousand kilometers long from its northern to southern limits. Third Platoon is four hundred kilometers to our southeast, and there's a swath of spotted terraforming stations and settlements between us and them. The airfield we raided two nights ago is almost five hundred kilometers to our west-southwest. Faint red tracks mark the trajectories of the Shrikes we spotted over the last thirty-six hours, and it's very clear they're covering the continent in an overlapping patrol pattern.

"We destroyed or damaged every last ship at that airfield," Sergeant Fallon says when she looks at the data I'm sharing via our local near-field TacLink. "Wherever those birds are coming from, it ain't that place."

"They have more than one airbase, then," I say. "That Navigator class holds two full wings of Shrikes. They must have unloaded both onto the planet when they got here."

"Plus whatever they stashed here before everything blew up back home."

"That's a cheery thought." The idea of five or six prestaged Shrike wings patrolling this place does not fill me with a great deal of calmness.

The map shows five settlements on Arcadia's only continent, or at least the part of it we've scouted via drop ships and drones so far. They are all arranged in a line that strings from north to south on the western part of the continent. The biggest of the colony towns is the one in the center of that line, with two smaller towns to the north and two to the south, each roughly two hundred kilometers from each other. The airbase we raided two days ago was next to the second northernmost settlement.

"All that space, and they cluster together within a thousand klicks," Sergeant Fallon comments. "Makes no fucking sense."

"Makes a lot of sense," I say. I still feel weird correcting my old squad leader, whose military experience vastly exceeds mine. But she hasn't been out in the Colonies much, and she doesn't really have an idea of why they do what they do out here.

"How so?"

"Supply lines. Easier to share stuff and shuffle personnel if you don't have to go halfway around the moon to deliver it. All the colonies work that way. They set up a central settlement and then expand out from there as the colony grows."

"Three Actual, this is One Actual, do you read?" I send back to Third Platoon, four hundred klicks away and moving across the landscape in their Blackfly at just under the speed of sound.

"One Actual, loud and clear. Looks like you people kicked over the hornet's nest the other night."

"We did what we were told to do. What's the word on Second and Fourth Platoons?" I ask.

"Second Platoon checked in eight hours ago. They took out an ammo depot near one of the settlements. Haven't heard from

Rogue Actual or anyone else from Fourth Platoon since shortly after planetfall."

"Copy that, Three Actual. Keep us in the link once you set up shop at the alternate deployment point."

"Will do. Three Actual out."

I kill the comms link and frown. If I wasn't wearing a helmet, I'd be scratching my head right about now.

"We were flying under the radar perfectly fine," I say to Sergeant Fallon. "We could have scouted the whole continent without pegging their radar once. Why did he have to turn this into a combat mission and make us blow up that airbase? Now they know someone's sneaking around in their backyard. And they're fucking livid."

Sergeant Fallon shrugs. "If I were the betting type," she says, "I'd place good money on the possibility that this didn't turn into a combat mission. I'm pretty sure it was one from the start."

CHAPTER 25

—— FOX AND HOUNDS ——

"Rogue One, this is Rogue Three, come in. Over."

The chirp of an incoming emergency transmission on the command console startles me awake. I try to check my chrono, but my eyes are so blurry that it takes a good five seconds for me to start making out the softly glowing numbers. I've been asleep for two hours, but it feels like I got no rest at all.

"Sarge," I shout as I scramble to my feet. By the time I'm at the command console and reach for my helmet, Sergeant Fallon is already in the cargo bay.

"Rogue Three, this is Rogue One Actual. Go ahead," I say once my helmet is on my head and I've toggled into the company channel.

"One Actual, we have a major problem here. We just had to put the bird down in the weeds with a mechanical problem. Repeat, our ride is down. And we are in a shitty spot."

"Goddammit," I say. "Give me a TacLink update."

"TacLink coming your way. We are presently one-three-zero klicks to your southwest."

The TacLink map updates—much too slowly, for my taste—and I see the icon for Rogue Three pop up on the display. It sits on a plain just a few kilometers from the foot of the low mountain chain where we are currently parked with Rogue One, on the other side of the mountains and over a hundred kilometers north.

"Three Actual, that is a really bad spot. You have no line-of-sight coverage for fifty klicks."

"Tell me about it. The bird is fuel-starved. One engine quit on us at five thousand. We barely made it down before the other one turned off, too."

"You're on the ground with dead engines?" I shoot Sergeant Fallon a panicked look. Without the Blackfly's engines running, the polychromatic armor is switched off, and without its active stealth technology, the drop ship is just a flat black spacecraft the size of a small building.

"Affirmative," Rogue Three Actual replies. "We're a sitting duck."

Outside, the moon is shrouded in the darkness that comes with its lunar nightfall. It's a short night, only six hours, and it's not nearly as dark as an Earth night because the nearby planet is so luminous that it's as bright outside as the brightest full moon on Earth, only in shades of blue instead of silver. And this hemisphere of Arcadia will be back in the sunlight in less than an hour.

"Goddammit," I say again. "Sarge, go and shake Lieutenant Dorian awake. We need to get ready for emergency dustoff."

"Copy that," Sergeant Fallon replies, and disappears into the passageway to the cockpit.

"Can you fix your fuel system in the next forty-five minutes?" I ask Rogue Three Actual. "Because you'll be a glowing billboard in about an hour when the sun comes up."

"The pilot and the chief are working on it. But if they can't get it straightened out, we will need a quick evac. First Shrike that spots us is going to tear us to shreds."

"Stand by," I reply. "We're heading your way ASAP."

Behind me, Sergeant Fallon comes back into the cargo bay with Lieutenant Dorian in tow, who looks about as ragged and tired as I feel.

"Rogue Three's bird is down with a fuel line issue," I tell them. "They're just sitting out on the prairie with no cover, and we're going to have sunrise soon."

I bring up the TacLink map on the command console's screen to show them the location of Rogue Three. Lieutenant Dorian frowns and shakes his head.

"They're still there when the sun comes up, they are dead meat."

"So what are our options?" Sergeant Fallon asks.

"We go get them with this ship," our pilot says. Then he looks at me. "Do you agree?"

"Only thing we can do," I say. "Other than leaving them to fend for themselves. The Shrikes can tear them up from BVR with standoff munitions. They'll never even get to launch Tridents. Not sitting out in the open like that."

"I concur," Lieutenant Dorian says.

"We can't get two platoons into this thing. Unless you want to stay here with the troops and let the ship go out empty," Sergeant Fallon says.

"I don't want to bring them all back here," I say. The map doesn't show me a whole lot of options, but I know that I don't want to separate my platoon over a hundred klicks from their drop ship. But the topography isn't completely unfavorable. The mountain range extends to twenty klicks from where Rogue Three is sitting on the ground, and there are always spots where a drop ship can hide for a bit. Even circling around with polychrome armor active and wasting fuel is better than leaving a Blackfly and forty men and women out in the open for the Shrikes to use as live target practice. After the airbase raid, I doubt they'd cut us any slack at all.

"Here's what we'll do." I mark the map and zoom in on the area around the stranded Blackfly. "We'll load up the platoon and switch deployment points. We'll find a new spot right here, on the other side of the ridge, wherever we can find good cover. Then Lieutenant Dorian and the chief run out and fetch Rogue Three's crew and Third Platoon and bring them back to us. That way neither platoon is more than twenty klicks from the working bird."

"Did you raise Company?" Sergeant Fallon asks me. I shake my head.

"They're out of comms. So's Second Platoon. This one's all us, and right now."

"Then let's go," she says. "We don't have time to wait for the squads to get off the OPs. Think you can do a nighttime pickup on a steep ridgeline?"

"Half dead or fully drunk," Lieutenant Dorian replies, and Sergeant Fallon grins.

Fifteen minutes later, we are racing south at five hundred knots, burning precious fuel at a prodigious rate again. All three squads are back in the hold, and the floor between the seat rows is cluttered with hastily loaded gear, in flagrant violation of safety procedures. I'm back at the command console and monitoring our tactical display.

"Shrike flight at four o'clock," Lieutenant Dorian warns. "Forty klicks out, on a parallel heading."

"Is he running active radar?"

"Negative."

"Let's hope he doesn't look too closely to his left." I check the icon for the enemy ground attack bird, a bright red inverted V keeping pace with us thirty kilometers to the west, and try to will its trajectory away from ours.

"Sixty klicks to target zone. ETA four minutes."

Lieutenant Dorian dips the nose of our Blackfly, and we descend even lower, until the mountain ridge on our right side is roughly at the level of the drop ship's wingtips. It's easier to hide the ship in the ground clutter than in the open sky at twenty thousand feet, but the lower and faster we go, the quicker the fuel goes. Lieutenant Dorian already detached the two outboard auxiliary tanks at the deployment point we just left fifteen minutes ago, sacrificing the little puddle of fuel left in them in exchange for eliminating the risk of a Shrike spotting two drop tanks tumbling to the ground out of nowhere.

"Get ready," I send to my squad leaders. "Out of the bird and perimeter security. Take all the Tridents in the hold. I don't want the skids to be in the dirt for longer than fifteen seconds."

Lieutenant Dorian threads our ship through the mountain valley between the two ridges, which is much narrower down here than up north where we set up camp earlier. The Blackfly banks from left to right and then to the left again at alarming pitch rates. Then the nose of the ship pulls upward, and we scrub speed as our pilot aims to hit the landing spot in a hurry. Without the adrenaline in my system, I'd probably be sick as a dog right now.

We hit the ground roughly. The tail ramp opens, and Sergeant Fallon and the squad leaders are out of their seats before the ramp is even halfway down.

"Platoon, haul ass," Sergeant Fallon shouts. "First Squad to the left, Second to the right, Third down the center."

The light above the ramp turns from red to green. I watch anxiously as thirty-eight troopers and their squad leaders un-ass the drop ship faster than I've ever seen an entire platoon disembark.

"You have the deck," I send to Sergeant Fallon. "See you in a few minutes."

She gives me a thumbs-up from outside and then turns to follow the squads out into the morning twilight.

"Ramp is clear," the crew chief sends to the cockpit. "Go, go, go."

The engines increase their pitch again, and the ground outside falls away as Lieutenant Dorian hauls the Blackfly around and toward the west. Then we are over the top of the nearby ridge and moving forward at full throttle again.

"Twenty klicks," Lieutenant Dorian says. I know he's as tired as I am, but whenever he's behind the stick, he sounds as cool and collected as if he's sitting in a RecFac lounge chair. I decide on the spot that I'll suggest him for a Distinguished Flying Cross at the very least if we make it back to Earth after all this.

"Rogue Three, this is Rogue One Actual. We are almost on top of you. Coming from the east at two hundred feet AGL. ETA one minute, thirty seconds."

"One Actual, Three Actual. Copy that."

When we skim over the next row of low hills, Third Platoon's stranded drop ship is plainly visible on low-light magnified optics even from over ten kilometers away. They're on a gently sloping rolling plain, and there's absolutely no cover of any kind to hide the very obvious shape of the Blackfly. As we get to within five kilometers, the passive infrared sensors show clusters of personnel, Third Platoon's troopers prone on the ground in a circle around the ship for perimeter coverage.

"Shit," Lieutenant Dorian says. "The Shrike is changing course."

I look at the TacLink map again. The red V representing the patrolling Shrike has started a turn to the south, and the line marking his projected course is bending closer and closer to the spot where Third Platoon's Blackfly is sitting on the ground, immobile and defenseless.

"Did he see them?"

"I don't think so," Lieutenant Dorian replies. "But if he gets within ten klicks of that ship, he will, unless the pilot got his wings from a surplus store."

"Three Actual, there's a Shrike in the neighborhood, and he's close. Do not waste any time boarding this ship, you understand?"

"One Actual, affirmative," Third Platoon's leader replies tersely.

When we are directly overhead, our pilot makes a low pass over the stranded Blackfly Three, then circles the site once before pulling the ship into a hover. We descend with the tail ramp opening in midair.

Then the skids of Blackfly One hit the ground with a thump. I unbuckle my harness and thunder down the ramp at a run.

"Grayson, that Shrike is changing course again," Lieutenant Dorian warns. "He's making a big loop to the east. He'll pass within five klicks of us in two minutes."

"Tell me you have some Tridents up," I yell into the platoon-level channel. "Incoming air from two-six-zero degrees, coming in fast."

Half the platoon is lined up to board the ship, the other half spread out in a semicircle facing west. We are in the most vulnerable phase of the process, both ships on the ground next to each other and presenting fat targets to anyone overhead, and that Shrike picked the worst possible moment and the worst possible patrol route.

On my TacLink, I hear the sharp chirp of a radar warning receiver, and my blood runs cold.

"He saw us," Lieutenant Dorian says. "He's sweeping us with his active. Coming in straight now from two-six-five degrees, CBDR."

"MANPADS, go hot," Lieutenant Horner orders. "Shoot him down."

I tuck my rifle under my arm and dash away from the drop ship to go prone, find some cover on the grassy slope we're on. Half the platoon is in the ship, but we will never get the hold full and the Blackfly underway before the Shrike gets into firing range. If I'm going to eat it in the next thirty seconds, it won't be while strapped into a chair and looking at a console. Ahead in the semidarkness, I hear the electronic whine of two Trident launchers firing up their guidance systems as their gunners scan the sky for targets. I've been on the receiving end of attack ship runs many times before, but I've never felt this helpless in my life, with a platoon of troops all around me and no way to avert what's about to happen.

The Shrike streaks in from the west in a ground-attack profile. He's descending at full speed from almost thirty thousand feet to under ten thousand in less than a minute. I track him on the TacLink screen, the distance between us rapidly decreasing, and hold my breath for the ground-attack munitions that I'm sure will leave the Shrike's wings to blow this slope and everything on it into ragged bits.

The cannon shells explode to my right in an earsplitting cacophony. They carve a meter-wide trench into the ground and rake across the nearby bulk of Blackfly Three, which shudders and rocks on its skids under the hammer blows from the cannon shells. Shards of armor fly off the drop ship's hull and sail through the air. A few seconds later, I hear the unmistakable ripping roar of the Shrike's multibarreled cannon in the distance, the sound arriving after the supersonic armor-piercing shells. I try to make myself meld with the ground, knowing full well that my battle armor has no chance of stopping a shell of that caliber. To my right, some rounds explode on the ground right next to Lieutenant Dorian's Blackfly One, and I can hear the shrapnel pinging off the cockpit and the portside armor like angry hail.

Thirty or forty meters in front of me and to my left, a single Trident launcher belches out a missile, which ignites its main motor a second later. The slender missile shoots off into the sky, too fast to follow with the naked eye. The incoming Shrike banks hard to the left and starts ejecting countermeasures, but a few seconds later, there's a muted flash in the sky, followed by a much brighter one. Then the sharp report of the warhead detonations reaches my helmet microphones. My augmented vision shows the Shrike in the distance, trailing a plume of fire, banking hard and then leveling out again. It flies off to the south, clearly damaged by the Trident, but still in the air.

"We have got to go," Lieutenant Dorian shouts. "We're going to have every Shrike above this hemisphere on our heads in a few minutes."

I get up on shaky legs and look around. Blackfly Three is burning ahead and to my right. The cannon shells pierced the side armor on the port side and ignited both auxiliary tanks on the port wing. The bulk of Third Platoon's drop ship managed to shield Blackfly One, so our ship is merely scuffed a little by shrapnel, but the other ship is a complete write-off. I see troopers running up Blackfly Three's tail ramp to check for casualties. A few seconds later, they emerge from the hold again.

"Lieutenant Wood and the chief are dead," someone reports. "Can't get them out. Whole front section's on fire."

"Get out of there before the internal fuel goes," Lieutenant Horner shouts.

"Board the fucking ship," I yell. "Do it now. Leave the dead."

We took more casualties in the Shrike's attack run than just Blackfly Three's pilot and crew chief. Three SI troopers are on the ground, unmoving. Half a dozen of their comrades rush over and drag the unconscious or dead troopers over to the ramp of Blackfly One, where others help hoist them into the cargo hold. It's costing us precious seconds, but I can't tell these men to leave their fellow troopers behind. I run up the ramp and past the rows of troopers who have thrown themselves into sling seats haphazardly.

"All aboard," the crew chief sends as soon as my boots are off the dirt. Lieutenant Dorian throttles up and yanks the Blackfly off the ground.

"More active radar from the west," he reports. "We won't be able to hide from that, polychrome or not."

I don't bother to reply. He knows his business far better than I do, so I leave him to it. To my left, the cargo hold is chaos as the SI troopers are tending to their wounded or dead squad mates. All I can do is plug myself into the console in front of me and see what's coming our way.

To the west, I see the detection cones from two separate sets of search radar. Whatever strange reluctance the renegade force has had to employ active radiation, it seems to have gotten over it. The electronic warfare suite built into the Blackfly identifies the transmitters as air-to-ground dynamic phased array radar from Shrike attack aircraft. The radar coverage cones are overlapping, suggesting a formation in close proximity.

"Two more from two-seven-zero, closing fast," I send to our pilot.

"I saw," Lieutenant Dorian replies. "That's not good. I'm taking us south."

The ship banks to the right and drops a few hundred feet to try to hide in the return radar clutter from the ground. I briefly wonder what Lieutenant Dorian is doing—turning south and giving the Shrikes a broadside scan of our ship instead of ducking behind the nearest mountain ridge—but then I realize that he's playing fox to their hounds, leading them away from the spot where we have an entire platoon sitting on the ground.

Now that they know where we are, I figure that I can't do much more damage with a high-powered burst transmission. I send a TacLink update as an electronic plea for help out into the dawning morning, all the sensor data from First and Second Squads bundled in a half-second burst transmission that goes out from the Blackfly's transmitter at thousands of watts. If Second and Fourth Platoons are within five hundred kilometers with their comms turned on, they'll probably hear us. Even if we die in the next five minutes, they may be able to use our recon data to extract some payback from the colonists.

On the plot, the two incoming Shrikes track south, following our movement. As stealthy as the Blackfly is, the polychromatic armor is no good against high-energy radar at close range. We need to get away from those Shrikes and disappear in the background noise again, but we are running out of time and space. They are faster, and they are closing in. We're more hare than fox right now, and the hounds are running us down. But despite it all, underneath the fear, I feel eerily calm.

The Shrikes are now within thirty kilometers, well within the range of the Fleet's standard air-to-air missiles. I keep my eyes on the TacLink map, which is constantly updated with the data from the drop ship's sensors. Any second, there will be two or three little red V shapes coming from those Shrike icons, and then we'll be falling out of the sky in a fireball a few seconds later.

But the missiles don't come. Instead, the Shrikes keep tracking our course and pulling closer, their fire-control radars making our threat receiver go ballistic with warning yelps.

Twenty kilometers. Eighteen. Sixteen. They either want to make absolutely sure we have no time to evade their missiles, or they intend to hose us out of the sky with gunfire. And if they do that—

Fourteen kilometers. Thirteen.

"They're not geared for air-to-air," I send to Lieutenant Dorian. "They're closing in for cannon kills. They have no AA on the wings."

"Well, neither do we," he replies. "Can't stop and turn around to shoot back, can I? Not that I'd come out ahead in that pissing match."

"Hey, Lieutenants," the platoon sergeant sends. "We have some AA back here. Anyone ever try to shoot Tridents off a cargo ramp in flight?"

Lieutenant Dorian barks a laugh. "Not to my knowledge, Sarge."

"They use an expeller charge," I say. "No back blast. I don't see why you couldn't."

Eleven kilometers.

"Do it," I say. "Chief, can you pop open the ramp just a meter and a half? Just enough for a Trident launcher to clear a shot?"

"Holy shit," the crew chief replies. "In flight?" Then he laughs as well. "We'll be violating safety regs that haven't even been written yet."

"We have two loaded launchers back here," the platoon sergeant says. "Crack that ramp open and hold her steady for ten seconds so the gunners can track. Santiago, Keenan, grab those Tridents," he sends to the platoon. "We're going to play mobile AA battery. Everyone else, clear the back of the ramp. Move it if you don't want to die today."

Ten kilometers. The two red icons behind us are closing the distance steadily. I'm now convinced they have no missiles on the wings and intend to shoot us down with their cannons, otherwise we'd be a flaming wreck on the ground already.

To my left, the ramp opens, and the sudden rushing wind noise in the hold is louder than the subdued roar from our engines. The platoon sergeant is at the back of the hold with Corporal Santiago and Private Keenan. Each of them has a Trident launcher tube on his shoulder. They aim them out of the meter-wide crack in the tail ramp and turn on their targeting modules.

"Eight klicks out," I yell. "Moving from four to five o'clock high."

"Got it," Santiago says. "Tracking target. Target acquired and locked."

"Target acquired and locked," Private Keenan shouts.

"Their guns have a three-kilometer range," I say. "Let them get to five so they have less time to evade."

The Tridents are mean little missiles. One warhead is generally not enough to bring down a Shrike, which is heavily armored and stuffed with redundant systems, but we can at least screw up their gun run and maybe even break something mission-critical.

"Six kilometers," I announce to everyone. We are thundering across the surface of Arcadia at seven hundred knots and three hundred feet of altitude, faster and lower than I've ever flown in a drop ship, not even with Halley on the stick.

"Five kilometers," I shout. "Weapons free, weapons free."

The two Trident launchers bellow almost simultaneously. The expeller charges kick the meter-and-a-half-long missiles out of their tubes and into the semidarkness outside. A second later, their motors kick in, and they streak off into the night, faster than fleeting thoughts.

The Shrikes are lining up for their gun run in our wake when the missiles take them completely by surprise. Tridents have a homing warhead that reads the laser beams emitted from the launcher's targeting module, and they don't set off threat-warning systems until they are already in their terminal intercept phase. In this case, that's half a second before the submunitions hit their targets.

Above and behind us, there's a bright flash, and then a fiery bloom as the left Shrike completely disintegrates. We are racing away from the sound and can't hear the explosion, but there's no doubt that the Shrike is gone. It falls out of the sky with no control or coordination, a flaming comet of wreckage that starts losing cohesion in midair right before the whole burning mess plows into the ground six kilometers behind us and makes another fireball billow into the sky. One of the submunitions must have pierced the armor right over a fuel tank or ammo cassette.

The second Shrike shudders from a hit as well, but that one isn't nearly as spectacular. There's a brief streak of smoke coming from one of the engine nozzles, but it stops almost immediately, no doubt put out by the Shrike's fire-suppressant system. But the attack craft breaks off its run abruptly. The pilot flings his bird into a sharp wing-over turn to starboard and races away from us at a ninety-degree angle.

"Splash one," I announce to cheers. "Second one got winged, but he's still in the air. He killed his run."

"He's coming around to our right," Lieutenant Dorian warns. "He's going to go wide to avoid our six. We won't be able to pull that trick off again."

"Reload those launchers," I tell the gunners. "Dorian, turn the bird and show him our ass end again."

"On it. But he won't come close to our six again, I can guarantee you that."

Our ship smoothly banks to the left and makes a sweeping turn to the east until our nose is pointed at the nearby mountain ridge. The drop ship's threat detector yowls again to alert us of the fire-control radar that is painting our ship. At this range, there is no stealth tech for us to hide behind, and the Shrike has more speed and maneuverability than we do.

"He's coming around high for a deflecting shot," Lieutenant Dorian says. "Now at eight o'clock high."

For the next minute or two, Lieutenant Dorian keeps changing course to present our tail to the Shrike and give the gunners in the cargo hold another shot with their Tridents, but the Shrike pilot is too aware and skilled to take the same punch on the nose twice. Inexorably, he closes the distance to our drop ship, always keeping above and to the side, and there's nothing we can do about it. If we climb, he has us in his sights right away, and there's nowhere else we can run or hide behind.

"Incoming," Lieutenant Dorian says. "Hold on back there."

The Shrike is three kilometers out when he sends the first burst of cannon fire our way. At the last second, our pilot jerks the Blackfly violently to the left. A bright stream of large-caliber tracers streaks past the drop ship on our port side, missing the ship by less than two meters. Then the Shrike thunders by above us, already starting his turn for the next attack run.

"I can't keep this up forever," Lieutenant Dorian sends. It's the first time I've heard stress in his voice since we left *Portsmouth*.

My TacLink display lets out a bleep to alert me of a new contact. I look at the map and see two missiles coming in from the outer edge of the scale, beyond visual range. Their little V shapes are blue, not red. A second or two later, there's a new targeting radar lighting up our threat receivers. Something is coming in from the south and shooting missiles—but not at us.

"Blackfly One, this is Blackfly Two," a familiar female voice comes over the company channel. "Keep up evasive. I'll get the bastard off your back."

"Affirmative," Lieutenant Dorian sends back. I let out a joyful whoop that makes heads turn toward me in the cargo hold. I've never been so relieved to hear Halley's voice.

The Shrike breaks off its attack run to evade the missiles that are coming at it at five times the speed of sound. The pilot kicks out countermeasures and banks his ship hard right and then left, still mindful to stay out of the firing cone from our tail end. The two missiles streak across the plot and whip around sharply to pursue the Shrike, too fast to see with the naked eye. I watch the plot as one of the blue missile icons disappears. The other one follows the Shrike for a second or two before it, too, blinks out of existence. A few seconds later, I hear the faint little crack of a warhead explosion. The Shrike soars back into the sky, unmolested. Halley must have fired her missiles at maximum range to draw the Shrike's attention, and now she has it. The explosive joy I felt at hearing my wife's voice dissipates as the attack craft turns toward the new threat.

"Blackfly Two, he has no AA ordnance," I send. "Guns only."

"Copy that," Halley replies coolly.

Halley is coming in with her polychromatic armor turned off and her fire-control radar locked onto the Shrike. She's at full throttle and zooming across the scope of my tactical map. The Shrike pilot is in a long right-hand turn to use his speed advantage and get behind her, but she has the tighter turning radius and turns right with him.

"Here's something you can't do, motherfucker," she says.

Her Blackfly's nose veers sharply to the right, accelerating her starboard turn, until it almost looks like she's skidding sideways. Then the launchers on her ship's wingtips pump out two more missiles. They shoot toward the Shrike, which drops countermeasures and tries to turn in to the incoming missiles. Both Tridents fly true and converge with the Shrike's hull in a bright little fireball. The attack ship rolls over to starboard until it flies inverted. The pilot tries to right his stricken ship. He rolls it back upright and arrests his steep descent maybe a hundred feet off the ground. The Shrike is trailing a long tail of fire. The pilot seems to have decided to quit before his ship blows up. There's another muted pyrotechnic flash by the cockpit, and the escape module shoots up and away from the Shrike, right before a stream of tracers from Halley's cannons reaches out and blots the pilotless attack ship out of the sky for good. The Shrike cartwheels into the ground and blows up in a huge fireball.

"Splash two," Halley says. She sounds satisfied. I relay the news to the two platoons in my comms circuit, and a cheer goes up as if we had just been approved for two months of shore leave.

"Blackfly Two, thanks for the assist," Lieutenant Dorian sends.

"Assist, my ass," Halley replies. "You'd be a smoking hole in the ground if I had gotten here ten seconds later."

"I can't argue with that in any conceivable way," our pilot concedes. "Thank you."

"Close your tail ramp and follow me. We need to clear this datum before they get smart and come back with AA missiles on the racks."

In the distance, the triple canopy of a Fleet eject-capsule parachute blooms in the morning sky. I train the optics from Blackfly One's sensor array on it and zoom in on the cockpit capsule, a titanium clamshell that will protect the pilot until he hits the ground safely.

"There's a chute at five o'clock low," I say. "Eight klicks out. The Shrike jock got out."

"Circle around, go full EMCON, and dogleg it around to where you dropped First Platoon, behind the mountain ridge," Halley sends to Lieutenant Dorian.

"Affirmative, ma'am," he replies.

"Don't get detected again. I am out of air-to-air, and I won't be able to pull that little trick again. I will have my guys collect the Shrike jock and then rendezvous with you at First Platoon's DP."

I watch Halley's Blackfly Two on our starboard as she turns on her polychromatic armor again and turns off her radar. Then her ship banks to the right and soars off toward the spot where the chute is obvious against the morning sky even from eight kilometers away.

"Your wife," Lieutenant Dorian says. "She's all right. I'd say you married way up, Grayson."

"Yeah," I say. The adrenaline is still flooding my brain, and I am very glad that I'm currently firmly strapped into a jump seat, or my knees would give out under me and dump me on the floor of the cargo hold in a very undignified way. "I'm the luckiest son of a bitch alive."

CHAPTER 26

——— GOOD COP, BAD COP ———

We get back to First Platoon's landing zone thirty minutes later. Our run from the Shrikes brought us sixty kilometers south, and Lieutenant Dorian backtracks our course on the other side of the mountain and very low to the ground to avoid detection.

"The aux tank is dry," Lieutenant Dorian reports when we're on the ground and the ramp is open again. Third Platoon are filing out of the ship, carrying their dead and assisting their wounded.

"Less to drag around with us," I say. "Right?"

"Trouble is that we also dipped into the onboard tanks. We're down to seventy percent."

"How much do we need to get into orbit and back on track toward the task force?" I ask.

"I wouldn't want to try it with less than what we have right now, and preferably with a full tank. And that's with one platoon on board, not two."

"Well, shit."

I unbuckle my safety harness and get up. My legs feel odd, like they're not used to bipedal locomotion anymore. I stagger down the ramp and pull my helmet off to breathe some unfiltered morning air.

Sergeant Fallon trots up to me and nods at the bodies Third Platoon's troopers are laying out in the dirt a few dozen meters away.

"What the hell happened? Once you guys were over the ridge, we couldn't get shit on TacLink."

"We saved Third Platoon's asses. Snatched them off the ground in the middle of a Shrike strafing run."

Sergeant Fallon winces. "That's a tough day at the office."

"Blackfly Three is toast. Pilot and crew chief burned up with the wreck. And Third Platoon has three KIA."

"What about the Shrike?"

"We clipped it with a pair of Tridents. Then another pair of Shrikes came in just as we were off the ground. And those motherfuckers chased us for thirty klicks. Did you know you can launch Tridents from an open tail ramp?"

Sergeant Fallon laughs and shakes her head.

"You scored an air-to-air kill on a Shrike. From a moving drop ship."

"I didn't. But Corporal Santiago and Private Keenan did."

"Holy hell." She laughs again. "I think that's a first. And then what?"

The other Blackfly appears above the ridge to our east with startling suddenness, the engines barely louder than a spirited conversation. I nod at it and exhale sharply.

"And then Blackfly Two saved all our asses."

We watch as the drop ship swoops in for a landing. The ship sets down fifty meters from Blackfly One, the skids kissing the ground so lightly they barely kick up any dust. Then the war machine settles on the skids, like a raptor hunkering down over a kill, and the engine noise recedes.

"One of the Shrike pilots bailed," I say to Sergeant Fallon, barely needing to raise my voice over the engine drone. "Looks like we have ourselves our first traitor brigade POW."

Sergeant Fallon perks up. "Really now. Let's go say hello."

"And quite possibly good-bye," I add, and glance over to the spot where the platoon medics are working on the dead and injured troopers.

The captured pilot stands off to the side, fifty meters from the Blackfly. He has his wrists locked together with a set of flex cuffs, and two SI troopers are flanking him. Halley is pacing in front of him, fixing him with an icy glare. Sergeant Fallon and I walk over to where they are standing to join the interrogation.

"Have a seat, Captain." The rank designation comes out of Halley's mouth with a heaping dollop of acid. She points to a nearby supply crate.

The Shrike pilot is a tall guy with thinning hair. He's supporting his left arm with his right. I can tell he's trying to look tough, but he can't quite pull it off at the sight of all the armed SI troopers milling around and shooting him very unfriendly looks. The name tape on his flight suit says BEALS.

"I think I'd rather stand," Captain Beals says. "So you don't just shoot me in the back of the head."

"Oh, for fuck's sake." Halley nods at the two SI troopers on either side of Captain Beals, and they yank him down to the ground by the sleeves of his flight suit. He yelps out with pain, but makes no effort to get up again.

"Trust me, motherfucker. If I wanted to shoot you, I would have done it on the ground where you landed," she says. "Save the weight for the trip back here."

"What's your unit, Captain?" I ask. He turns his head to look at me. I must not seem very threatening—or he may have decided on the spot that my rank doesn't merit cooperation—because he just shakes his head with a smirk.

"I'm not telling you a goddamn thing other than rank and name and service num—"

Sergeant Fallon steps forward and kicks him in the middle of the chest with one solid, well-placed boot sole. He flies backward off the supply crate and lands hard on the rocky ground. Before he can even start to get back up, she pulls her sidearm from her thigh holster. The pilot starts to get up, but freezes when he sees the targeting laser of the pistol in the middle of his chest.

"Here's how this is going to work, sport," she says. "You will answer the lieutenant and the captain here very promptly and truthfully. If you do not, I will start using you as a backstop for some target practice. Don't believe me, open your fucking mouth with attitude again."

Captain Beals swallows whatever words of protest he was about to blurt out. He looks at me and Halley, and the defiant expression on his face is gone.

"She has shot people for less," I say.

"You can't torture or injure me on purpose," he says very neutrally and carefully. "That's a war crime."

Sergeant Fallon sighs and lowers herself into a squat right in front of him, and he flinches. She reaches out with her gun hand and taps him on the head with the weapon, and he flinches again, only harder.

"One," she says. "We aren't at war with you. Ain't no treaty that covers this sort of shit, unless you went and joined the SRA or the Euros. Did you join the SRA or the Euros, Captain?"

He shakes his head.

"Two," she says, and taps him on the head with her gun again. "Don't be talking law. The law is not your friend right now. If the law is still in effect, you motherfuckers are all guilty of high treason, desertion in wartime, and theft of crucial assets, and we can hold a field tribunal and shoot every single one of you legally, on the spot. And if the law is not in effect anymore, I can do whatever the fuck I want to you. Do you understand me?"

The captain nods slowly. He looks like he wants to argue the point, but he's smart enough to hold his tongue.

"Three," she says, and reaches out again to tap him with the gun. He flinches away from the weapon, and she smiles without humor.

"You and your flyboy friends used your stolen Shrikes to kill three of our men and injure a few more. Those guys over there with the rifles? You killed their friends. I don't think any of them would be sad to see me put one between your eyes and leave you here to rot. And you destroyed one of our rides, which is worth—how much is one of those Blackflies worth, Captain Halley?" she asks in our direction.

"A trillion kabillion dollars," Halley replies.

"A trillion kabillion dollars," Sergeant Fallon repeats to Captain Beals, stern-faced. "And they're priceless to me, because we need them to get off this rock and back home once we are done with you people."

"You raided our airbase," Captain Beals replies carefully. "You killed twenty-seven personnel and damaged twelve Shrikes. You didn't even warn us."

"We did that," Sergeant Fallon says. "And we were in the right because of this." She points to the NAC flag patch on her armor. "Because we are with the Commonwealth Defense Corps. And whatever you people call yourselves now, you are not it. Not anymore. So everything we do to you is legal. And everything you do to us is criminal activity."

"We were under orders to leave Earth. From the president of the Commonwealth."

"That's bullshit," I interject. "Those were illegal orders. And you don't follow those. That's the first thing they teach you in NCO school, for fuck's sake. A fresh corporal one year out of boot camp knows that."

"The guy who is giving the orders around here isn't the president of the Commonwealth," Halley says. "He stopped being that when he left his post and went through that Alcubierre node. So try again, Captain."

Captain Beals stares at Halley, but doesn't reply.

"What is your unit, Captain?" I ask again. His eyes dart to me, then to Sergeant Fallon—or more precisely, the pistol in her hand. She studies him without emotion, like someone might look at an interesting scientific specimen, which is somehow more unsettling than if she had clear anger on her face.

"Strike Fighter Squadron 22," he says after a moment.

"Off NACS *Pollux*?" I ask, and he nods.

"We're dirtside now. Redeployed."

"All the squadrons from *Pollux* are down here now?"

Captain Beals nods.

"How many?"

"Four," he says. "We dispersed them on the moon."

"Which base did we hit the other day?"

"That was Strike Fighter Squadron 85," Captain Beals replies. "You took out all their ships except for one."

"Yeah, we were in a hurry," Sergeant Fallon says. "We'll try to do better next time."

"They're all on alert now. You can't pull that off again. Not with what you have here." Captain Beals nods at the nearby SI troopers.

"Why didn't you run radar from the beginning?" Halley asks. "In fact, why aren't you lighting up the approaches to the moon? We made it all the way from the node to this place without picking up any active radiation. Why did you choose to stay blind out here?"

Captain Beals looks at her and raises an eyebrow. "You mean you haven't figured that out yet?"

"Figured what out?"

He laughs quietly before replying. "It's how the Lankies find us. They're attracted to radio waves. Radar in particular. Comms relays. Everything that puts out more than a few dozen watts. Using radar in space is like turning on a flashlight in a dark room. Like hanging out a welcome sign."

"Son of a bitch," I say. For a second or two, I have to suppress the urge to take the pistol from Sergeant Fallon's hand and smack it against the side of the pilot's head to wipe the smarmy little smile out of the corners of his mouth. "How very fucking nice of you all to share that bit of intel before you left us all to the Lankies."

"It doesn't matter," Captain Beals says. "Not for the Solar System. You can't turn all that shit back off and stay quiet forever. Besides, they already know where you are. It's too late to hide."

"That's why you don't have any perimeter security worth a shit," Sergeant Fallon muses. "You're not expecting human visitors. You're geared to fight Lankies. You figured we'd be gone by now."

Captain Beals just shrugs, that little smirk still in the corners of his mouth.

"Four Shrike wings, minus the one we sidelined," I say. "How many ground troops?"

Captain Beals looks up at me, then glances at Sergeant Fallon, who is still holding the pistol, and who is in striking distance of his head with it. She gives him an encouraging nod.

"One battalion, plus the garrison company that was here already."

"Bullshit," I say. "A Navigator can haul a whole regiment. You came here with a million tons of passenger tonnage and a supercarrier, and you only brought a battalion with you?"

"It's true. We had to clear space for gear and civvies. Lots of dependent families. Flight deck was ass-to-nose with supplies and spare parts. You have no idea what kind of a mess that was."

"My heart breaks for you," Halley says dryly. "Bet you that wasn't shit compared to the mess you left the rest of us with."

"We were under orders," he says. "You get an order from the president and the joint chiefs to evacuate the system, you follow it. Simple as that."

"I get an order from the president and the joint chiefs to abandon billions of people to the Lankies, I tell them to go fuck themselves," Halley replies sharply. "Simple as that."

Sergeant Fallon gets up from her crouching position and holsters her pistol.

"I want to take this asshole back home with us," she says. "I want to take him to Detroit and drop him in the middle of the PRC. See what the hood rats think of his orders from the goddamn president."

"I have no particular issue with that idea," Halley says, and nods over toward the SI troopers, who are carrying three body bags up the ramp of Blackfly One's cargo hold. "We have the space for another passenger or two. I'll even help you push him out of the fucking ship."

The computer in my armor bleeps a warning tone. I put on my helmet again to check the visor display for the cause of the alert. On the TacLink map, a radar search cone is moving in our direction from the northwest. Almost simultaneously, Lieutenant Dorian sends a warning through the company channel.

"Enemy air coming in from three-two-zero degrees. Forty klicks out, running active ground radar."

Behind us, Blackfly One's engines are starting up with a low whoosh.

Halley and I exchange glances. Then she starts running back toward her ship, putting her helmet back on her head along the way.

"Get everyone on board for dustoff right now," she shouts into the Company channel. "Split Third Platoon between both ships. And hog-tie that Shrike jock so he can't hit any buttons."

Three minutes later, our two-ship formation is flying away from the patrolling Shrike's radar cone at low altitude, polychromatic armor active. Unless the Shrikes have already spotted us and locked their fire-control radar on us, we can hide from them easily enough. But that requires staying in motion, burning precious fuel we don't have to spare. Sooner or later, we'll be stranded somewhere with dry tanks, and then all the stealth technology won't do us a bit of good.

Halley and Lieutenant Dorian spend the next twenty minutes threading a course between the likely detection bubbles of two patrolling Shrikes. They are focusing their search efforts on the low mountain ridge where we set up our last two deployment points, and we take a westerly course and leave the shelter of the mountains behind reluctantly. With nothing better to do, I watch the optical feed from our passive gear again as it maps the landscape outside and translates it into coordinates and icons on the TacLink map. But as we stay aloft and on the move for an hour and then another, I can't help but wonder to what end I am collecting recon data that nobody else will get to see.

Finally, our pilots find an acceptable new deployment point to put down the Blackflies again, hundreds of kilometers to the northwest of our old landing spot. It's a forested plateau dotted with little lakes, and the terrain is just hilly enough to offer a radar shadow to hide in. Halley and Lieutenant Dorian set down their ships in two separate clearings a few hundred meters apart.

"You know the drill," Sergeant Fallon announces to the platoon-and-a-half in the cargo hold. "Perimeter security, three-sixty degrees. Eyes and ears, people."

Outside, the engines come to a stop. A few moments later, Lieutenant Dorian comes out of the cockpit passage. I unplug myself from the console, take my helmet off, and follow him down the ramp and into the sunlight.

"What's the fuel situation?" I ask.

"Thirty percent, plus the emergency reserve," he says, and I suck in air sharply and imitate a flinch.

"We are hauling so much weight around at low level, I'm not sure I could even make orbit with what's left. Not with sixty troops packed into the back of the ship."

"Well, shit," I say. "I guess we need to be looking for a fuel stop on this rock."

"I suspect they won't be greeting us with open arms if we just show up at the nearest Shrike base for a refill," Lieutenant Dorian replies.

———————

"I'm down to two-thirds," Halley says when we set up our little command post in the woods between Blackfly One and Two. Our three platoons are dispersed in the woods, as much for keeping them out of harm's way in case the drop ships get spotted from the air as for physical security.

"We spend another day dodging Shrikes, we'll be down to nothing," Lieutenant Dorian says. "And then we'll have no mobility beyond our boots."

"Remember Willoughby?" I ask Halley.

"What about it?"

"Well, they had spare fuel at the terraforming stations. We saw at least three of those that were cold. You think they have fuel storage there?"

"They wouldn't leave fifty thousand gallons of JP-101 in the ground," Halley says. "Not in a place like this."

"Then we need to find a different fuel source. Or put what's left to better use than running away until we can't."

"What did you have in mind, Lieutenant?" Halley asks me.

"Let me talk to that Shrike jock again," I say.

"What can I do for you, Lieutenant?" Captain Beals says, in a tone of voice that makes it very clear that he's not terribly interested in doing anything for me at this time. He looks past me and eyes Sergeant Fallon nervously, who is sitting on a fallen tree fifty meters away and opening a meal pouch with her combat knife in a very unsubtle manner. We are in a clearing in the nearby woods, just barely out of sight and earshot of the drop ship and the SI troopers gathered around it.

"I'm not going to play good cop, bad cop with you, Captain," I say. "I'm not half as good at threatening people as Sergeant Fallon. I'm planning on appealing to your self-interest."

"Oh," he says, with a sardonic little inflection. "Well, I wish you the best of luck with that, Lieutenant."

"You better hope I'm successful. Because if I lose my patience with you, I'll stop being a moderating influence on the master sergeant over there."

He glances over at Sergeant Fallon again and quickly averts his gaze.

"What do you want?"

"You're a Shrike jock. You know the maps for this place by heart. I want you to sit down with me at the command console and mark every airbase and settlement on this continent, along with troop strengths and defensive measures."

Captain Beals barks a laugh. "You want me to give you the entire defense setup of Arcadia. Sell out my comrades and help you kill them easier."

"Pretty much," I reply.

"Why the fuck would I want to do that? Because then you'll keep that battle bitch over there from carving me up with her knife?" He shakes his head. "They'll find you sooner or later. And then they'll mow you down for what you did back at the 85th base. They may get me, too, but I'd rather go that way than get skinned by Sergeant Psycho over there."

I look at the captain, who is sitting on the ground cross-legged with his wrists flex-cuffed together. Then I crouch down in front of him like Sergeant Fallon did a few hours ago. He looks up at me warily.

"Let's stop the feather-preening. Let me lay this out for you. The Fleet—the real Fleet—knows where you are. Both of them do. The SRA are pulling on the same rope with us right now, and they have a lot more ships left than we do. Sooner or later, they'll come for the stuff you stole. Or just to fuck up your little paradise, out of spite."

Captain Beals looks at me, but doesn't say anything snippy in response.

"When they come, this is going to end in one of two ways for you. You're going to die in battle, or they'll capture you and put you in front of a military tribunal. I don't think I need to tell you how that'll go for you," I say.

He looks over toward Sergeant Fallon again, who is calmly eating out of the ration pouch on her lap. "But this is where you come in and play good cop."

"I'm not good," I reply. "I only want to get off this rock and back home with my wife. I don't give a shit about you. But I'm counting on the fact that you don't want to die, either."

"Who the hell does?" he replies. "So what are you going to dangle in front of me, to get me to rat out my comrades?"

"We pull this mission off, I'll testify that you provided instrumental assistance to us. You come back home with us, and I'll put in a good word at your tribunal. You won't be here when the Fleet shows up and kills or arrests everyone on this rock for desertion and high treason. And you'll be spared a blindfold and a firing squad."

"And if you lose? What if I give you the information you want and you all get killed?"

"Then you're no worse off than before. From where I'm sitting, you can't lose either way. Or you can just take your chances with the Fleet or the Lankies, whoever shows up here first. But someone will show up, because everyone already knows where you went. We are just the recon team, and we took out a quarter of your offensive airpower. Once the rest of the Fleet shows up, or the SRA decide to get themselves a nice, pre-terraformed colony for their own use, you people are fucked."

"You may be wrong all around," Captain Beals says.

"Or your bosses may be," I reply. "They were already wrong twice. They thought nobody could track where you went, and they thought Earth was about to fall anyway. You really want to put all your chips on their call again?"

Captain Beals looks past me and chews on his lower lip. He stares off into the woods between the two drop ships for a little while. I get up from my crouching stance and step back a little. The forest we're in is another pine grove, strong trees at least twenty meters tall. If it weren't for the giant blue orb on the horizon in the distance, it would look and feel like Earth.

Another empty and clean world, and we bring death and destruction to it the first chance we get, I think.

"They're looking for you. They'll capture you and haul you in, and then they'll put me up against the wall when you tell them I've talked. Sorry, Lieutenant. I think I'd rather take my chances with them. And maybe the rest of you will be too busy with the Lankies to come calling here."

I close my eyes and try to control the sudden rage that is flooding me.

Selling each other out for little favors, for tiny scraps from the tables of our masters. Is that all we've ever done? Is that all we'll ever do, even with the world going to shit and our exterminators at the door? Billions of lives are riding on the outcome of Mars, and this waste of biomass in a flight suit is willing to sell all of them out to save his own hide?

Something in my brain just gives way. Until now, I've never fully understood why and how Sergeant Fallon lost her idealism and turned into the person she is, but now I begin to get my head around it.

I turn around and walk away from Captain Beals.

"Master Sergeant," I shout, and Sergeant Fallon looks my way.

"Sir."

"Take out your sidearm and shoot this man in the head."

Behind me, I hear a yelp of protest and surprise.

"Yes, sir," Sergeant Fallon says. She puts aside her ration bag and stands up. Then she starts walking over to where Captain Beals is sitting on the ground. As she passes me, she unsnaps the retention hood of her sidearm's holster. She looks at me as I pass her, maybe looking for a sign that I am bluffing, that I need her to be bad cop to my good cop for a minute, but I avert my gaze and keep walking. Behind me, I hear a pistol leaving its holster, and then the racking of a slide.

"Stop!" Captain Beals's shout is almost a scream. "Lieutenant, stop! I'll tell you what you want to know. I'll take your deal. Just stop."

For just a second, I let the rage control me as I consider just letting Sergeant Fallon go ahead with it and rid us of the captain's dead weight to haul around. Then reason takes over. I have more lives to think about than just mine and Sergeant Fallon's.

I turn around. Sergeant Fallon has almost reached the captain, and he's looking up at her with wide, terrified eyes. She raises her weapon, and he lets out an inarticulate noise of fear.

"Master Sergeant," I shout. "Hold fire."

She looks over at me, her targeting laser never wavering from the captain's forehead.

"Sir."

I look at the terrified captain and the cold-as-a-glacier master sergeant. I've never been so fully aware of the fact that I have someone's life in my hands. If I give the word, Sergeant Fallon is going to shoot this officer with the same lack of hesitation she'd show if I told her to smash a wasp.

I feel my rage subsiding a little, no longer seizing my brain in a stranglehold. Whatever I've become in this armor, this uniform, under this flag—I'm not yet the kind of man who can order the execution of a prisoner who's sitting before me with his wrists bound together, and I hope I never will be.

"Deal's off," I say to the captain. "You tell me what you know, you get to keep sucking down air for now. But I won't vouch for you when the Fleet comes. That was your decision, not mine."

He lets out a shaky breath and nods.

"Master Sergeant," I say. "Haul that piece of shit over to Blackfly One. If he tries to run, you will shoot him without warning."

"Yes, sir," she replies. Then she holsters her weapon with a smooth motion. She picks the captain up off the ground, and he gets to his feet and almost falls back down because his knees are shaking. Sergeant Fallon shoots me a look and a curt smile.

Nice job, she mouths.

I turn around and walk off toward the drop ship, not wanting to clue her in on the fact that this wasn't at all a round of good cop, bad cop, but a last-second stay of execution.

CHAPTER 27

— MORE BALLS THAN BRAINS —

Captain Beals has a sizable audience standing behind him when I have Sergeant Fallon deposit him in the command console's jump seat. Halley and Lieutenant Dorian are in the hold with us, and the two lieutenants commanding Second and Third Platoons are here as well.

"Look, don't touch," Sergeant Fallon warns. "If you go into a comms menu, I'll blow your brains all over that bulkhead. Do you copy?"

Captain Beals nods silently. The air of tough-guy bravado he was assuming earlier has dissipated. He puts his hands in his lap, wrists still shackled together with flex cuffs.

I bring up the TacLink screen with our known-world recon data, which has expanded a little with our run from the Shrikes and repositioning. Now we are at the northernmost end of the crescent of surveyed ground, two hundred kilometers from the nearest colony settlement.

"All right, Captain. Start putting labels on stuff," I say.

He studies the map for a few moments and then points at the closest settlement.

"New Eden," he says. Behind me, Halley lets out a derisive little snort.

"Ten thousand settlers," he continues. "Each settlement has an airbase with a Shrike squadron. New Eden, that's Strike Fighter Squadron 91. Twelve ships, plus a few spares."

"What about the SI garrison?"

"One company," he says. "One platoon in the admin building in town, two at the airfield, one at the terraformer. It's the same arrangement everywhere else."

He points out the other towns on the map, which make an irregular line from north to south.

"Tranquility," he says. "That's the place you hit three days ago. Strike Fighter Squadron 85. That one in the middle is Arcadia City. The capital. That's where the president and battalion command sit. Strike Fighter Squadron 22, that's my unit."

"Now short two Shrikes," Halley comments with some satisfaction in her voice.

Captain Beals ignores her jab and points to the next settlement, directly south of Arcadia City.

"Midland. Ten thousand settlers, one company of SI, same deal as the other towns. Home of Strike Fighter Squadron 35. And then all the way south, Landing. They have Strike Fighter Squadron 5."

He looks at me and shrugs. "That's it. Are we good now?"

"Not quite," I say. "You're saying the SI companies are all split three ways and deployed piecemeal?"

"Yes," he replies. "That's what I'm saying. They rotate them through so every platoon gets to stay in town one week out of four. Main base is the airfield, and the platoon at the admin building pulls local security."

"What about AA emplacements? Missile batteries? Radar coverage?" Halley asks. "And I still find it hard to believe that you have a carrier and a dozen freighters, and you only took along a lousy battalion to garrison the place."

"We had fifty thousand dependents to haul," Captain Beals says. "And food, and equipment, and all the shit that middle-class 'burber civvies take along when you tell them to bring only essentials."

"So our dear former president is in Arcadia City?" I ask.

"Yeah. The administration is set up in the main admin building."

"Does he have special security, or is the admin building platoon guarding him?"

"Both," Captain Beals says. "He's got those CSS bodyguards. Don't know how many, but I never see him with fewer than four. And they have a tactical team. Twenty guys at least. They do their small-arms training at the airbase."

"What about armor? We killed two Mules at Tranquility. What else do they have?"

"The airbase grunts have MAVs for patrol. And they keep a platoon of Mules per town. Four units. But no anti-air, and they keep the radar at the airbase cold for Lanky EMCON."

"Interesting," Sergeant Fallon says.

"Very interesting," Halley agrees.

"Master Sergeant," I say to Sergeant Fallon. "Take the captain outside and put him in the care of the biggest, most ill-tempered privates in your field of vision. But don't let them break him too much. We may need more intel in a little bit."

"That's a solid copy, sir," she says, and pulls Captain Beals from his jump seat. "Be right back, sirs. Just gonna take out the garbage."

"Situation," Halley says. "We are hiding out on a hostile moon, and the garrison is on the lookout for us. We have three platoons, two drop ships to transport them, and one full fuel load between those two ships. The pickup is four days away, and we don't have enough fuel to reach the rendezvous point. This is a little less than ideal, tactically speaking."

The other platoon leaders chuckle at this. Sergeant Fallon shakes her head with a smile that says *kids these days*.

"Have you tried to raise Company again, Lieutenant?" Halley asks me.

"Three times since we landed," I say. "No reply yet. Wherever the major and his SEALs are, they're either out of radio range, or they don't want to talk to us. I sure as shit hope it's not the latter."

"I'm fine with that," Sergeant Fallon says. "Saves me from having to ignore another idiot order. Our tactical situation wouldn't be less than ideal if the major hadn't ordered us to blow our cover. Loudly. Sorry, ma'am," she says to Halley. "Do continue."

"Options," Halley says. "Let's hear them."

"We can keep running until the fuel is gone," Lieutenant Dorian says. "Use the rest of it to spread out the squads and go to ground. Then hide out and do hit-and-runs until the rest of the Fleet shows up."

"That may be months," Lieutenant Wolfe says. Second Platoon's leader frowns and runs a hand through his reddish buzz cut. "That may be never, actually. If we lose Mars, they won't have anything to send after us."

"It's an option," Halley replies. "Other ideas?"

"We could raid the nearest airfield and fill up the drop ships from their fuel tanks," Lieutenant Hanscom suggests.

"They're all on alert now. You want us to fight off a prepared garrison platoon or two? I don't think they'll let us sit on the ground long enough to fill up," I say.

"Shrikes will shoot us to shit before we get off the ground again." Lieutenant Dorian shakes his head. "Not feeling too great about that option. I'd rather fly my bird dry and walk, to be honest."

"It's an option," Halley repeats. "Let's hear them all before we decide what not to do. Lieutenant Dorian?"

Blackfly One's pilot looks at the TacLink display over the command console and purses his lips.

"Transfer all the fuel to one of the drop ships. Use that to make orbit with one platoon and get to the rendezvous point. Fill up and then return to pick up the next platoon and refill the other ship with auxiliary tanks." He looks at the other pilots and shrugs. "I wouldn't give that one great odds. They probably have their whole task force out of the dock and on alert by now. But it's better than running around down here until they catch us."

"We'd have to stay alive for another four days without switching positions again," Halley says. "And then the two platoons we leave here would have to stay with the drop ships for another four days. What are our odds of staying in this place for eight days undetected, with three squadrons of Shrikes combing the place for us?"

Lieutenant Dorian shrugs again. "It's an option, right?" he says.

"Yeah, it's an option." Halley looks at me. "What are your thoughts, Lieutenant?"

I look at the TacLink display again, where the map is blown up to maximum size and updated with all the intel Captain Beals gave us a few minutes earlier.

Five settlements, I think. And four of them with airbases and garrisons on full alert.

I make my brain switch gears a little, and pretend I'm on an SRA-controlled world. I'm the mission's combat controller, and I have to come up with a threat assessment and targeting priorities for the infantry.

What would I do if these were Russians or Chinese?

The answer pops into my head almost automatically. My analytical, dispassionate professional brain has the answer very quickly, and it clashes very much with my emotional preferences. But this is the only way to get out of this that won't invariably end up with everyone dead.

I point at the center of the map and poke the settlement labeled ARCADIA CITY with my finger.

"That's the way," I say. "The only way to win this thing. We go in and kick them where it hurts."

"That is nuts," Lieutenant Hanscom says. "That's their main command and control facility."

"Yes," I say. "That's kind of the point."

The other squad leaders and Lieutenant Dorian all start talking at the same time. I look over at Sergeant Fallon, who just returns my gaze with a raised eyebrow.

"Keep going," Halley says, in that tone she uses when she doesn't agree with me in the least but feels the need to let me state my case. Only usually this tone comes up in discussions about plans for our next leave, not our survival and that of everyone with us.

"Arcadia City is the only one of the settlements that doesn't have an airbase parked right next to it," I say. "We can't take on a base full of Shrikes. Not with them all aware that we are here and looking to break their shit. We can't take on a full garrison battalion with three platoons."

I zoom in on the map and spin the recon image of the main admin building around for everyone to see from all angles. It's a boxy concrete bunker without windows, built for resilience and as an air-raid shelter for the colony leadership, standard colonial prefab architecture.

"But we don't need to take them all on at once. We can take on a platoon and a handful of CSS agents. We hit them hard with all three platoons and take control of their main C3 hub on this moon. If we get our hands on their command staff, we can maybe even make them stand down. They're all gormless career throat-cutters like that asshole out there." I nod toward the spot where several SI troopers are guarding Captain Beals outside. "The next Shrike base is two hundred klicks away. They're flying patrols all over this rock looking for us. We can assault that place and take it over before they can get a flight of Shrikes halfway there."

"Hold a gun to the president's head," Halley says with a thin smile. "Can you imagine? We could get three squadrons of Shrikes and a full battalion to stand down."

"At the very least we could force a stalemate. They can't strafe us with those Shrikes if we're sitting in their command facility, in the middle of their main town. With ten thousand civvies all around us."

"And even if we fail, we'll fuck their shit up in a monumental way," Lieutenant Dorian says. "Beats the hell out of getting run down like a pack of PRC dumpster dogs."

For a few moments, there's silence in the cargo hold as everyone looks at the TacNet screen, as if we're all waiting for it to unlock some previously invisible secret. Then Sergeant Fallon clears her throat, and all heads turn in her direction.

"That would be an incredibly aggressive and reckless thing to do. And only a totally irresponsible gung-ho podhead moron with more balls than brains would even think about it."

She smiles grimly. "Naturally, I'm very much in love with that plan, Lieutenant."

Halley lets out an exasperated little huff, but she smiles as she does it. "All right, gentlemen," she says. "Let's put the lieutenant's aggressive and reckless plan to a vote. Who here also has more balls than brains and thinks we should go out with a bang?"

Lieutenant Dorian and Sergeant Fallon both raise their hands. Lieutenant Wolfe follows suit after a few seconds. Lieutenant Hanscom only shakes his head with a frown.

Halley raises her hand as well.

"Oh, goddamn it," Lieutenant Hanscom huffs. Then he raises his hand, too.

"We're all a bunch of idiots," Halley says. "Now that we settled the if, let's get to work on the how. Get that asshole Shrike jock back over here. We're gonna need some more intel."

We have more computing power in the drop ships' tactical integrated neural network computers than existed on the entire planet fifty years ago, and somehow mission planning goes better when you're outside in the fresh air and drawing diagrams and maps into the dirt with a pointy stick.

"Two reinforced platoons," Sergeant Fallon says. "We pad First and Second with the combat-ready squads from Third. We'll leave the wounded here with a squad to take care of them. If we pull this off, we'll send for them later. If we don't, they'll wait for *Portsmouth* to reach the pickup azimuth and then do maximum-power burst comms to let them know what went down here."

"That's five full squads per platoon, plus an extra squad in reserve."

"We'll have full boats on the way in," Lieutenant Dorian says. "Almost sixty troops per ship."

Halley squats in front of the diagram of our target zone and points to the rock representing the admin building.

"It's a standard colonial Class IV hard shelter. Steel doors and reinforced concrete vestibules up front. We'll come in from here"—she scratches flight paths into the dirt—"and blow open the doors with MARS antiarmor loads. I don't want to waste whatever I have left in the cannon cassettes just to play master key."

"Wingtip launchers?" I ask, and she nods.

"Wish we had some pylon racks. With the MARS tubes on the wingtips, there's no space for Tridents. It's one or the other."

"First Platoon clears the building. Second Platoon takes up firing positions here on the building corners. Squads here, here, and here." Lieutenant Wolfe marks the positions for his men.

"Second Platoon will hold the perimeter," Sergeant Fallon says. "Things get too hot out there, they will fall back to the building entrance and defend from within while First Platoon does their business inside. I don't intend to drag this out until their reinforcements show up, but you never know. And if you see any Mules, you take those fuckers out. Last thing we need is an armor platoon running interference and picking us off with 35mm fire."

"Have no fear," Halley replies. "We see any from the air on ingress, they're priority targets."

"No word from the major and the SEAL platoon?" Lieutenant Dorian asks, and I shake my head.

"Not a thing."

"Fuck the SEALs," Sergeant Fallon says. "We don't need 'em."

We spend the next fifteen minutes drilling the battle plan—simple as it is—until everyone knows the sequence from top to bottom. We get up to spread the word to the troops, and Halley erases our dirt-drawn diagrams with her boot sole.

"It's Friday," I say to her when Sergeant Fallon and the other officers are out of earshot. "We could be in the RecFac on Luna right now. Or back home in the living unit."

"Drinking shitty soy beer and waiting for the world to end," she says. "Instead, you may get a chance to put a bullet into the former president of the NAC. Be a part of history."

"Or be a part of the local soil."

She laughs. "It's a shit plan, but it's the least shitty option we have right now. I'm happy to be a part of it."

She walks over to me and puts a hand on the chest plate of my armor.

"Quit your worries, Andrew. Even if we don't make it, I'll be fine with it. Because you're here with me, and we get to go on our terms." She pauses for a brief moment. "And if you call me 'sappy,' you'll be going into battle with a fat lip, Lieutenant Grayson."

She touches her fingers to her mouth and then presses them lightly against my lips.

"Break a leg," she says. Then she turns around and walks off toward Blackfly Two.

Over by Blackfly One, First Platoon is gathered by the tail ramp, and forty troopers are looking over toward me expectantly. I draw in a long, slow breath of cool forest air and let it out with equal leisure. Then I walk over to my men to let them in on all the ways I will risk their lives again today.

CHAPTER 28

– THE BATTLE OF ARCADIA CITY –

"Fifteen percent fuel," Lieutenant Dorian says from the cockpit in his usual calm voice. "One way or the other, this will be a one-way trip."

We are at five hundred feet and five hundred knots, as low and fast as the hilly terrain will allow. The cargo hold of Blackfly One is wall-to-wall with SI troopers in heavy battle armor. We ditched the food and supply pallets and the body bags back at the staging point with the wounded and the guard squad, so there's a bit more space in here than before, but the extra dozen troopers from Third Platoon have managed to fill it right up again.

"I hate going heavy," Sergeant Fallon grumbles from her jump seat to my left. "All that shit just slows you down when you're in a hurry."

"You'll be glad for it once we get incoming fire," I reply. "I love going heavy."

Our battle armor is modular. We can add or subtract armor protection as required by the mission. We usually go with the medium kit, which is hardshell only. The light kit is the same thing, only with the leg and arm protection removed. The heavy kit is the hardshell with added ballistic trauma plates, quarter-inch-thick laminate panels that can stop anything you can shoot from a handheld weapon, and some of the light crew-served stuff besides. The downside of the heavy kit is the extra thirty pounds it adds to your load, and the increased bulk of the armor.

We raided the well-stocked armory of the Blackfly for armor panel modules and ammunition, and every single trooper in the cargo hold is carrying at least twice the usual ammunition load. I traded my usual M-66C for a PDW, which is sitting in the arms bracket next to my seat. The PDW is not as powerful as the carbine, but it's easier to maneuver with one hand and in tight quarters. I can also carry an obscene amount of ammunition for it. The magazine pouches on my armor are stuffed with ten of the long and skinny five-hundred-round PDW magazines, and there are five more in the dump pouch on my side. If I die today, it probably won't be from a lack of shooting back.

"Double-check the ammo," I tell the squad leaders. "I want everyone to carry at least four HEAT grenades and two thermobarics. Gonna be a lot of closed hatches in that place once the shooting starts."

"Five minutes to drop," Lieutenant Dorian announces. "Ten klicks out."

Sergeant Fallon unbuckles herself from her jump seat and stands up. Then she raises her visor and signals "eyes on me." Every set of eyeballs in the cargo hold swivels toward her.

"Rules of engagement," she shouts. "If they hold a weapon, you shoot them. If they fire at you, you shoot them a lot. If they don't do what you say right when you say it, you shoot them. Do not give them the benefit of the doubt, because they won't return that favor."

She pats her carbine grimly.

"These people have sold out their species to sit here and set up Pleasantville for themselves. They have no incentive to surrender. And they don't have a bit of honor in their bones. Because if they did, they wouldn't be here. You want to go home? You hit them so hard they have no time to think straight. Show them what happens when rear-echelon garrison troops go up against hard-ass grunts with nothing to lose."

The troops let out a cheer.

"Make it hurt. Make them pay. Let's do this and go home. I'm tired of fucking around with these people."

"I do love your motivational pep talks," I send to Sergeant Fallon on a private channel when she sits back down. She doesn't reply directly. Instead, she scratches the side of her helmet with her middle finger.

I shift my attention to the tactical screen and transfer the feed to my helmet visor. We are approaching Arcadia City from the west, away from the patrolling Shrikes that are still combing the mountain range far to the east for us. The wide loop around the city cost us most of our remaining fuel, but with any luck, they'll never even suspect we're there until we put skids down right in front of the admin center and blow their doors wide open.

"Two minutes," Lieutenant Dorian says. "Shrike search radar eighty klicks out from bearing one-one-zero, moving south. No active radar at the settlement."

On the optical feed, I can see the first colonial housing units through the green-tinted low-light magnification. The sun set an hour ago, and now the only light outside is the ghostly glow of nearby Leonidas c, painting the landscape in luminescent blue. Other than that unusual tint to the night sky, the place looks so much like Earth that it hurts.

"One minute."

To our right, Halley's Blackfly Two is gliding across the landscape behind and slightly below us, a hundred meters away. The polychromatic armor renders the ship all but invisible, and the only way I can even be sure she's in formation with us is the ID tag my computer has put over the spot where her ship seems to fade in and out of existence. I know that she is practically one with her ship right now, fully in her place of competence.

Our ship pops up a few dozen feet to clear the tall perimeter fence of the settlement. Then we settle back down to worryingly low altitude. The domed houses of the settlement fly by underneath and beside us, and it seems we're clearing the top of the low-slung buildings by only a few feet. I can see people in the streets below, streetlights illuminating intersections, and light vehicles in the roads.

"Ten seconds," Lieutenant Dorian shouts over the intercom, and the red light above the tail ramp starts blinking. Up ahead, the large three-story admin building looms in the darkness, the antenna farm on its roof blinking its red anticollision lights. Our pilot pulls the drop ship up sharply to scrub speed, then whips the tail around, spinning the ship around its vertical axis until we are facing back the way we came. Then we are hovering above the plaza in front of the admin building. To our left, Halley's Blackfly Two performs the same maneuver at the end of the block, less than a hundred meters away. Our crew chief hits the button for the tail ramp, which starts opening with a hiss.

"Firing HEAT," Lieutenant Dorian announces.

The MARS launchers on the wingtips disgorge their payloads with their characteristic pop-whoosh report, and four HEAT warheads streak toward the reinforced entrance doors of the admin building at supersonic speed. The rockets tear into the laminate steel of the doors and blow them apart in a bright explosion that spews shrapnel and concrete dust outward into the plaza in a huge, angry plume. Some of the debris comes back far enough to pelt the cockpit armor of our drop ship, where it deflects with a sound like hail on a steel deck.

The light above the ramp jumps from blinking red to green.

"Follow me," Sergeant Fallon shouts, and rushes down the ramp. In her wake, First Platoon follows, then the rest of Third Platoon. I unbuckle my safety harness, grab my PDW from its clamp, and work the charging handle to chamber a round. Then I set the selector switch to full-auto fire and follow my troops down the ramp.

"Hold is clear," I hear the crew chief bellowing behind me when I've cleared the bottom of the ramp, and Blackfly One's engines increase their pitch again as Lieutenant Dorian wastes no time getting his ship off the ground once more.

Up ahead, black smoke billows from the open entrance vestibule of the admin building. From inside, I can hear the base alarm blaring.

Inside the entrance vestibule, things are a mess. The HEAT warheads from the MARS launchers have blown apart the doors and wrecked the hallway beyond. Burning debris is littering the floor fifty meters into the building. As I cross the threshold of the entrance vestibule, gunfire erupts in the hallway ahead.

"Contact left," Sergeant Humphrey sends from the front of the group. Instantly, everyone's TacLink screens update with red icons that show the locations of the spotted hostiles. Through Humphrey's camera feed, I see the outlines of SI troopers in fatigues down the hallway, firing at First Squad with M-66 rifles. First Squad returns fire, and the volume from our guns is considerably higher than that from the defenders. The hallway up ahead reverberates with the reports from a dozen weapons on automatic fire.

"We're in," I send to Lieutenant Dorian. "Making our way to the control center."

"Second Platoon is in position," Lieutenant Wolfe sends. "Do not take your time in there. We're going to have Shrikes overhead before you know it."

"First Squad, left hallway," Sergeant Fallon shouts. "Second Squad, right hallway. Third and Fourth, follow me upstairs." Then she turns on her suit's PA system and barks out an announcement that echoes through the entire building.

"Commonwealth Defense Corps," she bellows. "Drop your weapons and raise your hands. All armed personnel will be shot on sight. There will not be another warning."

To my left, there's movement in one of the rooms. Then a targeting laser streaks across my helmet visor, and I drop and roll to my left just in time to avoid a burst of rifle fire. I aim my PDW at the doorway from my awkward position on the ground and fire a long burst into the room beyond. In front of me, one of First Squad's troopers, Private

Carr, comes back around the corner of the hallway and brings his own weapon to bear. He sends three short bursts into the room, then thinks better of it, and pulls a grenade off his harness. He activates it with his thumb and then chucks it around the corner of the doorway and into the room with an almost casual motion. The grenade explodes with an earsplitting boom, sending debris and dust out into the hallway toward us.

"You okay, LT?" Carr asks, and I give him a thumbs-up. Then I pick myself off the rubble-strewn ground and point my weapon at the doorway again.

"On three," I tell Carr. "You take right. I take left."

He gives me a thumbs-up of his own and takes up position to the right of the door.

"One. Two. Three."

We both enter the room simultaneously, weapons raised and ready. I turn to the left and cover that side of the room, and Carr moves to the right. The room is an office—shelves of reference material, a desk, framed pictures and certificates askew on the walls or shattered on the floor. There's a weapons rack on the far wall, and I know even before we see the dead bodies that this is a security office.

"Clear," Private Carr says.

The two colonial constables are lying in pools of blood in the corner of the room where they had taken up firing positions behind an overturned desk. One of them has a rifle next to him, an M-66C carbine. The other is clutching a pistol. We take the guns, clear them, and throw them to the other side of the room. I look around the room before we leave it, at the personal and professional artifacts strewn all over the place by the explosion and the gunfire, and I have a brief flashback to Constable Guest's office on New Svalbard, which was laid out almost exactly like this one.

First and Second Squads advance down the hallways on the ground floor of the admin building, clearing rooms one at a time. Upstairs, automatic weapons fire and grenade explosions punctuate the progress of Third and Fourth Squads, who are doing the same on the upper floor. They may have a garrison platoon in this building, but they are dispersed and not prepared for the fight we brought right into their sanctuary, and my reinforced platoon pushes their advantage without mercy.

"We are at the ops center," Gunnery Sergeant Philbrick reports. "No casualties so far."

"Breach it and use flash-bangs," I send. "We'll need the comms gear in there."

"Copy that. Going in soft."

The flash-bang grenades are by design much louder than our anti-personnel grenades. When Philbrick and First Squad breach the ops center hatch and toss a pair of them into the room, the detonation is so loud that it feels like the walls of the hallway are bowing out from the sonic energy. None of the troops we have faced so far are in fully sealed armor, and without the benefit of an automatic hearing filter, anyone in that room still alive is going to have permanent hearing loss once they regain consciousness.

"Ground force, Blackfly Two," Halley sends. The transmission is weak and full of static, even though I know that Blackfly Two is overhead and at the most a few kilometers from us. The walls of the admin building are thick ferroconcrete, which doesn't like to let radio waves through.

"Blackfly Two, go ahead," I reply.

"We have active radar from Shrikes coming in from the north and south," she says. "I can't engage at range, so we are going to stay in the weeds until you need us. I'd say you have ten minutes before they are on top of us."

"Copy that, Blackfly Two. Keep low and good luck. Rogue Three, did you copy that?"

"Loud and clear," Lieutenant Hanscom says from his blocking position outside the building. "We've warned off the civvies. There's plenty of them out here, but they're staying away from the building. We have Trident teams up on the northeast and southwest corners." In the background of the transmission, I hear the colony's alert sirens wailing.

"Keep our backs clear for just a few minutes longer. We're taking control of the ops center."

I sprint down the corridor to my left to catch up with Gunny Philbrick and First Squad.

"Fallon, this is Grayson. How is it going up there?"

"It's a big party," the reply comes. "There are civvies with handguns and PDWs up here. Must be the CSS agents."

"If you come across the president, try to get him alive."

"Be happy to, if he doesn't shoot at us."

There are at least four or five bodies of fallen garrison troopers in the corridor. None of them are even wearing hardshell. Our attack took them completely by surprise, which is almost unforgivable. They knew they had a hostile presence on their moon, and the main protective platoon tasked with keeping their main command center safe wasn't fully battle ready when we showed up.

Two of First Squad's troopers, Giddings and Keenan, are hunkered down covering both sides of the hallway just in front of the ops center hatch, which is blown off its hinges and lying on the floor just inside the room. I step on top and over the hatch and into the ops center.

"So far, so good," Gunny Philbrick says. He's unloading sidearms and PDWs and tossing them into a pile in the corner of the room. First Squad's troopers are busy tying up garrison personnel with flex cuffs. There are half a dozen people in the room, two in civilian overalls and four in fatigues. Two more uniformed troops are motionless on the floor. Sergeant Humphrey checks them for weapons and then cuffs them anyway. The ops center people look shocked and scared. One of them is bleeding from a gash in the forehead.

"They got at least one call out," I tell Philbrick. "We have Shrikes coming in."

"They can't reach us in here," Philbrick says. "But they can fuck up things for Second Platoon outside."

I point at the comms console.

"They have multi-megawatt gear and a huge stinking antenna array on the roof. Get someone on there and send an update to Company and Fourth Platoon. Let them know what we're doing if they haven't figured it out already. No sense hiding now."

"Copy that," Philbrick says. "On it."

"I need some help up here," Sergeant Fallon sends over the Company channel. "We've got a whole bunch of people who got smart and surrendered. I don't have the manpower to keep a lid on them."

"Send two troopers down with them to the central staircase. We'll meet them down there and take over the prisoners. Got just the space for 'em."

"That's a solid copy," Sergeant Fallon replies.

"Humphrey, Rogers, with me," I say on my way out, and the two SI troopers follow me, weapons at the ready.

The central staircase well still carries the sound of gunfire from the floors above as Third and Fourth Squads under Sergeant Fallon clear the building of armed resistance. On the other side of the ground floor, Second Squad under Sergeant Wilsey is busy clearing the rest of the rooms.

One of Third Squad's troopers, Corporal Gregory, comes down the stairs a few moments later, followed by half a dozen handcuffed civilians. Another Third Squad trooper brings up the rear, weapon aimed at the gaggle of civvies. They're mostly fit men of fighting age, and their haircuts mark them as police or security forces—careful and martial-looking buzz cuts with slightly longer hair on the crown of the head, a time-consuming cut that would be too much trouble for a military barber.

"Protective detail," Corporal Gregory explains. "Some of it, anyway. We potted three before the rest put down their guns."

One of the civilians doesn't look like a cop at all. He's slightly over-weight and has the ruddy-faced look of a 'burber with access to—and a love for— lots of clean and safe alcohol.

"You." I point. "What's your name and function?"

One of his protectors answers for him.

"That's the secretary of interior security," he says, as if I just asked the dumbest question in the world.

I look at the CSS agent's face, and a jolt of recognition goes through my brain like a lightning bolt. The CSS agent in front of me interro-gated me on Independence last year, right after *Indy* made her suicide run past Mars and back to Earth. The last time I saw this man, both our noses were broken and bleeding.

"Special Agent Green," I say. "I can't tell you how very glad I am to find you here."

He looks at me, puzzled, and I open my helmet visor so he can see my face.

"Andrew Grayson," I say. "We had the pleasure last year, on Independence Station." I tap the bridge of my nose.

To Agent Green's credit, he doesn't show any fear or panic. Instead, his eyes just narrow, and there's a disbelieving little smirk on his face.

"Yes," he says. "I remember. The belligerent staff sergeant with the strong right cross."

"How many CSS agents are in the protection detail for this building, and where's the former president?"

Agent Green grins. "Go fuck yourself."

I return his grin without humor.

"Sergeant Humphrey," I say. "Take these people to the ops center and place them with the other prisoners. Beware of Agent Green. He's quick and mean. If he tries any tough-guy shit, shoot him in the spine," I add, echoing the words Agent Green spoke to the cops on Independence when they led me off.

"Copy that," Sergeant Humphrey replies. She gestures down the hallway with the muzzle of her rifle.

"Move along, folks," she addresses our captives. "And no funny shit. I'm quicker and meaner than the lot of you put together."

The CSS agents and the secretary of interior security march off obediently. Agent Green gives me a glance as he passes me, and the smirk is still on his face. It occurs to me that even in armor and holding an automatic weapon, I must not seem terribly intimidating.

"Enemy air, bearing zero-zero-three, right on the deck," Lieutenant Dorian warns on the Company channel.

The enemy Shrikes announce themselves a few seconds later with a thundering high-speed overflight of Arcadia City at extremely low levels. Unlike the Blackflies, the Shrikes are loud—so loud that I can hear the engine roars and supersonic cracks through the half-meter concrete ceiling of the admin center. A few seconds later, I see the blue V icons of outgoing missiles coming from our Trident teams and chasing the Shrikes across the city.

"Engaging," Lieutenant Wolfe says. "There's activity on the main drag. Looks like Mules, coming up the street from the south."

"Hold them off, but retreat to the admin center before they tear you up," I say. "We have the lower two levels cleared."

"Copy that, Rogue One. Not looking to earn any Purple Hearts today."

Both of the missiles our teams launched are locking on to a single Shrike. It dodges the first triplet of submunitions, but the second merges with the icon on my screen. In the distance, I hear a muffled boom.

"Hit," Lieutenant Wolfe sends. "He's damaged. Breaking off to the north."

"Now they know we have Tridents on the ground," I reply. "Watch yourselves."

"The Mules are unloading troops," one of the Second Platoon troopers reports. "We have incoming ground troops from grid Delta One-Three."

"Things are about to get sporty outside," I tell Sergeant Fallon. "What's the holdup on the third floor?"

"Sons of bitches don't know when it's time to pack it in," Sergeant Fallon replies over the sound of gunfire. "They're defending the back staircase like they have the national treasury back there. Give me three minutes."

Outside, there's a sudden fusillade of gunfire. I check the tactical feed and see at least a dozen red icons advancing up the main east–west street of the settlement toward the admin plaza. The troopers of Second Platoon are redeploying from the building corners to meet the new threat. On the far side of the plaza, a Mule rolls into the square, its autocannon swiveling toward the building vestibule. I'm in the main intersection of the corridor, with a clear view out into the plaza through the ruined main doors of the admin building, and for a short and terrifying moment, my magnified vision is locked directly onto the muzzle end of a 35mm autocannon. I dart into the hallway to my right in what seems like slow motion. A second or two later, the corridor intersection to my left explodes in a burst of shrapnel and concrete shards, and the pressure from the detonation flings me to the ground like a giant hand. I land on the hard concrete of the hallway floor and skid for a meter or two before I get my bearings.

"Mule's firing through the open door," I warn the rest of the platoon. "Nobody come down that central staircase. They have line of sight on the whole corridor from outside. Blackfly One, we could use a hand here."

"Copy," Lieutenant Dorian's static-riddled answer comes. "Rolling in hot."

I watch as the icon for our platoon's drop ship pops up on the tactical map to our west and then rapidly moves across the TacLink map toward the admin plaza. Then there's the deep, rolling staccato of cannon fire outside. I toggle into the optical feed from Second Platoon and see the Mule that just rolled into the plaza rocked by the impacts of heavy-caliber autocannon shells. There's a dull explosion inside, and one of the panels on top of the Mule flies off. Black smoke pours out of the gap in the armor.

Another Shrike comes streaking in from the north. I barely have time to shout a futile warning before the icon for the hostile attack jet and our drop shop are almost on top of each other. I hear the roaring ripsaw sound of a Shrike cannon outside. The TacLink display is alive with multiple fire-control radar cones, and there's no more stealth to be had in the sky above Arcadia City right now.

"Motherf—" I hear on the company channel. Then there's an inarticulate angry shout, and Blackfly One careens out of the sky and slams into a nearby cluster of colonial housing units at four hundred knots. The fireball from the impact lights up the sky outside. A second later, the crash of the explosion reaches my helmet microphones, a low thunder that makes my heart miss a beat in my chest. I am barely aware of the curse I shout into my helmet headset at the top of my lungs.

Behind the destroyed Mule, two more enter the admin plaza, guns swiveling and pumping out shells in short bursts. The audio feed on the Company channel turns into pandemonium as Second Platoon troops engage the new enemy and try to get clear of the incoming fire. With the Mules and the incoming infantry pouring into the plaza, there's no chance of them reaching the safety of the admin building, unless the gods of battle see fit to work a miracle and strike down a platoon of troops and three armored vehicles for us.

"Blackfly One is down," Halley sends. "Engaging with cannons."

I want to scream into the company channel, tell her to abort that run, tell her there are three Shrikes overhead and waiting for her to break stealth and give them something to shoot at. But there's no time, and I know she wouldn't listen anyway.

Another burst of cannon fire churns up the pavement on the admin plaza. It rakes across the bulk of one of the Mules from nose to tail ramp, and the Mule disappears in a violent explosion that sprays armor bits against the admin building more than fifty meters away.

I can't take my eyes away from the TacLink screen for the inevitable outcome of Halley's incredibly brave and foolish gun run. Two Shrikes home in on her suddenly visible drop ship from her port and starboard sides. I watch as she banks hard to the right, into the path of the Shrike coming at her from the south. There's the thunderous roar of a rotary cannon again, but Blackfly Two does not fall out of the sky. Instead, there's a firecracker chain of explosions as the salvo from the Shrike misses and rakes across a row of colonial housing units. Halley and the Shrike pass each other on opposite headings and maybe a hundred feet of vertical separation. Then she pulls her ship up and whips the tail around until she's flying backward at three hundred knots.

"Fuck right the hell off," she says. I hear the thunder of her Blackfly's cannons. The tracers from her guns reach out and touch the firefly exhaust of the Shrike's engines, glowing at full throttle. The Shrike rolls into a starboard bank and keeps rolling, until it's flying inverted, a long trail of flames gushing from its engines. Then it plows into the town below, digging a trench of fiery destruction across half a dozen houses.

On the ground, two more Mules push their way past the wrecks of their destroyed company mates and roll into the admin plaza, gun mounts turning. They dash toward the entrance vestibule of the admin building and lower their tail ramps. I know that one of those things usually transports a squad of troops, which means we'll have force parity on this floor of the admin building in just a minute or two.

"Incoming infantry," I shout into the Company channel, even though my information gets transmitted to everyone as soon as it pops up on my screen, and my verbal warning is entirely redundant. "Second Squad, cover the building entrance."

The situation is slipping out of our hands. We have the building mostly under our control, but the Shrikes are dominating the space outside the building, and the squads in those Mules are going to tie us down once they make it into the building, and there's not a damned thing I can do about it with what I have at my disposal.

Outside, the second Shrike homes in on Halley's ship. It barrels across the town at rooftop height, fire-control radar locked on to the Blackfly. Halley drops her ship down to what looks like an impossibly low level. She's racing down the settlement's main north–south street with just a few feet of air between the belly armor of the ship and the concrete of the road surface. The burst from the Shrike's cannons mostly passes over her ship, but two or three grenades glance off her dorsal armor in bright showers of sparks.

"Son of a bitch," she sends, almost conversationally. Then she pulls her Blackfly up in a near-vertical climb. The drop ship shoots up five, six, seven hundred feet into the night air. At the apex of its climb, Halley hits the rudder and flips it around on the ship's wingtip, then shoots back toward the ground in the opposite direction. Another burst from the Shrike fails to anticipate her sudden change in direction and rakes a row of buildings below and behind her.

I know how this will end. There are three Shrikes on the plot, homing in on one very exposed drop ship. Halley is a superb pilot, likely the best drop ship jock in the Fleet, but bravery and skill will only tilt the odds so far. She bobs and weaves, dips down into the shelter of the city streets and changes direction almost as quickly as an ATV on the ground, but I know that she can't fight off three Shrikes at once forever.

Outside, the gunfire picks up. Second Platoon is engaged with the garrison troops from the Mule platoon, and the flat and featureless plaza outside does not make for a drawn-out and tactically flexible firefight. It's just two groups of rifle-armed grunts shooting it out at under a hundred meters of distance. Another one of the Mules brews up from three simultaneous MARS rocket hits. The fourth Mule backs up at full speed, running over a few of its own troops, spewing grenades from its roof-mounted autocannon. On my screen, a third of Second Platoon's troopers are off the grid, dead or wounded. We are holding the line, but paying dearly.

In the entrance vestibule, human silhouettes emerge in the smoke and dust. They don't correspond with any of the friendly icons on my TacLink screen. I aim my PDW around the corner and cut loose with a long burst of automatic fire. One of the silhouettes stumbles and drops to the ground. Then there's return fire peppering the strikes to my left, and I withdraw around the corner.

"Second Squad," I shout. "Building entrance, now."

Outside, the two remaining Shrikes chase down Halley, bracketing her drop ship with bursts from their cannons. She changes direction and altitude, but the Shrikes have the speed advantage, and they have latched on to her with their fire-control radars. They use their cannons indiscriminately now, sending tracers into the settlement below with every burst they miss.

On the other side of the hallway intersection, some of the troopers from Second Squad have answered my call. Corporal Ponton and his fire team take up position and unload their rifles toward the entrance in short bursts. One of the troopers puts a rifle grenade downrange, which arcs through the corridor and detonates just in front of the vestibule. The return fire slacks off. Then the Mule outside contributes its 35mm cannon to the conflict. The armor-piercing grenades scream up the hallway and pulverize the staircase behind us. The trooper who fired the rifle grenade catches one of the cannon rounds between helmet and chest armor, and bits of armor and tissue spray everywhere in a grisly explosion of laminate and viscera.

"Fall back!" I shout. "Get out of that line of fire. Re-form the line at the end of the corridor."

I scramble backward, away from the smoking corpse of Second Squad's trooper, and eject the empty magazine from my PDW. I pull a fresh one from the mag pouch on my armor and slap it into the weapon on autopilot.

"We're about to lose the ground floor," I send to the rest of the platoon.

Halley's drop ship is still running from the Shrikes, but she's out of space and altitude. A burst of cannon fire connects with her tail section and blows off one of the vertical stabilizers. The ship yaws violently, but then rights itself only a few feet above the ground. I don't want to watch her die, but I can't take my eyes off the TacLink display, even though there are hostile troops just twenty yards from me around the corridor bend, and I'm not likely to live very much longer myself.

Blackfly Two's end comes just a few seconds later. Halley rights her stricken ship and pulls it up in a forty-five-degree ascent to gain altitude, and the two Shrikes home in on her like sharks smelling blood in the water. She dodges the first burst from the cannons again, but the second hits her bird square amidships, blows off one of the wings, and explodes the starboard engines.

"Bailing," she announces.

Then the icon for Blackfly Two winks out of existence, a thousand feet above Arcadia City and two kilometers from where my platoon troops are fighting for their lives, and I feel like I've just caught a round from an autocannon to the chest myself. My visual feed from Blackfly Two ends abruptly and with finality.

I want to charge around the corner and empty my PDW, engage the enemy until I too wink out of existence. Instead, I work the charging handle and stumble backward, toward the sanctuary of the ops center, where Philbrick and his squad have set up their fighting position. Then someone else is grabbing me by the arms from behind and pulling me backward. A human shape in battle armor appears around the corner, and I raise my PDW to bring the targeting laser up, but before I can pull the trigger, there's a burst of weapons fire behind me, and the figure in front of me falls to the ground in a hail of fléchette impacts.

"Fall back," Sergeant Humphrey shouts behind me. "Fall back to the next section."

"That Mule is murdering us," I say.

Outside, Second Platoon is fighting a fierce close-range action against the platoon that disembarked from the Mules a few minutes ago. The plaza is mostly clear—our squads have sought the shelter of the streets and alleys on the far side of the admin plaza to get out of the line of fire of the Mule's autocannon. I scan the spot on the TacLink map where Halley's ship got blasted out of the sky, two kilometers away, but there's nothing. Either her emergency transponder broke, or she didn't make it out of the ship before it blew up around her. But even if she's on the ground, she's too far away, and there's a platoon of hostile troops between us and her.

"Fire in the hole!" I hear on the Company channel.

Below us, there's a dull and powerful explosion. It's coming from one end of the building, from the basement underneath the admin center, and it makes the dust and rubble on the floor jump.

"The fuck was that?" Corporal Giddings exclaims.

"Fallon, this is Grayson," I send. "What the hell is happening up there? We are locking horns with the garrison company down on the ground floor."

"Top floors are clear," she replies. "We got a bunch of them, but some got away. There's an elevator at the back of the building. We jacked the doors and tossed about five kilos of boom down the shaft just now."

"Did you get the boss?"

"That's a negative."

Outside, one of the Shrikes makes another attack run. It comes thundering up the east–west road and rakes a street corner with its cannon. Another blue icon on the screen goes out, this one labeled 2/1-5 WILLIAMS T. Another one of Second Platoon's troopers is gone, and three more icons in the same spot flash WOUNDED/ MEDICAL. Three seconds and a hundred rounds from the Shrike's cannon, and an entire fire team is out of action, half a squad gone. Somewhere else nearby, a Trident streaks into the sky and gives chase. The Shrike pilot banks hard right, but the submunition darts can pull much higher acceleration in a turn, and he's too fast and low for evasive action. All three darts strike home. The Shrike cartwheels into the streets below, exploding and spewing burning fuel and wreckage for two blocks. I should be horrified at the carnage this battle is causing among the civvies down here, but I have no sympathy left for these people.

Let the bastard burn, I think. *Let it all go to hell.* If I could order a kinetic strike from orbit onto this city right now, I would do it with grim joy.

In front of us, at the main corridor intersection, someone tosses a grenade around the corner. It explodes with a sharp crack and fills the hallway up ahead with shrapnel and dust, but it's too far away for the payload to reach us. Two, three, then four enemy troops dash into the hallway ahead, right on the tails of the explosion. I bring up my PDW and fire a long burst down the hallway. To my left and right, Giddings and Humphrey fire their own weapons. Giddings shoots a few short bursts from his M-66, then switches to the grenade launcher and lobs a grenade down the hallway without the customary "fire in the hole" warning. It arcs down the corridor and lands right in the middle of the enemy fire team. The explosion obscures my view of the hallway section briefly, and when the dust clears, the enemy fire team is down, splayed out on the ground.

"Hold this corridor," I tell Giddings and Humphrey. "Hold it until Third and Fourth Squads come down from the top floors. We let them past that intersection, they can split us up and chew us up piecemeal."

Giddings and Humphrey send their acknowledgments. I remove the empty magazine from my PDW, toss it aside, and reload the weapon with a fresh magazine from my dump pouch. Then I run back to the admin building's ops center, twenty meters down the corridor.

"President and his entourage are in the basement shelter," Philbrick reports. His armor is caked with concrete dust. "They closed the blast doors and sealed themselves in. We didn't get to them in time."

"Can we crack that door?"

"Not with what we have with us. HEAT grenades won't cut it. Sorry, Lieutenant."

"If they've closed the blast doors, you'll need a pocket nuke to get in," Agent Green says from his spot by the back wall of the ops center, where he is sitting on the ground in a row with the other prisoners. "That shelter is hardened against nuclear strikes. They have supplies and ammo in there to be cozy for two years." He looks satisfied.

"That won't make a bit of a difference to you," I tell him.

"I've done my job. The president is safe. You fucked up yours, I think."

The situation on my TacLink screen strongly supports Agent Green's assessment. I've led the platoon into a bad spot, a windowless concrete coffin with only one way in and out. Without the command staff in our custody, we have no leverage. Outside, the Shrikes are mauling Second Platoon, and we are about to have our forces split and defeated in detail by the garrison force, and I have nothing left to stop it. All we can do at this point is to dig in and sell ourselves as expensively as possible. But there will be no escape for us from this city, or this moon, or the system. When *Portsmouth* and *Berlin* show up at the pickup azimuth in a few days, there won't be anyone left to evacuate. The drop ships are down, a quarter of my troops are dead or wounded, and Halley is gone.

"Central staircase is a mess," Sergeant Fallon reports. "We are coming down the east and west stairwells."

"Copy. Have Third Squad link up with Second, and Fourth with First. We are holding the line in front of the ops center."

The gunfire in the corridor outside intensifies. On my TacLink screen, there are two red icons for every blue one on the ground floor.

"There are more Mules rolling in," Lieutenant Wolfe reports from outside. "Two from the north, two from the south. We don't have enough HEAT rounds left to hold them off."

This is it, I think. I am out of ideas, and there are no options left other than to hold our ground and die in place. There's another platoon of troops rolling in, too much for our dispersed squads to handle. I made a call, and it was a bad one, and I got everyone else to go along with it.

The building lights flicker once, then go dark. A second later, the red emergency lighting comes on. I open the Company-level channel.

"They cut the mains in the admin building."

"Not just there," Lieutenant Wolfe replies. "Whole city just went—Jesus."

Outside, on Lieutenant Wolfe's video feed coming in on my TacLink screen, there's a bright sun in the sky beyond the city, even though the planetary sunrise isn't due for another six hours. The fireball in the eastern sky is so bright that the filters on Lieutenant Wolfe's optical feed kick in, and there's only one thing that can make the visor filters go active at that range. Several seconds later, the shock wave from the detonation washes over the city, enough to make the floor shake under my boots even at that range. The noise from the blast is deep and infernally loud, like a world-ending beast clearing its throat.

"Radiological alert," one of Second Platoon's troopers shouts. "Nuclear detonation."

On the TacLink screen, a symbol nobody ever wants to see pops up just five kilometers to the east—the bright orange inverted triangle signifying a nuclear warhead explosion. Outside, a roiling red mushroom cloud billows and rises above the city, ominous and terrifying to see at such close range. I've seen plenty of nukes deployed in battle, but always against Lankies, and never so close to an occupied human settlement. The mushroom cloud rising in the distance feels like an obscene violation.

All over the admin center, the gunfire slacks off as more and more troops on both sides become aware of what has just happened.

A new voice cuts in to the comms, on the NAC's priority emergency channel. There's heavy static in the background, but I recognize the speaker at once.

"Attention, renegade forces. Attention, renegade forces. This is Major Khaled Masoud of the NAC Defense Corps Special Operations Command."

"Son of a bitch," I say to the room in general. Our troopers are standing around, looking shell-shocked. The prisoners sitting lined up against the wall don't have the benefit of TacLink displays or video feeds, but nobody could have missed the characteristic deep and long-lasting rumble from the nuclear detonation. Even Agent Green suddenly looks anxious and concerned.

"Put him on speaker," I tell Gunny Philbrick, who dashes to the comms console.

"Building or floor?"

"Everything."

"The force under my command has just detonated a kiloton-size nuclear charge right underneath terraforming plant Arcadia One, five kilometers outside of Arcadia City. The sole power source for your capital city is now a glowing radioactive cloud," Major Masoud continues. "This is just the first strike, a demonstration of our resolve. Over the course of the last five days, my teams have placed nuclear demolition charges on every one of your active terraformers. They are very small and extremely well shielded, you have very little chance of finding them, and they are tamper-proof beyond the skill of your EOD personnel. That is a guarantee."

There's dead silence on all channels. All the gunfire in and around the admin center has ceased.

"This is an order to the leadership of this moon and all troops under their command. You will cease resisting the lawful and proper authority of the North American Commonwealth Defense Corps forces. You will lay down your weapons as of this moment. You will order any and all forces under your control to stand down. If you fail to do so, I will not hesitate to light off every one of the twenty-four nuclear demolition charges my teams have planted on this moon. If you choose to continue this fight, I will destroy your planetary infrastructure and your fusion power generation network irreparably. I will turn your stolen little paradise into an irradiated wasteland and leave you in it until the Lankies come for you or you all die of radiation poisoning. This is not a boast or a threat. It is a statement of fact."

"Damn," Philbrick murmurs next to me.

"I knew he was cold," I say. "I had no idea just how cold."

"The Fleet in orbit will stand down and wait for orders from the senior NAC commander in this system, to be transferred back to the Solar System. I don't want your personnel or your leadership. All I want are those orbital assets. Surrender and turn them over to us. Fail to do it, and they will have no ground left to land on. If you are tempted to doubt my resolve, look five kilometers to the east of Arcadia City.

"You have five minutes to respond on this channel. If you do not agree to these terms, fail to reply, or continue hostilities, I will initiate the nuclear demolition of your fusion plants one by one in three-minute intervals. And I will go to my death with a smile and the knowledge that you are going to freeze and starve in the dark. You left us at the mercy of the Lankies a year ago, and paying you back in kind for that act of treason would be a true joy. Five minutes starting now. Major Masoud out."

"Damn," Gunny Philbrick says again, this time with a disbelieving chuckle.

Behind me, Agent Green laughs out loud. I turn around, and he grins at me from his seated position on the floor.

"Now that's fighting dirty," he says. Next to him, the secretary of interior security looks like he wants to throw up.

"I hope your idiot president turns him down," I say, and mean it.

The reply comes four and a half very tense minutes later.

"Attention, NAC commander. This is General Stockett, Chief of Staff of the Arcadia Defense Corps." The voice sounds tired and harried.

"We accept your terms. I repeat, we accept your terms. There are sixty thousand civilians living near those fusion plants. Do not set off any more nukes on this moon. All Arcadia Defense Force units, stand down. That is a direct order. Transmit to all subunits as necessary. NAC commander, we are standing by for further instructions on this channel."

"Holy shit," Gunny Philbrick says into the sudden upswell of whistling and cheering in the ops center and the hallway outside. "We fucking won."

On my TacLink display, there are dozens of blinking blue icons signifying wounded or dead troopers. A third or more of the people under my command have been hurt or killed in the last fifteen minutes. It's the most violent and merciless small-unit fight I've experienced in my service time. The city streets outside are chaos, panicked civilians everywhere. The mushroom cloud in the distance is still billowing into the night sky, thinning out as it rises higher and higher. Never before have I seen a nuclear weapon used against other humans in battle, right near a civilian settlement.

"We didn't win," I say. "Nobody did."

CHAPTER 29

——— AFTERMATH ———

Outside, I only have one concern. I don't care about the civilians flooding the admin plaza, or the sullen renegade troops stacking their weapons by the entrance of the admin center under the watchful eyes of Second Platoon—or what's left of them. All I have on my mind is the coordinate two kilometers in the distance where Halley's drop ship went down thirty minutes ago in the middle of the short and ferocious battle. There's a quartet of Mules outside on the plaza, but there are troops and civvies all around them, and the streets are too packed for an eight-wheeled armored vehicle. Instead, I hang my PDW from its sling across my chest, and start running toward the northwest.

Pieces of Blackfly One rained down over a two-block area. I see one of the engines, still smoldering, embedded in the roof of a burning house. Shards of armor and bits of wing are scattered all over the street. The bulk of Halley's ship crashed into what looks like a little park, small trees and neatly planted bushes destroyed by the impact of the seventy-ton drop ship and the subsequent fire.

I don't want to see what's in the cockpit, but I have to know. I draw in shallow, painful breaths as I walk around the shattered hull, ignoring the burning patches of fuel I'm walking through.

The nose of the ship is staved in, and all the cockpit glass shattered. But where the pilot seat used to be, there's just a clamshell-shaped hole in the front of the ship where the rescue module used to be. I get weak-kneed with the sudden relief that floods through me, the first positive emotion I've had in a while. It feels utterly selfish in light of all the dead Rogue Company troopers who have been shot or blown apart by cannon rounds or burned up in the cockpits of their ships, but I am more grateful than I've ever been in my life that I didn't have to find the burned and mangled remains of my wife in that cockpit.

———————

The rescue module came down a few hundred meters away in someone's front yard. The triple-canopy chute of the capsule is partially draped over the roof of the house like an untidy overgarment. The clamshell halves are blown open, but there's no Halley inside.

I call for my wife and check the alleys around the house, then the next street over, then the street next to that one. All over town, black and sooty ashes have started to fall, and I don't need to see the radiological alert from my suit to know that this is the beginning of the radioactive fallout from the nearby nuclear explosion.

There's a group of civilians at the end of the next streets, half a dozen men and women wearing signal-colored wet-weather ponchos. I trot up to them and shine the light from my helmet in their direction to make myself noticed. They look scared and bewildered.

"The drop ship that crashed right over there," I say, and point with the barrel of my PDW. "Where's the pilot that was in the rescue capsule? Did you see her?"

"We did," one of the men says. "Pulled her out of that capsule. She was hurt pretty badly."

"What did you do with her?" I shout.

"One of the neighbors drove her to the hospital," the man says, eyeing my hand on the grip of my PDW. "We're not savages here, you know."

"Where's the hospital?"

"Quarter kilometer that way," he says and points south. "Two-story building, white with a red cross on the side. Can't miss it."

I want to say thank you, but find that the words won't come out. Instead, I nod at the group and point over to the nearest house.

"You need to get under a solid roof. This fallout is radioactive. Get inside and do a full decon, or you'll be puking out your bloody insides in a few days."

The settlement hospital is probably the busiest place in town tonight. Two of the garrison's Mules are unloading wounded troops in front of the building, and medics are helping them inside or carrying them. I push my way through the crowd at the entrance waiting in line for the decontamination lock just inside the building. Nobody argues with me when I skip to the head of the line in my battle armor.

The decon cycle takes three minutes, which are the longest three minutes of my life so far. Then the light on the decon lock goes green, and I step out of the lock and into the facility, which is in a state of controlled chaos. There are injured troops on stretchers lining the hallways and packing the first few rooms I poke my head into.

"What are you looking for, trooper? Are you injured?"

A stern-faced, harried-looking woman in a medical outfit stops me as I try to check the next room.

"I'm looking for the pilot someone brought in maybe twenty, thirty minutes ago. Female, dark hair, tall."

"This look like a Fleet rehab facility to you? With visiting hours? We are stitching people back together right now. Wouldn't have to if you hadn't started a shooting war in the middle of a civilian settlement."

She puts her hand on the chest plate of my armor and tries to push me away from the door.

"Don't," I growl.

She gives my gun on its sling a concerned look and pulls her hand away from my armor. Then she looks around, doubtlessly for help to deal with this irate knucklehead soldier who showed up in a medical facility armed to the teeth.

"They're stacking the arrivals wherever they can find them. If she came in half an hour ago, she's probably in the surgery queue up in the A hallway on the second floor."

"Thank you," I say, and run over to the staircase without waiting for an answer.

Halley is almost as tall as I am, but she looks strangely tiny on the stretcher. The left sleeve and leg of her flight suit have been cut away, and she's wearing bulky gel stabilizers on both limbs on her left side. The left side of her face is swollen and colored in vivid shades of purple and black, but she's still recognizably Halley. Her hair is matted with blood and sticking to her skull. There's an automatic med injector strapped to her right forearm, and she's barely conscious, probably in a deep and warm painkiller haze.

"Hey," I say, and kneel down next to her stretcher. I can't take her hand because it's tied down, so I just stroke her forehead. Where my hand touches her hair, it comes away with half-congealed blood. "Hey, you."

Her eyelids flutter a little, and I can see that she's trying to focus.

"Huh," she says, more an exhalation than a word.

"You look like hammered shit," I say.

"Mmmmh," she replies, with the tiniest of smiles in the corners of her mouth. "Goddamn capsule broke my goddamn leg," she mumbles.

"And your arm, and a bunch of other stuff."

"Had better days," she says.

"I haven't," I reply, and she smiles groggily.

"Did we win?"

I consider her question for a moment.

"We didn't lose," I say. "They surrendered. Masoud set off a nuclear demo charge on the main terraformer."

"Nukes," Halley mumbles. "Jesus. Can't believe I slept through that."

I look at my bruised and battered wife, one of two drop ship pilots left alive on this mission. We've lost so many today, and I will grieve for Lieutenant Dorian and all the dead troopers from First and Second Platoons later, when the smoke and the adrenaline have settled and I am alone with my thoughts again. But right now, I am selfishly and unapologetically happy that Halley is alive.

She grimaces and fumbles for the button that controls the med injector. I take her hand, put it back onto the stretcher, and push the button for her.

"Thanks," she murmurs. "'s good stuff."

"I'm familiar with it," I reply, but she's already drifting off.

"I'll be back for you later," I say, and she mumbles inarticulate assent.

———

The SEALs arrive in their drop ship half an hour later, while we are busy stacking captured weapons on the plaza. I've never hated any one group of my own podhead community as much as I loathe the Space-Air-Land commandos that come trotting down the ramp of their Blackfly, clad head to toe in HEBA suits.

"They've been in bug suits all along," I say to Sergeant Fallon. "They spent the last week in stealth and sneaking around while we were busy sticking our collective dicks into the local beehives."

"The term you are looking for is 'cannon fodder,'" Sergeant Fallon says. "Motherfucker used us as bait. We were the diversion. So his

SOCOM heroes could sneak around undetected and stick nukes every-where while the Shrikes were busy chasing us down."

Major Masoud brings up the rear. He's in a bug suit as well, but he's carrying his helmet under his arm. He stops at the top of the ramp and looks around with an unsmiling face. Then he puts the helmet on his head, and a second later, the personality projector built into the HEBA suits makes his face appear on the outside of the helmet, making it look like the bug suit dome has an actual visor. Then he trots down the ramp and steps onto the ash-covered asphalt of the admin plaza. I throw the M-66 in my hands onto a pile of identical weapons and walk over to where the SEALs are getting their bearings.

"Lieutenant," Major Masoud says. "I'm happy that my instinct about you was correct. You almost pulled this off without the SEAL platoon."

I have the sudden impulse to unhook my PDW from its carrying sling and put a hundred-round burst into the major's face. But with Halley alive, my sense of self-preservation has returned, and I have no interest in getting shot on the spot by his SEALs in this irradiated shithole.

"You used me," I say. "You used the whole SI detachment. Three platoons of distraction. So you and your boys could bring the place to its knees."

"Yes, I did," he says. "I needed their eyes on your platoon so they wouldn't look where it counted. And make no mistake, Lieutenant, I'd do it again tomorrow."

"We lost thirty-eight men and three drop ships," I say.

"And we got off easy," he replies. "We won. And we got it done with minimal casualties. Do you have any idea how many we would have lost if the Fleet had staged a full task force for the raid? Gone head-to-head against those ships in orbit? Thousands of lives, Lieutenant. Yes, I'll trade thirty-eight troopers and a handful of drop ships for that."

I glare at him, murder in my heart.

"You were willing to nuke every single terraforming plant on this moon?"

He nods. "Believe it. Although I bluffed a little. We only had time to set the charges on fourteen of them. We had to cut things short when you staged your assault." He smiles a very sparse smile. "That was excellent initiative. When we get back, I'm putting you and the other platoon leaders in for some major awards."

"I don't want any," I say. "I don't want a thing from you. I don't do your kind of war."

Major Masoud shakes his head.

"There's no 'my kind of war,'" he says. "There's only war. It's about breaking the enemy as quickly and thoroughly as possible, by any means necessary. That's all it is. That's our business, Lieutenant."

"You were looking forward to this. You came here just to stomp these people and make them bleed."

"I came here to win the battle," he says. "So we can take it to the Lankies and win the war."

"I'll believe that when I see you in formation with the rest of us to drop onto Mars. With all those kids they're training as cannon fodder for you and your high-speed brotherhood here."

"You will," he says. "*Portsmouth* and *Berlin* will be in orbit in two days and take command of the renegade task force for the transit back to Earth. And then we'll get ready for the main event. With the gear in orbit here, we'll double the Fleet's combat power. We're bringing back a supercarrier and six capital ships, Lieutenant. We'll both be on the ground on Mars in a month or two."

"Yes sir," I say, and sketch a cursory salute that's just on this side of insubordination. I know he's right, and I hate the knowledge, the near certainty that I would have made the exact same trade in his stead. A hundred dead and three drop ships gone, traded for a quarter-million tons of first-rate warships to take into battle against the Lankies. A hundred deaths for the chance to save hundreds of millions, maybe the entire human race. I'll come to terms with it later. But right now I am angry at the man who made that call for us all, without letting us in on the whole plan.

"Your wife doing all right?" Sergeant Fallon asks a little later, when we've finished stacking rifles and sitting down in the shell-marked vestibule of the admin building. I'm so tired I don't even have the energy to open a ration bag—not that it's advisable to eat outside when irradiated particles are falling from the sky.

"She has more broken bones than intact ones," I say. "The ejection capsule closed on her arm and leg when she bailed. Crushed them both in half a dozen places. Broke her hip, too."

"They'll stitch her back together," she replies. Then she stretches out her leg—the artificial one—and gives her titanium shinbone a good rap with her armored fist.

"I didn't get a scratch on me this time," I say. "Nothing. Not even a bruised knuckle. I've had guys blown in half right in front of me, and I didn't shed a drop of blood. Doesn't seem right, does it?"

"You've bled your share," she says. "You have credit."

We watch the scene in front of us—the troops clearing rubble and carting away weapons and body bags, the civvies milling around in radiation ponchos, the smoke still pouring into the nighttime sky from the dozens of fires our battle kindled. We turned a paradise into something worse than the shittiest PRC on Earth, a post-apocalyptic, irradiated urban wasteland. The population of Arcadia City has already begun the evacuation to the other settlements, because this place isn't livable anymore, and won't be for decades to come. And I have no doubt that Major Masoud would have let the other settlements suffer a similar fate if the chief of staff hadn't taken charge and surrendered his troops unilaterally, without word from the president, who is still in his hiding hole deep underneath the admin center. I know that what we did was necessary, but I can't bring myself to say that it was right.

There's only war, I hear Major Masoud in my head. And it occurs to me that despite all his experience and his Medal of Honor, the major is wrong about the nature of this profession to which he dedicated his life. There's war against the Lankies, which is right and necessary and a question of survival. And then there's war against our own—the SRA, the renegades, the welfare rats, the smaller nations on Earth—which is stupid and wasteful and demoralizing to the extreme. I'm willing to risk and give my life fighting the former, but I am tired to the bone of fighting the latter.

"I'm going to go check on the troops," I say, and get up. "They've had a shit day."

Sergeant Fallon shakes her head.

"That's what you don't get yet," she says. "We've all had a rough day. But those guys and girls are already sharing battle stories in the shower. It's how you get over shit like seeing your buddy get blown to pieces in front of your eyes without losing your fucking mind." She stands up and brushes the concrete dust from her leg armor.

"And in twenty years, if we still exist as a species, they'll be having drinks at their reunions. And you know how they will remember today? They'll say it was one of the best days of their lives."

She pats me on the arm and nods toward the rubble-strewn hallway in front of us.

"Come on, Lieutenant. You've earned a shower and a drink."

"I'm right behind you," I say. She nods and walks into the building. I watch as she makes her way down the hallway and disappears around the corner of the intersection.

On the western horizon, the bright blue orb of Leonidas c takes up most of the sky. On the eastern horizon, the far-off system sun creeps across the peaks of the low mountain chain where we sought refuge just two days ago. The sky in the middle graduates from blue to black to red in the span of fifty degrees. This was a beautiful place before the commandos set off that nuke, and it will be beautiful again, far prettier than most of what Earth has to offer to a low-rent hood rat like me. But right now I can't wait to go back to our overcrowded, filthy old Earth.

Two months until Mars, I think. And now we may actually have a sliver of a chance.

——— ACKNOWLEDGMENTS ———

Acknowledgments are terrifying to write. Regardless of how long you take or how many times you read over them, you end up forgetting someone you meant to thank. That's because nobody writes a novel in a solitary vacuum, and the number of people that had a role in the making of the novel in your hands is as high the personnel roster of a Fleet carrier.

Major thanks to my friends at 47North, the small, hardworking, dedicated, and professional team that has published four of these novels so far: Britt Rogers, Alex Carr, Ben Smith, Adrienne Lombardo, and Jason Kirk. The FRONTLINES series wouldn't be what it is without you, and I'll have drinks with you all in bars with historic urinals ANY TIME.

Thanks as always to my writer friends, the Daydrinkers: Claire Humphrey, Julie Day, Erica Hildebrand, Chang Terhune, and Scott H. Andrews. Our semi-regular long weekends together keep me on track and help see things in perspective, even if they're hell on my liver. Team Pantybear forever!

Some of you may be aware of the circumstances surrounding *Lines of Departure's* 2015 Hugo nomination for Best Novel, and my subsequent withdrawing of the novel from consideration. In the wake of

Sasquan, I feel compelled to offer thanks and appreciation to everyone who voiced their support.

Firstly, thanks are due to my awesome publisher 47North, who supported me in my decision even though it cost them the first Hugo nomination for the house. Thank you, Adrienne and Jason.

I want to thank my friend John Scalzi for his kind words both before the shortlist was made public, and after I withdrew my nomination. (And thank you for the most excellent bottle of single malt.)

Thank you to George R.R. Martin, who did a wonderful thing for the SF/F community in general and me and Annie Bellet in particular at the absolutely epic Hugo Losers party, and who was very kind and gracious throughout.

Thanks to the Atomic Nerds, Jess and Tom, for yet another excellent bottle of single malt, craftily dressed up by Tamara to look like a Hugo rocket (albeit one that had a repeated high-speed interface with an asteroid).

Thank you to everyone who sent me messages of support, whether via email, Facebook, Twitter, or in person. There were so many of you that I can't list you all, but you know who you are, and you have my gratitude.

And lastly, thank you to my readers. You keep buying these books, and I get to keep writing them, and if that setup works well for all of you, it sure works for me.

SEMPER FI FUND

ACKNOWLEDGMENTS:

While I was writing this novel, I decided to raffle off some of the names of the troopers in Andrew's company, so I started a little contest on my blog. The naming rights for the platoon troopers fetched a total of almost $1,300 for the Semper Fi Fund, which provides immediate assistance and lifetime support for wounded, critically ill and injured service members, veterans & their families. Here are the names of the donors who got to name Spaceborne Infantry troopers:

SSGT Welch, Scott
SGT Wilsey, Martin
CPL Ponton, Chad
CPL Sharps, Nick
CPL Nealis, Rob
PFC Von der Linden, Meg
PFC Whipkey, Sean
PFC Mekker, Anthony
PVT Best, Daniel
PVT Gilroy, Alden
PVT Harris, Devin
PVT Minie, Christopher
PVT Oakley, Stan
PVT Schneider, Kurt

—— ABOUT THE AUTHOR ——

Photo © 2013 Robin Kloos

Marko Kloos was born and raised in Germany, in and around the city of Münster. In the past, he has been a soldier, bookseller, freight dockworker, and corporate IT administrator before he decided that he wasn't cut out for anything other than making stuff up for a living.

Marko writes primarily science fiction and fantasy, his first genre love ever since his youth, when he spent his allowance mostly on German SF pulp serials. He likes bookstores, kind people, October in New England, Scotch, and long walks on the beach with Scotch.

Marko lives in New Hampshire with his wife, two children, and a roving pack of vicious dachshunds.